The Making of
Theodore Roosevelt

by Robert Louis DeMayo

Robert Louis DeMayo

Copies of this book can be ordered at:
Available from Amazon.com
and other retailers.

Edited by: Nina Rehfeld
Nina@txture.com

This is a work of fiction.

In the fall of 1878, twenty year old Theodore Roosevelt made the first of three trips to northern Maine where he was guided through the wilderness by two seasoned woodsmen: William Wingate Sewall and Wilmot Dow. It was here that Theodore learned to be an outdoorsman and to feel comfortable with the tough men who worked in the backwoods.

These journeys to Maine transformed Theodore from a sickly, depressed boy, to a young man who was ready to take on the world. Roosevelt would later comment on Sewall, "There is no one who could more clearly give the account of me when I was a young man and ever since."

Between his three visits, which all took place within a year, Roosevelt covered over one-thousand miles of virgin forest, frozen lakes and cedar swamps. These explorations were undertaken by foot, snowshoe, canoe, sleigh and buckboard, in all sorts of weather, and through difficult terrain. This story is also about how Theodore met his first wife, Alice Hathaway Lee, and follows their courtship. Alice was his first, passionate love, and during his trips to Maine she was always on his mind.

In the 60's my father bought some land from William Sewall's grandson; as a boy I roamed the same woods as Theodore and grew up listening to the many stories of his time in Maine from William Sewall's descendants and the offspring of the woodsman who knew him. In this account I have tried to imagine what these journeys were like, and have taken some creative license in doing so, but at the same time stayed true to the original experience. Even so, all characters other than Theodore Roosevelt, Alice Lee, Dickey Saltonstall, Bill and David Sewall and Wilmot Dow are the invention of the author, and all conversation, except where it is quoting other text, is the invention of the author.

I hope you enjoy learning about this fascinating time in Theodore Roosevelt's life — and northern Maine — as much as I have.

Sincerely yours,

Robert Louis DeMayo

"When you get among the rough, poor, honest,
hard-working people they are almost all, both men
and women, believers in Roosevelt."
(William Wingate Sewall)

"There are good men and bad men of all nationalities, creeds and colors;
and if this world of ours is ever to become what we hope some day it
may become, it must be by the general recognition that the man's heart
and soul, the man's worth and actions, determine his standing".
(Theodore Roosevelt)
Letter, Oyster Bay, NY
September 1, 1903

"Historians, seeking one after the other for centuries to come to explore
the mysteries of the paradoxical career of Theodore Roosevelt, will have
more to say of William Wingate Sewall than his Maine neighbors or even
the statesmen, scientists, and men of letters who drew him into their
councils. For "Bill" Sewall was guide, philosopher and friend to
Theodore Roosevelt in that period in his life when a man's character,
emerging from the shelter of home traditions and inherited beliefs, is
most like wax under the contact of men and events."
(Sholem Asch)

for

Cleo Sewall
fellow historian and long-time friend

and

Ron DeMayo
my father and life-long friend.

I would also like to thank some the people who made this book possible: notably Nina Rehfeld, whose tireless edits brought the story to life; David and Cleo Sewall, whose tales of their ancestor helped me see it for the great story it is; Cheryl Anne Gonzalo for her information on Morgans; and Ray & Jeanette Gallagher and Solomon & Monica Shaw for their edits and comments on logging and the Maine woods.

Robert Louis DeMayo

Chapter One
Northern Maine 1878

In early September a steam train slowly made its way through the rolling hills of Northern Maine. Although the lower states of New England still enjoyed a fading summer, this far north the trees had already begun to turn and now appeared ready to burst with color as the wind threw them about.

Farms spread out on either side of the train, each with a trail of smoke coming from their chimneys. Stacked by the house entrances was cord after cord of wood, ready to be moved under cover in preparation for the harsh winter about to set in.

Every hour or so, the train pulled into a station with a loud whistle and a blast of steam. A casual observer would have noticed that as the day proceeded the passengers thinned out, and the further north the train reached it carried fewer and fewer travelers.

By late afternoon, with the exception of one cabin, everyone on board was either a railroad employee, or had the rougher look of a workman returning home.

Still, the land appeared disciplined; complete with meadows and pastures and the occasional grove of apple trees. Most of the pines had been cleared away for lumber or heating fuel, but there were still maple, oak and beech, each displaying its own colors. The fields looked well kept and the animals grazed peacefully within their fenced yards.

And then that changed.

It was so abrupt that those few travelers still riding the train felt there almost should have been an announcement. A minute ago they had ridden through a familiar landscape of farms and gentle hills, now they were plunged into a sudden, confusing darkness.

From either side a towering forest seemed to close in. Light faded and the colors disappeared. Massive pines shot up all around them, their upper extremities stretching beyond the view of the train windows, the lower branches covered with moss.

The forest seemed ancient and untouched by man.

The train wasn't large by any standard, with little more than a dozen cars, but as it entered these woods it seemed to have shrunk to the size of a toy.

Altogether there were half a dozen freight cars, several third-class cars, one dining car, one-first class car. All but one cabin in first class was empty. In the occupied compartment sat three well-dressed young men at the cusp of their twenties. They all sported fashionable whiskers and sat amidst their numerous trunks and bags.

Two of them were playing a game of cards among the polished oak panels and brass of their cabin. They were using one of their trunks as a table and leaned forward as they dropped their excess cards.

As the train entered the forest and the sun's reflections on the wood and metal abruptly faded, they both looked up into the sudden gloom.

"I know we are heading into the wilderness, but really, they should have provided better lighting," murmured Emlen, the taller of the two card players. He had a strong Harvard accent and a cocky air about him. Having done this journey a few years earlier and being the elder of the two by one year he considered himself the authority on their destination.

The other player was Emlen's cousin West. He was currently studying medicine and felt out of place on this journey, a fact he attempted to cover up by pointing out how quaint or simple everything looked.

Other than agreeing with Emlen's comment about the darkened room West appeared bored and uninterested in the forest they were passing through.

The third young man, Theodore, was also a cousin. He had been absorbed with a book he was reading, but looked out the window when the light faded and now stared at the forest, seemingly enchanted with the ancient tangle of trees.

After several minutes of rapt attention to the forest outside, Theodore took off his glasses and rubbed his temples. He had dark circles around his eyes and looked like he hadn't been sleeping. Something in his life was aging him and he looked older than his twenty years.

For a minute he looked over the other two young men, but then decided the forest was more interesting and went back to watching it pass by.

For mile after mile the dense woods continued.

Emlen finally lay down his cards, stood, and impatiently began moving about the cabin. He was dressed in fashion; his three piece suit was immaculate.

He paused for a moment to pull a watch from his vest pocket and check the time.

He muttered, "The train is running late."

West looked up at Theodore and noticed the book he was still holding in the gloom.

Behind him he spied a light switch on the wall and he leaned over and flicked it. The cabin was suddenly filled with a soft glow.

Theodore returned to his book and smiled appreciatively.

The forest continued to pass by.

Emlen noticed Theodore occasionally returning his gaze to the wilderness and said with a mock voice of importance, "I hope you realize the significance of those trees. Almost all of New England's forests were clear-cut in the last two-hundred years; first to build England's ships, and then for housing and to heat homes — but not here."

Theodore looked up and smiled and said, "Why, thank you, Mr. Cutler."

West perked up and shouted, "*Touché*", and Emlen blushed slightly. Mr. Arthur Cutler had been Theodore's tutor in the years before Harvard, and his cousins knew him as well. He was only nine years older but his stern presence hinted at more. Mr. Cutler had been to Maine numerous times and as if to balance his scholarly side he maintained he also felt at home in the wilderness — a renaissance man.

West then did his own best imitation of Mr. Cutler, "Gentlemen, we are off to the wilds of Aroostook County…"

Later the scenery opened up and they found themselves traveling along a long lake with a majestic mountain rising up on its far bank.

Emlen nudged Theodore.

"That is Mount Katahdin — it is the highest point in Maine and the beginning of a mountain range that stretches south for two thousand miles."

At once Theodore sat up straighter and looked at the mountain.

Emlen continued, "Thoreau wrote about Katahdin."

Theodore promptly cleared his throat and recited a line from Thoreau's *Ktaadn*, "*…some hours only of travel in this direction will carry the curious to the verge of a primitive forest, more interesting, perhaps, on all accounts, than they would reach by going a thousand miles westward.*"

Looking at his cousins, Emlen added, "We should climb it."

"Really Emlen," said West with a yawn, "I do not plan on doing anything more exerting than fishing on this visit."

Looking over the cabin as if it were not fit for men of their social status he added, "I still cannot see why we are here in the first place. There is plenty of good fishing much closer to New York City."

Emlen took up his position as the authority again, and held up a finger for emphasis.

"This is a unique experience. Do you realize that you are going to a place that is just now experiencing the axe? It runs by the old rules and those places are disappearing fast."

West decided to push his cousin and said, "They sure are pretty trees, Emlen, but as far as I am concerned it should be more civilization and fewer trees."

Emlen shook his head in dismay.

"How can you say that after having been to Island Falls before?"

Then, in a more serious tone, he addressed him again.

"West, these are not just pretty trees; what we have been passing through is one of the last stands of virgin forest in the Northeast."

West grinned, "I for one do not think there is a virgin within a hundred miles of us."

Emlen replied, "This is the frontier. You should show it some respect."

West laughed. "The frontier?" he asked sarcastically. "Why, that is two thousand miles to the west of us where Custer got himself killed by the Indians. These are just woods."

Looking to Theodore for support he added, ""Besides, cousin Theodore has traveled all over the world. What would he fear in these woods?"

Theodore looked up from his book and gave them his full attention. "This area is actually quite different," he said, his straight teeth chopping his words as he spoke.

Slowly, he set the book down. He stared out the window for a solid minute before continuing, his cousins waiting patiently, both noticing his pale complexion, and how he had wheezed slightly when speaking.

He took off his thick glasses and polished them clean, then looked out again as if a clearer view of the forest might help him make his point.

"Temperature drops of twenty-five below zero are common, the woods are full of bear and moose; and the Indian still roams free north of us."

He stared hard at the other young men before making his final statement.

"The land here is still untamed."

After this he remained silent, as if there was nothing left to say.

After several minutes West sighed, "Could someone please tell me how much longer we have on this journey?"

Emlen replied, "Island Falls is so remote it will take us two full days to get there; the European-North American Train Line does not even go that far."

West began to recoil, as if he feared what his cousin would say. He sadly asked, "If the train doesn't go to Island Falls then how will we get there?"

Emlen reluctantly said, "The last thirty-six miles will be completed in a buckboard and that will take six or seven hours."

West placed a folded blanket under his bottom.

"My arse will not forgive me for leaving New York City."

Emlen ignored him and turned to Theodore.

"Our guide will be a man named William Sewall."

In a teasing voice he addressed West.

"You remember Mr. Sewall I take it?"

West looked down submissively and Emlen continued, "I would advise you to monitor that type of foul language when you are around him."

A bit arrogantly, Theodore asked, "Is that so? Why?"

Emlen replied, "Because he does not approve of it, that is why."

Although Theodore did not believe in cussing, he didn't like being told what to do either.

A bit shocked, he asked, "Who does this Mr. Sewall think he is? I believe he is a commoner, is he not?"

Emlen stroked his whiskers nervously, hesitant to speak.

Theodore asked, "Does he know we are Roosevelts?"

Ignoring the second question, Emlen answered, "William Wingate Sewall is the man to know if you are going to Aroostook country. He is the best backwoodsman around."

Then West blurted out, "And he does not give a *damn* if we are Roosevelts."

After that Emlen looked uncomfortable and didn't speak for a while. He finally muttered about getting something warm to drink.

West looked around hopefully. "Surely there must be a porter that could do that?"

They stared at the empty hallway until Emlen volunteered and departed.

Once Emlen was gone West seemed to relax. He turned to Theodore and eyed him from the viewpoint of the Doctor he was training to be. Although the young man looked focused and alert, his complexion was ashen and his eyes sunken.

"I can see the strain this journey is taking on you, Theodore," said West, "and knowing your medical history I am surprised your family allowed it."

At this Theodore glanced out the window, a resigned look on his face. "Of course my mother thought it a bad idea, but with my father's passing I seem to be in charge of my own destiny."

West waited a moment and then said, "I remember last summer, when you returned from your trip abroad, your father was worried about your physical condition."

Theodore nodded in agreement.

"Yes, we traveled all through Europe and the Middle East. What great adventures we had, all of us, but my health failed me constantly. Still, it was a great time for father and I." Abruptly, the young man trailed off into thought, lost in memories.

West nodded once and then sat uncomfortably until Theodore looked up at him again.

"Besides," he added, "when we returned I began studying under Mr. Cutler's direction, and I must say that man could not stop talking about northern Maine when around my father. He thought…among other things…that the cold air up north might be good for my lungs."

Even as he spoke Theodore began to wheeze with a bad asthma attack. He struggled to regain his composure, his face flushed from the exertion.

West had caught a note of sarcasm in Theodore's last statement and asked, "What would 'among other things' be referring to?"

"Well," started Theodore, "It appears my former tutor saw a veneer of, let's call it snobbism, developing in me and" - he pointed at West - "some of my cousins, and he thought this adventure might help us grow."

"Goodness," said West with a laugh.

Theodore shook his head, weighing Mr. Cutler's opinion in his own mind.

West now looked irritated and finally asked, "How so?"

Theodore stared him in the eye and answered, "Because Mr. Sewall was humbly born, of course."

In the silence that followed Emlen returned, surprised to see his two cousins wearing angered expressions.

Theodore blurted out, "What can you tell me about William Sewall other than the fact that he was humbly born?"

Emlen was a bit surprised by the question, but then, with a weak smile, he held up his hands in protest.

"I think you will find Mr. Sewall is much more than a simple man."

Theodore stared out the window for several minutes, obviously agitated.

Finally he asked again, "Can you tell me anything of interest about this Mr. Sewall, besides the facts of his birth?"

Emlen paused and took in a deep breath of air, and then he began talking about the Maine woodsman.

"William Sewall is quite an enigma to me. He has the strength of a bear, and it is true he is a commoner; but he also has a love of epic poetry — the man actually shouts verses of Longfellow as he chops down trees."

Theodore looked down at the book he was reading: THE SAGA OF KING OLAF by H.W. LONGFELLOW.

He smiled as he lifted his head and again stared out the window.

Robert Louis DeMayo

Chapter Two
Mattawamkeag Station

As the three Roosevelt cousins stepped off the train a strong northern wind assaulted them; West actually turned back as if ready to retreat to the safety of his cabin. The platform was alive with windblown leaves that swirled about in dust devils, and all around them tall trees swayed as if drunken.

Porters unloaded several large trunks, all belonging to the young men, while a few passengers boarded for the return journey south.

From a nearby bench, a local man gawked at the fancy clothing of the three New Yorkers.

"Taint likely 'dem suits's gonna last long 'round *heya*," he muttered.

The young men gave the man a confused look, trying in vain to make sense of his strong accent, and then returned to supervising the unloading of their gear.

When all was ready they looked about expectantly.

"Are we to walk to Island Falls?" asked West.

"Certainly not," replied Emlen. "Mr. Cutler wrote to Mr. Sewall, informing him of our arrival. There should be transportation waiting for us."

Theodore looked down the length of the station platform and saw a buckboard parked in the shade of a large oak tree. On the bench was a man slumped on his side sleeping. Two horses, still in their harnesses, grazed nearby.

"I believe that may be our ride there," he said.

The three young men walked to the buckboard where Emlen uncomfortably shook the driver awake. He sat up, rubbing his eyes and yawning, and finally said, "I'm guessin' you're the Rusavalts."

Not waiting for a reply, he put on his hat and said, "Okay then, git yur gear and let's get goin'."

West seemed offended.

"Surely there must be someone here who can do that."

The man grinned, exposing several dark holes in his smile and asked, "You mean other'n you?"

West looked to Emlen for help, but after a glimpse at the driver — who never offered his name and didn't seem ready to lend a hand — he returned to their pile of trunks.

Emlen and Theodore followed and together they carried their trunks and loaded them onto the buckboard.

Over the next seven hours they rode the buckboard over the rough road to Island Falls. Although winter had not yet set in the ground was already frozen and the ride was incredibly rough.

There were two large wheels on either side of the flatbed, and a low side railing to prevent injury from them. The driver sat on a bench up front, leaving the Roosevelts on their bottoms, facing forward, with their legs in front of them as they fought to stay centered.

The driver didn't speak again the entire time.

The few houses they passed were closed up tight against the chilled fall air, some even had shutters closed. The smoke from their fires hung low.

By the time they pulled up to William Sewall's large, white-clapboarded farmhouse in Island Falls evening was setting in and they were all exhausted.

Still dazed from the rough journey, the three young men were arranging their now rumpled clothes in the back of the buckboard as a tall, bearded man exited the house and walked onto the porch.

He had wide shoulders, stooped slightly, and looked like he had stepped out of some long-gone era. He was dressed in black with a wide brimmed hat. The man's dark hair had a reddish tinge to it, and his beard looked unruly and in desperate need of a trim.

From the description he'd been given Theodore knew the man was William Sewall, but his first reaction was intimidation. Here was a character that could have easily stepped out of *the Saga of King Olaf*. Theodore felt like West, ready to retreat to the safety of the train.

Mr. Sewall had a hint of a smile in his deep, gray-blue eyes as he looked over the young men. He stared at their impractical clothing, and then at the numerous trunks, and shook his head slightly.

In just a few strides he was down the stairs and beside the buckboard, his hand extended.

Emlen and Theodore hopped down to greet him.

"Mr. Sewall, I am Emlen. You showed me around several years ago when I came here with my cousin, West."

The tall man gave a grim smile and said, "*Ayuh*".

Theodore stood confused, not realizing Sewall had just affirmed his statement with a Maine *yes*.

The Mainer grabbed Emlen's hand and the younger man winced slightly, fighting not to cry out from the large man's steel grip. Then Mr. Sewall glanced at West and simply nodded.

"Hope you boys had a comfortable journey," said Mr. Sewall, unaware of how the word "boys" stung the pride of both Emlen and West.

Theodore shook hands with Mr. Sewall, but held his tongue and they simply nodded at each other.

The horses in front of the buckboard were stepping about nervously, exhausted after the long journey; Theodore walked to them and quietly stroked their necks. They responded to his touch and settled down.

Suddenly he turned and started wheezing.

It was then that Mr. Sewall remembered some of the text from the letter he'd received from Arthur Cutler. "He may not be strong," Mr. Cutler had written, "but he is all grit. And be warned, he will kill himself before he says he is tired."

Sewall stood straight, his face taciturn, and thought how he was not interested in having the heir of the Roosevelt family drop dead under his watch.

He sized Theodore up, thinking, "Bad eyes, weak heart... that pale youngster won't last three days with me."

As he watched another coughing fit overtook Theodore.

"Mighty piddlin'," thought Sewall.

While Theodore and West busied themselves with the luggage, Emlen stood by Mr. Sewall. As Theodore walked by, lugging a heavy trunk to the porch, another coughing fit overtook him. The trunk slipped from his hands and dropped with a loud clunk. With a grim face, he cleared his throat and picked it up again.

Mr. Sewall paid no mind to Theodore's fit and remarked instead, "That one doesn't say much."

Emlen nodded.

"Well, Mr. Sewall, I am sure you are aware Mr. Roosevelt senior passed away about six months ago."

The tall woodsman bowed his head and touched the brim of his hat, and Emlen nodded in acceptance. The two stood in silence while the wind cleared their thoughts.

Emlen finally said, "It was Mr. Roosevelt senior's wish that his son experience this area, and that it be done under your guidance. An acquaintance of his — a Mr. Cutler — had often spoken to him of you."

Sewall looked uncomfortable.

"Cutler's a decent man."

Again Mr. Sewall thought of Cutler's letter, whose final note read: "Just give him a chance. And watch to see how his lungs hold up. Who knows, they might work well with the cold air."

When Theodore returned for another trunk Mr. Sewall stopped him and gestured for Emlen to take over.

Mr. Sewall said, "Why don't you rest for a minute, Mr. Roosevelt."

Theodore looked down, uneasily. "I still think someone is talking about my father when I hear, 'Mr. Roosevelt'."

Then he added, "And please do not worry about my health, Mr. Sewall, I am stronger than I appear."

Mr. Sewall leaned back with a deep, throaty laugh, which startled Theodore.

"Mr. Sewall? We don't have any need for fancy titles here. We are in the woods now, and you can just call me Bill."

Theodore stood awkwardly, not used to sudden familiarity with strangers. Mr. Sewall placed a large hand on the young man's shoulder and steered him toward the house.

"Let's get you settled and then we can talk about how I'm gonna entertain you in these Maine woods."

Chapter Three
Island Falls

As they stepped onto the porch of the Sewall homestead, West commented sarcastically, "Civilization at last."

Completed just eight years before, the two-and-a-half story house was the pride of Island Falls, but it failed to impress the young New Yorker.

"Don't get too comfortable," Sewall replied. "We'll be spendin' most of our time campin', or at my huntin' lodge on Mattawamkeag Lake."

West looked at Emlen and frowned.

A large pile of recently split kindling sat near the entrance; logs had been split into pieces no more than a foot long and two inches wide.

"What a wonderful smell," said Theodore as he picked up a piece of the wood.

"Cedar," said Mr. Sewall, "Great for startin' a fire, but it burns too quick to heat a house."

"Then why chop so much of it?" asked West.

Sewall looked over the young man.

"Because it's a long winter, son," he said.

Theodore grinned at Mr. Sewall. He liked this man. Then he went to appraise the house.

"It looks solidly built, Mr. Sewall. I am sure it is warm in the winter."

Mr. Sewall nodded.

"Well, that was my goal," he said as he grabbed a trunk and headed for the stairs. "I built it for my ailing parents. I guess I owed it to my dad; he once built the first house in Island Falls back in 1841. He got to spend two good years in this one before the Lord took him."

Mr. Sewall looked up at the house with pride.

"I doubt it's the best house in Aroostook County, but it suits us fine."

West snickered.

"Are there many houses in this...settlement?" he asked and nudged Emlen. "Just how far would you have to go to collect one thousand people?"

Mr. Sewall frowned at the tone of the comment. He unceremoniously handed West the trunk he was carrying and got another for himself. The weight that was so suddenly handed to him almost toppled West. He barely succeeded in not dropping it.

"Well, I wouldn't call it a city," Mr. Sewall said, "but there are close to 150 people living in the area."

He opened the door and stood aside to let the three young men enter the house. Once the small group was inside he stepped after them and shut it as they all set down what they were carrying. The Kerosene lamp on the table and the fireplace in the corner only dimly lit the room, and they stood blinking while their eyes adjusted to the dark.

Eventually Theodore made out a tall figure leaning against the far wall, smiling patiently as he watched them. In his hand he held a knife and it flashed with a reflection of the lamp while he slowly whittled a soft piece of cedar.

"Gentlemen," said Mr. Sewall. "I'd like to acquaint you with my nephew, Wilmot Dow. He'll be helpin' me to introduce you to the area."

Emlen and West sheepishly nodded.

Wilmot was about as big as Mr. Sewall, and appeared just as rugged. He looked only a few years older than the Roosevelts, but something in his eyes hinted that he'd seen more of life than they had. He grinned, but didn't say anything.

Theodore strode forward—his hand extended—and shook Dow's confidently.

"Mr. Dow, it is a pleasure."

Wilmot shook his hand and smiled at Theodore's exuberance. "Mr. Roosevelt," he said as he motioned toward the kitchen.

"I've prepared a bite to eat. Once you've stowed your gear why don't you come down. You've gotta be hungry after that long haul."

Mr. Sewall smiled.

"Mighty kind of you, Wilmot; I'll show them their room while you heat things up."

Emlen looked at West.

"Did he say *room*? As in *one* room?"

Mr. Sewall chuckled as he grabbed two of the larger pieces of luggage—one in each hand—and started up the staircase. The three followed, each with their own load, and on the second floor West dropped his case heavily. But Mr. Sewall shook his head.

"One more floor to go, son."

The top floor of the Sewall house was an open attic with three beds ready for the guests. Sewall bent low so he wouldn't bang his head, and he smiled when he backed out a few minutes later.

"I'll see you gentlemen down-stairs when you're ready."

Emlen and West wore forced smiles on their faces.

"Thank you Mr. Sewall, we will be down shortly," Emlen said politely.

As soon as the door was shut West jumped up and shouted, "He has put us in the bloody attic. Can you believe this?"

Theodore looked around but kept quiet while he tested the bounce of his bed.

"The next time we come this way we really must find better accommodations," declared West.

Emlen looked restless, having earlier acted as their guide and authority on Island Falls; he now tried to be the peace maker.

"Perhaps we should remember that we are not here for the luxury."

West looked at him sarcastically.

Theodore walked to a chimney that rose through the center of the room and put his hand on it, feeling the warmth coming through the bricks.

"I would think this to be one of the warmest rooms in the house," he said.

West shook his head. "Cousin Theodore, you really have no sense of your place in society."

At the table Wilmot ladled out venison stew with potatoes and carrots. The food was straight off the stove and it steamed and filled the room with a rich aroma. Theodore dug in with an appetite and for once his cousins were silent as they also filled their stomachs.

West had begun to ridicule Wilmot—a lad only a few years older than him—for having to do a woman's job, but had fallen silent when Mr. Sewall asked, "You do realize you don't have to eat it, don't you?"

Now Theodore called over to Wilmot.

"Mr. Dow, this stew is simply delicious."

Wilmot nodded graciously, smiled, and with pride said, "Ayuh."

The good food soon drowned out all conversation, and after they had all finished the five men continued to sit sat in silence. Outside the wind howled against the windows.

Finally Emlen could stand it no longer. He had been ready to return to the wilderness, but the quaint house in Island Falls did not satisfy that yearning. During his earlier trip a few years ago and he had been in the shadow of Mr. Cutler and had not been able to establish an adult relationship with Mr. Sewall.

Although he respected Mr. Sewall, Emlen was a Harvard man and not quite comfortable conversing with common folk. He tried to find the intellectual in Mr. Sewall.

"So, Mr. Sewall," he said, "we are told you are the man to know here. What do you plan on teaching us?"

Mr. Sewall laughed.

"Well, I don't knows what I could really teach you three, bein' Harvard men and all. I'm sure each of you is better educated than I. In fact, except for a couple terms at a one-room school house, I've had no schoolin' at all."

Wilmot sat a bit straighter in his chair, unhappy with his uncle's assessment of himself.

"Uncle, you are cuttin' yourself short. I know for a fact that you can read and write."

"Well, I owe that to my sisters," replied Mr. Sewall.

Truly flabbergasted, Emlen pushed the point.

"What is it like to be in so remote a place and not know about what is happening currently in society?"

Mr. Sewall let out a deep laugh that seemed to shake the entire house.

"And what use would I have for current events?"

West piped in.

"Have you heard, Mr. Sewall, that the Greeks have declared war on Turkey?"

Wilmot leaned forward and smiled, "We declare war on 'em every fall."

As he leaned back he winked at Theodore.

West looked exasperated. "That is not what..."

Emlen felt it was his duty to inform Mr. Sewall on what actually was happening around the world.

He continued, "Have you heard of the attempt to assassinate Emperor William I of Germany?"

Mr. Sewall thought for a minute before replying.

"I never really had a use for the Emperor of Germany."

Frustrated, Emlen tried again. "Surely some of the new things of the world must have importance to you? Have you not heard of the Paris World Exhibition? Or the electric street lighting in London? Why, a German engineer has built a motorized tricycle that rides with a top speed of seven miles per hour."

Mr. Sewall looked Emlen in the eye and smiled.

"If you examined the road you came in on today you would have to agree that the best way to get around here is on foot or horseback."

Both West and Emlen's faces betrayed irritation at the man's quick wit. Mr. Sewall was enjoying himself while Wilmot and Theodore watched the show. Wilmot stood up and made the rounds with a pan and ladle and served everyone more soup.

West noticed a simple ring, carved out of a Walnut, in the center of the table. He tried it on and chuckled to himself at how primitive it was. Then he questioned the Mainer again.

"Okay, I see your point. How about this? Mannlicher has produced a repeater rifle. Surely a rifle would have importance to you—especially a repeater."

Wilmot, who sat back down, leaned forward again. He was a young man of few words, but he sure enjoyed saying what he had to say.

"Just how many bullets do you think it takes to kill a deer?" As he sat back he did his best not to smile.

West looked uncomfortable. He tapped his finger on the table, a slight knocking sound coming from the walnut ring as it made contact.

He noticed Mr. Sewall was examining him with a frown and turned to Wilmot to escape his gaze. West asked, "Are you saying you can do it with one shot?"

Wilmot didn't reply.

Mr. Sewall answered for him.

"Wilmot here is the best shot in the county. I've rarely seen him take a second shot."

West stroked his whiskers, exasperated.

"Impressive. But forgive me; I simply can't see how one can live without the exchange of opinions."

Now Mr. Sewall sat forward and held up a finger.

"Hold on a minute, young fella. You've been askin' me about the need to keep up on current events, not opinions."

West looked up confused.

"So what kind of opinions do you have?"

Mr. Sewall was silent for a minute before replying.

"Well, if we were to talk about my opinions, I might tell you how I feel about anything from Queen Victoria proclaiming herself the Empress of India to the conduct of the southern African Boer War."

West looked nervous and started banging the ring harder. Sewall continued, now with a slight note of anger.

"And if you pushed me harder, I might tell you my opinions on the Civil War, but I'm startin' to feel the conversation tonight is a bit too interrogatory."

West looked down, but Emlen followed up with the next inquiry, trying to play the part of the peacemaker.

"Please, Mr. Sewall, tell us your thoughts on the Civil War."

Mr. Sewall was quiet again; the other men noticed a look of sadness pass over his features. He then stared at the walnut ring on West's finger.

"Well, my first thought would be that I'd really like you to stop poundin' that ring. It came back from the war on the finger of a good friend of mine, Ben Brown, after he spent a hard time in the confederate prison camp in Andersonville. He never really recovered from his ordeal and that ring is one of the only mementoes I have of him."

Quickly, West took off the ring; his face blushed and while Mr. Sewall continued he stared at his hands.

"And secondly, my thoughts would go to my brother, George, who died in the winter of '61 of diphtheria while stationed in Bangor." He paused and continued in a lower voice. "Our little settlement here had only forty-two eligible men at the time and every one of them enlisted."

Mr. Sewall drew a breath and held up his finger again.

"One of them, George Robinson, even saved the life of Secretary of State Seward on the night of Lincoln's assassination. That was my neighbor, livin' just over there."

Mr. Sewall raised his hand and pointed east, then sat back and took another deep breath.

"Who would have thought a Mainer would come all the way from a remote place like this to do a great deed like that," said Emlen, as if it was an apology.

West had understood that he had offended his host, and sincerely he said, "My regrets, Mr. Sewall, if I have been inconsiderate."

Mr. Sewall exhaled and relaxed.

"No need, young man. We are all treated equally here. And everyone is allowed to voice their opinions under this roof, whatever they be."

Sensing an uncomfortable tension in the air, Theodore inquired about Sewall's childhood.

"I do have the distinction of being the first person born in Island Falls—that would be back in April 1845," started Mr. Sewall. "I got my first rifle at seven and rode on my first log drive at sixteen."

Theodore smiled as he looked at the tall stranger, a man who had been raised in circumstances so different from his own. This figure that seemed to pay allegiance to no one had gotten his attention.

"And who were your teachers?" he asked.

"I was the tenth child so I had plenty of older brothers and sisters, but I also knew the Indians that lived in the area. One of them taught me to make a birch bark canoe."

Theodore smiled and said, "Raised among savages, how interesting."

Mr. Sewall reddened and replied, "Well, I never called 'em savages myself, and I wasn't really raised by 'em, though I do remember Tomah who camped within two hundred feet of my father's house one winter.

"He lived with his squaw and our first winter he furnished us with meat in exchange for flour, vegetables and cornmeal."

"Did he teach you things?" asked Theodore.

Mr. Sewall shook his head. "Not me, but he taught my older brothers—and they taught me everything they knew. Tomah taught my brother David all about the woods and wild animals; in the end David could hunt and fish almost as well as an Indian."

"Seems like a good education to me."

Mr. Sewall nodded.

"I reckon it was if you aimed to be a hunter, trapper or woodsman. We lived a good distance from everything; Patten was eleven miles away by spotted line."

Seeing the confusion on his guest's faces, he added, "A spotted line is simply a trail through the woods that's connected by hatchet marks on the tree trunks."

He continued, "Eventually my father widened the trail so oxen could make it. When the water was high provisions could be brought part way by canoe, but at other times they had to be carried on men's back—most of the poor folk that moved this way couldn't afford horses.

West looked on with barely concealed disgust, "That must have been absolutely horrible."

Mr. Sewall laughed deeply, "Fish and wild animals were abundant in the woods and we were never really hungry or of want for anything."

Then he pointed to the empty serving pot that had held the venison stew and said dramatically, "But even when I reflect way back I don't remember anyone makin' a better venison stew than Wilmot."

Everyone took the hint and applauded Wilmot for the fine meal. In the commotion, Theodore leaned close to Mr. Sewall and said in a low voice, "I see clearly why you do not care for high society. I envy you."

Mr. Sewall nodded and quietly replied, "I have always been glad that I was destined to live at this time, although I feel that I would have enjoyed living a hundred years sooner."

Nostalgically he added, "All the tales of pioneers are dear to me, and I have always believed I could have gotten along peaceably with the Indians of old."

Theodore raised his fists triumphantly.

"Well said, sir."

Emlen and West had overheard the last part of the exchange and were fairly speechless.

Sensing that the conversation had come to an end, Wilmot stood and began to collect the dishes, but Sewall reached out to his arm and stopped him.

"Wilmot, I noticed you also split up a good pile of kindlin' for us."

"Yes I did, Uncle, I don't want Gram gettin' cold while we are off and thought it might make it easier for her to tend the fire—I also loaded the wood ring with hardwood."

Mr. Sewall nodded appreciatively and then turned to the Roosevelts.

"I suppose this's as good a time as any to tell you our camp rules— and when I say camp I mean this house as well as the huntin' camp."

The three young men looked up expectantly.

"Counting Wilmot and myself there are four of us livin' in this house. My mother is elderly and doesn't get around much, but you'll meet my sister, Sarah, tomorrow, and I believe you will find her a capable manager of the house."

He paused before continuing.

"Still, I'm a single man, as is Wilmot here, so everyone pitches in with the day to day chores."

He looked hard at West and Emlen. "And that means everyone."

Then he turned to Theodore and asked, "Would you mind helpin' me clear the table and do the dishes?"

His cousins snickered at the thought of the heir to the Roosevelt Empire doing dishes, but Theodore happily agreed.

Next Mr. Sewall looked over Emlen and West.

"Do you young men mind stackin' the wood Wilmot so kindly chopped this afternoon?"

After a moment of silence West asked, "Why can we not just chop some more wood?"

Mr. Sewall stared at them sternly and then replied, "Because I don't knows that I trust you with an axe; that's why."

Looking defeated they followed Wilmot outside.

When Mr. Sewall and Theodore were alone in the kitchen, the Mainer had a proposal.

"From this house it's 'bout five miles down some fast water to Mattawamkeag Lake. I plan on setting up some tents on the far side of the lake and basing there for a few days with you gentlemen."

Theodore nodded and waited for Mr. Sewall to continue.

"Once we've settled in, I'm thinkin' of sendin' Emlen and West off with Wilmot while you and I go off in a separate direction."

Theodore was silent while he thought over the idea.

"Will they be in good hands with him?" he asked.

"Wilmot is a better hunter, trapper and all-around woodsman than I ever was—they'll be fine."

Theodore dried the dishes as Mr. Sewall washed them.

"Then I think it is a fine idea. When do we all set out?"

Mr. Sewall smiled as he hung the dish rag to dry by the fire.

"Well, tomorrow is Sunday so we'll observe the day of the lord, but Monday we'll be headin' out before first light, so have your clothes ready."

Theodore turned and headed for the stairs.

"Very well, sir. I thank you for the dinner and your hospitality."

Robert Louis DeMayo

Chapter Four
The Northern Woods

In a slow-moving flow William Sewall paddled a canoe upstream, moving from one eddy to the next. The sun had not yet risen and the water appeared alive through the swirls of mist it exhaled.

Their expedition had started well when they took Sewall's *bateau* down the river to Mattawamkeag Lake, but then rain kept the three Roosevelts and two Maine guides confined to their camp on the lake for several days.

Since they'd first arrived, this was the first time Theodore had managed to get away from West and Emlen.. His cousins had been content to play whist and euchre and fish for trout, but Theodore had been restless and the senior guide had picked up on it.

Soon the river they were on widened — and slowed even more — and the banks that had been barely visible against the edges of the shady river disappeared.

Sewall looked around with a surprised expression and said, "Been some busy beavers at work here."

With a deep, carefree stroke he steered them between the clumps of earth — often topped with grasses and wildflowers — that clogged the area they were passing through. Out of the fog also appeared the gnawed-off stumps of trees and floating debris.

It was still so dark on the water that only the closest features of the landscape were easily visible. One object turned out to be a large snapping turtle, and Theodore almost upset the canoe when he realized what the thing he had taken for an obstacle actually was.

Next they entered a grove of swamped cedar trees, covered with moss; the trees spread out all around them and Theodore found he had no more conception of which way the water flowed; the trees dimmed the light even further and he could barely see.

"Mr. Sewall, if you do not mind me asking, how do you know where we are going?"

Sewall had followed a path that only he appeared to be acquainted with, but on the next open stretch he stowed the paddle and let the canoe coast.

Then he raised his finger to his lips and said, "Listen."

At first Theodore heard nothing, but then somewhere ahead of them he heard water gurgling.

Sewall bent down and smiled.

"That sound is how my father found the place that was to become Island Falls. He was camped nearby—he knew it was close—but he hadn't found it yet.

"My dad was an early riser and when he woke that morning he listened, and just like the sound of water you can hear now he heard those falls."

The gurgling turned out to come from a beaver dam. After they had portaged their canoe around it Sewall carefully lowered the boat back into the water and they headed out onto a larger lake.

Here Theodore took advantage of the low glow of the immanent dawn and sky-lighted the few birds they encountered. Since the beginning of their journey he'd been documenting everything in his journal, struggling to see the ink on the paper.

His first entry had been about an owl, hooting across the lake they'd first set forth on. Then later a pair of loons sent their sad calls across the quiet water. He would note whatever animal he perceived; it didn't matter if it was big or small, mammal or bird, even if he only heard it. The morning chill was sharp and Theodore's breath kept fogging his glasses, forcing him to clean them repeatedly.

The tops of the surrounding hills were now greeting the sunrise. The poplar and birch lifted their leaves and flashed their lighter colors, and the spruce and pine reached up, their crowns painted gold by the first rays of sunlight.

As the day lightened around them a large bird flew overhead. Theodore asked, "Would that have been a partridge or a grouse?"

Sewall grinned, "It would'a been breakfast if I could'a gotten my hands on it." After a pause he added, "I'm not sure what other folks call them, but I call 'em ruffed grouse."

Theodore said, "I recently published a book titled *The Summer Birds of Adirondacks* in which I documented ninety-seven different birds. Before I left I could even mimic most of them."

Sewall stroked his beard and grinned.

"Well, ain't that somethin'. And what do you say to them birds when you talk back?"

Theodore knew he was being played with but answered the best he could.

"I hope they hear me saying, 'Come out and see me so I can see what you are'."

He blushed slightly and added, "I have a love of nature, and I find myself drawn to it—would you like me to try to call out a partridge?"

Sewall laughed, and then shrugged and nodded.

Theodore cupped his hands and let out a soft cooing sound—one that was remarkably like a partridge—that floated across the water. He repeated this for several minutes, but with no luck.

Then, just as Sewall picked up his paddle, one flew low in their direction, forcing both men to duck.

Theodore scrambled for the gun, but Bill steadied his arm and calmly suggested, "Why don't we wait a lil' bit before breakin' out the guns?"

The younger man agreed with reluctance.

Gesturing to a bank of overgrown willows, Sewall explained, "If we pull in by that stand of vegetation we'll stay dry." While he guided them to shore Theodore started to pack his belongings into a canvas backpack.

Sewall steadied the canoe while Theodore stumbled out onto dry land, then got out himself and pulled the craft into the bushes.

"I need to check some of my traps. Would you like to stay and wait or come with me?"

Theodore looked slightly offended.

"Come with you, of course."

Sewall shrugged, grabbed a worn woodsman's axe from the floor of the canoe, and then set off through the dark tangle of green, following a faint game trail.

Soon the growth closed in around them and made steady movement difficult. Theodore stumbled repeatedly and was surprised when he looked ahead and saw Sewall weaving easily through the thickets.

Although imposingly tall in the dense brush, Sewall moved with barely a sound; his bright, red woolen shirt the only beacon to draw ones attention.

At times he used the sharp blade of his axe to eliminate a branch in his way, but he tended to feel his way through the dense area, careful not to waste his energy.

Once Theodore heard him mutter a verse, the lines possibly from the Song of Hiawatha, "*And beyond them stood the forest, stood the groves of singing pine-trees, green in summer, white in winter, ever sighing, ever singing . . .*"

Sewall stopped suddenly when a flash of white caught his eye; silently he watched a white-tail deer bound away through the brush ahead. He smiled at its gracefulness.

Suddenly a gun cracked and he jumped. Looking back he saw Theodore, about fifteen feet away, behind a smoking barrel, a look of dismay on his face.

"I took a shot," proclaimed Theodore.

Sewall nodded seriously.

"I can see that."

He turned and simply looked in the direction the deer had fled, trying to control his agitation.

Theodore thought Sewall was staring at the animal and came crashing up behind him.

Sewall nimbly ducked under a low limb without even turning around and thus got out of Theodore's way.

The young man was wheezing and as he stumbled forward his gun barrel swung everywhere.

He pounced in front of Sewall, raised his gun and shouted, "Where is the game, sir?"

As he did he caught the top of his backpack on a low branch. It lifted him off his feet, and as he came down he landed on his back with a loud thud.

Sewall scrambled to make sure he was not in the line of fire of Theodore's gun, and then extended his hand to help him up. He smiled patiently while Theodore brushed himself off.

"I believe the game has fled the area for the morning" Theodore said breathlessly. "I guess there is no sense in us staying here."

Again, Sewall looked ahead on the trail. He stopped and cocked his head, then turned to the left where a red squirrel sounded its warning.

"Yes, it seems that doe is movin' deeper into the swamp."

Theodore nodded and stared at his gun, "I am sorry, Mr. Sewall, I am usually a better shot."

Sewall scowled at him. "You have more than that to be sorry for. Seems we should return to the canoe right away and make our way back to the camp with your cousins."

Theodore looked up, his face flushed with impatience.

"Why are you threatening our expedition? Are you angry that I missed that deer?"

Sewall exhaled. "I may be a simple man, but I have rules that I live by. One of them involves safety, and another killing."

Theodore nodded gravely and didn't speak.

"First, you always let your partner know when you're going to discharge—especially if you're firin' anywhere near him."

The older man stared at Theodore until the younger man finally lifted his eyes and acknowledged this rule. Bowing to authority was something the young man was not accustomed to.

Defiantly, he asked, "How can I be expected to collect specimens under these conditions?"

Sewall said softly, "You'll collect enough before we're through, but you won't shoot 'til you get a nod for me. Is that understood?"

"Fine," said Theodore. "And how should I alert you?"

"Any one of your bird calls will do," said Sewall. "The birds might not know the difference, but I can still tell it's you."

Theodore turned away, angered by the comment, but after a slight hesitation he nodded again.

Sewall added, "And don't go killin' something you don't want to carry. If we have to cover dry land, I'll be carryin' the canoe—anything you shoot is goin' on your shoulders."

Sewall watched closely to assess Theodore's reaction to criticism. Before they went any deeper into the bush he needed to size up the odd young man.

It took some time for them both to cool off and they walked in silence. When Theodore was once more in control of himself he turned to Sewall.

"Alright, I understand your reasoning," Theodore said apologetically. "You will not have a problem with me in these areas again."

He then put on his best smile.

"Just please tell me how to exit this miserable brush? It seems like a dead end. What are we doing here anyway?"

Sewall nodded. "Well, as I mentioned, I have traps in the area; when we're done checkin' 'em we'll go back to the lake."

Theodore started coughing roughly, his breath exiting in frozen puffs of air. Sewall listened as the sounds echoed through the woods.

"Maybe we should slow our pace a bit" he suggested as he watched Theodore try to regain composure.

"Do not be ridiculous!" the young man snapped. "Let us please just find some country that is a bit more open."

A few minutes later they could see a long hill rising up on their left. The sun's rays were just creeping over the top of it, and long shafts of sunlight filtered through the misty morning air.

"We can follow that ridge-line up out of these thickets; it should be a bit warmer up there as well."

Theodore cleaned his glasses between coughing fits.

"Really, Mr. Sewall, I am not bothered by the temperature at all. I just find the terrain a bit difficult."

Sewall laughed, "With some luck the other animals will think you're a moose and stay put."

Theodore's scowl told the Mainer that he didn't appreciate his humor.

"I would think the temperature is below freezing. What do you think?"

Sewall wrinkled his face as he sniffed the air.

"I reckon its cold," he said with a smile and added, "but not unusual for fall."

The older man stopped and looked over Theodore.

"You sure you're holdin' out okay?"

Theodore stiffened.

"Yes. I am fine. Shall we proceed?"

Sewall didn't answer; in his mind he was again contemplating what exactly to do with the young man behind him. So much potential and so much power; and at such a malleable age! He'd initially decided to just set off and see how well they traveled together, but now they had come to a crossroad.

Bill wondered if he should bring Theodore to a logging camp. Most loggers he knew were good men of honor, but they were also men of discipline and they might not feel like catering to a rich New Yorker.

Sewall took the lead and soon found another game trail. This one lead away from the thickets.

As he exited onto a hardwood ridge Sewall knelt and leaned against his axe. He watched Theodore catch up, crashing and stumbling through the brush. Twice he went down to his knees.

"You might want to try actually watchin' where you step," Sewall advised. "It'll keep you from fallin' and you won't make as much noise."

Theodore looked up, a sharp reply on the tip of his tongue, but then he checked himself and smiled.

"I suppose you are right," he said. Then he looked down at the tangle of willows that had tripped him up. "How do you suggest I make my way through this brush? It truly is miserable."

Sewall looked down, studying their trail. "There are animals all around us and they move through it fairly gracefully. I suggest you mimic them."

The young man stared at him in confusion.

Sewall pointed in the direction they had just come.

"If you look along the line I just followed you'll see that there's a rabbit run down close to the ground. When I walked I stepped high and then placed my foot on the run."

Theodore nodded.

"And when we first exited the canoe I followed a trail that a moose had made," continued Sewall. "I stepped to the side of his tracks so as not to sink in, but I used his trail."

Theodore looked back in the direction they had come and looked over the trail. Before they continued he backtracked about twenty feet to reexamine their path. Looking at Sewall, he said seriously, "I can see it now; there is a trail. I will dedicate more of my attention to it."

Sewall laughed and slapped his large hand down on Theodore's shoulder. "Good lad, let's keep movin'."

The trail they followed now went steadily uphill, but was much easier to navigate. Large stands of poplar shivered in the cold air, their grey-white bark making the already chilly morning appear even more frigid.

Sewall doubled his pace over a section of smooth, glacier-worn granite and Theodore appeared behind him, his concentration focused on the placement of each foot.

He hardly took note of his own labored breathing. But Sewall heard him take a huge lungful of air, exhale and take another one.

Sewall turned. "Are you okay, Mr. Roosevelt?"

Theodore motioned ahead, gesturing for Sewall to continue.

Soon he was on Sewall's heals, his face concentrated. He could feel his lungs responding ever better to the cold air. Not used to being able to fill his lungs, he now inhaled deeply and exhaled evenly.

He grinned.

Suddenly breathing was enjoyable.

Five hundred yards up the slope the light of the sun hit the hill they climbed; the entire section looked warm and inviting.

Theodore increased his pace and stepped in front of Sewall. "Race you to the light..." he said and off he ran.

Sewall laughed, taken by surprise. He chased the suddenly energized man, shouting from behind.

"Was it a *challenge* that King Olaf heard blowing in on the wind?"

Theodore laughed, panting. "I would not recommend quoting Longfellow on this slope."

At the top of the ridge they came to a stop, sweat on their brows. Theodore had his hands on his knees, but he was glowing and breathing deeply.

"Nicely done, sir," said Sewall, grinning and wiping his forehead.

Theodore slowed his breathing as he surveyed the land around them, taking in each geographical feature like he was trying to memorize it.

"Such a fine day, Mr. Sewall, would you not agree?"

Sewall nodded, still catching his breath, and then said, "It's just the two of us now, please, call me Bill."

With awkwardness, Theodore said, "Okay...Bill, what is our destination? How far are we going today?"

The Mainer looked a bit uncertain.

"Well, I thought we'd just turn around soon and head back to Island Falls. I suppose we could also go to the camp and join the others."

Theodore stared at him without speaking and Bill noticed the dour expression.

"Actually, I didn't plan on being out in the open for long. Didn't even bring a tarp," the older man muttered.

He reluctantly added, "Also, Mr. Cutler warned me not to expose you to too much bad weather. Maybe you should take it easy, sir."

Again, Theodore stared at him without speaking.

Finally, he said in a serious voice.

"Mr. Sewall, I do not wish to return yet. And despite the fact that you are my senior *I* am paying for this expedition."

Sewall paused to think for a minute before replying. "You have a point there. My traps won't take but ten minutes to check and the day is young. What would you like to do?"

Theodore relaxed; his mind now ready to turn to the task. "What are our options, other than returning to the hunting camp or Island Falls?"

Sewall considered their choices.

"Well, we could just rough it and improvise a camp wherever it suited us. Or we could continue on and stop for the night at one of the logging camps…but it's a fair distance and we can't cover all of it on water."

Theodore stood and shouldered his pack.

"A logging camp?" he exclaimed. "Splendid! I have always wanted to visit one. If you still need to check your traps we best get moving."

Bill smiled as he watched him, secretly pleased by his gumption.

After checking the traps — which all turned out to be empty — they headed back to the canoe. This time when they passed through the thick vegetation Theodore did his best to mimic Sewall's earlier movements and followed the game trails with a slow, high step.

They got back on the water and over the next four hours kept a good pace. Sewall did all the paddling and the few times they had to portage around rapids Theodore tried to be helpful by carrying gear. At one point Bill had to carry the canoe almost a mile, balancing it expertly, until they came to another lake.

Theodore was breathing hard, but his cough had faded. Around them the clear fall sky was awash in the colors of autumn and gusts of wind helped to push them across the lakes.

"You live in a beautiful place, Mr. Sewall…I mean Bill."

Sewall grinned. "Why thank you. I'm quite partial to it if I don't say so myself."

In the late afternoon Sewall again balanced the canoe on his shoulders while they portaged through a shallow section of a stream. Theodore hopped from rock to rock, attempting to keep his boots dry.

Ahead on the shore a white-tailed buck snorted at them defiantly, and then it turned and was gone. Its grayish winter coat blended so perfectly with the woods that if it hadn't been for the white tail flagging as the buck bounded away, Theodore would have missed it.

He stared after it, memorizing detail with his naturalist's eye: the white coloring on the throat and eye rings, the main beam of the antlers as they spread forward, the ten-point wrack , about three feet wide.

The sight had stopped Theodore dead in his tracks.

"What a fine animal!"

Sewall lowered the canoe so one end rested on the ground, then he looked in the direction the deer had fled, and agreed, "It would'a made a fine donation to the camp kitchen, but I'm afraid only Wilmot could'a got a shot off that quick."

Theodore looked at the gun that was still slung over his shoulder.

"After the botched attempt I made at shooting that deer earlier I would have been ashamed to try."

Sewall laughed.

"Don't take it too hard. Get used to the country first and then you can try your hand at huntin' it."

With a curt nod, the Mainer hosted the canoe up over his head and expertly balanced it. For the next half mile he steadily marched forward, finally setting it down when they reached another alpine lake — the source of the stream they'd been following.

On the far shore ahead they could barely make out a long building made from large, unpeeled logs. It appeared to be constructed as two separate cabins with a covered area in between. Each building had its own stove pipe chimney with a trail of smoke flowing out of it.

To their right was a small cove with a pleasant field behind it. Sewall looked at it and saw several partridge shuffle about.

"Theodore, I think we should make one last detour before we arrive at the cabin. You know, out here you really shouldn't knock on someone's door empty handed."

Then Sewall smiled and asked, "Do you think you could help me with something?" Theodore shrugged. "Sure."

A few minutes later, Sewall steered their canoe along the shore, his rifle ready between his legs. He took one powerful stroke that sent them coasting, then stowed the paddle, raised his hand and nodded.

At his signal Theodore did his best partridge call.

Soon a curious bird jumped up on a log and Bill quickly and smoothly sighted it in and shot it.

Theodore went to grab the paddle, but Sewall stopped him, "Just keep callin', we can come back later."

They followed the entire length of the cove, then came back and did it again. Finally, Sewall went ashore a few times and with the certainty of a bloodhound picked out the downed fowl.

In the end they had eight.

Theodore was overjoyed. "Eight birds with ten shots! Excellent work, I must say."

Sewall accepted the praise.

"To me, partridge is right next to turkey," said Sewall as he cut free the breast meat from the birds.

"Not much else worth eatin' on these except the breast," he said, "but they'll be tasty."

After wrapping the meat in a cloth he stowed it in the canoe and added, "When I was a boy we never had turkey — only partridge. On Christmas mornings my brothers and I would just go out and not come back 'til we had gotten some. One year we had company and we came back with twelve — with what else we had it was a pretty good dinner."

Theodore looked over the lake, and noted how the late afternoon rays reflected off it and said, "I bet it was, Bill."

After a few minutes they were back on the water heading for the camp as if they had never stopped.

Chapter Five
The Logging Camp

On the shore of a sprawling lake sat the logging camp. The main structure was made of large, notched spruce logs that were chinked with moss and mud, and all the trees around it had been cleared away. Behind it sat other buildings - stables and a workshop for the blacksmith.

Bill and Theodore stared at the quiet camp from the water, hesitating before they beached. The lake appeared larger if you were on the water. Its low banks were mellowed by a weak tide that sank into the slate shoreline with a soft hiss. Further along the slate gave away to cat-a-nine tails, and behind that a quiet stream flowed out through a grassy area.

They'd accomplished a lot in the last few hours, covering over fifteen miles, and Bill no longer doubted that where he would lead the young man would follow.

The Mainer pointed to the covered area between the two cabins and said, "That's a dingle, it's where they store their supplies. The building on the right is where the camp boss lives with the cook; and the men take their meals there. The rest of the crew lives in the cabin on the left, and that's where they keep their gear as well."

He looked at the cabins and thought: if this young lad really wants to experience something of the area, then he's about to have his wish granted.

With a grin on his face and a ballad on his lips Bill dipped his paddle into the water and sent them landward. As the front end of the canoe glided onto the beach, he nimbly stepped across its bow onto the shore and hoisted it up from the water.

He then waited for Theodore to get out and together the two men approached the cabins.

Stepping into the dingle, Bill walked to the door on the right and paused.

"This's Cecil's place. I was afraid he might'a moved on already — he normally sets up on the Aroostook River for his winter camp."

Bill looked over the yard and then at the stables and added, "Looks like our timing is good. There's a fire goin' and the crews are still out in the woods."

He appeared hesitant as he waited to knock and looked over the yard again.

"Doesn't look like there's a full crew here either — that's good for us too."

He knocked and stepped back.

A nervous expression clouded Theodore's face when he heard a deep voice yelling from inside that this cabin was reserved for the cook and camp boss.

Bill leaned over to Theodore and said with a smile, "Be warned, the sign of a good Maine woodsman is you can smell 'im half a mile off."

The door was opened by a mountain of a man; as tall as Sewall, but twice as broad. His beard covered most of his face, and he did indeed smell ripe.

He smiled wide as he looked at Sewall.

"Bill Sewall! What brings you to our neck-a-the-woods? Couldn't believe my ears when I heard that knock...we don't get much company here, no."

He crinkled his brow, looked around and said, "Don't mean there's not a lot to do anyway." His eyes scanned the back yard. "Now where's that Coty run off to?"

Bill extended his hand and shook the man's huge paw. "Good to see you, Cecil. We're just passin' through, and we're hopin' to bunk down for a night."

At this the giant in the low doorway looked a bit uncomfortable.

He diverted his gaze to Theodore, unabashedly summing him up and then said, "I wouldn't a minded, Bill, 'specially if it was just you — you know you're always welcome here — but I've already sent most of my supplies up the Oxbow. If you'd come by in a few days we wouldn't even be here."

Cecil scratched his thick beard and added, "You know how it is."

"I figured as much. That's why I brought along something for the pot. I bet Coty could do wonders with these."

Bill lowered his sack from his shoulder, dug into it and pulled out the cloth bundle of partridge breasts. He unwrapped it and showed Cecil.

At the mention of Coty's name Cecil looked around again, this time with an expression of annoyance.

"Wish I knew where that bluenose was, I could use some help 'bout now."

Without warning he hollered, "Coty!"

Then he looked over the breasts.

"All ready for cookin'," said Bill.

"You sure brought along a few," Cecil said, smiling so wide Theodore could see a few missing molars.

Then Cecil's eyes lit up as he made a connection.

"That must'a been the shootin' we heard earlier. There were so many shots I was 'fraid the animals were shootin' back."

His gaze wandered back to the meat in Bill's hands.

"Of course, if you'd really wanted to make me happy, you would'a brought some Soldier Beans — you know my weak spot for your bean hole beans."

Bill shrugged.

"It really was a last minute thing — us comin' by." He held up his finger and added, "But I promise the next time I come by we'll have some beans."

Cecil laughed and then became somber as he stared down at Theodore and asked, "But what about this young buck? What can he contribute?"

Without hesitation Theodore stepped forward with his hand extended and introduced himself.

"Theodore Roosevelt of New York City, at your service."

A bit reluctantly, the big man shook his hand and said simply. "The name's Cecil."

Then he added in an apologetic tone, "All due respect, Mr. Roosevelt, but this ain't a hotel."

Theodore nodded and said, "I would be grateful for whatever hospitality you could provide."

Cecil laughed. "Oh, you might be surprised at what you're settin' yourself up for."

"Regardless," said Theodore, "I would not be a burden."

Cecil looked him over again. "Well, nobody gets a free ride here — I don't care who you're in New York City. If I give you a bunk, you'll have to work for it."

The younger man nodded even as Bill began to protest.

"Hold on, Cecil. He did help me get the birds."

Cecil smiled and gave Bill a strange look; not really certain why he would be speaking for the young man.

"Really," he said. "And how many did he shoot?"

Sewall averted Cecil's gaze and said, "Well, I did the shootin'."

Cecil nodded, seriously, "And who cleaned 'em?"

Bill stared at his boots.

"Well, I guess I did that too."

Confused, Cecil scratched his beard.

"So what exactly did young Mr. Roosevelt do?"

After a pause Bill said, "Well, he called 'em out, he did."

Cecil stared in disbelief, trying not to laugh.

"He called 'em?" he questioned.

He scratched his head and looked at Sewall again.

Sewall simply nodded.

"Did he use their first name when he called 'em? Or did he just say, 'hey bird'?"

Bill couldn't seem to get out a reply, while Cecil began to just fall apart laughing at his own joke.

Theodore waited for Cecil's yelps to fade. Then he said, "Please, Cecil, allow me to help."

The woodsman drew a breath, looked at a large pile of logs, and gestured to them with his thumb.

"I guess I could use some of those logs cut and split into firewood," he explained. "I always like to leave a good supply of wood when I depart a place in case anyone stops by."

He paused and added, "That is if you're so inclined to stay the night."

Again, Bill began to protest, but Theodore interjected by speaking directly to Cecil. "I would be glad to do it."

Cecil said, "I'll have Coty set you up."

Then he turned and started shouting for Coty again. Theodore quietly said to Bill, "Mr. Sewall, I feel my bird calling abilities will be the joke of the evening if I do not contribute in some other way."

Bill conceded. "Just be careful with the axe."

As Theodore started toward the wood pile Cecil turned and said, "A bit of advice; I've only got one crew out there but stay out of their way when they come in. They've been right out straight and might be a bit irritable."

With that he stuck his head inside the cabin and shouted again, this time in French.

Soon a young man came running around the corner. He had long, unkempt brown hair, looked about twenty and sported a sparse beard. He was also wearing a buckskin suit.

Cecil shouted, "And where you been, you lazy Frenchie?"

Coty looked back defiantly, "I was cleaning de root cellar—like you tell me to do."

Cecil lightened up. "Oh, yeah. Good boy."

Then he added, "Okay, Bluenose, you and Mr. Roosevelt go make some firewood."

Coty led Theodore around to the side of the cabin where he grabbed a large two-handled wood saw. The blade had been recently sharpened and oiled and looked ready to go.

"I tink it easiest if we pull one log out and work as a team."

Theodore nodded and helped him drag a log until it hung off the end of the pile by about six feet. The log was eighteen inches across and Coty marked a spot about two feet in.

"We saw here; den we split later."

Theodore tightly gripped one side of the saw, Coty the other, and then they slowly started drawing the blade over the log. At first it went slowly, but as they fell into a rhythm they picked up their pace. Soon they were halfway through, and just as Theodore was beginning to feel the strain the log broke free and dropped by their feet.

Theodore inhaled the soft scent of the wood while Coty marked where the next one was to be cut and they began again. After fifteen minutes they stopped to catch their wind and move the cut sections to the side. Theodore was breathing hard, but strong. Once two more logs had been sawed free they set down the saw and Coty pulled an axe out of a nearby chopping block.

Next Coty took a log and set it up on the chopping block. He turned it slightly so he could split it along the natural grain of the wood and stepped back.

Just as he was hefting the axe, Theodore asked, "Would you mind if I did some of the splitting?"

The young man in the buckskins smiled at the request and handed over the axe. Theodore smiled confidently as he lifted the axe, then he quickly—and rather erratically—swung at the log.

The axe fell on a slight angle and shot out to one side while the log was launched to the other. Theodore still held the handle tightly and the momentum sent the blade whizzing close by his shins.

Coty raised his eyebrows in surprise at the crazy attempt, and before Theodore could try again he politely grabbed the axe, lifted it and said, "Imagine where de axe lands before you strike. Picture it in your mind."

He retrieved the log, placed it back on the chopping block and rotated it to where he wanted it. Then he lifted the axe as if it weighed nothing and with only the slightest pause, the axe went up, descended, and then bit deep into the wood — all in one fluid movement — and split it down the middle.

Theodore smiled, showing a mouthful of straight teeth.

"Now that is what an axe is for."

Coty smiled and sat down on the log.

"I use an axe since I was a boy."

Theodore nodded, "It looks it."

Then Coty placed another log on the block, gave the axe back to Theodore, and said, "You try again."

Roosevelt did, and this time his blade bit deep into the log, but didn't quite split it. Coty ripped the logs apart with his hands and gave the axe back to Theodore.

"Good," said Coty, "now again." With that he placed another log on the block and they kept at it for about thirty minutes, splitting all the logs they'd cut.

As they caught their breath Theodore asked, "Why does he call you 'Bluenose'?"

Coty spat, "Dis is what dey call us Frenchmen — or at least de ones from Nova Scotia. I tink dey mean we are always out in de cold and our nose turns blue — I don't really know."

"He calls you Frenchie, too. Are you from France?"

At this Coty laughed, "Dis is a difficult question. Many years ago my ancestor came over to Hudson Bay. They say he arrived with de first boat of trappers to come to dis *New World*. I don't know dis man's name, only that he liked the land and he stay here.

"Eventually he took an Indian wife and dey had children. Dese children were raised as Indians, but also learned European ways. Dey learn to speak French. Dis went on for generations — over 150 years."

Coty had reached into his pocket and had pulled out what looked like a charred tail.

Theodore stared at it, intrigued. "Please tell me, what could that be?"

Coty grinned and chewed off the end of it.

"It is muskrat's tail. I trap some and cook dem last night, but I save de tail for a snack today."

He smacked his lips. "De fat and gristle make it tasty; my *moder* always saved it for me when I was young."

Coty held it up. "After hundreds of years I tink my French blood is diluted, but still I speak French. I know I am not from France, but am I French?

Reluctantly, he asked, "How many Frenchmen do you know dat love to chew on de muskrat's tail?"

Theodore said, "None that I have met."

Coty shifted uncomfortably, "Well, all de ones here do."

"Today we are called, *Courier de Brah*, or Runners of de Woods. In de end our European blood helped us survive de diseases dat wiped out many of our neighboring tribes.

"Our territory had always been large because as trappers we follow de game, but our identity was often confused. We were not European, but also not Indian.

"I believe it is dis reason that he calls me names—he doesn't understand me, or my people."

Theodore nodded. "He seems pretty demanding."

"Of dat please have no concern," said Coty. "He is demanding of everyone here. It is de way."

Coty looked over the lake. "This land may look peaceful, but it is easy to die here. Even at my age, I have seen many strong men die. And some of dem were very careful men also."

"Death strikes at the most inopportune time," said Theodore. "And it is not always as easy to face the future as bravely as we face the present."

Coty shrugged, "When it is your time you have no choice—all you can do is accept. Once your spirit believes it is time to go you cannot stop it."

He smacked his lips again and wiped his chin with his sleeve. Smiling, he added, "Dat is why we live well today."

The two young men then collected the wood they had split and began stacking it in the dingle. When they returned for another load the sound of bells drew their attention across the lake.

Out of the woods, by the shore of the lake about a half mile off, four large oxen appeared—lumbering forward in yokes that pulled immense weight. The bells on their harnesses tinkled clearly across the water.

Soon a sturdy sled came into view with a large load of logs piled on it. It creaked and swayed but the huge runner plowed over any brush it encountered and it continued on smoothly.

From where Theodore stood the load seemed too big for the animals, but they continued forward, steadily treading down a rough logging road that followed the lake shoreline.

A woodsman walked to the side of the oxen, a set of long reigns in his hand. Through whistles and shouts, and tugs on the reigns, he directed the load to the camp. Behind it followed several woodsmen, their axes and saws casually balanced on their shoulders.

Coty squinted to see who the driver was. "Dat's Barry; give him some distance when he come in."

Theodore nodded.

Suddenly Cecil's voice boomed from inside and Coty disappeared in that direction.

Theodore continued to watch Barry slowly direct the oxen to the end of a clearing by the lake shore and unload the logs. In the early evening chill the animals moved with determination and strength. Steam lifted off their hides as they trod along the muddy track.

Once relieved of their load they became lively, suddenly feeling the closeness of their night quarters behind the cabin—just beyond where Theodore had been chopping the logs.

When Barry pointed them at the corral the oxen started to run, despite the harnesses. He put all his might into stopping them, but only managed to slow them a little.

The other woodsmen had gone ahead, and now they scrambled out of the way as they saw Barry and the oxen moving in their direction.

Theodore heard Barry shout several commands, but they meant nothing to him until he noticed the oxen were moving directly towards him—and they were coming fast.

As he watched the animals seemed to grow in size, and he thought it best to step backwards, out of the way of the oncoming show.

But the wet mud under his boot gave and instead of moving away from them he found himself slipping into the track, directly in the path of the oxen. They were almost upon him as he scrambled for all he was worth; Barry nearly choked the oxen into a stop, and they finally came to a halt.

Bent with exhaustion, Barry pulled hard on the reigns while he shouted.

"Hey, four-eyes, get outa da way!"

Somehow Theodore scrambled out from under the oxen, but any fright he had felt evaporated after hearing Barry's words.

Instead of trying to get away, he now stood up in the path of the oxen to prevent them from moving forward again.

He looked Barry in the eye.

"You will address me as Mr. Roosevelt."

Barry glared at him.

"I don't care who ya'are..." said Barry, and he would have said more if he hadn't been interrupted by Sewall who had suddenly appeared on the scene.

"What's the problem here, Barry?" asked Sewall.

Barry motioned at Theodore.

"That young man almost got himself killed. That's my problem, Bill, if you're askin'."

Bill stepped forward, ready to defend his young charge, but Theodore steadied him.

"Barry is correct. I was at fault and I apologize."

A bit uncertain, Barry nodded.

"Well, these knuckleheads *heya* got a bit excited 'bout *dinnah* and were ready to go for it."

Theodore smiled, but then turned serious.

"But I will not tolerate being called 'four-eyes'," he added.

Barry stared back.

The oxen stepped about nervously.

Finally Barry nodded, but warned, "Well, Mr. Roosevelt, if ya slip in front of my oxen again they may be calling *you* the late Mr. Roosevelt."

Theodore grinned, a dozen different thoughts racing through his mind. And although Bill feared he'd been offended — or hurt by the unintended reference to his departed father — the young man only said, "Fair enough, sir, fair enough."

Bill and Theodore stayed out of the way while the men took their meal, and after Cecil had led them into the cabin where the crew lived, stowed their gear in one of the bunks.

The bunk room had a floor made of rough cut timber, and a woodstove near the middle of the room. The stove pipe ascended to the ceiling where it met a circular metal flange. It was primitive, but fairly spacious.

After Barry had had some food and a few drags off his pipe he calmed down. He'd eaten his grub quietly, not making eye contact with anyone. Once in the bunk room he sat not too far from what they called the stink pole – a long, narrow log where everyone hung their wet clothes to dry

Bill had noticed him watching Theodore.

The two other woodsmen were now talking to Theodore, comparing their knowledge with his. Although he was green in many ways, he'd read everything he could on the wilderness and knew many facts.

There were six bunk beds, all made from peeled logs, and one man lay back on a top bunk listening to the conversation; from time to time he threw out a comment.

"What kind'a name is Ruusavelt?" he asked. "I *nevah* heard such a strange name in my life."

Theodore said, "The evidence suggests that Claes van Rosenvelt — the ancestor to the American Roosevelt family — came from the Tholen region of the Netherlands, where they were land owners."

After an awkward silence the woodsman mumbled, "Hmm."

Then Theodore asked him his name, and where his family hailed from.

"Reckon I don't rightly know where we all come from," was his reply.

Then he added with a laugh, "I just know ya can't get *theya* from *heya.*"

Theodore noticed an animal skin on the wall and asked what is was.

"Peekunk," replied one of the woodsmen.

"Peekunk?" asked Theodore.

"That's an Indian name", another said, "we call it a fisher cat."

Theodore examined the pelt.

"It doesn't look like a cat to me."

Bill approached the pelt, looked it over and said, "That's a fisher — or an American fisher to be exact. My brother and I used to trap them when we were young."

Then he added, "And you're correct, it's not a cat at all."

From the bunk a man grumbled, "Don't know what you're talkin' 'bout Bill — that *theya* is a Peekunk."

As the other woodsmen shuffled to the bed he added, "That young fella can sure ask a lot of questions."

Later, most of the woodsmen were in their bunks, at times they still threw out a comment, but they were settling down. A kerosene lamp burned on a small table by the door, although it had been turned down low. Theodore had remained by the stove, cleaning his gear.

Barry sat up and asked, "Mr. Roosevelt, have ya *evah* heard a snowy owl screech?"

At this everyone became silent. A woodsman in the bunk shook his head slightly, as if to say the question was a bad idea.

Barry smiled in anticipation.

"Well, I have heard owls, but I do not believe I have heard a Snowy Owl," admitted Theodore. "In the Adirondacks I saw a Great Horned Owl, but did not have the opportunity to hear its call."

Barry nodded gravely.

"So ya don't think ya could mimic one?"

Theodore shook his head. "No, I do not believe I could."

Barry seemed to accept that and then casually asked, "As you are *closah* to the stove would ya mind gettin' my extra shirt? It's hangin' on that peg in the *cornah*."

Suddenly all eyes were on Theodore

He looked to Bill for an explanation, but the older man was in the other cabin talking with Cecil. Coty was out back scrubbing a cast iron pan.

"Certainly," said Theodore as he stood and walked to the corner. He reached for the shirt and was about to grab it when a blood-curdling scream erupted just above him.

He dove to the ground, and when he looked up, he saw a large Snowy Owl sitting on a rafter in the corner of the ceiling. It hopped around nervously as it stared at him.

The woodsmen all laughed as Theodore scrambled to his feet and backed away, subconsciously placing his hand over his beating heart. Barry was howling with laughter.

Cecil stepped forward. "Who's buggin' Whitey?"

Theodore raised his hand sheepishly.

"My apologies, Cecil, I did not know about…Whitey."

Someone by the bed shouted, "Barry set 'im up."

Feigning embarrassment, Barry waved it away.

"I just asked the lad to get me my shirt."

Cecil shook his head angrily.

"You scare away Whitey and we'll be overrun with rats. Anyone here want that?"

The laughter faded into a submissive silence.

Up in the corner Whitey settled down.

Out of the quietness there now came the sound of scratching and everyone looked at the back wall of the cabin.

"What is causing that?" asked Theodore.

Barry perked up. "I'm thinkin' it's a bear."

Someone by the bed mumbled, "Here we go again."

Instead of slinking away, Theodore stood up eagerly.

"Really, a bear? I would so like to see one."

Barry shook his head from side to side.

"Well, I wouldn't recommend it. We got some mighty big bear in these parts and we wouldn't want to scare ya, Mr. Roosevelt. In fact I wouldn't even go outside to relieve myself on a night when there are bear about."

All eyes fell on Theodore.

In the silence they could hear something roughly gouging one of the logs. From the inside it did sound imposing.

Cheerfully, Theodore put on his boots.

"Please, someone lead me to this bear."

Reluctantly, Barry sat up.

"Well, if ya really want to see a bear then I'll go with ya. But I can't be responsible if ya get eaten."

Then he grabbed an axe and opened the door, saying, "Someone might want to lock this *aftah* us."

Theodore had picked up on the serious tone and suddenly looked a bit sheepish.

"Should I bring my rifle?" he asked.

Barry looked at it and shook his head.

"That wouldn't even slow down a big bear. Let's just be quiet and see what's out there."

Sewall had watched the whole conversation, but was sitting back, seemingly unconcerned.

Once outside it was cold and quiet. When Barry shut the door there was only the crunch of leaves under their boots and the wind — and then they heard the scratching coming from behind the cabin.

Barry and Theodore moved slowly, trying not to make any noise. The ruckus from the back carried well, and it sounded like something was trying to tear through the cabin itself. Suddenly the safety of the cabin felt a long way off.

Theodore banged into some gear that leaned against the building and the sound abruptly stopped. The men too would stop and hold their breath here. But when they rounded the corner there was nothing there.

That bear must'a heard the racket you made and lit out a here quick-like," said Barry.

Theodore looked at the dark forest surrounding them, but couldn't see anything. "He must have moved very quickly I would think."

"Oh yes, they *ah* fast," said Barry.

Then he pointed at the scratch marks on a high log near the roof. "And look how big he must'a been to reach all the way up there."

Theodore stepped closer and looked up to examine the damage.

"You say a bear was responsible for those marks?" he asked.

The woodsman stepped closer and looked the marks over. "Yes sir, most definitely."

Theodore looked at the ground and then scanned the surrounding area again.

"Nothing else could have made those marks?"

Barry shook his head.

Theodore took another close look at the scratches in the logs, which were about two feet above his head, near the overhang of the roof.

"Well, do you suppose that bear could have been holding a porcupine when he did it? You know, like a tool?"

Barry sounded confused as he asked, "What?"

"Well, those marks were obviously made by a porcupine, so I am assuming if a bear was responsible for them then he must have been holding up that porcupine so he could do his work."

Barry nodded seriously, until he figured out that Theodore was playing with him. At once his face broke into a grin. He grabbed Theodore by the arm and shook his hand vigorously.

"We may've gotten off to a bad start, Mr. Roosevelt, but you're okay in my book."

Theodore smiled back, his teeth shining in the moonlight.

When they reentered the cabin Barry had his arm over the younger man's shoulder. "Don't worry, govnah," he said to Cecil, "We scared that bear right out of here."

When the men were all bedded down the cabin was oddly quiet. Cecil and Coty slept in the other cabin, and with more than half of the bunks empty the bunk room felt fairly spacious.

The men slept in most of their clothing, anything wet had been left on the stink pole by the fire. Coty seemed to just live in his buckskins, and he slept in them as well.

Cecil damped down the wood stove and blew out the Kerosene lamp as he left, and the heat creaking through the stove pipe was the only sound for a while.

Suddenly there was a flurry of wings followed by a loud screech.

"Sounds like Whitey found his *dinnah*," said one of the woodsmen.

The owl moved about in the darkness, possibly pursuing something, until someone yelled,

"Settle down Whitey, we're tryin' to sleep here."

Chapter Six
A Night in the Open

By three o'clock a weak sun looked ready to drop over the horizon. A cold wind blew across the land, whispering winter's arrival, and banged hollowly in now naked tree branches.

Bill Sewall steered the canoe across an alpine lake. His destination was a swampy grove of spruce with a hardwood ridge behind it, but the water ahead was blocked with floating debris and he was having trouble getting there.

Theodore sat up front, searching the shore for animals and occasionally pushing away a dead log. He thought about the overnight at the logging camp while Bill paddled.

"How far away is Cecil's winter camp?" asked Theodore.

Bill thought for a moment.

"I reckon it's about fifty five miles, maybe sixty, but gettin' there would depend on which time of the year you went. In the summer it's a long way off unless you've got a horse. In the winter you'd need a sleigh and some good weather."

To the left sat a large beaver dam, but there were no animals in sight. Theodore raised his gun. He looked through the sight and then, to Bill's relief, set it down again.

Slowly, Bill moved them closer to the shore, but here the water became stagnant and clogged with debris. Eventually the canoe bottomed out in mud.

Bill looked at the shore — still fifty feet away — and sighed. "This entire end of the lake is all muck. We can't get around it."

He then looked at the sky and the pale Fall sun — this far north already looking like a winter sun — that was now being accosted by clouds.

"Some of them clouds don't look so good."

Theodore cocked his head up and assessed the weather. "Do you think it will rain?"

Bill shrugged.

Theodore persisted. "It feels cold. Could it snow this early in the year this far north?"

Bill reflected. "When my father, Levi, first came to Island Falls — that would have been in July of Forty-Two — he claimed he saw snow flurries at night."

And then, without another word, Bill swung his legs over the side of the canoe and stood up to his waist in mud.

He sucked in his breath and fought for his footing.

"Thunderation, this is cold!"

Theodore was dumbfounded.

"Mr. Sewall what are you doing?"

"Well, I can't paddle through this muck, and we need to get to that shore. I guess I couldn't think of any other way to get there."

Fighting to hold his chest out of water, he was breathing hard. "I'm in it now though, and we'll get her out in just a minute."

Slowly, he made his way around to the front of the canoe and grabbed a rope. After tying one end to the bow he continued towards the shore until he had run out about twenty feet.

When he turned to pull the canoe towards him he sank deeper. From the neck down he was now covered with black mud, and only with great effort did he slowly move the canoe.

Theodore sat there, looking uncomfortable, while Sewall worked like an ox to pull the young man in the boat ashore. When Bill finally reached the shore he got solid footing under him, and he slowly brought the canoe closer.

They reached land after all and Theodore climbed out.

Bill was covered from head to foot with mud. He looked exhausted, but his spirits were only slightly dampened.

"I guess I wouldn't mind a little rain right now."

Theodore thanked him for his efforts as Bill grabbed the front of the canoe and started pulling it down the trail. Theodore followed him, but then stopped and took out his notebook to sketch a chickadee perched on a low spruce branch.

Had he paid equal mind to Bill he might have noted that the older man's face was flush with exertion. Meanwhile the sun had all but disappeared.

When the rain started the temperature had dropped so much that even Bill was surprised it didn't snow. He doubled his pace, working hard to get the canoe up a long hill, alternating between carrying and dragging it.

His breath shot out of his mouth in white puffs that were quickly dispersed by the rain. At least most of the mud had washed off, he thought, as he struggled along.

Behind him walked Theodore, apparently lost in thought with his head sheltered under a hood. Suddenly he stopped and took in the situation.

"Mr. Sewall...I am sorry, Bill. Exactly how far are we from your hunting camp on Mattawamkeag Lake?"

Bill stood up straight and fought to catch his breath.

"It's still a good distance, sir. In fact, with this weather turnin' on us I'm not certain we'll make it today."

The tall Mainer stared at the ground as if he had failed the younger man. Theodore took a long look at Bill; he was a living image of the day's exertion. Although he had a strong disposition toward ignoring discomfort, the freezing rain was doing its best to wear him down.

"This is because of me, is it not?" asked Theodore.

Sewall's expression turned to confusion.

"Excuse me, sir?"

"I just realized that because I was distracted with my observations, I was blind to the efforts you have been making to get us to shelter — is this not correct?"

Bill held his face up into the icy rain, exhausted and unsure of what to say.

Theodore extended his hand.

"You have my apologies, Mr. Sewall. It will not happen again."

Bill somehow shrugged off his fatigue and laughed uproariously. He grabbed Theodore's shoulder and shouted through the rain. "You sure can be peculiar, Mr. Roosevelt. Let's see if we can't come up with some shelter."

Theodore nodded. "Is there any chance of a fire?"

Again the woodsman laughed.

"Not unless King Olaf sends a lightning bolt...or I get real lucky."

At the top of the hill was a mound of granite. Bill walked around it and noticed one side was flat - it even had a bit of an overhang to it.

He gestured for Theodore to come over and said, "We're goin' to make a shelter here. That rock face is out of the wind and luckily there's a good tree that we can use."

Theodore looked over the site and then felt the rainfall pick up. On the ground he noticed the rock face only offered a little protection. He began to ready his mind for a rough night.

"Looks like it is going to be a wet one," said Theodore.

Bill smiled. "Well, I think we can improve that a little."

He gestured for Theodore to step aside and with several well-placed strokes he began chopping into a pine tree, about four feet off the ground. The tree itself was twenty five feet tall.

Soon he was more than half way through and he stepped behind the tree and notched it so it would fall the way he intended. After some more work it was ready to go.

Bill motioned for Theodore to step behind the tree and shouted, "Give it a push."

Theodore put his weight into it and soon the tree came crashing down, almost on top of their intended site.

Theodore stared at the scene in confusion, but Bill moved into action, trimming up all the branches on the underside. He left a few to support the trunk, and while Theodore watched a small shelter began to take shape, the felled tree acting like an extension to the overhang of the rock.

"We'll use some of the limbs for bedding, and throw the rest above us for more coverage."

As a final touch they lifted the canoe and placed it upside down on the tree. Bill grabbed a few remaining spruce limbs and lay them vertically in front of the entrance to act as wind brakes.

"Very impressive," said Theodore.

"Don't get carried away," said Sewall. "It's still goin' to be a cold night if I can't get a fire lit."

Grabbing a small bundle from his sack he set to work.

Theodore watched him make his preparations, and after a few minutes he asked, "Bill, why did you not ask me for help today?"

Bill looked up from his task.

"Guess I wasn't raised to ask for help."

Theodore laughed. "Since I was born I have always been surrounded by servants ready to help. I guess I never thought about just not asking for help."

"As you know," said Bill, "I had many older siblings, and between them — and my father — I learned to be self-sufficient and to never give up to hardships."

The younger man nodded.

"So you never quit a task you have started?"

Bill smiled. "Oh, I've quit a few when I had to. What I'm saying is I was raised by men who fared rough and hard, and the man who flinched or whined was thought very little of by his companions."

Theodore nodded. He took off his fogged glasses and began to polish the lenses while Bill resumed trying to start a fire.

In his sack he'd stored some dried tinder and a waterproof container, and he now added a pine knot he'd taken from the tree. From the waterproof container he pulled a metal tin, out of which he poured a handful of matches.

Once he had everything ready he turned to Theodore. "Snap off a few of those dried branches for me, if you don't mind," requested Bill, "and break them up nice and small."

Theodore did as requested and handed them over.

Bill placed the dried twigs over the tinder, and then got the pine knot ready. He checked the direction of the wind again.

Then he struck the match and it took.

Quickly he held the pine knot over the flickering fire, after a minute a wisp of smoke floated up, and then a steady flame. Bill set the tinder to flame and added the dried branches Theodore had handed him.

After making sure it had all taken he sat back with a proud smile.

"Not much of a fire, but it'll help."

Bill stowed his fire starting gear back in his sack. He was careful to make sure the matches remained dry.

"Always good to have somethin' dry to burn for when you're in a pinch like this."

With the fire taking root, Bill settled back. They had a nice bedding of pine boughs under them; not only was it comfortable, but it kept them off the ground—away from the water—as well. With a satisfied smile and said, "Those men back at the loggin' camp are good examples of how I was raised."

Theodore listened expectantly as Bill talked.

"You may have seen 'em relaxin', but their morals carry right through the day."

Bill stepped into the rain to grab a few logs and then added them to the fire. They were green, but the fire was burning strong enough that they eventually took; their sap sizzled as it heated up.

He continued. "I've worked the loggin' camps and it's a tough routine. You eat breakfast before daylight and work as soon as you can see—and you work until it's too dark to make out your axe.

"Counting us, there was only seven men at Cecil's that night—in high season there could be twenty-five—up at the Oxbow in winter-time it might be thirty. And that's a much smaller camp! When you have that many men livin' and workin' together you have to have rules. If you are ever sent to do something you better do it, and if you are expected to be somewhere at a certain time you better be there."

"Good for your word!" exclaimed Theodore.

"Ayuh," said Bill seriously, "And I gave you my word to be a good guide and that's what I'm tryin' to do."

Theodore tried to say something, but Bill, not usually a man of many words, seemed to be on a roll.

"Remember, up in the deep woods it's not all about money. The men that work in those camps work hard because they love the life. They may need money, but they'll give it away for a just cause. I've seen men work to the bone for seven months and then give their share to a friend to help with his family. That was the way the old time people dealt with community life up here in the woods.

"You've got to remember most of those woodsmen are family men. They come out here for five or six months—right through the winter—and work hard so their families have food on the table."

Theodore pondered these words.

"I believe the morals of the men you talk about to be of the highest standard. And there are lessons there that I hope to learn from, but I have one request from you before our journey is over."

Bill eyed him curiously.

"I am not here to be pampered—I wish to learn something from you—and I cannot do that if you treat this like a social outing. After hearing how your fellow men treat each other I have come to the conclusion that up until now you have not held me to the same standards. In the future, if I can be helpful, please instruct me on how."

Bill smiled. "Very well, no more kid gloves—and we'll see how well you keep up."

"I think my father would have liked you, Mr. Sewall," said Theodore just before he began to cough. He controlled it quickly, but Bill stared at him with a concerned expression that angered Roosevelt.

"As I have already stated, you are not to worry about my health either, Bill, I will be fine." With a sigh he added, "Mr. Cutler worries too much."

Bill nodded. "Well, your asthma seems to fare well in our lovely Maine weather. What other health issues do you have? If you don't mind my askin'."

Theodore thought for a minute while he added some wood to the fire. It was burning well now and took the chill off of both of them, but they were still thoroughly drenched. Outside the shelter the rain still came down hard, but they were fairly dry now.

"When I was just a child I fell into a snow bank and I have had a chronic ear ailment since then..." Bill grunted.

"And also I had a close call with diphtheria."

At this Bill looked up and said, "Diphtheria almost got me too. I was never discouraged and never thought I was going to die; though at times I did think I was quite near it. The doctor said my heart weakened and stopped beating at three different times, not for long at a time of course."

Theodore smiled.

"Well, you have me beat there. I do not believe my heart has ever actually stopped."

Eventually the rain stopped. Outside, everything steamed. Their shelter may have been adequate, but it really wasn't conducive to sleeping so they sat awake talking all night.

Later in the evening the cold set in; the temperature dropped and the water froze on the branches all around them. The two men observed the woods in the steaming twilight for a while, without speaking, but in the end Theodore broke the silence.

"You know," he started, "my father did a good many things in his life, but I do not know if he ever roughed it like this."

Bill laughed, and then said, "Forgive me, for I know your father passed away six months ago, but I am not familiar with how."

Young Roosevelt nodded.

"The doctors said it was an intestinal blockage, but really it was the political arena. After losing his last election he seemed visibly aged. He wanted to do so much and I think he could not accept not being reelected. What was worse was his opponent slandered him and my father was deeply disappointed that people actually believed the lies they had heard. "

Theodore adjusted a pine bow underneath him and continued. "They tried to hide it all from me and I was not sent for until the end—I had been at Harvard while my father suffered at our home in New

York—but I had read some stuff in the papers and knew he had had a rough time of it."

Here Theodore paused. "When they finally told me how ill he was I took the first train back, but I arrived two hours after he died."

Sewall shook his head. "That's a shame, son."

After a moment he added, "My father took a blow at the same age, but luckily, that's how I ended up here."

"How is that?" asked Theodore.

"You see," began Bill, "my father was a shoemaker from Phippsburg, Maine, but after twenty years he decided to be his own man and buy a woolen mill. He applied for insurance and a man was sent up from New York. Unfortunately, the day before he arrived there was a fire that burned down the mill.

"My father had always been poor with a lot of mouths to feed, but after putting his savings into the mill, he found that despite living prudently he could not support a family. So he decided to go where land was cheaper. He swore if he were ever to own a home it would be out here."

Bill grabbed the canoe suspended above him and shook it, making water flow down aver its edges. "And what a fine home it is."

Theodore looked around.

"It is practical and it serves its purpose. I can see nothing wrong with it."

Sewall laughed deeply. "It's nice to be with someone who is not easily discouraged."

Theodore nodded. "There is really not much point to it, is there? I have never believed it did any good to flinch or yield from any blow, nor does it lighten the blow to cease from working."

Now Bill nodded in agreement and then asked, "So tell me, do you have plans for when you finish at Harvard?"

Theodore paused before he replied.

"How I wish my father was here to discuss it."

"You took your father's counsel seriously?"

"Even now, I cannot take a serious step without first thinking what father would do."

"What was his advice when you went to college?" asked Bill.

Theodore smiled. "Take care of your morals first, your health next, and finally your studies."

Bill grinned. "I would have liked your father."

He fell silent and stared out at the rain that had started up again and finally added, "What decisions trouble you so much you need his counsel? If you don't mind my askin'."

Theodore smiled good-naturedly.

"I am torn between the life of a scientist studying natural history and that of a civil servant."

Bill nodded. "Are you drawn to politics?"

"At my father's funeral there was such an outpouring of love for the man. They called him 'Greatheart' you know. There in line, side by side, were the wealthiest men of New York next to some of the city's poorest."

Again, Bill smiled in agreement and then asked, "And in life, did your father treat all men equally?"

Theodore's face lit up as he thought of him.

"He acknowledged no man his superior unless it was by merit, and no man his inferior unless by demerit."

"Your father sounds like he was a straight shooter. I guess that's what you need to be a good politician."

Theodore looked around as if to make sure no one was within earshot.

He then leaned forward and said in a low voice, "You may laugh at me, Bill, but I believe one day I may be the President of the United States."

Bill raised his eyebrows and became somber and then replied with a smile. "Well, sir, we are a long way from the White House tonight."

Theodore grinned back. "Indeed we are; and I hope our future holds a few nights that are warmer than this one."

Bill laughed. "Oh, this ain't cold; back in '61 we had what they called `the cold Friday'. The temperature had dropped to 40 below when the only thermometer burst."

Theodore pulled his jacket close around him and moved a bit closer to the fire while he pondered what such unforgiving weather might feel like.

When the sun finally dawned its first rays reflected off the ice that coated everything. Theodore watched it sparkle, thinking how young and alive the world looked.

Chapter Seven
The Bear

Bill advanced through the forest with bearlike tread, stomping along confidently. Theodore followed him, wiry and nervous, cocking his gun and aiming at anything that moved. They each now wore fresh clothing and looked ready for whatever adventure lay in store.

A dense forest of pines gave way to a grove of apple trees, overgrown, but still producing fruit. The ground was littered with tracks from animals who foraged through the fallen fruit, leaving the soft earth bare.

Bill picked a couple of apples and shared them with Theodore.

"The bear love these apples," he said.

Theodore took a big bite and smiled.

"How could you blame them," he said, munching on the sweet fruit. "How did this orchard get here, anyway?"

Bill looked around sadly.

"A few years back there was a farm here. A man came up from New York and thought he'd try his hand at bein' a Mainer. He brought his wife with him and they did okay at first, but after their first winter they didn't have the stomach for it and left."

He pointed to the trees. "At least he planted these before he headed out."

Bill sat down on a log and, chewing his apple, asked, "Did you ever talk to your father about your indecision about a career?"

"Yes, I did," answered Theodore. "He was supportive, but never really said what he thought would be best."

Bill scratched his beard. "Well, what did he say?"

"He said if I wished to become a man of the sciences I should make sure that I intensely desired to do scientific work. We both knew he had enough money for me to do whatever I wanted, but he frowned on not doing something to the best of one's abilities."

Bill smiled. "All or nothing, eh?"

"Yes, something along those lines," said Theodore. "He also gave me a piece of advice that I have always remembered, namely, that if I was not going to earn much money I must even things out by not spending much. He warned me that if I went into a scientific career I must definitely abandon all thought of the enjoyment that could accompany a money-making career, and must find my pleasures elsewhere."

Bill grunted in response and then nodded towards the woods behind apple orchard. "I've got a few bear traps set nearby. Do you mind takin' a detour to check them?"

Theodore agreed eagerly. "Certainly! I had hoped to come across a bear on this excursion."

"The traps are good size so mind your step when we get close," warned Bill.

But Theodore had taken out a pad to take some notes, and as he walked he was careless, concerned more with what he was writing than where he was going.

"I believe there are no grizzlies in this area," said Theodore, "only the smaller black bear, correct?"

He snagged his toe on something and stumbled forward, and only barely caught himself. He glimpsed Bill's scowl and put away his notes.

Bill replied, "You might want to concentrate more on where you're placin' your feet than which bear's about."

Then he added, "There may be no Grizzlies, but a bear's a bear. You be careful as we approach them traps, and if there's one in it you do exactly as I say."

Near the far end of the orchard the pines took over and Bill turned and walked into the forest. He proceeded cautiously with Theodore behind him until he was about fifty feet in.

Suddenly he motioned for Theodore to stop.

In a circular area ahead was a large black bear with one hind leg caught in a trap. His thrashing had torn up all of the vegetation in a circle around him, and his leg was raw from the teeth of the trap.

The trap's chain had wrapped several times around a large stump while the bear was fighting to get free, leaving only a few feet of slack. The animal half stood, the chain weighing down over one shoulder and pinning him, and growled at them.

The bear's eyes rolled in its head as it searched for a way out, and then eyed the men as they approached just as cunningly.

This bear looks mean, thought Bill. He studied it for a solid minute with an apprehensive expression on his face.

Then he warned Theodore. "This old bear looks like trouble; you better keep your distance."

Theodore looked over the bear, which didn't seem too big as it cowered behind the stump.

"It does not seem so imposing, Bill," said Theodore, taking a step closer.

"That bear's four hundred pounds if he's fifty," said Bill. He noticed Theodore had moved closer again and added, "and I said to keep your distance."

Theodore raised his gun and asked, "Would you allow me to shoot it?"

Bill shook his head.

"That wouldn't really be sportin' with it chained like that."

As he saw Theodore frown he added, "Besides, a bullet hole would ruin the pelt."

"Come now," Theodore pressed, anxious for action, "I will pay you for the pelt."

But Bill shook his head again.

"I'm sorry, Mr. Roosevelt, but I'm not goin' to change my ways just because you've got money."

Theodore looked slightly hurt as he asked, "What do you plan on doing if you are not going to shoot it?"

Bill scratched his chin.

"Well, I normally just come up behind 'em and give 'em a thump on the head with this," said Bill as he held up a hatchet with a handle about a foot and a half long.

As if the bear understood his words it roared in anger and tried to stand on its hind legs. The chain dropped off his shoulder and now rested in the crook of his arm.

Bill took a closer look at the wounded animal.

"That bear might not be a grizzly, but it will still kill you if you don't keep your wits."

"Okay, Bill, I hear you," said Theodore. He lowered his gun, stepped back a bit, and then took out his notepad and began to sketch the bear.

Bill surveyed the ring of torn up vegetation and moved Theodore back to just beyond the edge of it, even though the bear seemed limited to the stump he was chained to. Theodore smiled patiently, feeling Bill was being overprotective.

Then Bill slowly began to circle the bear.

Cowering, his injury now apparent, the bear moved behind the stump, dragging the trapped paw—just out of Theodore's view. Frustrated, the younger man lowered his pad and moved closer to a better observation post.

As Bill got nearer the bear glanced back and forth between the two men. It tried to stand again and the chain slid onto its paw.

Its eyes narrowed as Bill raised the hatchet; and then—in a very human-like motion—the bear grabbed the chain with its paw and snapped it. The motion made a wave ripple down the chain and around the stump. In fact, it moved with enough momentum that it lifted all three lengths of the chain that surrounded the tree up into the air and then in a pile by the bear's feet.

Suddenly the bear had plenty of free reign.

It lunged past Bill so fast the Mainer had no time to react, and aimed straight for Theodore who had slowly moved forward into the bear's newly extended reach.

Theodore looked up from his sketch and saw the bear charging. He had no time to run; simply fell backward. The bear's eyes were locked on his.

"Watch out!" shouted Bill.

The bear came to a stop and rose up on its hind legs, its forepaws extended over his head. It took a swipe at Theodore, who was still falling, its sharp claws ripping his shirt but not penetrating the flesh.

Theodore hit the ground and looked up at the angry bear, towering over him. Now it looked formidable—very formidable—as its mouth opened wide showing teeth and dripping saliva.

The bear prepared to pounce, its jaw snapping.

Suddenly Bill appeared behind it and drove his hatchet into the back of the bear's head. The first stroke killed the bear, but Bill yanked out the hatchet and buried it again just to be safe.

Blood splattered Theodore. He was frozen in place on the ground, shocked. The bear still stood above him, leaning forward against the limit of the chain.

And then Bill pushed the carcass to the side where it crashed with a thud, dead.

The bear had already hit the ground when Theodore snapped to and scrambled backward.

"I...I can...I cannot believe..." he stammered.

Bill knelt next to him and calmed him. He gestured for Theodore to be silent.

The men sat panting for a minute; the bear lying dead by their feet.

Eventually Theodore said, "I cannot believe how fast he was."

Bill nodded. "Ayuh."

Finally Bill shook his head from side to side.

"In all my years," he said, "I never did see a bear pull a stunt like that. Did you see how he untangled the chain?"

Theodore shook his head slowly as his guide continued, "I must admit that was something I didn't foresee."

Theodore looked at Bill, then at his ripped shirt, and finally at the dead bear.

"I guess I did not foresee it either."

Bill took one look at the stunned expression on the young man's face and burst out laughing, and after a short pause Theodore joined him.

As they stood, brushing the dirt off their clothing, Bill asked again, "Are you sure you're okay, Mr. Roosevelt?"

Theodore smiled. "Considering you just saved my life, I think it's about time you started calling me Theodore."

Bill smiled back. "Okay, Theodore," then he added, "Now don't get too relaxed. We still got a bear to skin."

Robert Louis DeMayo

Chapter Eight
Bible Point

On the shore of Mattawamkeag Lake Theodore sat reading his Bible in a warm patch of sunlight. The site he'd chosen overlooked the confluence of the West Branch of the Mattawamkeag River and First Brook.

The West Branch had deposited fine sand and silt during the seasonal floods along its banks, and supported a magical forest of ferns and Silver Maple.

In the water before him ducks swam about, and several turtles basked on a dead log that floated just off shore. Behind him a forest of beech and birch shivered in the easy breeze — somewhere in their depths several songbirds called out a melody that drifted through the air.

After three weeks in the deep woods Theodore looked a bit different than when he'd arrived from New York. He'd allowed his facial hair to grow and altogether he now sported a rougher look.

Those who knew him would later comment that the biggest difference was in his eyes. They now held more confidence as they should considering he'd just completed something most of his Harvard classmates could never have dreamed of. Over the last few weeks he had embraced nature on its own level, and his body had responded well to it. He could only wonder now what the future held in store.

All he knew was that he felt proud of himself for what he'd accomplished, and the burden of his father's death had lifted somewhat and now seemed as if the grief and loneliness might actually be bearable.

He took a deep breath, set down his Bible and looked at the forest around him, as if seeing it for the first time.

The lake stretched out in front of him, but in his mind he pictured the land beyond that he'd spent the last few weeks exploring; his scientific intellect drifting through the rich assortment of plant and animal species he'd encountered.

He thought of the broad uplands that rose high enough to give an unobstructed view of majestic Mount Katahdin, and the wetlands, the small ponds and rivers, that they'd traversed using Bill Sewall's canoe.

Suddenly, he was startled as a shadow passed over, immediately followed by the whoosh of sizeable wings. A bald eagle swooped down just in front of him and expertly snatched a large trout out of the water.

The huge bird worked its wings to gain altitude again, not even glancing at the fish that struggled vainly in its talons. A minute later it landed in the crown of an ancient Hemlock on an island in the middle of the lake.

While taking in the scene Theodore noticed a canoe making its way toward him. Even at a distance he had no trouble making out Bill's tall figure, or recognizing his slow, methodical strokes.

When Bill got closer he hailed him.

"Hello Theodore! I'm on my way to check on your cousins; they're fishing out by the point—hopefully not gettin' into any trouble. I'll be passin' by again in an hour if you'd prefer to stay a bit longer."

Theodore grinned.

"I feel like I could stay here forever."

He motioned to a trail that led off into the forest and said, "I was planning on hiking back, but a ride would give me more time here."

"Can you wait an hour?" asked Bill.

Theodore skipped a flat rock across the water.

"Easily," said Theodore, "stop and visit now if you have time."

Bill ran the canoe ashore and stepped out.

"Oh, I think I've always got time for a Sunday visit."

The older man sat down next to Theodore and then lay back into a bed of ferns. The weeks in the wilderness had well established their friendship and neither of them felt the need to jump into conversation.

Eventually Bill sat up and noticed the Bible.

"Have you been findin' any truths in your readin'?" he inquired.

Theodore smiled and patted the Bible.

"I have always believed a thorough knowledge of the Bible is worth more than a college education."

Bill shrugged. "Well, I could only guess at the value of a college education, but I do try to read when I can."

Theodore looked at the Bible. "I also believe we make part of us everything we read—the words and ideas stay with us."

Bill nodded and stared across the lake in thought.

Theodore mentioned the eagle that had just come through and pointed to the island.

Bill laughed.

"There was a time when I was obsessed with those tall Hemlocks on that isle," said Bill. "And those eagles were all that stood in my way from gettin' 'em."

They both assessed the tall pine forest that covered the island. The trees there seemed older and bigger than those along the shore.

"You see," started Bill, "the trees on that island are some of the easiest money around. All you'd have to do was drop 'em in the water and you could float 'em all the way to the lumber mill—wouldn't even need oxen."

After a minute curiosity got the best of Theodore and he asked, "Okay, so what stopped you?"

Bill smiled.

"Well, you'll remember I told you how we had Indians as neighbors when I was young, and I grew up with several as friends."

Theodore nodded.

"Maybe it was the fact that I was born here, or maybe just something about my disposition, but I always got along well with the Indians—we seemed to look at things the same way. And when I was old enough to go into the forest to make a livin' I somehow ended up with a loggin' crew that was all Indian."

Bill gestured to the island.

"During the winter we'd pile up logs on this lake and then take 'em downstream in river runs when the water was high in spring. I can't tell you how many times I passed that island with my crew.

"Each time I'd nod at the big trees and try to get 'em interested in taking 'em down, but whenever I did they'd get quiet and look at the Eagles nesting up top."

"Finally I asked 'em point blank why they didn't want to cut down the trees. And do you know what they said?"

Theodore raised his brows in anticipation.

Bill laughed. "They said the eagles wouldn't like it."

The two men laughed and then Bill added, "At the time I thought they were being sentimental, but I'll tell you something. You look around this lake now and it may look like an untouched place to you, but a keener eye will see that most of the big, old trees are gone—except for on that island.

"I've paddled this entire shore countless times and I can say with certainty, the only eagles nests here now are the ones on that island. Bald eagles were once abundant in Maine, but you don't see 'em as much now."

Theodore nodded. "You think if you had cut down those trees the eagles would have moved on?"

Bill said, "Who can say, but it sure seems that way. There's a delicate balance to the natural world and I'm glad my Indian crew knew enough not to let me mess it up."

Over the next hour they talked about what they'd accomplished during Theodore's visit. Although he was proud of the things they had done: the trip to the logging camp, the night they roughed it in the open, hunting partridge and cooking trout over a fire, Theodore still felt in many ways that it had been a bit of a failure when he looked at his hunting record.

Bill tried to convince him otherwise.

"Bill, I am embarrassed to say that with only a few exceptions I barely hit anything I aimed for. If we had been dependant on my hunting skills we would have starved."

Bill laughed. "Oh, you weren't that bad. And I feel you are now far safer with a gun than when you arrived, and that's more important."

"Well, I have seen you with a gun," said Theodore, "and I am not sure I will ever be that good."

Bill held up his finger. "You have to remember, I got my first gun when I was seven. The reason I got good was, my dad had some pretty strict rules that I had to follow: first I couldn't be around kids or have it loaded anywhere near the house. And second, he only gave me one bullet so I made sure it counted."

Theodore stared at the ground, obviously not encouraged.

"Don't take it so hard, Theodore," said Bill. "If you want to be a better shot all you have to do is practice. There has to be some place in New York where you can shoot, isn't there?"

Theodore thought for a minute before replying.

"Yes, in fact there is."

The older man nodded.

"Good, now as to your visit, I think you are forgettin' just how much you've accomplished. Remember our first day in the woods? We traveled a good twenty-five miles that day — and some of it through some pretty messy bogs. I maintain that that's a good, fair distance for any man to cover."

Theodore picked a fern and stripped it down to the stem while remembering the journey.

"Yes, I agree. I doubt my father would have believed I accomplished it from what he knew of my body and its faults."

Bill shook his head.

"I think you are being hard on yourself. I'm sure your father saw the same potential in you as I do now. More than likely he shared your frustration concerning your asthma and just waited for the day you broke through."

"You are right," said Theodore. "He would have marveled at my new physical condition. These Maine woods have certainly done wonders for me."

Then Bill grew quiet for a minute, collecting his thoughts. He walked to the lake's edge, picked up a mussel and examined it, and then skipped it across the water.

Theodore watched him. It seemed to him that Bill was hesitating. He said, "Mr. Sewall, if you have something on your mind, please say it. I believe we have gone beyond being shy with each other."

"Very well," said Bill. "You asked me to be straight with you regardin' your progress here, and seein' as you are leavin' tomorrow, I feel I should give you my assessment."

Theodore sat straight up. "Please, go on."

"I realize you are uncompromising when it comes to integrity, and in many ways you see things as black and white."

Bill hesitated for a moment before continuing.

"I also know you use your father's persona as a yardstick, basing your actions and decisions on what he would consider right and wrong."

Theodore frowned slightly, nervous about where these observations could be leading.

Bill held up his hand, cautioning him.

"Don't get me wrong, I see nothin' bad about that and it seems to have served you well in the past."

The older man took a deep breath before continuing.

"I guess what I'm tryin' to say is that you seem like you aren't really here for yourself as much as for your father."

Theodore looked up angrily.

"You do realize he only passed away six months ago?"

Bill nodded and placed a hand on Theodore's shoulder.

"Of course I do, son. I'm not sayin' you should forget him. I'm just suggestin' that if you should return to do this again you should make sure it's for you, Theodore."

Theodore looked up, confused. "I do not understand."

Again Bill paused.

"We did pretty well out there, all things considered. But the wilderness is a dangerous place and you've got to be focused," said Bill. "Between your note-takin', all the seekin' of your father's approval, and the high-society world you've left behind, you've got a lot goin' on inside your head."

Theodore agreed, but said nothing.

"Now, I've never been to New York City and I bet there are some things there that would eat me up, but you learn to deal with them every day. You know the rules there, you've tamed that jungle — but it's also tamed you.

"When you come up here next you've got to shake all that — forget your notebooks, and Harvard, and your family name and the rules you grew up with.

"When you come back you need to become untamed. If you don't, you'll always just be stumblin' through the woods. Just be observant and forget that other world — then you'll be ready to really take on the woods."

Bill stood and walked slowly to the canoe.

Once seated, he pushed off and said, "I'll be back in a while to pick you up. While I'm gone just think about what I said."

Theodore nodded and sat silently, not looking up until Bill was long gone.

He glanced at his Bible, but left it sitting in his lap.

Then he stared at the surrounding landscape, as if an answer might be there, willing to float to him on the gentle breeze. The beauty was breathtaking, but offered no solutions.

Finally, he just sat and listened.

He took in the sounds of nature and enjoyed the breeze and the sun caressing his skin.

After a while, however, he had the strange sensation that he wasn't alone. For an eerie moment he thought of his father and wondered if his spirit could be watching him, but then dismissed the thought.

But the feeling of being watched stayed with him, and soon it became so overpowering that he turned to look at the woods behind him — and that's when he saw the wolf.

The animal stood by the trunk of an old beech tree, almost blending into the surrounding forest. It didn't move at all and watched him curiously. The breeze ruffled its fur.

When their eyes met the wolf took a half step back. It was only about twenty feet away and Theodore took in every detail of its appearance: the grizzled color of its hair, the ears standing up alert, the intelligence in the eyes that held no menace — but no fear either.

Theodore wondered how long the wolf had been there.

Later on he realized he had no idea how long they'd stared at each other, though it seemed an eternity at the time. There had been a connection that he could never fully explain, but that stayed with him long after.

Eventually the wolf had lifted its nose, alarmed by some scent in the air, and then trotted off silently without looking back.

When Bill returned Theodore didn't mention the encounter. In fact he never mentioned it to anyone, believing deep inside that it was supposed to stay between him and the wolf.

But he never forgot it.

The next day he packed his things and began the long journey back to New York City — to the world of the tamed.

Robert Louis DeMayo

Chapter Nine
Harvard

Theodore leaped up a flight of steps, two at a time, moving with the same stride he'd tackled the Maine woods with just a short week ago.

Above a stone archway a sign read, PORCELLIAN SOCIAL CLUB.

Ivy clad stone walls rose all around, giving the building a druidic look. He paused for just a second before pushing open an ornate oak door.

Someone shouted, "It's Roosevelt!" and he found himself greeted by cheers from a room full of well-dressed young men, all about his age. Theodore smiled, flashing his straight teeth. He took a deep breath, stepped forward and started shaking hands.

To the left the room he had entered opened into a magnificent library; behind the men several billiard tables waited for players. The walls, tables, and floors were all made of oak, polished smooth. The wood's scent mixed well with that of good cigars and leather.

One of the smartly groomed young men shouted out and approached with his hand extended. Theodore recognized his friend Dick Saltonstall instantly and moved in his direction. Dickeys hair was slicked back stylishly, and his clothes were expensive and fashionable.

"Dickey!" Theodore exclaimed as he pumped the young man's hand.

"Roosevelt! I'd given you up for dead. Where have you been?"

Theodore grinned confidently, "The wilds of Aroostook County, Maine. You should come up with me next time."

Dickey put his free hand on his friend's shoulder and looked at him from under his brow.

"You, my friend, are the heir to the Roosevelt family! You're taking nine classes at Harvard, and you've just been accepted to the Porcellian! That's the highest social honor Harvard can bestow! What in God's name are you doing in the woods of northern Maine?"

Roosevelt smiled patiently, "It's a wilderness area, not just woods — Aroostook County is bigger than Connecticut and Rhode Island combined. I also spent some time in Penobscot County...we really covered a lot of ground."

Dickey waved away the fact as trivial.

He asked, "And how did it treat you?"

Theodore took a deep breath and then exhaled .

"It appears to have cleared my lungs a bit. In fact, I cannot remember when I felt better."

Dickey steered him over to a punch bowl and they each got a drink. While their backs were turned to the crowd Dickey produced a flask and poured some gin into his, but Roosevelt refused.

"It's good to see you didn't pick up any bad habits in the wilderness," said Dickey as he took a sip of his drink. He wore several expensive rings that flashed as his hand rose. Dickey came from money, and even in this Harvard crowd he stood out.

He watched his friend over the rim of his glass and noted that Roosevelt smiled but appeared a bit uncomfortable. He also kept looking at the door, furtively, as if he couldn't wait to take his leave.

"With your father gone I would think your house would be very quiet this year," said Dickey.

Theodore nodded. "Most of my family is away this holiday season...maybe it is for the better."

Dickey placed his hand on Theodore's shoulder and said, "Then for Christmas holidays I insist you visit my family at Chestnut Hill. I won't take no for an answer."

Theodore was overcome by a sudden urge to be alone. The motion of his train journey home was still mixed up with Bill Sewall's canoe as it rocked from side to side on an alpine lake. He imagined the brisk winds of the Maine woods still moving his hair all about.

He fumbled for a polite way to refuse. "I don't think so, Dickey, I ..."

Before he could finish his sentence a door opened in front of them and several older men entered. They appeared to be professors, but in the Porcellian Club they treated the younger men with respect.

One approached Theodore and extended his hand.

"Master Roosevelt, I was so glad to hear you were accepted to the Porcellian. Your father would have been proud."

Theodore lowered his head slightly and accepted the praise. "My father did believe in seeking out quality."

The older man nodded. "Rightly said, young man, and remember that to be like him you have to be associated with men of quality – and honor – like those of the Porcellian."

Theodore hesitated only a second before replying.

"Quality may be attained through breeding and upbringing, but honor is a bit different. My father would have said that to be a man of honor you must see the good in every man, regardless of status."

The professor seemed taken aback as he looked over Theodore.

Theodore added, "And even the poorest of men can afford to be honorable."

Dickey stared at his friend in disbelief as if he'd just gone mad. In the club everyone acted as equals, but there was still a matter of submission to one's elders, especially the professors.

The professor scoffed, "The common man? And what do you suppose you could learn from the common man?" asked the professor. "Be serious, young Roosevelt. You will need to be if you hope to move amongst the upper class."

For an instant Theodore was transported back to the Maine woods, to the trapped bear behind the apple orchard...

Bill stood next to him and said, "That bear might not be a grizzly, but it will still kill you if you don't keep your wits."

In his vision he watched himself as he continued to sketch, oblivious to what was going on with the bear or the chain.

He saw the bear watching him draw…and then, as if in slow motion he saw the bear raise and turn…it stared right at him…and then it lifted the chain and snapped the coils free…it came for him…he saw himself frozen, unable to move…and then saw Bill Sewall appearing behind the bear with his hatchet raised…he saw the blade impact the back of the bear's skull…and then again…and he felt the blood spray forward onto his face…

It felt so real his hand moved as if to wipe the blood away. Then, for a brief moment, he froze.

He caught himself and replied to the professor.

"I think there is much we can learn from the outdoors; and the men who work in that theatre."

The professor laughed.

"I think you will find little wisdom in the wild, or those who live there."

Roosevelt listened politely, but again his mind wandered back to the northern woods. This time to the night he'd spent in the shelter with Bill after their first visit to the logging camp…

The rain had started to come down hard, and Bill had looked around for more wood and found none. He had gestured to the hatchet.

"Well, I better chop up some more wood or this little fire of ours is goin' to go out."

Theodore coughed as he said, "Bill, allow me to chop the next load of wood."

A sad expression came over Bill's face as he considered the request. He remembered Theodore's cousins requesting the same thing, and after the time they'd spent in the woods he felt this young man deserved better treatment.

He also thought of the fine conversation they'd been having, and hated to ruin it.

Still, he couldn't let him do it.

"I don't think that would be wise, Theodore."

The young man's face turned red.

"Do I have to remind you who is in charge of this operation?" said Theodore.

Bill exhaled. "You can remind me all you want, but it doesn't mean I plan on changin' my mind."

Theodore was quiet for a few minutes.

"Give me one good reason why you do not want me to chop wood. You have seen that I can handle an axe."

Bill nodded. "I've seen you with an axe, but not a hatchet in the rain. We have a fair way to go and if you cut yourself with that hatchet I may have to carry you out of here."

The younger man sat silent.

"Try to remember," said Bill, "that out here it's the little mistakes that get you. Leave behind your fire kit, twist your ankle, forget your axe in a tree…any one of these mistakes can cost you your life."

He placed his hand on Theodore's shoulder.

"You usin' a hatchet in the rain is a risk I don't think we should take." He motioned around them.

"Even with this shelter we've already got a lot workin' against us. Things can change quickly in environments like this. And you may have a good disposition, but that won't get you through everything."

Theodore was quiet for a few more moments.

"I see. Thank you for explaining yourself to me."

Both men sat there quietly, watching the rain-soaked forest, the cold mist steaming off them…

Theodore again came around and noticed the confused expressions of the two men standing before him.

He shrugged good-naturedly. "I may have been off in the woods too long, my apologies.'

The professor extended his hand and wished him luck, and then left.

Dickey again placed a hand on his shoulder and looked into his eyes. "Theodore, you seem distracted. What is going on with you?"

Before he could reply a young woman stepped through the door and caught both of their attention. She had pale blue eyes and thick ropes of honey-colored hair piled high on her head. She looked to be not a day older than seventeen.

She smiled shyly as she moved through the room, trying not to acknowledge the fact that every young man in the room was watching her. She also seemed oblivious to the fact that women weren't normally allowed in the Porcellian Club.

Roosevelt noted her movements reminded him of a young doe as she came their way. He also saw from her dress and hair that she must come from a solid family as there appeared to be some money behind her.

Dickey called, "Alice! Come join us," and the men around him looked at him with resentment. She came up to Dickey and, to the envy of all, hugged him.

Dickey introduced her. "Theodore, this is Alice Lee, my cousin, and our neighbor at Chestnut Hill."

The young woman curtsied and extended her hand so Theodore could take it.

Dickey quickly added, "Alice, this is my best friend, Theodore Roosevelt."

Theodore held her hand, but couldn't seem to find any words. Alice was an inch shorter than him, but held herself perfectly erect as she gazed into his eyes with a mischievous look in her own.

"Hello, Mr. Roosevelt. I believe Dickey has spoken of you before. Were you not recently traipsing in the wild somewhere?"

Still, Theodore couldn't find his tongue.

With a panicked look he found he could hardly pronounce a word. He stammered weakly, "Yes."

Alice played with his shyness.

"*Yes*? That is it? Surely you must have more to say about your adventure. How did you find the area?"

Theodore stammered again. "B-beautiful."

She laughed lightly.

"*Beautiful?*" She looked at Dickey and raised her eyebrow.

"Dickey, is this not the Roosevelt you said studied Natural History? I would have thought he could produce a more scientific description than '*beautiful.*'"

Theodore was now so embarrassed and self-conscious that Dickey finally had to come to the rescue.

"I'm afraid he isn't really himself yet. He's seemed distracted all evening—most likely been away from society too long." He jostled his friend playfully.

"In fact, I invited him to Chestnut Hill for the holidays, but I can't seem to get him to commit. I know you will be there, Alice."

Suddenly Theodore found his voice again.

"No, you misunderstood me," he blurted out. "I would be glad to accept your invitation."

Dickey looked at Alice and then grinned at Theodore.

"Really?" he asked.

"Oh, that would be fun," interrupted Alice, "I do so love the holidays."

Dickey continued to watch his friend, and he smiled as he sarcastically added, "I'm glad I could persuade you."

"How could I turn down such a gracious host?" said Theodore, suddenly somewhat extroverted. "I think that staying away from Chestnut Hill during the holidays would be like trying to stay submerged in the Dead Sea."

Alice perked up. "And what was that like?"

Dickey stood between them.

"Enough you two—I've been waiting all season for Theodore to return and will not have him distracted with trivial conversation. Besides, we've got important business to discuss."

But the lively young woman would not be put off.

"How rude of you to just dismiss me like that!" said Alice as she playfully punched her cousin in the shoulder. Then she added, "Please, cousin, tell me what could be so important that it cannot wait?"

Dickey grinned. "Paddy Ryan is fighting William Miller and we need to get tickets. They call Miller 'The Professor' because he teaches his opponents a lesson."

Alice said excitedly, "I want to go."

Dickey shook his head.

"Easy cousin, fights aren't for ladies. Even in today's society you must respect your place."

Alice glared at him and he grew restless. "Besides", he added, "we are going for educational reasons."

She looked skeptically at them both.

"And what could that mean?"

Dickey tried to sound professional as he replied, "Well, Theodore is quite a boxer himself, and we've got to see some new technique."

"I am not buying it. You are taking me", she said firmly.

Dickey started to protest, but Theodore interrupted.

"Even President Lincoln felt that women should be allowed to vote—and if that is not equality, I do not know what is."

He looked at Alice and added, "Perhaps with the passing of the 13th amendment to the Constitution that will happen someday."Dickey stared at him, confused.

"The 13th amendment freed the slaves," said Dickey.

Theodore responded, "Of course it did, but it freed all of us from prejudice as well. Now blacks can be judged by their merit, or demerit, not by the color of their skin. It is my hope that someday women are judged in the same fashion."

"Roosevelt, what has gotten into you?" asked Dickey.

Alice curtsied. "I have a champion."

Chapter Ten
Chestnut Hill

The Saltonstall family mansion sat on a hill surrounded by ancient chestnut trees with an expansive lawn up front. The back lawn retreated down to a river where a breeze rippled the water.

The ground had just frozen and dried leaves blew about, which made the impressive house with its numerous smoking chimneys appear all the warmer. When Theodore had departed for Maine it had still felt like summer in Massachusetts; now fall was upon them and its bitter cold was in every breeze.

Dickey and Theodore arrived in Dickey's buggy, following a private lane to the entrance. The wind whistled through the cab and they both wore heavy overcoats, scarves, and hats to stay warm. Theodore also sported some sizeable sideburns.

A servant steadied the horses while they both exited the vehicle, and as they walked up to the door the buggy was led away. After stamping some life back into their stiff limbs on the stairs Dickey opened the door and entered without knocking.

A butler appeared and took their jackets and hats.

He nodded to Dickey with a brief "sir."

Then he turned to Theodore and said, "It is nice to see you again, Mr. Roosevelt."

Theodore thanked him and Dickey said, "Yes, Mr. Roosevelt has become a regular fixture here this holiday season, hasn't he?"

Dickey grinned, "I believe he likes the chestnuts."

Theodore flushed slightly.

The butler nodded to Theodore as he left the room.

"It is always a pleasure, Mr. Roosevelt."

Trying to act casual, Theodore walked to the window and stared at the luxurious estate next door. Just as impressive as Chestnut Hill, the Lee Mansion could have easily sat next to any Newport Estate.

Dickey watched him, now noticing his fancy clothes which had been hidden under the heavy overcoat.

"I do say you are dressing well these days."

"It never hurts to be in fashion," said Theodore with a grin as he tried not to look out the window that faced Alice's house.

He added, "I have actually just received my inheritance and I feel a bit guilty spending some of it on clothing."

Dickey laughed, "If I remember correctly your father did keep a somewhat extravagant wardrobe."

Theodore warmed at the memory. "Yes, I called him a 'dandy' one night before he went out with mother, and he teased me with the same wording whenever I got dressed up."

Nodding curtly, as if the matter was settled, Dickey said, "You keep up the good looks. It can't hurt you in today's society."

Then he looked out the window at the Lee Mansion.

"Perhaps we should stop by the Lee's and see what plans they have for the evening."

Again Theodore blushed and said, "I suppose it would be only proper."

Dickey smiled mischievously.

"Unless you feel you have been seeing too much of Alice lately. We could just stay in if you would rather."

Theodore finally gave in and smiled.

"Okay, Dickey, I admit it; I am completely enamored. I will do whatever I have to in order to win her affections."

Dickey put his hand on the young man's shoulder.

"Ease up, Roosevelt, you're doing fine. I was just having a little fun." Then he added, "And maybe I'm a little jealous — do you realize that on your last visit you spent so much time with Alice that I barely saw you?"

Theodore was silent for a minute and then words started spilling out of him.

"Dickey, I cannot stand to keep this secret anymore, I must tell someone. On my last visit here I asked Alice to marry me, and I am hoping she has an answer for me today. The suspense is simply killing me."

"My dear friend, Theodore, you are full of secrets," said Dickey, surprised. "I wish you luck; and I must say my cousin, Alice, would be a good match for you."

On the grounds next door Alice suddenly appeared and Theodore involuntarily held his breath. She was with another young woman with dark hair. They walked to a bench set with a nice view of the river, and began to unfold some blankets.

"There's Alice with my sister, Rose," said Dickey. "You head on over there, and I'll join you in a moment."

On the bench with blankets around them, Alice sat with Rose. Lengthy scarves and warm hats insured that the ladies would not catch a chill.

Theodore approached without his overcoat, which he'd left behind despite the cold so it wouldn't cover his new clothes. He truly was dressed in fashion: high glossy collar, silk cravats, and un-creased, cylindrical trousers.

"Hello, ladies," said Theodore. "Alice, I must say that you look as pretty as ever."

Alice acknowledged his praise, but was interrupted by Rose before she could respond.

"Theodore!" exclaimed Rose, "What is growing on the side of your head?"

Theodore flushed at the mention of his new sideburns.

"Why, they truly are the size of powder puffs," giggled Rose.

A look of panic came over Theodore.

Alice came to his rescue.

"Oh leave Teddy alone; I rather like them."

He glowed when she called him Teddy, but then looked embarrassed when he saw Dickey approaching.

"So its *Teddy* now, is it?"

Dickey smiled wide, having heard the new nickname; he knew it would make teasing material.

Alice gave him a mischievous grin and then turned to Rose with a pleading look. Rose understood. She stood up, grabbed her brother's arm, and led him away.

"Why don't we check on the dinner plans."

Dickey protested playfully. "I was just beginning to enjoy myself!" But Rose continued to tug on his arm. He followed reluctantly and called over his shoulder, "But I want some time with *Teddy!*" and Rose yanked his arm hard.

Alice lifted the blanket and motioned for Theodore to sit next to her. Once he did she covered his legs with it and pulled another blanket around their shoulders.

"I do so love the fall," said Alice. "When winter begins it makes me sad. Even now I cannot let this autumn weather go...that is why I am out here pretending it is still warm."

Theodore looked over the cold river below them, and the barren trees, but he was unable to comment on the weather. He tried to look casual, but was unable.

The color drained from his face and he quickly became pale. Then he gently grasped her hands and looked into her eyes—eyes that shown like jewels to him—as he blurted out, "Dear Alice, have you considered my proposal of marriage?"

Alice smiled politely and moved a bit closer to him.

"Oh, Teddy," she said lightly.

She paused as she looked into his eyes, hoping to find understanding. "We are so young; I think we should wait a bit."

"W...wait for what? It will not change how I feel."

Alice looked up as a gust of wind blew through the trees, sending dead leaves cart wheeling across the lawn. And then, with a casualness she did not feel, she added, "Perhaps in time you will know better what you wish to do for a profession. I think it might reassure me."

Theodore relaxed as he realized her hesitation was regarding his career, not something more personal.

"Well, as you know," he began, "I am drawn toward a career in science. I feel a connection with the wilderness and the plants and animals there."

Alice reached for a basket by her feet and took out a thermos. Then she opened it and poured him a cup of hot tea. She took her time as she put away the thermos, all of her movements very slow. She was delaying her response, and Theodore began to fidget.

Unhurriedly, she blew on the hot liquid which was sending spirals of steam in the air, took a sip, and then casually said, "But you have also mentioned an interest in politics."

Theodore nodded enthusiastically.

"Yes, this is true. I am drawn in both directions. Watching my father allowed me to see what good could be done by public service."

Shyly she looked at him before speaking.

Her eyelids fluttered as she said, "At least in politics you do not return home with the smells of the lab lingering on you."

Despite himself Theodore drew up a hand from under the blanket and sniffed it for the scent of formaldehyde.

She laughed. "Come now, I am not that sensitive — I was just teasing. But do you really see yourself as a scientist? Tucked away in a lab doing research?"

Theodore thought for a minute and then replied, "Well, I have never really liked the laboratory as much as I enjoy just observing nature. I do not want to study things through a microscope, but observing nature and animals does not make you a scientist at Harvard."

Then, as a memory overtook him, he added, "But politics has some bad sides as well."

The thought of his father's death, and how politics featured in it was on the tip of his tongue, but he kept his silence.

Staring at the ground he gathered his thoughts before speaking. In a weak voice he said, "I am also not the best public speaker."

The bench they sat on placed them side by side, almost touching. Alice laughed heartily at his comment and moved even closer to him.

"Do not worry, Teddy, you can practice your speeches on me."

With that she placed her hand on his leg — a gesture that made him dizzy.

"I adore you," Theodore said softly.

"And I you, Teddy," she replied, "but that is enough conversation about marriage or your profession. I want to enjoy the holiday with you and any more serious talk will simply ruin it for me. We will talk about it again in the spring."

He felt that he had won at least some kind of victory, and so he agreed.

"I will leave it for the moment, but I will not stop trying to win your favor."

She smiled warmly.

"And what will you do for me, Theodore Roosevelt?"

Theodore laid out his plan.

"In February I will return to northern Maine. This time I intend to hunt large game — possibly a caribou."

Alice did her best not to look shocked, or disappointed, that his attempt to win her favor would somehow be related to the Maine wood — or an animal for that matter.

"A caribou," she whispered, "Oh my."

The young man nodded enthusiastically.

"Yes! And I will bring you the head as a trophy. We can have it mounted and displayed where everyone can see it. Maybe right at the entrance to the Lee mansion."

Not certain how she felt about this prospect, she smiled and simply said, "That would be lovely, Teddy."

Chapter Eleven
Return

As the steam train pulled into the Mattawamkeag Station a large, bearded man waited patiently on the platform. The icy February wind howled around him, but he stood unflinching, seemingly impervious to the weather.

Theodore stepped gingerly onto the platform, which was covered with at least six inches of ice, and set down his trunk. He only had one trunk this time, and it was smaller than either of the trunks he'd brought last time.

He wore a heavy coat with good insulation and a scarf. On his head he sported a fashionable hat — but it was one that he had picked out with warmth in mind, not style.

When he saw Bill he took off the hat and immediately walked over with his hand extended. There was, Bill noted, a new momentum to his step. Although both men smiled widely, when they shook hands their voices were serious.

"Mr. Sewall," said Theodore.

Bill nodded and noticed how exuberant Theodore looked. He squeezed his hand a little and felt a strong grip respond.

"Mr. Roosevelt."

Theodore looked around as if expecting someone else.

"My nephew, Wilmot, wanted to come along, but I decided to take the *pung* and it won't fit three."

Theodore creased his brow in confusion.

"A pung?"

Bill cocked his head nostalgically.

"I reckon with all the new vehicles coming around its gettin' a bit outdated. But a pung is a one-horse, open sleigh. With all the snow we've gotten this year it really is the only way to get around."

Theodore looked over the platform, but there was no horse or sleigh in sight.

"I didn't want the train to scare Scout, so I tied her up 'round the other side of the station. We should be goin'."

"Here, lemme grab that for you," added Bill as he reached for Theodore's trunk.

With a casual gesture Theodore waved away Bill's attempt and hefted the trunk himself.

"Thank you, but I have it."

He lifted it a little higher than he had to, hinting that it felt quite light to him.

"I have been working out during my off time at Harvard and I think you will find my strength has improved quite a bit." He then pressed the trunk into the air several times to prove his point."

"That's the spirit."

Theodore nodded and added with a laugh, "Maybe this time you will teach me to use an axe properly."

Bill slapped him on the back. "Good lad."

Theodore continued, "I have also been going to the firing range twice a week — and it is a three mile walk each way."

"Well, that's good news if I ever heard any! I'm goin' to have to think up some good adventure now to put you to the test and see just how strong you've gotten."

The train was getting ready to depart and Bill glanced nervously up and down the platform.

"Do you have any other luggage, Mr. Roosevelt?"

Theodore shook his head.

"No, this is it — and I think you will find what I brought this time is much more practical."

"So you received my letter with the suggestions?"

"Yes," said Theodore. "It was very helpful. I cannot believe how casually I chose my dress on my last visit. This time I brought layers and wool."

"My advice may have been helpful, but it seems to me you've been followin' President Lincoln's."

Theodore pondered this for a moment but couldn't make the connection.

"Okay, Bill, which advice are you referring to?"

Bill had a spark in his eyes as he said, "Our former president once said that if he had eight hours to chop down a tree he would spend the first six sharpenin' his axe."

Theodore smiled wide.

"Yes. I have been sharpening my axe. I was also a bit nervous; in your letter you made the Maine winter sound very dangerous."

"Well, a little fear is a good thing. Besides, I wanted you to know what you were gettin' into. If we have to rough it this time, the temperatures are always goin' to be below zero."

Theodore beamed. "We have done cold nights before."

Bill let out his boisterous laugh and grabbed Theodore's shoulder to steer him around the corner where his horse and sleigh waited. "Ayuh, we certainly have!"

Scout was a beautiful young horse, chestnut brown with an untrimmed mane. Her frame was compact and muscular, and she watched Theodore nervously as he reached up to stroke her arched neck. She warmed instantly to his touch.

"This is Scout," said Bill. "She's as good a horse as I've ever owned, and she'll go the distance if you ask her."

He patted her snout.

"That's why we take good care of her — loyalty is not something to be casual about."

"She is a Morgan, is she not?" asked Theodore.

"Yes she is," replied Bill. "You know the breed?"

Theodore nodded.

"I know their trotting ability made them favored for harness racing."

Bill added, "They're good for a lot more than racing. Morgans are fearless and dependable — they were used in the Pony Express and as mounts for the cavalry in the Civil War."

While he talked, Bill walked around the horse checking her harness and the traces that connected her to the sleigh.

As Theodore looked over the sled he asked, "You said this is called a pung, did you not?"

Bill simply nodded and continued checking it over.

"Do you think the term could be related to *tow-pung*, which comes from the Algonquian region?"

The Mainer grinned at his young charge and said, "It's good to have you back."

Theodore was still on a line of thought, "I am serious, Bill. It is akin to the Micmac word, *tobagun*, which means a 'drag made with skin'."

Scout neighed and got both of their attention.

"She can be nervous when she first meets someone, but she seems to like you. Talk to her while I check out the sleigh if you don't mind."

He explained. "She just loves runnin' in the woods, especially in winter with a sleigh behind her. Once we get going my biggest job is keepin' her speed down — that is until we get out of town and the snow gets deep. But waitin' around isn't her thing; and lots of people make her nervous."

Bill seemed satisfied with the condition of the harness, and he offered Scout a bucket with some grain in it. She eagerly went to it.

"We came in yesterday and the new snow on the road hadn't been broken yet, "said Bill. "It took us the better part of the day."

Theodore looked over the contraption behind Scout with interest. The sleigh was of a simple design, but sturdily built. On top of two solid runners sat an open box with little more than a bench for two to sit on. The back featured a shelf where Bill tied down Theodore's trunk.

The sleigh remained flat when moving, but the runners were smooth and offered little friction. When Theodore climbed aboard he noticed that the seats were so low in the sleigh that the sides came up to his shoulders, effectively sheltering him from the wind.

Bill untied Scout from the hitching post.

Before he put the trunk away, Bill made sure Theodore was wearing all the warm clothing he needed.

"It'll be cold when we first start out," said Bill. "Scout loves these town streets because she can really get the sled movin'. I've got a warm blanket to go over our legs, but you're gonna want everything buttoned up tight."

Theodore nodded and did the buttons on his coat up to his chin, and then smiled with satisfaction over his smart choice of clothes.

If it wasn't for the reappearing vision of Alice that seemed to be haunting him, he could have been content in the moment. But once again his thoughts wandered to her and he envisioned her bundled on the bench at Chestnut Hill, smiling shyly.

Bill shouted, "Tally-ho!" and as soon as Scout heard the command she fell into an excited trot onto the snow-covered road. Bill raised the reigns to command their direction, and Theodore held on for dear life. He didn't trust the stability of the sled and gripped the sides for support.

The streets of the town that had grown around the station were covered with a thick layer of hard-packed snow. As Scout picked up momentum, the sleigh cruised along behind her, lightly swinging out to the left or right when she encountered an obstacle.

On the corners she dug her hooves in deeper as the centrifugal momentum whipped the sleigh outward. But Scout ducked her head low and smoothly navigated the forces at work, keeping the sleigh at an even speed.

Theodore watched her and couldn't help yelling for joy. He nodded to Bill.

"She does indeed appear to enjoy her work."

"Yes she does," said Bill. Then he shouted.

"Go on, Scout! Show 'im what you got."

And the proud horsed raced through the streets.

Once they had left the town behind the forest closed in, the trees heavy with snow-laden branches. For mile after mile all they encountered was frozen fields, wind-swept icy lakes, creaking tress; and an intimidating silence.

For a while they just cruised along, their faces flushed from the cold, but the rest of their bodies warmed by the woolen blanket. They had both also put on thick scarves.

But the further they pushed into the wilderness, the worse the road got. More snow had come down since Bill had ridden through the day before and it was slow going. Soon they were breaking trail through three feet of fresh snow with drifts up to six.

Now and then Bill stopped and let Scout catch her breath. During one of the pauses he broke the silence with a question.

"So, Theodore, do you remember what we talked about at Bible Point just before you left?"

Theodore gave him a quizzical look.

"Bible point?"

Bill laughed.

"Ayuh. That's what I've named the place on the lake where you often retreated to read your Bible."

Theodore nodded. "Very fitting."

And then he added, "And yes, I remember our entire conversation like it was yesterday. Are you referring to my state of mind when I returned here?"

Bill said nothing, but the twinkle in his eye said he was.

For a minute the young man hesitated.

"It has been a year now since my father passed away. I think I can say now that I am here for myself, not him."

Bill smiled and relaxed slightly.

"That's good. And what have you been up to other than your studies?"

Now Theodore's eyes lit up.

"Actually, I have been courting a young woman. I plan on returning with a trophy caribou for her. You should see her, Bill, she really is someone special."

Bill nodded; a concerned look now in his eyes.

Theodore looked over the cold landscape they passed through, a dazed expression on his face as he said, "Alice Hathaway Lee…I plan on marrying her, Bill."

Chapter Twelve
The Frozen Woods

The Maine woods were still in the grip of winter as Bill, Wilmot and Theodore set out on their first excursion. The evergreens were heavy with snow and it lay deep on the ground, crunching under their boots in the sub-zero temperatures.

They hiked in a line through a stand of young birch whose branches whipped them each in passing. Their path was little more than a game trail, most likely blazed by deer.

Theodore stumbled along behind his two Maine guides, a bit angered at how much trouble he was having in spite of the training regiments he'd developed at Harvard.

It had been his intension to excel on this visit, not repeat his last poor performance, but throughout the first few miles he'd had trouble breathing, and he had fallen several times already.

He rubbed a fresh laceration on his face, made from a birch branch that caught him when he was distracted. Every so often he had to stop and clear his throat loudly.

Eventually he got control of his breathing, and after making a determined effort to concentrate on his foot placement he no longer stumbled.

Bill seemed to notice the improvement.

"If you're through gufflin' we might pick up the pace."

Theodore was about to reply when he saw a red squirrel nearby. The squirrel would have been hard to miss as it stood on a branch broadcasting a warning through the forest about the three intruders.

"That would be fine, Bill, if you could just wait one moment."

He nodded toward the squirrel. "I understand it is just a red squirrel, but I realized when I got back home last time that I do not have a specimen for my collection of the wildlife in this area."

Bill nodded and then stepped back.

"Go ahead, take your shot."

Using the low-caliber rifle he carried Theodore sighted in on the animal, about twenty feet away, and fired.

It dropped into the snow and lay there, unmoving.

"Nice shot," said Bill.

Theodore stepped up to the squirrel and opened the canvas backpack he carried.

"Better make sure he's dead before you handle him," Bill cautioned. "I got bit good one time by an undead squirrel when I was young,"

Theodore nudged the animal and said, "I think I have this one covered."

Then he wrapped it in a cloth and stowed it. Before he was done he also entered notes about the location, time and weather, and then stowed his notebook with the squirrel in his backpack.

His business finished, Theodore shouldered his pack and stood. The other two men stood silently, waiting.

Taking in their location, Theodore drew a deep breath, looked around and said, "There is something scary about the woods in winter, but still I find them intoxicating."

The scenery, Theodore thought, was nothing short of magical, as he walked through a hushed land of white and green. The wind was suspiciously absent, and the air had a tangible crispness to it, filled with the scent of pine.

Bill warned, "They are indeed intoxicatin', but if you stop for too long after sweatin', you'll catch a chill."

Both Wilmot and Bill turned and started down the trail again, and Theodore followed. Barely a hundred steps later Theodore requested another stop so he could sketch an Arctic woodpecker.

Bill sighed, obviously not happy with the delays.

"My apologies," said Theodore, "but there does not appear to be much other game about, so I thought I would study the smaller ones that appear to have stayed through the winter."

Bill was silent for a minute.

"Theodore, may I speak frankly?" he asked.

Theodore took off his fogged glasses and cleaned them.

"Mr. Sewall, I would expect no less from you."

"Well, sir, there is plenty of game about, but there are several reasons why you're not seein' it."

Theodore stood his ground defiantly.

"Please, Mr. Sewall, tell me what they could be."

Again, Bill let a few moments pass as he pondered his response.

"Do you remember when I showed you how to walk through the brush, followin' game trails so you wouldn't continuously fall?"

The young man nodded, "Of course I do, but we are in open ground, with the exception of all the snow, and there is nothing similar in the terrain."

Bill nodded.

"Ayuh, I agree, there are no obstructions from the brush, but there is still a way to move through this landscape without soundin' like an elephant."

He looked at Theodore and added, "These winter woods were made for stealth."

Theodore absorbed the comment silently. Then he said,

"I see. And aside from my tread, what other suggestions do you have that might help us see more game?"

Bill could see he'd ruffled the young man's feathers and was hesitant to continue.

Wilmot spoke for his uncle.

"It might help if you didn't fire off that gun every twenty minutes," said Wilmot. "At least not until we see something sizeable."

Theodore considered the request, but before he could reply Bill had an idea.

"Theodore, if what you'd like to do is see game, then I suggest you follow me for just a few minutes and try it my way. I'm sure I can put you close to something."

Theodore smiled. "That would be smashing."

Bill nodded and continued down the trail, but now he watched the periphery a bit more carefully.

Soon he stopped and pointed at a set of tracks.

In a low voice he said, "These tracks are fresh. Do you see how they have not been filled in by any recent snow?"

Theodore examined them and then nodded.

"Well, just inside of these woods is a deer—a big buck by the looks of it. Would you like to see it?"

Again, Theodore nodded.

"Very well," said Bill. "We are goin' to leave everything with Wilmot; includin' your gun and backpack. I want your hands free and nothin' on your back."

Theodore handed it all over to Wilmot.

Bill continued. "And when we step into the woods I want you to move the way I do—step in my footsteps, and try your best to be utterly quiet—and no sneezin' or coughin' if you can help it."

Pointing at Theodore's coat he added, "Don't let the branches rub against your clothin' either, a deer will hear it no problem."

Bill then set off into the deep snow. He moved slowly, taking high steps through the drifts and weaving through the pine branches carefully.

The tracks led into a grove of thick pines, none over twenty feet high, with lots of low bows.

Wilmot was now out of sight and the wind had died down completely. It was utterly quiet.

One after the other the two men waded through the thick snow, the tracks trailing off ahead of them. Bill followed the hoof prints as they wound through the trees and Theodore gingerly stepped in the woodsman's tracks.

Soon they noticed some branches ahead were swaying erratically, suddenly relieved of their snow load. The buck had brushed past them mere moments before.

Without turning, Bill gestured for Theodore to come closer and whispered, "The white-tailed deer is one of the most curious animals we've got here. Now that we're this close he's gonna hear us no matter how quiet we are, but sooner or later he will wait to see what we are. Don't move fast when you see him."

They continued for awhile, their concentration fixed on the woods ahead and all sense of time disappearing in the winter maze of pines. The tracks wove through the area with no discernable destination. They seemed to be guided by curiosity only.

Deep in the grove all was still, but ten feet above them it whistled through the crowns, blowing fine crystals of snow into the sun's rays.

Theodore was so enchanted with the beauty of the forest that he had almost forgotten their purpose when they stepped around an ancient spruce and confronted a ten-point buck. It jumped in place as they came into view, surprised at seeing humans this close, and then snorted.

The buck was in its prime, and although it seemed as tightly wound as a spring, for a minute it stood defiantly.

Theodore and the buck stood unmoving, staring at each other. Neither flinched while the trees around them swayed in the wind, and then a nearby branch cracked loudly, spooked the deer and sent it bounding out of sight with a few leaps.

Theodore watched the white tail flag.

"What a magnificent specimen," he whispered in awe.

Bill nodded, "Just remember, they're all around us — you just have to learn how to tread quietly and with reverence when you are in *the haunts of Nature.*"

Recognizing the words from Longfellow's *Song of Hiawatha*, Theodore recited the next stanza.

"Love the sunshine of the meadow, love the shadow of the forest, love the wind among the branches..."

Bill joined him, *"And the rain-shower and the snow-storm ... and the rushing of great rivers through their palisades of pine trees ...and the thunder in the mountains, whose innumerable echoes flap like eagles in their eyries..."*

Theodore stopped and let Bill finish.

He looked at Theodore with a smile and said quietly, *"Listen to these wild traditions, to this Song of Hiawatha!"*

Robert Louis DeMayo

Chapter Thirteen
Caribou Chase

The Maine woods were in a deep freeze. The tree branches were covered with a layer of clear ice and the frozen leaves looked like crystals. They clinked like chimes when the cold wind blew through, and when they dropped, the made the sound of a footstep in the snow.

The weight of the ice had proven too much for some of the lower branches. They lay on the ground, defeated, among ice-coated twigs that the wind had snapped off the tree tops.

Under the crust of ice lay a good three feet of soft snow. As Theodore soon discovered, it was no easy terrain to maneuver through. When he took a step he slowly placed all of his weight on the leg. It would hold for a moment, but then suddenly he broke through the surface and sank deeply into the snow. While trying to extricate the leg he broke through with the other until, in the end, he just stood in a deep hole.

Wilmot came over to him and examined his predicament. He walked in a pair of snowshoes, only sinking in about four inches.

He stopped and sat back on his haunches.

"Travelin' on a day like today is going to be miserable."

He laughed, "I'm sure that's why my uncle let me do the guidin' today."

He stood and gave Theodore a hand out of his hole.

Then Wilmot reached behind his head to retrieve another pair of snowshoes from his pack which he had brought along for Theodore.

"You get nowhere if you try to cover this terrain without snowshoes. You just keep post holin' and that's exhausting," said Wilmot, "and where the snow isn't deep the ice has everything locked down.

"At least there's enough snow to use these," he said as he handed the snowshoes to Theodore who examined them carefully. Wilmot added, "They take a little to get used to, but in the end there's no other way to move through deep snow.

"This ice is more dangerous than you'd think. You may do well in the mornin' when you're fresh, but later in the day your concentration might wane and you won't be as stable on your feet. Out here you don't want to be down with a broken leg, miles from shelter."

The snowshoes had a hardwood frame that was connected in a webbed pattern with rawhide lacings. The front end of the shoe was raised for easier maneuverability, and there was a leather pad in the center of the shoe where the user placed his boot when strapping them on.

"I have read about these and always wanted to try them," said Theodore.

Excitedly he noted the merits of the design. "By distributing the weight of a person over a larger area the snowshoes prevents a person's foot from sinking completely into the snow. The mechanism is called 'flotation'."

Wilmot strapped them onto Theodore's boots, trying not to laugh as the young man lectured him about the benefits of something he'd been using since he'd been five.

Theodore continued. "The trick is not to let the snowshoe accumulate snow, hence the latticework of the webbing."

The Maine guide nodded and watched while Theodore walked around practicing.

"What a functional design. It really does make a difference."

He stomped in place and then examined the grid-like patterns he left in his wake.

"My goodness!" he exclaimed. "I thought they would feel awkward and cumbersome, but they do not...how extraordinary!"

Wilmot fought to suppress a smile.

"Well, Mr. Roosevelt, you really need 'em when the snow is heavy."

Theodore stomped around some more, exhilarated. His breathing was heavy, but not strained.

"You could go anywhere with these," said Theodore.

Wilmot turned away, laughing, as they continued down the trail.

Later, they stopped and looked at a set of tracks.

Theodore studied them and ventured a guess, "A white-tailed deer?"

Wilmot shook his head and replied, "No, caribou — and those tracks are fresh."

Theodore perked up.

"How fortuitous!" he exclaimed. "Wilmot, I have promised my Alice that I would return with a trophy caribou head. Do you believe this caribou is of good size?"

Wilmot studied the tracks for several minutes.

"Ayuh," he answered. "I believe it is. But that animal could be halfway to Canada by now. They range farther than the deer."

Theodore took a deep breath and scrunched his eyebrows together as he concentrated.

"I want to go after it," he stated. "With these snowshoes we can go anywhere."

Wilmot lifted his head and looked away, trying his best to avoid looking at Theodore.

"I don't think it's a good idea," he said.

"The temperature is goin' to start droppin' soon and we don't know where those tracks will take us."

"Nonsense," declared Theodore. "The day is young and I am paying for this venture. Tell Mr. Sewall that I simply insisted. After all, it is really just a matter of time."

"Alright," Wilmot reluctantly agreed. "But first we need to redistribute our gear."

Theodore had a canvas backpack; Wilmot only carried a sack—like the one Bill often carried. Wilmot helped Theodore lower his pack and then rummaged through it and his own sack, taking stock of what they carried.

"You'll need to go lightly. I'll put my things in your pack and carry both loads."

"Also," added Wilmot, "your gun won't bring that caribou down, so we'll switch. Mine is a heavier caliber."

With that Wilmot reverently handed over his riffle.

Theodore took the rifle and marveled at it.

"I call it Old Reliable," said Wilmot, "she's a Sharp's business no. 45 and one of the best guns I ever had."

Theodore set his jaw as he put his arm through the gun strap, then he quickly cleaned his glasses and nodded sharply when he was ready.

"Let us get started," he said as he moved on in the direction of the tracks, lifting and lowering his new snowshoes in exaggerated movements.

The frozen land proved easily traversable with the snowshoes and the men made good time. The tracks stretched out clearly in front of them forming an obvious trail. The woods were quiet and Theodore felt as if there was nothing alive except himself, Wilmot and the caribou.

As they approached a rocky hill Wilmot cautioned Theodore not to make any noise. The hill was short and steep and looked to have a good vantage of what lay ahead, but the approach was thick with snow.

"Go up that hill, quietly, and you might get a shot at him on the other side," said Wilmot.

As Theodore started to step up the incline he lost his balance and clumsily fell backwards. There was a tearing sound and they could both see that the webbing on his snowshoe had broken. Worse, when he landed he fell on a stick and the sound of it cracking seemed to reverberate in the quiet country air.

They looked up the hill.

Wilmot whispered, "With that knoll between us I don't think he would'a heard you."

"Good," Theodore said quietly, relieved.

They both examined the broken snowshoe.

"Don't worry," said Wilmot. "I can fix it. Take it off and put on one of mine."

As soon as Theodore had replaced his broken snowshoe with Wilmot's he slowly side-stepped up the hill. Wilmot had taken off his other snowshoe and gingerly followed Theodore by stepping in his footsteps. Several times he broke through the snow and sank to his waist.

Theodore waited several times for Wilmot to catch up so they could survey the land together. When they reached the top they were rewarded with the sight of the caribou foraging quietly in a clearing below them. It was indeed a buck, and it wore a magnificent rack that curved forward over its head.

Theodore removed the safety of Wilmot's rifle, leveled the gun, and slowly crept over the crown of the hill on hands and knees.

He sighted in on the caribou. The animal sensed something was wrong but hadn't spotted the men.

It anxiously looked all around, raising its nose to smell the air. Exhaling in short bursts, its eyes scanned the area.

Just as Theodore pulled the trigger the animal, apparently startled by instinct, moved. The bullet winged it and almost knocked it off its feet, but the caribou got its footing and ran off, bucking once.

"Thunderation!" shouted Theodore.

Wilmot frowned as the animal bolted north, seemingly uninjured. Where they stood they could see a splatter of blood on the white snow.

He said, "That's the last we'll see of him."

Theodore stood dumbfounded.

He looked at Wilmot as if he'd insulted him.

"Out of the question!" he declared. "I wounded the animal and now I am duty-bound to finish it off."

Wilmot took off his hat, scratched his head, and paused before speaking. "Mr. Roosevelt, you'll never catch that animal — it's gone."

Theodore was unfazed.

"Indeed we will. The day is young and the animal is wounded. We will be upon him shortly."

Wilmot replaced his hat.

"All due respect, but we don't have the proper gear to overnight in this weather, sir, and that animal may not be mortally wounded."

It was as if Theodore didn't even hear him.

He stepped quickly down the other side of the hill; Wilmot tried to follow but kept breaking through.

Theodore yelled back, "Did you see that rack? I think it would look lovely in the Lee mansion!"

In his enthusiasm Theodore was just about running after the wounded caribou. Wilmot looked at the broken snowshoe he was carrying and shouted, "We need to slow down long enough for me to fix this snow shoe."

Theodore disagreed.

"Absolutely not; my caribou will get away."

Wilmot glanced at the ground, obviously not liking where any of this was going.

With a note of panic in his voice he shouted. "Wait!"

Theodore reluctantly stopped and glared at him.

"I will have this caribou," he shouted.

Wilmot thought hard for a moment, and then said with reluctance, "Okay, you go and I'll follow as soon as I've completed the repairs."

Theodore quickly started the spot where the caribou had been hit.

Wilmot shouted after him.

"Mr. Roosevelt, I do not feel comfortable with you running off alone."

"Do not be ridiculous," Theodore called back. "I will have *The Challenge of Thor* by my side."

Wilmot, perplexed, watched Theodore disappear around the side of the hill.

He sighed, took out some rawhide lacings and began to repair the webbing, but he was too anxious to complete his work quickly and catch up. The rawhide slipped from his nervous fingers several times.

He looked in the direction of Theodore's disappearance and mumbled, "If this goes wrong my uncle's gonna kill me."

When Theodore reached the clearing where the buck had stood he examined the blood splatter on the ground and then followed the tracks as they led off through a forest of frozen pines.

Soon the tracks reached another clearing, and Theodore could now see drops of blood dotting the snow along with the hoof prints.

"The animal is wounded," Theodore whispered to himself, "how long can it continue like that?"

He stayed on its trail, hour after hour, always close, but never in sight. The caribou continued to lose blood and Theodore was amazed at its stamina.

He decided to quicken his pace.

Soon he found himself on the shore of a frozen lake — and far across the ice, there was the caribou. It stood looking at him, pausing to see what the next move of his pursuer would be. After a moment it turned and walked away.

Even from the distance Theodore could tell it was limping.

He continued his chase.

Wilmot reached the shore of the frozen lake almost an hour after Theodore, panting heavily. The snowshoe was damaged worse than he'd thought and he'd been forced to stop repeatedly to fix it.

Instead of finding a smooth rhythm in the pursuit of his trustee he was forced to move at a ridiculously slow pace. He felt like he was barely making headway and knew if he didn't find Roosevelt — and some shelter — soon they would both be in trouble.

Wilmot could see both the caribou and human tracks stretching across the lake, but there was no other sign of either of them.

Wilmot glanced at the weak winter sun which was already nearing the horizon. A heavy gust of wind hit his side and he watched it blow away a section of track right in front of him.

He exhaled in frustration.

"Roosevelt, what are you doing?"

Miles away, Theodore was stubbornly following the caribou. It was now a mere 100 yards ahead of him, but it moved whenever he did, refusing to let the hunter reduce the distance between them. Both were getting tired from the long pursuit.

Theodore appeared to have forgotten that he was carrying a gun. His face was flushed and his whiskers were frosted from his exhalations.

He felt his mind slipping with exhaustion and recited a favorite poem by Longfellow — the Challenge of Thor — out loud, as he continued.

"I am the God Thor! ...I am the War God! ...I am the Thunderer!"

His eyes were fixed on the caribou; he saw nothing else around him.

Between breaths he yelled, *"Here amid icebergs rule I the nations!...This is my hammer, Miolner the mighty!"*

He stopped to clean his glasses, glared at the buck and muttered, *"Giants and sorcerers cannot withstand it."*

The caribou stopped as well and watched him.

When he started after it again, he shouted at it.

"Here in my Northland..." he gasped, *"My fastness and fortress..."* gasp, *"...rein I forever!"*

He stopped again, exhausted, but after a few breaths pushed on.

It had started snowing hard.

He realized the fresh snow was beginning to obscure the bloody tracks and quickened his pace regardless of his exhaustion. His legs throbbed and his lungs burned.

Visibility was waning quickly with the thickening snow flurries, and even though the caribou was only a short distance away, he began losing sight of it.

Theodore was now wheezing from the exertion and his recitations had become tortured shrieks.

"The wheels of my chariot roll in the thunder..." he huffed, *"the blows of my hammer Ring..."*

He had to stop. He struggled to breathe.

He looked around, suddenly confused, and cried, *"... earthquake!"*

He saw the caribou heading for a grove of trees, and despite his exertion Theodore tried to sprint for it.

With the last of his energy, he yelled, *"Here I defy thee!"* but then his body defied his will.

He stopped.

His legs buckled; then his lungs appeared to collapse, and he fell forward in the snow.

He lay like a fallen branch, half sunk in, and he didn't move for a long moment.

With the last of his strength he lifted his head and looked around.

Everything had turned white, and there was a silence about that suffocated him. The wind blew hard but he could no longer feel it on his skin.

Just ahead the caribou had stopped and watched him.

He was breathing hard, as was the caribou.

They stared at each other, questioning, no longer obsessed with reason or motive.

For a minute he forgot even the chase.

His body yearned to sleep, and then his head fell forward, into the snow.

Chapter Fourteen
Another Night in the Open

Wilmot was hurrying through the storm, hunched over like some snow demon as he ran. At the lake he'd taken off his snow shoes. The ice was now pocketed and gave enough traction that he didn't need them.

And now he finally made good time.

His gaze was pinned to the ground as he moved, concentrating hard on the rapidly disappearing tracks. The weather had worked itself into a white-out, and with the oncoming dusk a sudden drop in temperature descended over the land.

When he came upon Theodore, Wilmot was going so swiftly that he almost tripped over his body, which was now almost completely covered with snow to form a white hump.

His body was still warm and Wilmot figured he hadn't been down long. He felt for a pulse in the collapsed man's neck, and when he sensed the throb of the artery he slumped back in the snow and let out a breath of relief.

He called to him and tried gently to wake him, but Theodore was far away.

In his mind Theodore pictured Alice watching him as he walked toward a frozen horizon. She called his name repeatedly, but he could barely hear her voice. She said something about "the spring", but her light soprano was lost in the wind...and then it strangely morphed into Wilmot's deep voice.

"Mr. Roosevelt, sir. Wake up."

After a minute he came around.

His face was caked with ice and snow. Theodore opened his eyes and stared uncomprehendingly into the white-out that had descended around them. In less than an hour a foot of snow had come down and not one thing was recognizable to him.

He was also awakening to the last few minutes of daylight; the snowstorm had ushered in the evening. Theodore blinked repeatedly in the thickening gloom.

Wilmot noticed that Theodore's eyes were still unfocused as he fumbled to locate his glasses. As he spoke it became evident that his mind was still occupied with one thought, and he repeated it over and over.

"He is close, Wilmot, we cannot stop now."

Theodore squinted at his glasses that Wilmot had picked out of the snow and handed to him. They too were caked with ice, and what exactly to do with them appeared to confuse the young man.

"We are wasting time here," said Theodore.

He gave Wilmot a pleading look. "I saw him not ten feet away, Wilmot, watching me. We must continue the chase."

Wilmot held Theodore's gaze, trying to steady him. "You're goin' to be dead by mornin' if we don't get shelter and a fire soon."

Theodore looked shocked at the suggestion. He gazed down at his snow-covered clothes, barely realizing he had passed out.

"I feel fine. I see no reason to stop…"

Wilmot cut him off, "You are feverish, and if you have any sense left you better start listenin' to me."

Theodore seemed to reluctantly grasp his physical condition, but still he refused to quit.

"Wilmot, I am not afraid of this storm. I do not fear the weather," shouted Theodore, reviving himself a little.

With the adrenaline pumping through his veins, he added, "Why not go for it, Wilmot? What are you afraid of?"

This comment made the young Mainer smile. He crouched in front of Theodore, sheltering him as the wind howled around them. He never appeared rushed or impelled by the weather.

He said, "Mr. Roosevelt, we're not takin' shelter because we're afraid, we're doin' it because it's the sensible thing to do."

"Well, I do feel rather cold," replied Theodore weakly.

"Good," said Wilmot. "Now if you pull it together, and help me through this, I'll tell you about the only thing that really does scare me."

He looked around scornfully and added, "And it taint a snowstorm, that's for sure."

Theodore choked out a laugh, "Well that is something I would like to hear. Something you fear, eh?"

Wilmot asked, "Can you follow directions?"

Theodore nodded, but began to shiver as he struggled to stand up in the deep snow. Wilmot found his gun and slung both weapons over his left shoulder so he could support Theodore with his right.

After getting off the frozen lake they made it to the edge of the forest. Wilmot sat Theodore against a large pine tree trunk with the backpack leaning against his side.

He was now out of the wind, but not much warmer.

"I'm goin' to look for a shelter. You stay put."

Theodore still looked confused. Snowflakes silently sailed through the air all round them.

He began to sing, "*And beyond them stood the forest... Stood the groves of singing pine trees...green in summer, white in winter...ever sighing...ever singing.*"

Wilmot looked into his eyes again.

"Mr. Roosevelt, are you okay?"

Theodore raised his eyebrow, which was still thick with ice.

"Such a chase!" he exclaimed. "How intoxicating."

Wilmot pushed him back, gently, against the tree trunk.

"Just don't get up. Stay here, I'll be back."

Theodore nodded, leaned back and closed his eyes.

When Theodore reopened his eyes he saw earthen walls surrounding him. Roots protruded as if reaching for the two intruders; and the frozen dirt crumbled under him when he leaned against it.

They were out of the wind, in a shelter of some kind.

As he blinkingly looked around, he saw Wilmot's rifle hanging from one solid root. His pack sat on the ground a few feet away. Wilmot was sweeping the snow from the center of the enclosure with a freshly cut pine bow.

"Where are we?" asked Theodore.

Wilmot replied, "Looks like this big pine tipped with that last ice storm. She didn't want to let her roots go and tore up a big hole when she fell."

Theodore's mind cleared of the heavy fog that had numbed it as if he were in a dream. He looked over the burrow he had awoken in. The crater created by the fallen tree may have kept the wind down, but the snow still fell on the half of it that was uncovered and open. In the woods around them the wind had picked up and made the snow appear to be falling from all directions.

"I am surprised a bear does not live here. It seems appropriate," said Theodore.

Wilmot looked around and said, "Doesn't appear to be occupied."

He pulled a small bundle out of his gear and crouched near the open edge of their shelter. With precision he opened the bundle and neatly set aside its contents. It was now so cold that his fingers froze stiff; he had to interrupt himself several times to breathe warm air onto them.

"I'll make the fire right here and with the earth behind us we should be okay until mornin'."

He smiled at Theodore as he pulled out his tinder and matches. "I'm sure my uncle gave you his speech about the importance of a good fire kit?"

Theodore nodded and tried to smile, but his face was still numb from the cold. He then thought of something, obviously funny, because he grinned and in doing so thought he'd cracked his cheek.

"I bet that caribou is having a bad night."

Wilmot looked up from his task and said, "I bet he's doin' better than you. What I can't figure out is, why didn't you just stop chasing it?"

Theodore thought for a minute.

"He simply would not stop running."

Wilmot shook his head.

"That caribou stopped runnin' as soon as you stopped chasin' it. I'd guess it's not more than a few hundred yards away."

Theodore looked up. "Really?"

"Animals aren't stupid," continued Wilmot. "If they are injured they just rest as soon as they can."

Seeing Theodore's bewildered expression he continued, "Look at the storm and tell me what you see?"

Theodore peered into the darkness.

"All I see is wind and snow."

Wilmot smiled. "Exactly, and there's also darkness and the cold, but none of these are anything to fear. You may have forgotten that, but I guarantee the caribou didn't."

Pointing into the darkness he added, "To the caribou that's home."

He walked to the edge of the shelter and stood facing the wind. Breathing deeply and looking up, he noticed some of the dark storm clouds blowing off and a sharp horned moon trying to break through.

Theodore had never heard Wilmot quote anything before, but recognized the tone of respect in his voice when he did.

"I think I could turn and live with animals," he began, *"they are so placid and self contained. I stand and look at them long and long."*

Wilmot looked Theodore in the eye and asked, "Did you hear what I said about animals not fearing nature?"

Theodore nodded, his teeth chattering.

"Then what do you think the caribou is doing right now?"

Theodore thought of the wind and snow coming down, and the darkness enveloping everything. Then he remembered how comforting the snow had been when he passed out.

He smiled as he said, "Sleeping."

"That's right," said Wilmot. "Sleepin' like a baby."

Then he continued with the quote he'd started earlier.

"They do not sweat and whine about their condition."

Theodore glanced over and saw Wilmot looking him over, sizing him up.

"That is not Longfellow," said Theodore.

Wilmot nodded and continued, *"They do not lie awake in the dark and weep for their sins."*

Theodore tried to stand up, but Wilmot put a hand on his chest and gently held him in place.

"It's dark and you've lost your heat. If you go out there now you won't have a second chance."

Finally, sense returned to Theodore. He looked Wilmot in the eye and nodded.

Wilmot took off Theodore's rifle, which he was still carrying on his shoulder, and set it leaning against the roots of the fallen tree by the other rifle. He set Old Faithful next to it.

Then he sank to his knees next to his fire kit, retrieved a small container and produced a few matches. After selecting one, he put the others away.

The kindling was ready as he crouched to block the wind. Holding the match in the air, ready to strike, he paused and smiled. "Of course, if I don't get this fire goin' neither of us is gonna make it."

Then he struck the match and, cradling the flame from the wind, held it to the carefully prepared bundle of kindling.

It threatened to die at first, but then the flickering flame quickly grew from an unsteady dance to a small but steady blaze that hungrily devoured the kindling.

Wilmot leaned back contently and was about to say something when a movement caught his attention.

Their shelter lay at the edge of a meadow, about one hundred feet across. When Wilmot looked up he saw a flicker of movement, and then made out a rabbit standing in the clearing, watching them.

The rabbit was white, nearly invisible in its thick winter coat against the snow. Theodore could barely make out the thing that had caught Wilmot's attention, but he knew it must be something alive.

The animal sensed the men's attention and tensed.

When it finally bolted into the air to escape, Wilmot was ready. With one swift movement he grabbed and aimed his gun. The shot rang out and the animal dropped dead onto the snow.

Wilmot grinned.

"It's a whole different experience with a belly full of warm meat. We're eatin' rabbit tonight."

As he got up to collect their dinner he nodded at a small pile of dead wood he'd gathered.

"If you don't mind, Mr. Roosevelt, please add enough from that pile to keep the fire goin' 'til I'm back."

Theodore smiled. He had finally fully come around and shuffled toward the fire, albeit with stiff bones.

"I think it is time you started calling me Theodore," he said.

Later they crouched around the fire, eating singed pieces of rabbit. Wilmot had been correct and the meat was restoring strength and energy to their bones.

The storm had died off, but it remained bitterly cold. Every few minutes they had to stand and stomp the life back into their legs. The mist from their breath filled the air and frosted their facial hair.

"Are you ready to tell me what you fear, Wilmot?" asked Theodore.

Wilmot broke a small branch in half and added it to the fire. He looked Theodore in the eye and said, "You remember the lines I quoted earlier?"

"Yes, I do," replied Theodore. "Although I did not recognize them; I did not know you were a fan of verse, to be honest."

He laughed. "Well, my uncle and I have different opinions on what qualifies for verse. The two of you prefer the epic poets, but I tend to like Whitman."

Theodore nodded. "I have read some of Walt Whitman's verse."

"Uncle thinks he's too wild; too unrestrained."

"And what do you think?" asked Theodore.

"I believe the man has great insights into human nature. I believe he sees the truth."

Theodore thought about the lines he'd heard earlier.

"You stated before that you thought you could live with animals...are you saying you prefer their company?"

He nodded. "Let's just say that I prefer to be rid of the human qualities that are lacking in animals." He paused and looked up at Theodore. "So you want to know what I fear?"

Theodore nodded but held his tongue.

"What I fear most is to be trapped in the world of people—to lose this freedom...this independence that we find in nature."

They both looked out over the white landscape that had developed around them.

Wilmot continued.

"I fear that one day either this wilderness will be gone, or I will—for some reason—not be able to be part of it."

Theodore looked at him for some time before commenting. Then he said, "You fear society."

The Mainer nodded somberly, "I think Whitman saw the true benefits of honoring our animal instincts, and being part of nature, not just observers."

With that he sat up a bit straighter and started reciting again. This time he raised his voice and projected it into the darkness, "*They do not make me sick discussing their duty to God... Not one of them is dissatisfied... Not one is demented-with the mania of owning things!*"

The words echoed over the nearby hills and hung over the fire. Both men absorbed them slowly.

When Theodore looked up a short while later he noticed Wilmot was now standing. With a wild look in his eye Wilmot walked to the edge of their shelter and shouted into the night.

"*Not one kneels to another, nor to his kind that lived thousands of years ago... Not one is respectable...or unhappy over the whole earth!*"

When he was done he sat back. Theodore pondered the words, letting them repeat in his mind, but in the end he could not speak.

They sat silently by the fire, the trees around them occasionally cracking from the intense cold.

A pale, weak sun rose over the meadow which now lay under several feet of fresh snow. Theodore and Wilmot stood by the fire, stomping their feet to keep them from growing numb.

"Oh, how I wish I could take off these boots and warm my feet by the fire," said Theodore.

"I know," replied Wilmot, "But you've gotta be careful with your footwear. If your boots get too close to the fire they'll thaw, then you'd never get your foot back inside. You're much better off just keepin' 'em on."

They had spent the night stripping the nearby shrubbery of burnable material, but now that the sky was lightening they could see more fuel.

"I'm goin' to get a few more logs to turn this fire up one more time, and then we can have the last of the rabbit," said Wilmot. The frozen carcass didn't look too appetizing, but Theodore well remembered how well the meat had gone down and was already anticipating it.

When he looked over the frozen land around them Theodore saw no landmarks that might have helped him get his bearings.

"How can you tell where we are?" he asked.

Wilmot sniffed the air — in almost the same way that Bill had done — and then said, "I have an uncanny sense of direction that never fails me."

Theodore watched him, eager to learn his secret.

Then Wilmot laughed and pulled a small gadget out of his pocket. "It's called a compass."

Theodore joined his laughter and then Wilmot opened the compass to determine their location and the direction of Island Falls.

"Wilmot," said Theodore. He cleared his throat. "As you stated, the caribou is very close to us. At this point I am not willing to abandon the chase."

Wilmot turned to him in disbelief.

He chanced using his first name.

"Theodore, I really think we should be headin' back."

He was still speaking as Theodore put on his snowshoes. But he found it difficult to walk in them.

"My goodness, this hurts my feet today."

Wilmot nodded.

"You've most likely got a case of snowshoe feet. You won't be able to wear them snowshoes for more than an hour before it gets unbearable."

Theodore stood up straight and said, "We will see about that! I, for one, am not ready to quit."

The Mainer held his stare as he scraped up a pile of snow with his boot. As he pushed it over their low fire he said, "We've got a long way to go, sir, and when this fire is out we are committed."

Theodore watched the fire hiss as Wilmot strapped on his snowshoes. Then he shouldered his backpack and slung his riffle over a shoulder. When he was ready he gave Wilmot a curt nod.

Without asking for approval Wilmot started them in the direction of Island Falls. They had lost the trail of the caribou, and Wilmot's only concern now was getting them to safety.

As luck would have it, after only a few minutes Theodore pointed out tracks in the snow.

"That is him, Wilmot. There is my caribou."

Sure enough the tracks led away from a bloodied indentation in the snow where the animal had slept.

"He must have set off when he heard us comin'," said Wilmot.

Roosevelt took off like a bloodhound, his aching feet forgotten.

"Come on, Wilmot," he shouted. "He cannot be far."

As it turned out that was wishful thinking. For most of the morning they followed the tracks, but never again did they actually see the caribou.

By mid-morning both men were exhausted, encouraged only by Theodore's unfailing convictions. Somehow he had overcome the crippling pain of the snowshoes, and as they continued the pursuit he had shown the same enthusiasm as when they first started.

The day cleared and the light reflecting off the snow was blinding. As the sun warmed up the air, snow began dropping from the trees, falling in clumps with a dull thud.

Around noon they paused at the edge of a wooded area. Theodore retied his boots while Wilmot unloaded the backpack and assessed the last of their supplies.

"This ain't gonna get us far," he said grimly.

Then he smiled proudly and again quoted Whitman, defiantly, "*I stand in my place with my own day here.*"

From a distance they heard the sound of bells, and a voice shouting commands.

"That's a woodsman," stated Wilmot. "Sounds like he's got a team of oxen he's working this way."

About a hundred feet away a deer emerged from the woods, obviously moving away from the oxen and wagon, which were still a ways off but getting closer.

Wilmot nodded in the direction of the deer and whispered, "You feel like tryin' your hand again?"

Theodore nodded and took Wilmot's gun when he offered it. He sighted in on the deer, which was anxiously focused on the oxen and driver.

This time he exhaled slowly and then paused before he fired. The shot rang true and the doe dropped in its tracks.

Wilmot slapped his shoulder.

"That's the way to do it," he said as they made their way to the downed deer.

When they got to the deer it was still alive, although just barely. One of its back legs kicked weakly while it tried in vain to lift its head. Theodore raised his gun, but Wilmot stopped him. "That deer's gonna die in less than a minute—just let it happen."

The two men crouched a few paces away and watched the animal. The doe looked in their direction, but its eyes were unfocused and soon it dropped its head, dead.

Wilmot had killed many things in his day, but not Theodore—at least nothing this large. When the doe died he turned mournfully to Wilmot and asked, "Should we say something."

Wilmot smiled. "*And as to you Death, and you bitter hug of mortality, it is idle to try to alarm me.*"

Theodore looked at him, mystified.

"That's not from the Bible."

"Nobody said anything about the bible, sir, you just asked me to say something," said Wilmot. "How about – *I hear and behold God in every object, but understand God not in the least… I see something of God each hour of the twenty-four, and each moment then still.*"

Theodore said, "I have a feeling it is the best I am going to get." As they stood over the carcass, Wilmot asked, "Have you ever gutted a deer?"

Theodore looked a bit nervous, "I have prepared many animals for the laboratory, but never an animal this large."

The young Mainer nodded.

"Okay. Well, this is different because we are only concerned with what is edible. Our main concern here is to get as much meat as possible before the carcass freezes. We will cut off the lower limbs at the joints, take the best cuts of meat we can, and then wrap it all in the skin."

Wilmot handed him his knife.

"I'll let you do the messy part as it was your kill."

With that he showed Theodore where to cut and told him to pull out the inner organs.

"The heart and liver are considered delicacies, but we can't carry everything back so we are just goin' for good venison."

Once the deer was relived of its intestines and organs they peeled away the outer fur, and then Wilmot instructed Theodore on where the good cuts of meat were and how to extract them best.

As they were finishing up Theodore realized the sound of the bells had gotten closer. He could now make out the creaking of a harness. Looking across the clearing they could see a sled pulled by four oxen coming into view.

Wilmot took the venison and rolled it up tight in the fur, then tied the bundle with some strapping he had in his bag. It weighed about twenty five pounds, but was securely bound and there was no fear of anything getting through the fur to spoil the meat.

Looking at the sled that approached, Wilmot smiled.

"Now you're in for a treat. Here comes Bill's older brother, David."

The four oxen lumbered forward, muscles rippling and slapping against the sturdy leather harness and reins. Each team carried a heavy wood yoke that connected them to the sled, and they lined up one in front of the other.

Just ahead of the lead team — and slightly to the side — David directed them with whistles and shouts and the occasional crack of a whip. He also carried a set of reigns in his hand that he could attach when they were faced with difficult sections — or when he wanted to ride on the sled behind the team.

David's full beard was frosted over with snow flurries, and despite the cold he wore his sleeves rolled up to the elbow. He hadn't noticed Theodore and Wilmot yet and was all business.

The sled was sturdy enough to move a barn, but the size of the logs it was carrying made it look tiny. Virgin spruce trunks, two to three feet wide and twenty-five feet long — longer than the sled itself — were towering behind it. And they were stacked high as well, held down by chains and the low sidewalls of the sled.

David now saw Wilmot waving from about two hundred yards away. He waved back, and turned the oxen fully in their direction. Soon the entire show had moved into the clearing.

The snow was about three feet deep, but the hooves of the oxen and the runners of the heavy sled compacted it into four inches of hard packed ice. David had been able to walk the oxen through the forest, but when they hit the deep snow in the clearing he attached the reigns, climbed on the sled and steered from the top of the load.

Theodore noticed that David was a good twenty years older than Bill, in his early fifties, and he looked as tough as nails. He wasn't as tall as his younger brother, but with such a compact build it seemed like he could move the logs himself, without the help of the oxen.

A heavy shirt that he had pulled over a set of woolen underwear apparently sufficed to keep him warm in the Maine winter.

Theodore couldn't stop marveling at the sheer power required to move these logs from the backcountry to the civilized world, and he continued to stare silently after they had met up with David and introductions had been made.

"Mr. Sewall, I commend you on your ability to control these oxen and accomplish this task."

David looked over Theodore and asked, "And what the heck are you doin' out here boy? Freezin' your ass off, I would think."

Theodore looked at himself, and then at Wilmot, and realized how pathetic they appeared. They might have survived the deadly grip of a Maine winter night in the wilderness, but the struggle had left some scars. Their clothes were ragged and their faces gaunt. Theodore grabbed a harness for support and the ox in it leaned against him slightly. "I have had warmer nights," said Theodore.

David grinned. "I bet you have."

Then he added, "Up ahead I'm gonna drop this load by the river." He gestured to the logs behind him.

"After that I'll follow the trail out to the road. You boys want a ride; you just have to follow me for 'bout a mile. After that I'll let you ride on the sled."

It was agreed, and Theodore and Wilmot walked behind the oxen and sled, the venison bundle on Wilmot's shoulder. Theodore only now realized the relief he had felt when the wagon appeared. Thus far, he had not admitted to himself just how tired he was.

His feet were killing him, just as Wilmot had predicted, and now that they had a clear pathway he took off his snowshoes and limped behind the sled.

As they left the area Theodore looked off in the direction of the caribou tracks.

"Wilmot, do you think that caribou is still alive?"

Wilmot grinned.

"I think now that you're not chasin' him he's probably just takin' another big ole nap."

Theodore nodded, but walked on with his eyes on the ground; deep in battle within himself about whether abandoning the chase was the right decision. He asked himself if he would take up the chase again if he saw the bloody caribou tracks again.

Then he looked up and nodded in the direction of David.

"So David is your uncle as well?"

Wilmot answered, "Ayuh. My grandfather Levi had ten kids, so there are Sewalls all over this place."

Wilmot shed the irreverence as he added, "David was the oldest when they moved here. William wasn't born yet. It was young David who roamed the local woods with Tomah learnin' to hunt and fish.

"On one of his first trips to Island Falls, before Levi had even built his cabin, David was sent to help an old-timer drop some trees. David was just a young lad then."

Wilmot looked at his Uncle walking up ahead with the lead ox, talking to it like it was an old drinking buddy. "Get on over there you lazy..." He checked his language when he saw Theodore and Wilmot watching him.

Wilmot continued, "Anyway, this guy was a drunk and he started bossin' David around. After a while David got sick of it, and that's when the man pulled a knife on him.

"David wasn't havin' any of it. The guy was drunk so as soon as he had a chance David grabbed his gun and held it on him—said he'd be alright if he just handed his knife over, sat down and behaved."

Theodore smiled as he asked, "How did it all turn out?"

"Well, eventually the drunk dropped the knife and went back to the bottle. David said the next mornin' the man was so miserable that he wouldn't shut up until he shot him a partridge for breakfast."

Wilmot grinned as he added, "The guy never did get his knife back though."

The hard trail that the sled left in the snow was smooth and about a foot wide. Wilmot took a big step and slid forward on both feet.

"If we had some rope we could ski behind it."

Ahead the woods opened up to reveal a frozen river, about thirty yards across. David planned on leaving the logs where the water could do most of the work when it came time to float them downstream.

"You two hold back," he shouted. "That ice might not hold and it could be tricky gettin' back."

David moved just ahead of the lead ox and grabbed his harness. He stopped and the oxen stopped as well. Leaving them for a minute, David walked ahead and eyed the river, trying to decide where the ice was thickest.

He then returned and led the oxen onto the ice; the sled creaked under its load as it moved forward. Once on the ice the oxen stepped awkwardly, uncomfortable with the lack of traction.

The weight of the loaded sled took its toll on the ice and deep cracks appeared and raced across the ice. The noise spooked the oxen and they looked ready to panic.

They continued for about fifteen feet, until they were nearing the center of the river, then he swung them back around and pointed the team toward the shore. The immense load slowly pivoted and straightened out until it was perpendicular to the shore.

For the next few minutes David crawled over the sled as he took off the heavy chains that had helped keep the load in place. Now there were only low supports on each side that prevented the logs from falling off.

He then walked to the lead team and whispered. "Now this's the tricky part."

David stood slightly ahead and hit a lever that dropped the support on one side. The logs came loose and started to roll, then crash over onto the ice with a tremendous noise as David directed the oxen to move the sled forward.

The river echoed with the dull, heavy pounding of the logs as they bounced on the ice. While the oxen moved forward the last of the logs rolled off. .At first the ice held, but then a spider web of cracks appeared and spread in all directions.

As the first team of oxen reached the shore the ice gave way under the load. Under the sled an ice plate tilted and even though the sled was now empty, its weight added to the momentum.

David had kept his spot near the lead of the oxen. As the weight of the sinking sled began to pull them backward their eyes became wild with fright. David urged them forward with a shrill whistle.

They doubled down and pulled harder.

The lead team had good traction, but the second team was fighting the breaking ice beneath their hooves. As they sank deeper their nostrils flared and they exhaled hot burst of steam over the frigid water.

"Move, you lazy sons-a-whores!" shouted David.

If the sled went down, the oxen seemed to sense, they would go with it. Led by David's whooping and whistles they leaned into the harness with all their weight.

Slowly, the lead team pulled the others to more secure footing "That's better!" David hollered.

Encouraged by a second command, all four oxen pulled forward, and the sled straightened out.

With a final whistle the four oxen marched out of the river and onto the shore, pulling the sled from the hungry grip of water.

"Sorry I got your ride wet!" called David as the whole formation came to a halt on the shore, "But it's still better'n walkin'."

The sled had a solid platform—about ten by twenty feet—for them to ride on, and it sat four feet above the ground. David climbed up, the long reins in his hand, and smacked them on the oxen. Next he directed them to make a wide turn.

Before they climbed aboard David put up the low side walls again so they could hold on to them for support, and Wilmot tied the venison package to the side wall so he didn't have to worry about it falling off.

When Wilmot and Theodore had loaded and secured their packs and had stepped onto the sled themselves, David whistled, and the oxen pulled the sled to a slow but steady pace.

David pointed at one of the corner supports.

"You better grab one of those or you'll be pickin' yourself out of the snow in the woods someplace."

Theodore did as he was told just as the sled lurched. They were not moving along a flat path; indeed it appeared to Theodore that David was blazing his own road.

As soon as they were comfortable with the motion, Theodore and Wilmot climbed to the head of the sled and sat on either side of David, with their feet dangling as they watched the oxen plow forward.

"How do you know where the trail goes?"

David laughed as the sled bucked over the terrain. "There are no beaver dams in the roads...other'n that we goes where we want."

Soon they were back on the logging trail and the ride smoothed out some. It was a far cry from a road, but regular use by oxen and sled had cut a discernible path into the wilderness.

For the next three hours the oxen pulled them, tirelessly. Only once did David have to bring them to a halt, get off the sled and clear a pine that had toppled from the weight of the snow.

When they reached a wider road whose broad and flat surface hinted at regular traffic, David halted the oxen.

"You young fellas get off here. It's only a few miles to Island Falls."

Wilmot extended his hand to David.

"I know where we are, Uncle. Where are you goin' from here?"

He nodded in the other direction.

"I'm on my way up to Cecil's winter camp. I'll hold up down the road a bit and try to make it to just shy of Masadis by nightfall tomorrow."

Theodore had shouldered his pack and came marching over to extend his hand as well, while Wilmot was untying the venison package and their bags.

"I want to thank you, Mr. Sewall, for taking us out."

"You think I had a choice there, do you?" hollered David with a laugh. "If I'd let either of you get into any more trouble than you already were in, my brother would never let me live it down."

Theodore stood back sheepishly until David added, "Just relax there, govnah, you can ride with me anytime. You just listen to Wilmot. He's a good man and he's quick on his feet."

Theodore stared at Wilmot and said, "He has got nothing left to prove to me."

David whistled and whipped his hand in a circle gesture. The oxen dutifully pulled the sled around and they headed north.

Chapter Fifteen
A one-horse, open sleigh

Bill Sewall sat on his front porch in Island Falls whittling a stick down to nothing. There was a concerned expression on his face and every few minutes he looked up to let his eyes scan the horizon.

Eventually he cocked his head to the side in the direction of the river. Soon a faint wheezing filled the air and when Bill next lifted his gaze he saw Theodore and Wilmot coming into view. In the few minutes it took for them to reach the porch his face had become dark with anger.

From fifty feet away Wilmot could tell he was in trouble with his uncle. Bill had gotten to his feet and was facing the on comers with his hands on his hips. As the approached the porch he towered above them, blocking the stairs.

"Wilmot. We had arranged to meet here yesterday," Bill said sternly. "Where have you been?"

"Sir," blurted Wilmot, "we came upon..."

Theodore stepped in front of him and cut him off.

"Mr. Sewall, the fault is mine. I wounded a caribou and decided the honorable thing to do was finish it off."

Then he added proudly, "I tracked it myself."

Bill stared at the men with an angered expression for an eternity.

"And where is this caribou?" he finally demanded.

Theodore lowered his head and cleared his throat, "I am afraid that in the end it did not need finishing after all—it just ran off and left us behind."

"Not for lack of tryin', I might add," said Wilmot. "Even this mornin', after a rough night in the open, he picked up the chase again."

Bill stared at Theodore from under lowered brows for a full minute, looking over his clothes, his complexion, his face. "Theodore, I can see how weak you are even now. You must monitor your health when in the wild."

But Theodore was still too elated to take heed of Bill's concern.

"You should have seen the rack on it. What an animal!"

Bill turned without reply and led them into the house, where plates were set for an evening meal.

"You were expecting us?" asked Theodore when he saw the plates.

Bill grumbled, "If Wilmot didn't bring you in tonight I'd a known you were in some serious trouble. So I guess I would'a just eaten all I could and then set out after you."

Then his voice cleared and his tone turned serious.

"Theodore, considering your current condition I think we should just stay around town for a few days. You need rest. I wouldn't want to push you too hard."

While he spoke Bill dished out a serving of venison stew. He held the steaming bowl forward and then paused and said, "You know there would a been no way for me to find you if you'd had trouble. Not unless I stumbled upon your tracks which taint likely in all that snow."

Both men stared at the bowl, watching it move with his gestures like they were starving dogs.

"Reckless!" said Bill, the bowl still held in mid-air. "And reckless men die in the wild."

No one said a word. Theodore, who all but drooled as he stared at the stew, finally interjected. "I think some of that stew would do a lot to revive us."

Bill drew the bowl closer to himself.

"Oh, you want some of this, do you?" he asked. "After making me wait for the two of you to casually come strolling in, a day late?"

Wilmot touched his uncle's arm.

"Uncle, I'm sorry we caused you distress. We took shelter when the storm hit; and one way or another I would've brought him in today."

Bill set down the bowl in front of Theodore and filled one for Wilmot. Once he'd set the second bowl down he said somberly, "I'm not raising either of you boys to die in the cold. Now eat up."

Theodore attacked his bowl with a hunger so impatient he singed his lips and tongue on the steaming food. As he was chewing on the deliciously gamey meat, his spirits soared.

"Honestly, Bill," he said, chomping on a chunk of venison, "I feel great. Let me just have another bowl of this stew, a warm bed for the night, and I will be ready in the morning."

"You better be ready when we set out," Bill replied, stirring the stew in his bowl to help it cool. "We've got to go up the road a good ways —

maybe forty miles — and then we'll be following a loggin' road along the Aroostook River to the Oxbow; and that'll be for another fifteen miles."

"I'm going to need some new snowshoes," said Theodore with a glance at Bill before he wolfed down the next bite.

Both Wilmot and Bill burst out laughing.

"No, no," said Bill and leaned forward, obviously excited about the next journey they were to undertake. "We're taking the pung — you and I. It's close to a hundred mile round trip and at this time of year its one I wouldn't want to undertake on foot."

He sat up, dipped his spoon in his bowl and took a hearty mouthful.

"You goin' to Cecil's winter camp?" asked Wilmot, who had finished his meal and was wiping his mouth.

"Yes, if he'll have us."

Wilmot put his napkin down and nodded to Theodore. "You better take that venison with you; Cecil's probably got a hungry crew with winter's end approaching."

Bill took another spoonful, ate it silently and then asked, "And who shot the deer?"

"I did," stated Theodore.

He proudly looked Bill in the eye. "And with one shot."

Bill stared him down.

He said, "Just because you got a deer doesn't mean you get out a doin' dishes."

The next morning Bill was up early, but Wilmot was already busy in the kitchen when he came down. He had made a hearty bacon and egg breakfast and was filling a basket with a warm meal for their journey.

While Theodore finished his breakfast Bill stepped out of the warm house into a bitterly cold winter morning. The air was crisp; it cut into his nostrils and made his eyes water. He swung their gear onto the back bench of the pung and strapped it on.

Wilmot came out and handed him the newly wrapped venison package. He'd unpacked it, cleaned and trimmed the meat, and then bound it up tightly. Bill lashed it onto the back bench with their other gear.

Inside the pung the bench was raised slightly, allowing room to store things. Bill placed an axe and Wilmot's basket of food below them and a heavy wool blanket on the bench.

Scout was harnessed and ready to go. She stepped about eagerly, anticipating the journey ahead. Theodore soothed her and patted her gently. Bill allowed him to give her an apple — which she loved.

The sun peaked through the barren branches but there was little warmth in it. The morning chill was so heavy that when they did talk it muffled their voices.

When Theodore stepped outside he clearly felt the exhaustion in his body from the night out in the snow. His muscles ached from the chase and his bones felt stiff, but he made no mention of it.

He had buttoned up his heavy coat and put on his scarf. Bill was dressed for warmth as well. They climbed into the pung, laid the heavy blanket over their laps, and got as comfortable as the simple sled would allow.

There was little room to move, but they were snug. The sleigh didn't require much work if the driver and the horse worked well together.

Bill said in a hushed voice, "Scout here probably could make it to the camp in one day if the snow ain't too soft, but I'd rather do it in two, considering how cold it is. We'll stop somewhere along Benedict's Road and make camp, and then go up the Aroostook River to the Oxbow tomorrow."

With that he waved goodbye to Wilmot, raised the reigns just a little, and Scout eagerly set off with her usual enthusiasm through the settlement of Island Falls.

On the road north she slowed down a bit, as if she suspected a harder journey lay ahead. The road was clear and Scout fell into a steady pace. After an hour they came across the tracks from David's oxen and sleigh, which were easily visible and made a nice smooth trail for them to follow.

"You do have some good roads up here!" Theodore exclaimed and Bill laughed while working the reigns a little to steer the sled away from the edge of a steep bank.

Over the hissing of the runners on the ice he said, "Little over a hundred years ago, a general — and a brave one at that — led eleven hundred men through this area trying to get to get to Canada and invade the British Province of Quebec."

"They came this way?" asked Theodore.

"They built this road," answered Bill with a smile.

Theodore looked over, always eager for a good story.

"This was early in the American Revolutionary War when there were no good maps of the area. The men had to trudge through a swampy tangle of streams and lakes — just like the ones we explored last fall — except they covered over 350 miles of it — and were traveling with cannons and ammunition.

"They also had to deal with foul weather, difficult portages, and dwindling supplies as winter set in; it wasn't pretty."

Theodore's chest swelled with pride that he had himself endured some of that same hardship and adventure.

"How'd you like to try to get a cannon out to that logging camp we visited?" asked Bill.

"And what was their fate?" Theodore inquired eagerly, "Did the men stay loyal to the general?"

"Some died, others deserted," Bill continued, "and in the end the general reached Quebec with 600 starving soldiers.

"There he met up with another general and his troops, and together they sacked the city. But he said later that the journey through Maine haunted him for years to come."

Theodore nodded, his thoughts drifting back to the snow-covered, bloody tracks of the caribou, and the distant image of the caribou fading ahead of him.

Bill pointed to the road.

"This road was put through by that general. In the time since some sections have been improved; others are lost to history."

Theodore thought for a minute before speaking.

"And what of the general — has history forgotten him as well?"

Bill grinned.

"History knows him as Benedict Arnold, and so far history hasn't been very kind to him. But I know him as a road builder, and I have to say there have been times when he's made my life a lot easier."

As dusk approached Bill started to look for a place to camp. The side of the road was deep with snow and the woods looked inhospitable.

Then the sun left the land without notice and the temperature plummeted. Scout plodded along tirelessly, the road easy to navigate even in dark.

"I was hopin' to come across David on this road," said Bill. "If you saw him yesterday, just outside of Island Falls, he should be close."

Just as he said it a fire appeared ahead. In the cold darkness that had set in it was a warm beacon. Behind the fire sat the empty logging sled, to the side stood the oxen. They were downwind of the fire and looked ghostlike as the smoke floated across their white coats.

Bill slowed Scout down to a walk as they approached the fire. David heard the bells on Scout's harness and stood, peering into the darkness. When he saw them he turned and added several logs to the fire.

Bill brought the pung to a halt and Scout stepped about nervously. She eyed the oxen, which were getting the most out of the fire. Since David had added the wood it had flared up and they now leaned into the heat with their eyes closed.

The sled had been pulled so near to the fire that when it burned brightest the flame was dangerously close, but after several minutes it died down to a good bed of coals that David expertly kept alive.

The woodsman had placed his fire so the sled would create a draft and pull the warm air over him while he slept. It was well below freezing and he only had one blanket so he had to get it right.

Without the logs, the sled again looked its size. Underneath, between the runners, was a crawl space, about three feet high and ten feet wide—just enough for three men to sleep side by side. David had also fresh cut pine boughs on the ground to insulate from the cold beneath.

"Nice of you gentlemen to stop by," said David.

He was standing by the fire, and Theodore noted how even at night he went without a coat.

Bill climbed out of the pung, slapped his brother on the shoulder and said, "You made good time." He took off his gloves and stretched out his hands over the flames.

"Hey, little brother! Sit down and have some coffee."

Then he saw Theodore and added, "And you too... Mr. Roosevelt, isn't it?"

"Indeed it is."

Bill had Scout move the sled to the side, forming a two sided pen with David's larger sled. He then took her out of her harness and tied her to the side of the sled. While she ate some grain he put a fitted blanket over her.

"You did good today, Scout," Bill said to her as he stroked her mane. "Now you rest up for tomorrow."

The oxen were losing interest in the fire now that it was again dying down to coals. They curiously looked over to Scout, but they were tied off and couldn't get closer.

"Don't pay those lunkers no mind either," added Bill as he left to join Theodore by the fire.

David had left for a minute and then returned with an armful of pine boughs. "Didn't know I'd be havin' company," he said. "I'm gonna need a bigger bed." After disappearing under the sled he reemerged and took a seat by the fire.

David took a pan off the fire and poured its contents into a metal cup, "I've only got one cup with me," he said, "but I'd be happy to share."

From the pung, where he was getting the blanket, Bill called, "Not to worry, David, we've got our own supplies."

When he came back, in addition to the blanket he was carrying the wicker basket that Wilmot had prepared.

"Wilmot set us up before we left," said Bill.

With that he opened the basket and took out a warm thermos and several containers of food.

"Look at Mr. Fancy Pants!" exclaimed David.

"Easy, David, I've got plenty to share."

"Oh, just settle down, Bill. You know I was just teasin' you. You boys get over here, out-a-the-wind, and I'll get this fire crankin' up."

Later, they lay under the sled — side by side with Theodore in the middle — the runners on each side acting as wind-blocks and a solid roof over their head. At the front end the fire emitted a warmth that floated back and right over them, the bed of pine boughs under them proved sufficient to keep the frozen earth at bay as well.

Theodore reckoned it had to be 20 below and marveled at how the Sewalls seemed to take it in stride. He settled into his bed comfortably and noticed he could barely even make out his breath.

The oxen had quieted down, and Scout slept standing between the sled and the pung.

"Mr. Sewall, would you mind if I asked you a question?" asked Theodore.

David laughed. "You can ask me anythin' you want but it don't mean I'm gonna answer you."

Theodore thought for a minute.

"Bill was talking about Benedict Arnold and how he built this road we are on, and I was wondering how you felt about it."

David focused on the underside of the sled, above him.

"Well if you're askin' about the road we're on, then I'll tell you it's a pretty good road."

After a pause, he added, "If you want to know how I feel about that Arnold fella, well then that's another matter."

Theodore rolled onto his side and looked at David.

"Surely you would not argue against judging him for his merits as well as his demerits."

David looked at Theodore with disbelief.

"You do realize you are talking about the biggest traitor this country has ever experienced?"

Theodore nodded, "I do, I just feel like all sides of a man should be known before you judge him."

The old Mainer shook his head.

"Here's the problem I have with that," he said. "Sure, he did some great things for America before he turned traitor. He was brave, he was smart, but before he turned there had to be a period when he wasn't straight with the people around him. And that meant he'd a been talkin' with weasel words."

Theodore looked at him, a bewildered expression on his face.

"What are *weasel* words? What did you mean by that?"

David was quiet for a while as he thought it over. He rolled on his stomach and grabbed a stick and used it to stoke the fire. Theodore remained on his side.

"I can't give you a good example," David said, "but I know in the future you'll recognize 'em when you hear 'em."

Then he added, "A weasel word sucks the truth out of what's said like a weasel sucks the innards out of an egg and leaves only the shell."

"So you do not think you could be impartial when it came to judging a traitor?" asked Theodore.

David shook his head, "When he started being deceitful, or not fulfilling his obligations—when he started using *weasel words* – then in my eye he forfeited the right to stand by my side."

He gestured around them.

"This isn't country were you can survive without people you can depend on. I guess I'm just sayin' I wouldn't want him in my crew."

Theodore creased his brow as he thought over the reply, then added, "Thank you, Mr. Sewall."

David grinned, the firelight casting a glow on his face.

"You're welcome, Mr. Roosevelt."

The next morning they were up with the sun, attaching harnesses and coaxing the animals into place.

Scout was anxious to be moving as usual, but the oxen seemed stiff and slow, unmotivated to budge in the morning chill. David shoved them and cursed while trying to get them into a formation.

Theodore stood to the side of the pung, watching the oxen stumble about. He then soothed Scout as Bill began to put her in her harness.

Bill explained that soon they would come upon a logging road that turned away from the main road and followed the Aroostook River.

They'd be on that road for about fifteen miles until they came to a place called the Oxbow. That was where Cecil's winter camp lay.

David left quickly, but Bill took his time and made them a breakfast of some sausage Wilmot had packed for them. Theodore joined Bill by the fire.

"We can go a lot faster than David and those lunkers, so we might as well give him a head start," said Bill.

Then he looked over at Scout and added, "They leave a mighty fine path in their wake, don't they?"

Scout whinnied, not all that happy about the delay for breakfast.

Eventually they did get going, and on David's tracks they made good time. An hour later they saw the sled tracks take a left hand turn and they started to follow them onto a snow-covered trail that skirted the river. David's tracks were clearly visible ahead of them.

After a few miles they came upon David, who stood beside his sled looking down a section of the trail that dropped steeply into a gulch; on the far side of the gulch, it rose up at the same angle.

Bill whistled and said, "That there is what we refer to as a *pitch*."

David agreed, "I'd say it's about the worst one on this trail. And it gets worse..."

He nodded down the hill and Bill saw a large log leaning against a tree, blocking the way.

Bill said, "That log must'a dropped off a sleigh that came through."

David turned to get one of his oxen out of the harness, while Bill grabbed several lengths of chain and an axe.

As he walked by Theodore he said, "We'll have that cleared out in a few minutes."

And then they heard the sound of bells coming from across the pitch. In the distance a sled came into view. There were two oxen up front pulling it, and a woodsman sat on top of a load of logs directing the team with some reigns. In the early morning he rode along peacefully.

David hollered out a greeting and the man looked in their direction, shielding his eyes against the rising sun behind them.

"I think that's Sherman," said Bill.

Bill dropped the chain and said, "He can't see a thing with the sun in his eyes like that."

Bill looked down the pitch, which still lay deep in shadow. It was a drop of at least fifty feet to the bottom and there'd be no way to stop before the oxen and sled hit the fallen tree at the bottom. "And that's a big load to be pulling with only two oxen."

"He's gonna hit that tree," David called as he started running down the hill with his axe in hand. He shouted at Bill as he ran. "Get that ox ready to help with the mess."

Just as Sherman's sled started to drop into the pitch he realized what he was getting into—but it was too late. He pulled hard on the reins, but instead, the weight of the logs forced the oxen forward into a trot.

David was halfway down the pitch on the other side when he heard Sherman scream, and then the oxen bellow in fear. He saw Sherman jumping clear off the charging sled at the last minute.

David skidded to a halt just before he reached the bottom and watched in horror as the oxen charged toward him. The tree lay in the middle of the road, at a forty-five degree angle, pointing away from the oxen. If they hadn't been harnessed the oxen may have simply each gone around one side of it.

But their wooden yoke prevented that and as they each passed on one side the yoke rode up the tree trunk, rising as the oxen's momentum pushed it.

The weight of the sled from behind forced the yoke up even higher, and within seconds both oxen were in the air; their hind feet dangled just off the ground, the yoke threatened to choke them. With wild eyes they helplessly kicked and snorted and blew snot their panicked moans echoing over the surrounding hills.

Under them, the sled now hit the log. The abrupt stop caused the logs it was carrying to shoot forward, and if the oxen hadn't been up in the air they would have been killed. Instead the logs noisily landed under them in a pile.

David had reached the accident site and jumped onto the log. He clambered up until he reached the yoke. On either side hung a suffocating ox, their eyes bulging. Quickly, he raised his axe high and brought it down as hard as he could in the center of the yoke.

The yoke was made of hardwood and was about two feet thick, but David's first swing rang true and deep and it split the wood — unceremoniously dropping both oxen to the ground.

They scrambled to their feet and off the log pile and shook their sweaty hides, still spooked. They were each still wearing the broken half of a yoke but otherwise unhurt. Sherman appeared, took their broken yoke off and led them away.

Bill arrived with one of the oxen and started chaining one of the logs to drag it clear. David set down his axe and helped him.

When Sherman had tied the two oxen to a tree a few yards away and returned, David teased, "Well, Sherman, that's a hell of a way to start the day."

"Ain't it!" replied Sherman with a grin.

He looked back at his animals; his oxen were still on their feet, although they looked a bit shaken. The team had a disgruntled look, as if they'd expected better treatment.

After Bill's ox had disappeared up the pitch with a log in tow they sent Sherman's oxen up one at a time with two more logs. While he waited for them to return, David chained the log that had caused the accident and when the oxen returned he hauled it off with their help. After several more trips the road was clear.

David turned to Bill and said, "You better tell Cecil I may be late comin' in. Sherman and I still got some sortin' to do here."

Bill offered to help, but David declined.

"You go ahead," said David. "This might look bad, but we've got plenty of muscle and I'll be along shortly."

Soon Theodore and Bill were back in the pung, making good time. They were now blazing their own trail. Luckily, the previous sled traffic had left a hard base and they only broke trail through a few inches of new snow.

Even still Theodore realized quickly that this ride was going to be much rougher. The trail they followed along the Aroostook River and had been blazed by successive teams and sleds, but it still cut through the wilderness in the middle of winter.

"We will be goin' up river about fifteen more miles," said Bill. "At any other time of the year it would be quite a journey, but thanks to the sleds that have come before us we'll have a pretty good trail to follow."

The surrounding woods were thick with snow, Scout continued on showing little sign of tiring. She held her head high and trotted along effortlessly through the snow-covered terrain.

Bill noticed how Theodore was watching Scout.

"You can see why military men prefer Morgans. There's something unstoppable in their attitude."

He watched how Scout charged down a rolling hill and then used the momentum to come up over the other side.

He added, "In the civil war, General Sheridan used them at the battle of Rienzi, and Stonewall Jackson did the same at the battle of Little Sorrel."

"You are implying they have an aggressive attitude?" asked Theodore.

"Not at all," replied Bill. "They simply get the job done. If I had to sum them up in a word I'd say they are *survivors*." He chuckled. "Did you know that the only Cavalry survivor of Custer's Last Stand was a horse named Comanche? Actually Comanche was a Morgan-Mustang mix, but he still had to be a survivor to come out of that."

Just as Bill finished speaking he pointed to their side. About thirty feet away, running parallel to them, was a mother moose and her calf.

Scout had come upon them so quickly that they'd ended up running alongside the pung, rather than running away from it. The calf was all gangly; its limbs appeared a size to big. Theodore had a tough time figuring which direction it was heading as it crashed along.

The moose looked at Scout with curiosity, but when she saw Bill and Theodore sitting behind in the pung she panicked and quickly veered off into the woods, the white of her eyes showing.

Throughout the day they continued along the Aroostook River. Several times Bill had to stop Scout and move fallen limbs out of their way, but they were covering a good amount of distance. Twice Theodore observed deer as they silently slipped away into the white forest, and once he saw a wolf.

The wolf had seemed more like a ghost, as it trotted away, darting in and out of view in the silent woods. Just before it disappeared into the woods it stopped and watched them drive by.

Theodore thought the wolf was long gone when several miles down the trail they passed through a clearing and there it stood again, watching them.

At the time Bill was busy directing Scout away from a dead branch hanging over the trail and didn't see it.

"That there is what we call a widow maker," said Bill as they swerved around it. "These big branches come down sometimes and you're better off not bein' around when they do."

Theodore smiled as he looked around at the forest. It was old and appeared to have always existed in this deep winter they rode through. Some of the pines were so large that they sheltered wide areas under their branches completely – there was not a spot of snow. On the snow around them, there were animal tracks everywhere.

"I know you are used to all of this, Bill, but I do not think I have ever seen a grander or more beautiful sight than these northern woods in winter.

Bill smiled. "Have'ta agree with you there."

Chapter Sixteen
The Winter Camp

Theodore and Bill approached the log cabin in the pung, their faces flushed from the cold. The sun hovered above the horizon, dim and weak, and dropped out of sight just as they pulled up.

With stiff movements they both climbed out of the sled. Scout stepped in place after halting, not quite ready to cease moving. "That's a good girl," said Bill as he caressed her mane and looked her over.

From under his seat he took out a fitted blanket and a smaller piece of fabric which he used to wipe down her sweaty neck.

"Can't let you catch a chill after all that work, can I?" said Bill affectionately.

While Theodore unstrapped the venison and their bags from the back, Bill dressed Scout in her blanket which enclosed all but her head and legs. Again she stepped in place, her head held high and alert, "You did just great, girl, now settle down."

Now that the sun had set there was little light to see by, but Bill knew the camp well and guided Scout to a large covered stable made from unpeeled logs. Next to it was a blacksmith's barn, sided with rough-cut timber.

There was a fenced corral where several oxen ate from a manger, and more oxen in a sheltered area. The animals all watched them approach, their bodies steaming in the cold night air.

To the side was a separate stall where Bill placed Scout. He closed the gate so she could move around freely.

"All the comforts of home," he said as she walked in and went to work on some hay at the far end.

Outside, the snow had started again and had covered all evidence of the woodsmen's presence other than their animals and several large wooden sleds. It was coming down so hard that it had already filled in the sled tracks from their arrival a few minutes ago.

The cabin itself sat low, one side of the roof extending almost to the ground, and it was topped with three feet of snow.

A four foot chimney made of small cut logs in the middle of the roof allowed the smoke to escape, and the smoke carried men's voices from inside the cabin. Theodore heaved the dressed-out venison over his shoulder, while Bill went back and grabbed his sack—which seemed heavier than usual—from the floor of the pung.

As they walked to the door Bill paused. "I must warn you, Theodore, that this camp will be very different from the one we stayed in last fall. There will be a full crew in here and quarters will be tight."

Theodore nodded.

"These men are descended straight from the old Pilgrim and Puritan stock. They're tough and most likely more than a little grumpy after wintering over."

The young man stiffened slightly.

"Bill, I can assure you, there is no reason to worry about me."

The tall man smiled.

"I realize that. I'm just lettin' you know what you're walkin' into— this crew can be tough."

Then he added, "It's also goin' to be smoky inside. I hope your asthma doesn't bother you too much."

Theodore gave Bill a frustrated expression which told the older man that he didn't want him worrying about his health.

The door opened and they were greeted by a very hairy Cecil. He leaned out and looked at them, surprised.

"Bill Sewall again!" shouted Cecil. "It's mighty cold weather for social walkin'."

He shook Bill's hand and nodded to Theodore.

Then he eyed the venison.

"From the look a that package on yer shoulder I'd bet you're gonna want to bunk down again."

Bill laughed.

"Well, we happened to be in the neighborhood and thought we'd bring by some fresh meat."

"Ayuh, I appreciate that, but I've got two crews in there—that's twenty odd men plus the two of you."

Bill held up his palms.

"Come on, Cecil, we won't take up much room."

Theodore added, "I would be happy to cut some wood."

Cecil nodded pensively and looked at the package of meat. "Who shot the deer?"

Theodore excitedly stated, "I did."

"Good," said Cecil. "And who dressed it out?"

Bill sheepishly nodded at Theodore, knowing where this was going. "He did."

For a solid minute Cecil stared at the ground, thinking hard, as if pressed to make a difficult decision.

Finally he looked up with a grin and said, "Doesn't sound like you've done much, Bill."

Bill looked at him awkwardly, but Cecil smiled even wider and put an arm over Bill's shoulder.

"You gentlemen are welcome here anytime; I was just messin' with ya."

Then he furrowed his brow and added, "Though I must admit that when I saw ya I was hopin' you'd brought up some of your bean hole beans. Don't get me wrong, we appreciate the meat, but we've all had our fair share of venison over the last eight months and we could'a used a change."

Cecil looked over his shoulder to make sure none of his men could hear him and said, "All the company sends up is salted cod and pickled beef."

Bill hefted the heavy sack by his side.

"Don't worry, Cecil, I've got all the fixin's for my bean hole beans and if I start 'em now they'll be ready for breakfast."

Cecil's face lit up, and as they stepped through the door he shouted, "Bean hole beans for breakfast, boys!" The room full of men cheered as one.

Theodore turned to Bill.

"So much for our rough reception."

Bill smiled and replied.

"Don't get cocky; there's still more men coming in."

Cecil overheard him and asked, "Any chance you saw that brother of yours? I was 'spectin' him as well."

"Yes, I did," replied Bill. "He's got Sherman with him, but you won't see 'em 'till tomorrow at the earliest."

For a moment Cecil looked serious.

"Everything okay?"

Bill grinned proudly.

"Nothin' David can't handle."

Inside, the cabin was dark, smoky and full of overpowering odors. Mixed with the smoke from the fire was an aroma that combined sweat, spruce boughs, fresh cut kindling, and a stew that brewed over the fire.

The cabin was sunk down in the ground and much smaller than the cabin they had visited earlier in the year. This one also looked a bit rougher and unfinished. The floor was dirt, but appeared to be well swept.

This structure was built around a fire pit which sat in the middle of the cabin; the intense cold of winter not allowing the fire to be near one end of the cabin. The remoteness of the cabin also necessitated only one building, so cook, camp boss and crew all slept under the same roof.

The fire itself had no chimney or flue, the smoke was casually escaping through the hole in the roof. To the side of the fire was the kitchen area with pots and stores of food.

One entire wall behind the fire pit was used as a communal bed. It extended from one end of the cabin to the other. This was the side of the cabin where the roof dropped low so when the men lay down it was just over their head. There was no mattress, just a bedding of spruce boughs and one long blanket.

A half-log hewn smooth served as a footboard and seat. All furniture was handmade, of wood, and constructed without any nails. A stack of wood sat by the door, and there was another one by the fire.

A young man in buckskins approached the fire to move a large cauldron of stew in place over the coals. The cauldron was suspended on a chain from a log tripod.

Theodore recognized Coty and strolled over to help him.

"I remember you from my last visit," he said as he held the tripod in place. Your name is Coty, is it not?"

Coty turned, smiled and embraced him warmly.

"Yes, I remember you also. Last fall I tink."

"Yes," nodded Theodore enthusiastically, "it was last fall." Theodore lifted the venison which he'd set on the ground by his feet and added, "We brought a doe to contribute to the pot, and Mr. Sewall is going to make something called 'Bean Hole Beans' for breakfast."

Coty beamed. "I have tasted dese bean hole beans of his. You will be more excited once you taste dem also."

Adjusting the cauldron one final time, Coty gestured to it with his thumb.

"I have de dinner meal prepared — rabbit stew — and dere is plenty."

He motioned for Theodore to follow him.

"Bring your venison, I have a rub we can put on it. Den it will be ready when we need it."

They stepped outside into a bitter cold. Coty untied the package of meat, placed it on a flat piece of wood that served as a chopping block, and cut away a few choice selections. Theodore could see the man's breath frosting instantly, and he marveled at the weather he had just arrived in.

Theodore took a deep breath and exhaled, amazed at how well his lungs were responding to the cold. In fact, even when he'd been inside and felt almost assaulted by the aromas and heavy smells he'd breathed with no problems.

The clouds had blown off and above them the sky was now filled with countless stars that glittered brightly. The barren branches on the trees above them stretched up, as if reaching for the heavens.

Coty wrapped up the rest of the meat, tied it to a rope that he tossed over the meat pole, and then hoisted it up out of the reach of any predators.

"De meat will freeze overnight, but I use it tomorrow for another stew," said Coty.

From somewhere along the lake the wind carried the sound of tinkling bells and creaking runners.

"Do you hear that?" asked Theodore.

Coty said, "Dat would be de last crew coming in—I tink it is Barry's—do you want to wait and watch dem come in?"

Theodore laughed.

"No, I have had that experience. Let us go inside."

Later in the evening all the crews had returned. There was barely room to move in the tight little cabin. Theodore and Bill tried to stay out of the way of the woodsmen; instead, they did their best to be helpful with cooking or anything else that Cecil needed.

"It is very different from what I would have expected, Bill." Theodore looked around and noticed they were in the company of others and added, "...I mean, Mr. Sewall."

Bill grinned at the young man's discomfort.

"Well," continued Theodore, "I imagined a bunch of men all lined up doing the same thing—like a work crew—but there really appears to be a lot of diversity regarding what is going on here."

Bill turned and they both watched the men throughout the cabin. A few were already sleeping on the big bed, simply worn out from the day's toil. Others sat by the fire, finishing their dinner, or cleaning a piece of gear—each man minding his own business. And there was always someone on the grindstone near the fire, sharpening an axe.

"Well, you have to remember that to these men reality is the business of cuttin' trees and drivin' logs down the brooks, streams and rivers to the sawmills," said Bill. "It takes a lot of different jobs to get a log down river from here."

Cecil, who was within earshot, added, "And there's more to it than just knockin' down a tree, limbin' it, and pushin' it in the water. You've also got to have teamsters, sawyers, landing men, filers, blacksmiths, swampers..."

Theodore held up his hand to halt Cecil, "I am afraid that at this point I do not know what half of those jobs even are."

Bill smiled as he said, "All you need to know is that one and all they are dedicated to lettin' the daylight into the swamp."

"Letting the daylight into the swamp?" repeated Theodore.

"That's right," said Bill.

Before he could say anything else Coty looked up from stirring his cauldron and added, "And don't forget a good cook."

One of the woodsmen made a rude comment and Coty fired back. "If you are so brave den cross my line!"

On the ground a line had been scratched in a circle around the cooking area. Suddenly Theodore realized that despite the activity in the cabin nobody but Coty and Cecil had stepped into that space.

Bill leaned closer to Theodore and explained.

"When you're in a camp that's this tight nobody goes near the fire or the food without permission from either the camp boss or cookie."

Coty beamed. "Is true, and if I catch you in my kitchen I can make you work." He looked at the woodsman who had made the rude comment. "And I could use a dishwasher very badly."

"I guess I never realized there was so much to it," said Theodore, turning back to Bill. "I also expected this place to be chaos and filled with restless woodsmen who could not wait to get away—but what I am observing is a gentle order directs things here."

"I'm a bit restless!" shouted one of the woodsmen in the bed and Theodore realized they'd all been listening to his conversation.

As if this was his cue Cecil looked at Bill and said with put-on formality, "Mr. Sewall, I do remember you mentioning something about bean hole beans."

Bill grinned, "I haven't forgotten, Cecil," and then he looked at Coty and added, "Coty, I was hopin' you could set me up with a good bean hole and pot."

Coty smiled, retrieved a large lidded pot from his cooking area, and gave it to Bill, "I have been waiting for you to say someting."

While Bill unpacked his sack full of supplies, Coty took a broom and swept clean a large piece of slate that lay a few feet from the fire. He lifted it, revealing a large hole in the dirt floor of the cabin — three feet deep by two feet wide.

Coty lined the bottom of the hole with smooth river stones, filled it about a foot deep with hot coals from the fire, and then added some chopped cedar, followed by some split logs of good dry hardwood.

"That's perfect, Coty," said Bill. "You just let that burn for about three hours and I'll get everything else ready."

Theodore stared at the hole, a bit uncertain of what was going on, when a deep voice by the stink pole asked a question.

"So, Mr. Roosevelt, d'ya think we *suffah* here?"

Theodore recognized Barry and moved over to shake the man's hand.

"On the contrary," he said, stretching out his hand to meet Barry's, "I envy you."

All the men within earshot laughed loudly.

Bill leaned forward.

"There's more to this lifestyle than sleigh rides and sleepin' in a cabin. I think you are just seein' the easy part of being a Maine woodsman."

"Of that I have no doubt," replied Theodore. "But I have always been drawn to nature — to be part of it. You can laugh, but it is why I study it."

Cecil had taken a seat by Bill and scratched his beard as he watched Theodore.

"Do you think you could live like this for eight months?" asked Cecil. "No showers, no newspapers...?" he grinned and added, "No women?"

A woodsman named Charley lamented, "Please don't remind me...oh, I miss my wife."

Theodore creased his brow as he contemplated Cecil's question. Finally he answered, "I could not see myself allotting that much time to an experiment."

Despite trying to be respectful several of the men lost control and burst out laughing.

Barry was laughing as well "Well, govnah," he finally said, "I think the problem is you are lookin' at this as an experiment, and not as an *experience*."

Laughter filled the room again. Theodore thought for a minute.

"And what experience would you have me partake in?"

"Where would you start?" asked Cecil. "We may all be Maine woodsmen, but some are choppers, some swampers."

Barry added, "And don't forget the river drivers. Now there's a job you'd *nevah* forget. There's your *experiment!*"

"And what does that entail?" asked Theodore over the laughs of the men.

Cecil cleared his throat and explained, "In the winter the riverbanks are piled high with spruce. When the ice goes out the drivers are there to ride and chase the logs downriver. Even small brooks take part in this great annual event, catchin' and holdin' water in dozens of head dams.

"Then the logs are sluiced from one dam to another until they reach a main drive on one of the big rivers. It takes a lot of determined men to work that operation and they've all got a different job to do."

Cecil gestured at Coty.

"Some even attempt — not always successfully — being cooks."

Coty lifted his head from the fire.

"I hear dis. Is dere someone here who can cook better?"

Nobody applied for the job. After a minute Theodore looked around nervously and addressed the room.

"Gentlemen, I do agree that all these professions are worth experiencing, but for me the next best thing is to be here with you."

Barry pushed the point.

"And ya could be content with that?"

"I am rarely content with any aspect of my life," said Theodore with a laugh.

Barry proudly stated, "I'd *rathah* live in this half-savage place than a town, *thaht's* for sure."

A few woodsmen shouted encouragement and Barry added, "Ya may think of this as a remote wilderness — or just woods — but I love it *heya.* I love the sounds the fir and hemlock snappin' and cracklin' at night from the *bittah* cold."

Barry lifted an axe and felt along its sharp edge, "And the day echoes with the sound of axes sinkin' deep, or the ping of a wedge slammin' home only to be followed by the swishin' of a tall fallin' spruce as it comes to silence in deep snow."

This seemed to strike home and they all sat in silence for a while listening to the fire and the wind howling around the corners of the cabin.

About an hour later Bill took several containers of beans, opened them with his knife, poured them into a smaller pot and covered them with water that Coty supplied. Then he placed the pot to the side of the fire over some hot coals.

Theodore came close to see what he was doing and Bill explained, "We're gonna cook these for 'bout 45 minutes — no longer or the beans will get mushy."

He looked at Coty and asked, "You reckon you can figure when that much time has gone by?" asked Bill.

Coty nodded. "Dis is not my first time cooking."

"Good," said Bill, and then he added sternly, "Cook 'em 'til the skins roll back when you blow on 'em. And watch these like your life depended on it…"

One of the woodsmen in the bunk yelled out, "Cause it does!" and everyone laughed.

Then Bill examined the hole and added some more hardwood. "We want that hole 'bout three quarters full of burnin' hot coals before we start thinkin' about addin' the beans."

Cecil looked over the operation with satisfaction and said, "Mr. Roosevelt, when you taste these beans in the mornin', you will see why we feel we have it made here."

With pride he added, "Few of us boys ever wanted to be soldiers or cowboys or policemen. To be a river man ridin' a heavin' log through white water was the secret ambition of most of us when we was young."

From the bunk a woodsman added, "Or to break a jam." And another added still, "Or steer a bateau through the spring flow!"

After each comment the cabin filled with the shouts of agreement.

Cecil nodded, "For us the loggin' camps had all the magic of the Land of Oz."

Bill laughed as well and added, "*I have given you lands to hunt in… I have given you streams to fish in… I have given you bear, and reindeer, and beaver… Why then are you not contented?*"

Theodore held up a hand of caution.

"Mr. Sewall, you are quoting my college alumnus again."

Now Bill grinned with pride.

"Well, Mr. Roosevelt, I shouldn't have to remind you that long before Mr. Longfellow went to Harvard he was a son of Maine."

The men who'd still been listening all cheered and Cecil playfully slapped Theodore's back.

Bill held up his finger and added, "And long after!" to another chorus of cheers.

As the night wore on more men went to bed and eventually it was just Theodore, Bill, Cecil and Coty sitting around the fire watching the hole full of hot coals.

With a satisfied smile Bill said, "I think she's just 'bout ready."

After emptying his supplies from his sack Bill moved the large bean pot between his legs and picked up several large pieces of salt pork and began cutting them into slabs—about two inches wide by one quarter inch thick. He placed them in the bottom of the bean pot and then peeled and cut onions in half and laid them on top of the pork.

Lastly, he poured the cooked beans in the smaller pot on top of the mix and added molasses, black pepper, dry mustard, and fresh butter on top.

"Would you mind helpin' me with this?" asked Bill when he had the lid securely on the bean pot, and Theodore and Coty jumped to his side.

Coty handed Bill a shovel and he removed all but one third of the coals, and then together—using a chain between them—they lowered the bean pot into the hole. There was still about six inches of space between the pot and the edge of the hole and they filled it in with hot coals and then placed more coals over the top of the pot.

Lastly they placed about two feet of dirt over the coals to completely fill the hole, and Coty laid the slab of slate over that to mark the spot. Then Coty lay down on a blanket to sleep a few feet from the fire.

Bill winked at Theodore, "Now you just wait 'till mornin'," and they both headed off to the community bunk.

The bed was twenty-five feet by six feet and could sleep twenty men if needed. Small boughs of balsam fir were layered on the bed floor and the men shared one long blanket. Coty had cut new bedding that day and the smell of it was almost overpowering.

As Theodore settled in he tested the bed.

"This does actually make a pleasantly perfumed mattress."

One of the men laughed and said, "With these guys we need all the perfume we can get."

All the men laughed in the darkness.

Chapter Seventeen
Beans and Trapping

"Oh, that smells good," groaned one of the woodsmen waking next to Theodore. The man beside him added, "Smells better'n Barry!"

Then he yelled, "When we eatin' them bean hole beans anyway?"

A thermometer was tacked on one of the logs, and when Theodore inspected it he saw it read -4 degrees. The men were all moving slowly, and the few words they spoke were surrounded by puffs of frost.

All around, men sat up slowly and started putting on the few items of clothing they hadn't slept in.

By the fire, Bill and Coty had just uncovered the buried pot and lifted it. With care Bill wiped away all traces of coal and ash, blowing the lid clean before he lifted it.

"You men just settle down," replied Bill. "It'll be ready when it's ready." With the lid removed the aroma of the beans floated throughout the cabin and tickled two dozen hungry stomachs. At once the men climbed out of the bed and fumbled for their grub kits. Theodore, too, stumbled awkwardly up out of the bunk and got in line.

Coty placed some fresh venison liver in a cast iron pan and smothered it with peeled onions. The onions seared as they hit the hot pan and flooded the cabin with more delicious odors.

When Bill looked up he was surprised to see all the men standing in line, quietly, their eyes fixed on the food.

"You'd think it was Christmas the way they're reactin'" said Cecil as he strategically moved closer to the food.

Coty started doling out food to the waiting men. He placed a heap of venison and onions on their plates, and then Bill added a ladle full of beans. They had barely finished serving the last men when the first came back for more.

"Dem beans was wicked good, Bill," said Barry.

During the second round Bill also dished out the bacon and onions that had settled to the bottom of the bean pot. The men looked determined to just keep lining up until it was all gone.

"No sense in having leftovers with this meal," said Cecil as he scraped up the last of the beans.

"I wouldn't a trusted you fellas to save us any once we hit the woods anyway," said Barry.

Cecil looked hurt.

"I thought you trusted me more than that."

Barry grinned. "Not when it comes to Bill's bean hole beans I don't."

It was still dark out as they wrapped up the meal with just about everyone shaking Bill's hand in thanks.

"Some of you still got a day ahead of you," lectured Cecil. "And I'd just-a-soon you're outdoors before you start fartin' up those beans."

Most of the men had already begun dressing for the day and preparing their gear, but now they stepped it up, heckling Cecil right back as they did.

Theodore approached Cecil and asked in a low voice, "Cecil, could you tell me where the lavatory is?"

Cecil suppressed a chuckle and nodded behind the building. "Just go 'round back, Mr. Roosevelt, and you'll see the outhouse."

He added, "Might be a bit cold, but it was cleaned and limed not too long ago."

Theodore nodded and made for the door when Barry's voice stopped him.

"Mr. Roosevelt, you're not goin' out *theya* now are ya? Before daylight and all..."

Having experienced Barry's humor before Theodore suspected a trick.

"Are you telling me there might be more bear out there gunning for me?"

Barry laughed uproariously.

"Oh, so you *remembah* that, do ya? No, I'm not jokin', I just don't want to see ya get hurt."

Theodore nodded politely.

"And what might be out there that would hurt me this time if you do not mind me asking; a rabid raccoon, perhaps?"

Barry looked around the cabin as if seeking support in his efforts to warn the young man from Harvard.

"Well, it'd be the wolves, of course."

From the back of the cabin Charley said, "Here we go again."

Theodore smiled.

"I will do my best to keep alert."

Barry offered him a gun as he walked out the door, but Theodore didn't take it. In fact, having once been a victim of Barry's teasing before, he didn't take any of it seriously.

The cold hit him like a fist as he stepped outside, and he was surprised at how it could be this much colder than inside the cabin, where everyone's breath puffed when they spoke.

Theodore leaned forward and pulled his coat tight against the back of his head.

In the predawn hour the woods were still filled with shadows. Under his boots the snow crunched loudly. Otherwise, all was still.

And then from across the lake he heard a wolf howl. He stared in that direction, silently, but his breathing was all he heard. His thoughts returned to Bible Point and the wolf he'd seen there.

As Theodore rounded the cabin he saw the outhouse.

He walked in that direction, but just as he stepped past a large spruce trunk something caught the corner of his eye that seized him with terror.

His shocked gaze fell on a large wolf, crouched and ready to spring, its mouth open, fangs bared.

Theodore dove to the side and scrambled through some low brush until he came upon a pine trunk. Without thinking twice he started up the tree like a porcupine with a dog after it, branches flying everywhere.

It was only after he was about fifteen feet in the air that he stopped. Arms and legs wrapped around the trunk, scratched and bleeding with sticks in his hair: he tried desperately, but in vain, to control his breathing.

He looked down to see where the predator was, and when his panicked gaze found the animal he noticed something strange about it.

The wolf still sat in the snow to the side of the spruce trunk — crouched and ready to spring. But it wasn't moving. In fact, as Theodore looked at it, it became obvious that the wolf was dead and had been for some time.

One of the woodsmen — most likely Barry — had set it there as a joke. Theodore interrupted his panting to draw a big sigh of relief and lowered himself to the ground. He walked over to the wolf and admired the taxidermist job.

The image of himself scrambling through the woods to flee from a dead animal made him grin. Then he thought of Barry and his face hardened.

When Theodore returned to the cabin every man stopped what he was doing and watched him, waiting to see how he'd take it. He looked around angrily until his eyes found Barry, and then his expression changed as he said with a grin, "I do believe that wolf helped with my constitution."

"Scared the shit right out a you, he did," shouted David to the disapproving stare of his brother, Bill. The rest of the woodsmen were rolling with laughter.

Barry stomped over and slapped a heavy hand on Theodore's shoulder.

"*Thaht* there wolf was gettin' into our supplies so we poisoned it." Then he grinned wide and added, "Before he froze solid we put 'im into that crouchin' position."

He shook Theodore's shoulder "Pretty realistic, wouldn't ya say?"

Bill stepped forward protectively and moved Theodore away. "Ayuh, very," he said, and then defensively added, "Mr. Roosevelt, you have to forgive them for their jokes. It really is the only sense of fun we have around here."

Theodore told his version of what had happened. The story greatly amused the other woodsmen, especially when he went on about how high he had climbed. Barry laughed so hard he had tears running down his cheeks.

"After that scare, I half expected to see some critter staring up at me from the seat in the outhouse," added Theodore.

"Oh, we might arrange somethin' for ya," said one of the woodsmen and everyone howled.

Coty led Theodore over the frozen landscape: they went on foot, following a ridgeline that began on the far side of the lake the cabin sat beside. The sun was high and each of them was freshly fed and warmly dressed.

When they'd left the cabin all but Bill and Cecil had set out to work. Two crews had departed in the early hours, and Coty had packed them with enough food to cover their next two meals.

Bill volunteered to help Cecil repair a roof leak, and when they stepped outside to assess the job Coty realized that he had some free time—a rare commodity at a logging camp.

"De crews will be away for most of de day so I want to do someting for you," said Coty as he motioned for Theodore to follow him.

Theodore nodded and followed silently.

After crossing the windswept lake they stopped to put on snowshoes. There were several inches of fresh snow on the ground and with the help of the shoes the walking was easy. Eventually the land tilted down again, and the brush got denser. In the distance Theodore could see a small lake, but before that stood an old forest of virgin cedar.

As he examined the forest, Theodore felt he was looking at an enchanted place. This land and the trees on it had never been logged and they towered up before them; their trunks were six to eight feet wide and covered with moss.

The tops of the cedars were covered with snow and iced over, in the tight grip of winter, but closer to the ground their branches became so dense that they created a canopy. Underneath it existed a sheltered world.

The men entered it as Coty led him along a deer trail that disappeared under the canopy. Theodore marveled at how warm it had suddenly become. He guessed that the temperature was at least fifty degrees above that on the lake.

The wet ground around the base of the moss-covered trees was unfrozen; steam rose up from it into the cold air. Up above, the sky was no longer visible.

"This is incredible," said Theodore.

"Even in de worst winters dis place does not freeze," said Coty.

Theodore marveled at the absence of lower branches under the canopy; then he saw that the ground was covered with deer prints. "I believe the white-tail deer may winter over in a place like this. I have read that they *yard up* for the winter in groups of hundreds...maybe even thousands."

"Yes. And many other aneemals come dis way. We will set some traps and check dem when we return later."

After taking off their snowshoes they proceeded on foot under the forest canopy, staying on the bare earth whenever possible. The ground here was muddy, but they made due by stepping on the roots of the cedar trees, which sprawled out all around them.

"I heard you talk about de caribou dat got away and wanted to bring you here," Coty said.

Theodore looked around, "It is certainly a unique environment, but it does not really look like the kind of terrain where one would find a caribou."

Coty laughed.

"I may live far from any cities, and it has been a long time since I have seen a woman, but it appears I know more than you on dis account."

Looking a bit unsettled, Theodore stopped to retie his snowshoes onto his backpack.

"And what would a caribou have to do with knowing a woman's mind?" asked Theodore.

Coty ignored the question and instead pointed at a well-used game trail that ran through an open area, almost a clearing, with the branches doming high above.

"Dis would be good place for one of de traps," said Coty."

Coty took off his own pack and proceeded to take out several metal traps and get them ready. They were each set off by a metal pad that sat between the sharp steel jaws. They shined from some secret animal fat rub he'd worked into the metal the night before.

Theodore noted that the traps were of a similar design to the ones Wilmot used.

"Wilmot calls them *lucivee* traps, but I was never certain if he was referring to an animal called a lucivee, or if he was actually saying, illusive."

Coty laughed.

"*Lucivee* is a nickname for an aneemal that haunts dese woods, but is rarely seen. I grew up knowing him as a *loup curvier*, or *Indian devil*."

"My goodness," said Theodore, "please tell me what this animal is."

"In English he is called a Canada lynx," replied Coty, "and he is what you need to win your woman's heart."

Theodore went to ask another question, but Coty silenced him by holding up his finger and then went to work on setting and placing the trap with deep concentration.

After he was finished he camouflaged it, and carefully backed away, erasing all evidence of his passing as he did. As he retreated he took out a small bottle and placed several drips of scent near the set trap.

Theodore watched it all with interest, but he was also still pondering Coty's comment.

Finally he asked, "Coty, I wish to understand your remark. What was wrong with bringing down a caribou for my Alice?"

The young man sat back on his haunches, brushed the dirt from his hands, and stared at Theodore without speaking for a moment.

"If you are courting a woman you must give her someting special. A caribou is a noble aneemal, but it will not make her feel. You must give a gift dat makes her *feel* someting."

More confused than ever, Theodore stood as they prepared to move on. With the traps in hand, Coty set out down the game trail, reading the tracks as he went.

Theodore followed, moving as quietly as he could.

After a few minutes Coty stopped and pointed to a track in the soft mud.

"Dis is him, de lynx," he said with a knowing smile. "A good-sized one as well — we will trap it together. Dis time you help."

Theodore nodded, and together they baited and set several more traps and placed them along the trail.

"We leave dis place now," said Coty. "I will take you to anoder place where we can rest."

With that Coty marched off, leading Theodore out of the cedar swamp and up a long incline. An hour later they were on the top of a granite ridge. It was colder than in the swamp, but the winter sun warmed them as they reclined on a smooth boulder.

Theodore took off his boots and socks and laid them to dry in the sun, a little fearful of Wilmot's warnings of how dangerous it could be to let your boots freeze once you took your feet out. Then he examined the heavy wool pants that he'd brought with him for this visit to Maine.

"These pants really are an improvement to the ones I wore last time," said Theodore as he stared at Coty's buckskins, "but I wonder how they would compare to your clothing over time."

"De buckskin is best," replied Coty with certainty. "You can make it yourself, it is warm, and it dries quickly."

Theodore nodded and looked again at his own woolen pants. "I am not convinced; wool is pretty good."

Coty added, "I am serious. Dis is de only clothes I own. What more do I need?"

With a smile he continued, "Dis visit we take care of your woman. Your…"

"Alice," said Theodore with a smile.

"Yes, your Alice. We make her someting nice. When you come back next we get you some buckskins."

The prospect appealed to Theodore greatly and it showed in his smile.

"I look forward to that, Coty."

Coty reached in his pocket and pulled out a grizzled muskrat tail and offered it to Theodore.

"I save dis; you want half?"

Theodore shook his head. "I am afraid I am still not ready for that."

Coty laughed. "If you come back when it is warmer we will go on de lake and take frogs, den I cook you some frog legs you will never forget."

The sun was warm and the wind was down so they lay back to nap. Theodore closed his eyes, but after several minutes he sat up and put his boots on. With a smile, he lay back again.

Later they both awoke to the sounds of several jays fighting over the remains of Coty's muskrat tail. From the position of the sun Coty could see several hours had passed.

Above them the wind blew through the barren trees and it was obvious that the weather had started to turn. Soon the sun disappeared behind dark clouds.

They began the journey back to the cabin, passing by the traps on the way. Although there had been only a slight breeze on their backs on their trip out, they now found themselves leaning into a harsh wind.

The warm, windless area under the canopy of the ancient cedar grove was a welcome relief and they stopped to rest a short way from where they'd seen the lynx tracks.

Coty heard a noise and cocked his head in that direction.

"I tink we have someting; I go look."

Minutes later he returned to inform Theodore that a good-sized lynx was in one of the traps, the steel jaws holding it firmly in place by its front paw.

They quietly made their way to it.

When it first saw them it glared in anger, the hair on its back rising straight up as it tried to back away.

As they got closer the cat's eyes became wild, darting back and forth as it looked for an avenue of escape. And then it crouched down low and watched them approach.

Theodore raised his gun to kill it, but Coty stopped him. "If you want dis pelt den do not shoot. You must kill it with a blow to de head."

Reaching into Theodore's pack, Coty took out a short handled axe — very similar to the one Bill had used to kill the bear — and handed it to Theodore.

"Move close to him, but not too close, and whack him with de dull end," said Coty.

Theodore did as he was told and slowly approached. The lynx was glaring at him and now letting out a low growl that seemed to pass through him. The intensity of the growl made the lynx seem more formidable than its size would have suggested.

He moved closer and the cat took a swipe at him with his free paw.

"Wait," warned Coty. "I will distract. When he look at me you hit his head with de axe."

As Coty moved forward the lynx shifted his attention. It hissed at Coty loudly and then growled again. Theodore moved in and struck quickly, and the lynx slumped to the ground with a thud.

Using a sharp knife he kept by his side, Coty poked the lynx to make sure it was dead, and then he severed the head.

Afterwards he showed Theodore how to gut it and properly strip the skin. Coty worked quickly and with confidence, but the skinning took time and though there was not much sense of daylight under the canopy, they both knew the sunlit hours were passing.

When he was finished, Coty used a few strips of leather and bundled the hide with the soft fur on the inside.

"It seems a waste to leave the meat," said Theodore as he looked down at the naked carcass.

"We do not eat predators," Coty said. "My family taught me it is bad luck." He saw the confused look on Theodore's face and added, "Do not worry; der are many aneemals dat will be grateful for dis meat."

He then knelt by the carcass and quickly said a prayer, the words of which only his Indian ancestors would have understood, but the meaning was plain to Theodore.

On the walk back they talked while crossing over a frozen river — Theodore led the way. He carried his pack with the axe in his hand, and Coty had the lynx pelt resting on his shoulder, the leather ties making it easy to carry.

The wind was howling now, and they leaned forward as they went, shouting over it when communicating.

Coty pointed out a hole in the ice and said, "Otters keep dese holes open all winter."

He added, "I would like to get an otter..."and suddenly said no more.

When Theodore turned to look back at him he found him nowhere in sight. The pelt lay on the ice, abandoned.

Theodore scanned the landscape in all directions, but there was no sign of Coty. Puzzled, he lifted the pelt and discovered a hole in the ice right under it. It was about one and a half feet wide — just big enough for a man to drop through.

Suddenly Theodore realized what had happened.

Dropping everything except the axe, Theodore looked at the water under the hole and determined which way the river was flowing. Then he carefully but swiftly walked downstream from the hole, scanning for Coty's body under the ice as he went.

Theodore felt panic welling up in his guts, and then suddenly he spotted a body under the ice. He could see Coty was still conscious, weakly clawing at six inches of ice; his eyes were filled with panic. The river didn't appear to be deep, but it moved fast. Theodore could see that Coty was trying to lodge his feet into the river bottom and stand, but the current swept him away again and again.

Theodore hurried ahead of Coty's body and tried to break through with the axe, but it was too thick to do it in one swing of the axe. By the time he was ready to strike again Coty had floated past.

He located Coty again, noticing with alarm how his eyes were no longer open, and he seemed limp. He ran ahead twenty feet and struck the surface as hard as he could.

Chunks of ice flew up as Theodore frantically hacked away at the frozen river. He saw a dark shape approach from beneath and he dropped the axe and jumped on the cracked surface as hard as he could.

He felt it give, and then he was up to his waist in the water and felt Coty's body float into his. The water wasn't that deep, but it moved along swiftly.

Coty was unconscious and cold as death. Theodore fought to lift his body out of the river, the water rushing around them and threatening to sweep them both away.

Finally he managed to pull him up onto the ice and laid him on his side, panting and shouting at Coty to wake up. His stomach churned in helpless panic. But then the young man began to come back to life, vomiting water and coughing.

Theodore helped Coty sit up. He was pale — almost blue — but managed a weak smile. "I sh...should have m...mentioned dat de otter always l...likes to have two h...holes in case one is b...blocked."

The sun was again nearing the horizon and the temperature had begun to drop sharply. Now the wind chill felt deadly and they both knew they were in trouble. Coty's buckskins were soaked, and in the few moments since Theodore had pulled him from the ice they had begun to freeze.

"We have to get you back to the camp," said Theodore, knowing that they were still several miles away. "Can you walk?"

Coty nodded.

"Should I stop and light a fire?" asked Theodore.

"I would not make it through de night with dese wet clothes," Coty said, his voice weak and raspy.

"Then we best get started," said Theodore as he threw Coty's arm over his shoulder. He grabbed his pack and shoved the lynx pelt out of their way with his foot but Coty gripped his arm weakly.

"You cannot leave dat, my friend. It would be an insult to the lynx."

Theodore interrupted him, his voice urgent and worried.

"I need to get you somewhere warm, I do not care about it anymore."

Coty sunk away from Theodore's support and grabbed the pelt. He held it to his chest.

"Just because you fear for my life doesn't mean we should live life differently," said Coty as he stiffly began to march. Theodore moved to his side and again placed Coty's arm over his shoulder. They made it off the river and onto the trail they had used earlier that day, their own tracks visible ahead of them.

"My people believe dat you sh...should live your life in a way dat de fear of death can n...never enter your heart," said Coty. He was shivering violently. "We will be fine if we do not s...stop."

Their clothes had frozen stiff on them. Theodore was soon unable to bend his legs and one arm, but what worried him more was that Coty's buckskins had frozen solid and he could barely move his limbs. As Theodore helped him shuffle along he could feel his body shivering, and his breathing had grown rapid.

"Tonight I s...show you how to m...make someting beautiful from dis p...pelt. I..." he tried to continue, but his chattering teeth interfered. The pelt had frozen to his chest, but it weighed nothing and Theodore hoped it might help insulate him.

As they reached the lake they could see the cabin on the other side, a comforting ribbon of smoke trailing through the hole in the roof.

Theodore stopped long enough to unsling his rifle from his stiff arm and struggled to fire three shots into the air. Then they continued.

"Almost there, Coty."

The light had begun to fade from Coty's eyes. Theodore mustered his last energy to cross the frozen lake. He was dead tired and had trouble supporting Coty, who he was now almost carrying.

Within a few minutes he could see several men racing across the lake to their aid.

Chapter Eighteen
The Old Timers

When Coty and Theodore finally stumbled into the cabin with the help of several woodsmen, they found it bursting with people and activity.

Cecil took one look at Coty, grabbed him and sat him down right near the fire, which he quickly cranked up. Within minutes he had a bowl of hot stew ready. Cecil fed him slowly, fussing over him like a parent.

"You stupid bluenose, what've you gotten yourself into?"

All Coty could manage to say was, "O...t...ter...hole."

"Shut up and eat the soup. How would I manage this camp without you? Ever thought of that, you selfish half-breed?"

Coty weakly smiled at Cecil's efforts at caring and settled back a little. He tried to set down the pelt and realized it was still frozen to him. In fact his buckskins were frozen so stiff he still couldn't bend his legs and they stuck out in front of him just begging for someone to trip over.

"Don't you worry 'bout that," said Cecil, motioning at the pelt. "It'll come loose in a few minutes and I'll thaw it out proper."

Looking around the first time since arriving, Coty noticed everyone staring.

He said, "Looks like a full house, boss."

Cecil spooned him some more stew.

"And here you are all frozen stiff and unable to help when I really need it. Boy, I've got some bad luck."

While they'd been gone, David had come in with Sherman, and there were also two new men—brothers.

They were old-timers; dressed entirely in furs, their white whiskers and long hair merged in a wild tangle behind their cheeks. They had spent most of their lives in the wilderness, and were actually so different from anyone Theodore had ever met that he had a hard time not staring at them.

Coty was laughing from his place by the fire as he thawed, soaking the ground around him. Water poured from his buckskins like someone had emptied a bucket on him.

"Smells like the *rivah*," said one of the woodsmen.

Cecil kept the fire burning hot, and in no time Coty was flushing red from the heat as he flexed his hand in response to the pins and needles that had set in.

Theodore helped himself to some food and watched the two old brothers while he ate.

They talked little and used unique gestures that they'd developed while on their own. All around them men organized their gear, ate, hung wet clothing on the stink pole and settled down, but those two just kept to themselves. They were obviously accustomed to the hustle and bustle of a logging camp, and knew when to stay out of the way.

When everyone had eaten Cecil introduced Theodore to the brothers who were named Fredrick and Hollis. Fredrick had a scar on his left cheek. Other than that they looked identical.

By the fire David and Barry shared some tobacco. Next to them Cecil doted on Coty and thawed the lynx pelt, slowly unraveling it by the fire. Bill retreated to a corner, allowing Theodore some space to talk to the old timers.

"And what task do you gentlemen perform in this logging operation?" asked Theodore.

The brothers both laughed at the question.

Fredrick glanced at Cecil as he answered.

"We don't do much a anythin' no more."

Hollis added, "No sir, them days is over."

Cecil leaned forward and interjected.

"You men cut yourself short."

Cecil pointed to the meal that he had just finished serving and said, "These men are hunters—you're eatin' meat they brought in. When they were younger they worked in the loggin' industry, but now they help keep it goin' by bringin' in meat from time to time."

Fredrick laughed.

"Oh, it's nothin' *regulah* like *thaht*. We just move 'round the woods now, and when we shows up *somewheya* we brings along somethin' ta eat."

Hollis nodded, "Makes us more welcome."

Theodore was intrigued.

"But surely you must have a home somewhere."

They looked at each other.

"Nope, all I've got is my *brothah*," said Fredrick. "Our daddy raised us at one of the camps and we *nevah* did want to see the city."

"So you have never been to a town?" asked Theodore.

Hollis chuckled at the thought.

"You kiddin'? If a trail even starts lookin' like a road we turns around."

Fredrick added, "No offense, but why would ya want to go to a place where the loon didn't laugh, or the bear and moose didn't roam free?"

"So what you crave is the wilderness?" asked Theodore, "The lack of civilization?"

"Civilization is for the vain," stated Fredrick.

The young Harvard student shook his head and asked, "What could you possibly mean by that?"

Hollis sat back, aware that his brother was about to go off on one of his rants.

"I'm told you come from New York City, *thaht* right?" started Fredrick. Theodore nodded and he continued. "Do ya think New York City will be there in one hundred years?"

Before Theodore could reply he added, "How 'bout one thousand, or ten thousand?"

Now Theodore looked a bit uncertain.

"The forest is a sentient thing. It watches us with patience and per-sis-tence; waitin' for us to move on before sendin' out fresh shoots."

Fredrick pointed at his brother and added, "Our ancestor came to this area *aftah* the Revolutionary War. We still know the spot." Hollis nodded in support.

"Over a hundred years ago he came *heya* with the appallin' notion of clearin' the land. The hills echoed with the sounds of saws and lumbermen as he built a big house with two stone fireplaces, and then a barn."

Hollis added, "And a schoolhouse."

"*Ayuh*, there were a few other farms in the area and they sent their children. The pastures were full of music from the bells of the Merino sheep that grazed *theya*."

Fredrick grinned as he looked at Theodore.

"Now if ya had asked any a those people what they had created they would a said they had *improved* the land. They might have even said they had brought *civilization* to this dark, immense forest.

"And maybe they had! One hundred years ago only a few small clearings broke this wilderness. In those days the jays and crows were the only sound that disrupted the quiet."

He slowly looked around the room and nodded at the woodsmen who'd been listening.

Then he said, "But were we to take ya back to the land formerly owned by our ancestor ya would see how relentless the growth of the forest is.

"Long ago it swallowed miles of stone fences. It tore the gates off the hinges, slowly, and *aftah* a time advanced right to the foundation of the house. There it paused at the very slab of granite that had served as a doorstep—the house beyond destroyed by fire in the distant past. In the yawning cellar hole a few decaying apple trees looked up sadly. All signs of man's efforts ob-lit-er-ated. Now ya tell me, where did the civilization go to?"

Theodore reflected on his words before replying.

"Surely you must believe that our lives have value, that we are not just wasting our time?"

"Well that's *anothah* subject, I was just sayin' that everythin'—even New York City—passes in time and that to believe otherwise is vanity. Even what we do, bringin' light into the swamp, is temporary."

Theodore smiled as he heard the phrase *Bringing light into the swamp* again.

"I *nevah* cease to marvel at what happens in the old clearings once we move on. Over a period of decades I've watched 'em grow back—sometimes several times—leavin' no trace of the havoc we wreaked. All through this il-limit-able wilderness the forest continues marchin' to erase any evidence of our passin'."

Fredrick leaned back and stretched before adding.

"I don't really know what else to tell ya, sir. This is the only life I've *evah* known."

He then said proudly, "To me, freedom is the roar of the wind as it blasts through the tops of the pines."

Hollis added, "It's livin' in a land where the only castles are built by beavers."

"Aha!" said Bill from his corner. "Like Mr. Longfellow stated, '*Who are the true nobles of the land...the true aristocrats...*"

From the back of the cabin David moaned, "Here we go again."

Bill ignored him and continued, "*Who need not bow their heads to kings... Nor doff to lords their hats... Who are they but the men of toil... Who cleave the forest down... And plant amid the wilderness...the forest and the town."*

Theodore took out his notebook to write something, standing at the same time, but he suddenly lost his equilibrium and almost fell forward. Bill moved quickly from the corner and caught him.

"I think that spell on the river was hard on your body too, "Bill said as he sat Theodore back down in his chair. He looked down at him, disapprovingly, "I shouldn'ta let you go off like that so soon after your ordeal with the caribou."

Theodore nodded and steadied himself. He looked at Cecil and asked, "Coty doing alright?" The camp boss nodded, but they could all see that his complexion was still pale.

Hollis patted Theodore's shoulder.

"*Ayuh*, we heard about your huntin' adventure. Cecil was just tellin' us before ya came in."

Theodore appeared lost in thought, recalling the chase in his mind.

"Yes, I believe I botched the entire thing. I still cannot believe it got away."

Bill shook his head and added, "Through no lack of effort, I might add. Wilmot says he was on the trail thirty-six hours!"

Hollis and Fredrick looked at each other, a slight smile on each of their faces as if they shared some private joke.

Hollis leaned forward and asked, "When ya were chasin' that caribou, did ya feel connected to the animal? As if there was nothin' else in the world?"

Theodore paused for a moment.

"Yes. There was nothing else."

He then astounded himself by adding, "Not even Alice."

Hollis nodded.

"And I bet even when ya were close ya didn't *remembah* that gun ya were carryin', did ya?"

Theodore flushed slightly and looked at the other men in the room.

"I had not realized it until just now, but no, after the first time I wounded the beast I never took another shot."

The brothers looked at each other again and smiled.

Fredrick pointed at his brother.

"I saved him once, the same way Wilmot saved you. Ya get that fever and it's tough to stop the chase."

Hollis laughed at the memory.

"Funny thing is," he said, "ya might'a caught that caribou if ya could've only stopped chasin' it."

Theodore stared at the ground, shaking his head.

"Wilmot said something similar. I just saw that rack and had to have it. I promised my Alice that I will return with a trophy for her."

Coty stood up stiffly and grabbed the lynx pelt. While everyone watched he slowly knelt in front of Theodore and stretched it out. His hands still shook slightly.

David came forward to inspect the pelt.

"That's a nice skin. Good work."

Theodore blushed with pride as he helped Coty lay out the pelt.

"We rub a mix into de skin to make it soft, and den we put it on a stretcher," explained Coty.

Coty moved to stand, but Cecil headed him off and returned with a container he grabbed from the kitchen area. He handed it to Coty, but he lacked the strength to open it and let Bill do it. The contents smelled wretched and Theodore turned his head away.

"Dis might smell bad now," said Coty, "but wait 'til you see how soft it makes de pelt. Did you tink of what you might make out of it?"

Now Theodore looked uncomfortable.

"Excuse me? I do not understand."

Coty laughed. "Well, you cannot just give her de hide as it is. Not if you are courting her. You must make it someting special."

Theodore looked to the old timers for support, but they just stared back expectantly.

Coty then lifted the cat's fur, weakly, and draped it over Theodore's shoulders. "I tink dis would make a good — what do you say? — shawl? Yes, a shawl."

Cecil appraised it. "And add a clasp on the front, something nice", he said.

Hollis lifted a tattered end that had formerly been a forearm. "Better trim it up a bit too."

"Good thing he didn't get a moose," hollered David from the corner.

"I would like to shoot a moose if the opportunity arises," said Theodore.

David shouted, "Bill, tell 'im about the time I got a moose and a bear with one shot."

Bill shook his head, "I've heard that story a few too many times — you tell him."

David came over and took a seat closer to Theodore and started his tale, "When I was a youngin I was friends with an Indian named Tomah."

He looked at the two brothers.

"You two knew Tomah didn't you?"

They both nodded.

Hollis added, "Tomah was a great tracker, but his eyesight wasn't *thaht* good."

"*Ayuh*, that's how I got involved. It was late in the winter and Tomah had come across some bear tracks — and the bear was following a moose."

"Tomah came and got me, and had me bring one of our oxen. He was wicked excited as he explained that sometimes the bear get desperate and they will stay on a moose 'til it gets cornered."

David looked around and grinned. This was obviously one of his favorite stories.

"Anyway, we tracked the bear that was trackin' the moose for a couple hours, and eventually come across 'em both at the end of a lake where it drained into a river. Here the water wasn't frozen and the moose was standin' shoulder deep in it.

"Tomah told me to just wait and watch, and soon enough that bear entered the water and swam toward the moose. Just before he reached him the moose went up on his back legs and started stompin' the bear.

"That bear never had a chance and was drowned pretty quick. Then Tomah had me shoot the moose — he would'a done it but for his eyes — and we used the ox to pull out both bodies."

"That is an incredible tale, Mr. Sewall!" exclaimed Theodore.

"It is every time we hear it," stated Barry from the communal bed.

"Alright everyone," said Cecil, "I think it's time we all called it a night. We've got an early day tomorrow."

Within a few minutes the men were all bedded down on the communal bed; fresh spruce boughs underneath them and one long blanket covering.

Theodore looked over the silent camp, comparing it to the estate that he'd been raised in. Fredrick and Hollis slept near the fire, which Coty still tended. He imagined that after their cold walk back Coty must have appreciated his job as the camp cook and its proximity to the fire. After several hours his buckskins had dried completely.

Still, Theodore noticed that Coty still shivered, and he slept very close to the glowing coals that night.

Bill lay near Theodore, his sack under his head as a pillow. He said in a low voice, "You must be aware that King Olaf trapped a lynx, and swore its fur would soon warm his beloved."

"The thought has crossed my mind, Mr. Sewall," said Theodore in the darkness.

The next morning they rode the pung back to the main road. Coty had said goodbye from his spot by the fire, which he now seemed reluctant to leave. The color had returned to his skin, but there was still something missing from his life force.

"He'll be okay," said Cecil. "It's almost impossible to kill one of those bluenoses."

The return journey in the pung started out fine: the weather was reasonably pleasant, hovering just above freezing. The sleigh hissed along over a three foot shroud of snow. But once they got a few miles from Cecil's camp the trail turned rougher.

"We had it easy comin' out, ridin' in the tracks of a few sleds that had just made the journey," said Bill, "but nobody's passed this way since the last snow fell and we're gonna have to brake trail the rest of the way."

"I am ready for anything, Bill," said Theodore, "I feel like I have enough health to last me to next summer."

The Mainer cautioned him, "Careful now, we still gotta long way to go. Don't get cocky on me."

Theodore smiled and replied, "Seriously, Bill, have you not noticed that the entire time I was in the camp my asthma did not bother me once?"

Sewall looked up at the dark clouds that gathered above them and warned, "You just save some of that energy. If we get hit with some weather while it's this warm there'll be hell to pay."

Theodore didn't understand until a while later when the soft snow flurries that had started to fall around them turned to sleet, making the trail too soft to support the pung with them both in it.

Scout repeatedly lost the trail and foundered in deep snow. Each time they had to hop down, unharness her, and drag the pung backward; then they hitched her up to her harness again and continued.

It was fatiguing work. They seemed to make little progress in light of all the delays and backtracking and they were getting completely soaked in the process. When they finally arrived in Island Falls they were both cold, tired and hungry.

Theodore did lose some of the zest he felt at the journey's start, but he never complained and Bill experienced a certain amount of pride in the young man's accomplishment.

At the train station Theodore stood with Bill while the few passengers disembarked the train. They had spent several nights at the Sewall house in Island Falls, and even one camping by Mattawamkeag Lake, but all too soon the time had come to go back to New York.

"I would like to thank you for your hospitality, again, Bill. It really was a great opportunity for me to get to know that crew up at the Oxbow camp."

Bill laughed. "I'm surprised that bunch of Aroostook woodsmen made such an impression on you. Don't get me wrong, I'd lay my life down for any of 'em, but they're mostly unlettered and I hadn't expected you to enjoy our visit with them fellas so much."

Theodore grinned. "In New York, or at Harvard, I might read about such things — or such people — but with you I was able to get first-hand accounts of backwoods life from the men who had lived it and knew what they were talking about. It really was priceless."

"It was my pleasure, Theodore," said Bill.

Then the older man paused.

"I didn't want to ruin our last night together, but there's something I feel I should say before you go."

"Goodness, Bill," said Theodore. "What is on your mind?"

Bill collected his thoughts and then said, "Well, the first time you came here, your head was — understandably — full of your father. I'm sure you remember our conversation."

Theodore nodded.

"But you do not think that was the problem this time, do you?"

Bill shook his head and Theodore answered for him.

"You think I was preoccupied this time with Alice, is that it?"

Bill smiled.

"It's not really the end of the world, but might I suggest that the next time you come visit, you come up here for yourself?"

The older man grinned and added, "It would do you good."

Theodore smiled and shook Bill's hand vigorously.

"I promise, Bill. I will do that."

Chapter Nineteen
Boxing Match

Dickey Saltonstall stood in the cool night air of the Harvard Campus, waiting impatiently. He scanned the courtyard approaches, saw Alice finally appearing, and waved to her.

A late winter storm had left a few inches of snow, but a path had been shoveled clear. Alice advanced with a light step, smiling broadly.

Her neck and ears were snuggled in a fur shawl that she wore with unmistakable pride. It had been cut from the lynx Theodore had trapped and, guided by Coty, tanned at the cabin.

All evidence of the animal's limbs was gone, and where the ends met by her collarbone they were held together by a gold clasp. The pelt covered her to just below the shoulders and encircled her slender neck.

Dickey could not stand tardiness, but he could not hold a grudge against his cousin.

"So I finally get to see this wild cat that Theodore trapped," he greeted her.

Alice lifted the lynx shawl and with a coy smile nestled her face in deeper. Her breath shot forward in puffs of mist, but she didn't seem cold. Theodore's gift looked good on her and the fur felt luxuriously soft on her shoulders.

As she spun in a circle to show it off Dickey noted how she glowed. He examined the garment up close and gave it some deserving praise.

"You know he hasn't stopped talking about his last trip to Maine since his return."

Alice snuggled her chin against the soft fur.

"Thank heavens he did not get the caribou; there is no way it could have been so soft."

"I think you're lacking imagination, cousin."

Alice gave him her best scowl.

"Dickey, there is no way I could go in public with a shawl made from a caribou—I would look like a cow."

Dickey laughed and then remembered the fight they were going to attend.

"Alice, we're late enough! We already missed the first bout."

"I am sorry I was delayed..." began Alice, but Dickey had already taken her by the arm and steered her toward the nearby gymnasium. "Let's go inside," he said. "I've saved us some great seats."

Inside, a large crowd occupied folding chairs surrounding a boxing ring. The arena was packed with men, alongside the alleys, and surrounding the ring; all anticipating the upcoming fight.

Suspended from two sides of the galley, a banner hung over the ring announcing: HARVARD ATHLETIC ASSOCIATION – LIGHT-WEIGHT BOXING CHAMPIONSHIP.

The noise from the galley intimidated Alice almost as much as the crowd on the floor. As she looked up she noticed it was where all the young people were, and a few women too. On the floor she seemed to be the only woman. As Dickey led her through the crowd, cutting a path with one outstretched hand, Alice kept close behind his back and whispered. "Is it normal to bring a woman onto the floor?"

He paused to turn and look at her sternly, "Well, you see cousin; I was in a difficult position. As a friend of Theodore's I had great ringside seats, but as your cousin – and protector for the evening – I thought I should sit with you in the galley, where the respectable women are."

Alice was squeezing by a particularly angry older gentleman who seemed irritated by getting a face full of lynx shawl as she edged past him.

"And then what do I owe this honor to, being the single woman on the floor?"

Dickey grinned. "Knowing you I figured you would not allow yourself to be so far from Theodore. And you never seem to be shy about breaking with tradition – you didn't complain when I snuck you into the Porcellian Club and that's only for men."

Now Alice giggled with excitement.

"Where is he, Dickey? I cannot see him."

"Let's just get to our seats before they start." Then he added, "The first fight was between Roosevelt and Coolidge. Last year Theodore gave him a tremendous thrashing."

"And how did he do tonight?" asked Alice anxiously.

Dickey grinned. "He displayed greater coolness and more skill than his opponent, I can say that much."

They had just found their seats and sat down when everyone stood and cheered, backed up by a roar from the galley. Theodore was returning from a break in the locker room. His small frame rippled with muscle from a vigorous training program he had been subjecting himself to.

He climbed under the rope and tested the bounce of the ring floor. Alice stared at his muscles and found herself speechless.

"He looks fresh," said Dickey. "Looks like they sponged him off between fights."

"Yes, he does," she whispered.

She watched Theodore and tried to gauge his chances in the fight from his stance, then from his expression, but found herself lost. The young man in the boxing ring appeared very different from the shy boy that quoted poetry to her at Chestnut Hill.

He threw several combinations and stretched his neck.

"He appears focused," was all she could manage to say, but in her mind she heard her cousin Rose saying, "What kind of society man boxes these days? I swear Harvard is turning him into a fraternity hoodlum."

As Theodore took his corner his eyes scanned the crowd, but he didn't see Alice. For a minute he turned to look again, but then gathered himself and went back to loosening up.

Soon the referee appeared and asked both fighters if they were ready. Roosevelt and Hanks both nodded and he made the announcement.

"Your attention, please! This next fight will be for the Harvard Athletic Boxing Association Light-Weight Belt between Theodore Roosevelt and C. S. Hanks."

The crowd around the ring suddenly appeared diminished as a wave of cries from the galley greeted the announcement. Hundreds of people stomped their feet, and the woodwork sounded like it might shatter.

Alice had never been to a fight before and shrank away from the noise and commotion.

The referee broke through the cheers.

"...weighing in at 135 pounds, Theodore Roosevelt, Jr...." his voice was drowned in the wild response from the galley. The referee then announced Hanks, but Alice heard none of it. She had been trying to catch Theodore's eye, but he had his back to them. Everyone around them was now on their feet.

Across the ring Hanks danced in place, taking swings and running through combinations.

"That's Hanks?" asked Alice, although she knew the answer. "Is he good?"

"He has endurance and that's dangerous," answered Dickey. Hank's strong body appeared bigger than Theodore's, and he looked fiercely focused.

Alice experienced a sinking feeling in her stomach.

"Oh, Dickey, I know he has been training a lot, but is he good enough? I would so hate to see him get hurt."

Dickey took a breath.

"We'll find out soon enough, won't we?"

The bell rang and both men approached each other.

Dickey nodded at Theodore's opponent.

"Hanks is the defending champion. He's a bit bigger and has a longer reach, but Theodore knew that coming into the fight. He says he can handle him."

Alice looked nervous. She brought her hands to her face as if to cover her eyes. She couldn't bear to look, but neither could she look away.

Finally she blurted, "Oh, this is horrible. I don't know if I can watch it."

Theodore was pursuing the bigger man in the ring, surprisingly acting as the aggressor.

Alice said, "Actually, he seems to be doing quite well."

Dickey agreed. "Yes, if he can stay close he will have a better chance by negating Hanks' longer reach."

After a moment's hesitation he added, "Theodore's real problem is, he can't wear his glasses."

Alice noticed that Theodore was squinting. Then he looked directly at her and their eyes met.

He smiled at her just as time was called and the bell rang. Roosevelt dropped his guard but Hanks didn't. Instead, Hanks landed a heavy blow on Theodore's nose, making it gush with blood. For a moment, Theodore was stunned.

The crowd started hooting and booing. The young men in the galley sounded ready to tear the roof off.

His manager handed him a towel to wipe away the blood. All around them the crowd continued to scream foul.

Hanks nodded apologetically at Theodore, who had snapped awake again. Moving to the center of the ring, Theodore raised his gloved hand and addressed the crowd in a commanding voice.

"It is all right. He did not hear the bell. It is okay."

The crowd still booed Hanks, but Theodore approached Hanks and touched gloves.

Hanks stared at the blood.

"Shouldn't we stop?" he asked.

Theodore wiped his nose with the towel, grinned, and stepped back at the ready.

"Certainly not, sir."

The crowd's sympathies swung toward Theodore. He had become the underdog and the galley cheered his every advance, even if it was only the slightest victory.

The wild cheers — and more importantly, seeing Alice — had charged Theodore up. Again and again he glanced over at her.

It made her nervous.

His determined grin, distorted by a smear of blood, and the fierce look in his eye frightened her.

Regardless of the crowd's support, the fight was a battle for Theodore. Hanks used his longer reach cleverly, and anyone who knew fighting would have said that Roosevelt was outclassed. But he was determined not to lose in front of Alice, and he held Hanks at bay by dodging his blows.

The fighters were now into the final rounds, and they were growing tired. Both were trying to break a stalemate in the ring; Hanks couldn't put Roosevelt down, and Theodore wouldn't give up. Painfully they fell into a rhythm that was distinctly gory; like wounded animals not ready to die.

Hanks circled with his right arm raised slightly, ready to strike, but Theodore watched alertly. When the blow fell Theodore darted out of the way, then came back with a combination. It was an exhausting game, and from their seats Dickey and Alice could hear Theodore begin to wheeze.

To Theodore, all had become the battle — even Alice had faded from his mind. Hanks circled, trying to force him into a corner, but he threw a combination just in time to stand his ground.

The bell announced the final round. Everything had started to blur.

Then, as Theodore ducked under an intended knock-out punch, he had a flash of the trapped black bear on its hind legs coming at him.

...he looked up from his sketch and saw the bear charging for him. With no time to run, he fell backwards, the bear's eyes locked on his. "Watch out!" shouted Bill.

The bear rose up on its hind legs, its forepaws extended over his head. It took a swipe at Theodore's falling body, its sharp   claws ripping his shirt but not penetrating the flesh...

Theodore stepped sideways and dodged a punch, a bit uncertain of where he was.

"Look alive, Roosevelt!" shouted Dickey.

But then he was back in the woods...

...he hit the ground and looked up at the angry bear, now towering over him. Now it looked formidable – very formidable – as its mouth opened wide showing teeth and dripping saliva.

It prepared to pounce on him, its jaw snapping.

Suddenly Bill appeared behind it and drove his hatchet into the back of the bear's head. Blood splattered Theodore, who was frozen in place on the ground, shocked...

Alice screamed. "Watch out, Theodore!"

Just in time he realized it was Hanks coming in with another punch.

Theodore shook his head like a dog, grinned, and tried to step it up again, but his breathing had become ragged.

He looked disoriented.

Hanks seemed to hesitate to put him down.

Again, Theodore's mind flashed back to Maine. This time he was on the caribou chase.

...everything had turned white, and there was a silence about that suffocated him. The wind blew hard but he could no longer feel it on his skin.

Just ahead the caribou had stopped and watched him.

He was breathing hard, as was the caribou.

They stared at each other, questioning, no longer obsessed with reason or motive.

For a minute he forgot even the chase.

His body yearned to sleep...

Roosevelt shook the vision from his head and went at Hanks again.

Through gritted teeth he snarled, "Here I defy thee!" as he crashed into Hanks and the battle continued.

Both men were swaying on their feet when the bell finally rang, and they shuffled to their corners with leaden legs.

Outside, Dickey was ecstatic as he described the fight to a friend who had arrived late. Theodore had showered and changed, but his face was still frightful.

"You should have seen it...Hanks couldn't put him out and Roosevelt wouldn't give up. It wasn't a fair fight to begin with, what with Hanks being bigger, but oh, Roosevelt showed himself a fighter."

Theodore stood there, wiping his bloody nose, a bit uncomfortable with all the attention. Alice snuggled against him and as they listened to Dickey speak she examined his cuts and bruises from up close.

"Listening to you go on, you would think he won," said the friend to Dickey.

Alice leaned forward and gently kissed Theodore's swollen face to the envy of all the men.

"He did win," she said.

Chapter Twenty
Courting

Back at Harvard, Theodore paced through his rooms, nervously stroking his whiskers. His fingers grazed his cheek and he flinched. The bruises on his face were still tender from his fight with Hanks.

Dickey watched him from a stuffed leather chair.

Young Roosevelt pleaded his case.

"I simply do not know what to do, Dickey, I have been as persistent as I dare, but Alice still will not consent to marriage."

Dickey flushed slightly, not used to talking about personal matters, even with friends.

"Has she given you any answer at all?"

Suddenly, Theodore looked hopeful.

"Yes, she says she wants to marry me…she only believes that we are still too young."

Dickey laughed.

"What's wrong with waiting a few years?"

Then he added, "And you *are* young! My advice to you is to do what she suggests and wait a few years."

Theodore flinched and blurted out, "Years? I cannot wait months!"

He face became grim and with a dour tone he said, "I fear that when I return to New York for the summer she might find another suitor."

"She's in love with you, Theodore," said Dickey, "it's obvious to anyone who sees you together."

Theodore stared at the polished floorboards, his mind flooded with the image of her pale, blue-grey eyes.

"I believe that also, but I cannot chance it."

He began pacing again, but stopped just as quickly.

He looked up, a new light in his eye. "I have it!"

Then he returned to pacing the room as he laid out his plan.

"I will have a party, here, in my rooms. I will invite Alice, and Rose of course. I should also invite several other couples so it is not too obvious."

Dickey surveyed the rooms, which truly were done up with taste. Theodore's sister had decorated them, sparing no expense, and they were furnished above and beyond those belonging to most other Harvard students.

"There certainly is enough space," said Dickey.

But then he looked over his friend's face which had turned an unhealthy yellow from bruising and added, "I would suggest, however, that you wait a few weeks to let your color return...you do look rather ghastly right now."

Theodore touched a cut on his lip and winced. "Perhaps you are correct."

But now that he had a plan of action he could not sit still. "Dickey, do you suppose your mother would consent to be a chaperon? With her presence Alice could not refuse."

"I think she would," replied Dickey.

"Then it is settled," said Theodore eagerly. "I will start on the invitations immediately, and I will make the evening one that will burn in her memory warmly whenever she thinks of me."

He added with a smile.

"I am sure that after this event she will be more than willing to consent to marriage."

Three weeks passed—a time that seemed an eternity to Theodore—but his bruises healed and by the night of the party he looked fine. He'd continued training and appeared healthy; his muscles bulged under his shirt and he'd regained his energetic step.

The food was catered by his favorite restaurant. The caterers had set up a long table and laid it out with hors d'oevres and a roasted duck. A waiter casually approached the guests offering to refill glasses with some excellent wine.

There were five other couples—all carefully chosen—plus Alice, himself and Mrs. Saltonstall. The furniture had been polished until the dark mahogany and oak was reflective, and every flat surface was covered with either candles or flowers.

Theodore surveyed his party with pride. His guests were engulfed in conversation, swirling their wine in fine crystal glasses as they gestured and joked.

Alice talked with her aunt, flashing her bright, upturned smile when she spoke, but kept glancing at Theodore.

Suddenly she stood before him, a small present in her hands. "Please, Teddy, open it."

He looked over her shoulder at the others as she whispered to him.

"Not in front of everyone. It is nothing special…just open it."

Theodore turned his back on the room and quickly opened the present. When unwrapped he found himself holding a pair of men's slippers.

He blushed.

"I just think of you sitting up late studying, your cold feet under the desk, and I wanted them to be warm," she said.

Then she saw her aunt approaching and took the slippers from him.

As she slipped away, she whispered, "I will put these in your dressing room."

Theodore smiled broadly as Mrs. Saltonstall approached.

She cocked her head and looked him in the eye. "Well, your party certainly seems a success."

He nodded enthusiastically. "Yes, indeed. Thank you for coming."

She smiled graciously.

"Theodore, I am so glad that you have been courting my niece. Alice is such a lovely young girl and the two of you look so good together."

Emboldened by her comments, Theodore told her of his plans to marry her.

Mrs. Saltonstall looked around the room, making certain nobody else was within earshot and said, "My dear Theodore, I do hope someday you marry Ms. Alice. But you have to remember she is only seventeen, and she has not yet even made her debut."

He nodded gravely, masking his surprise to be receiving warnings from someone he'd counted among his supporters.

"Yes, I realize that, but I love her and I know I am ready for marriage."

Alice entered the room and stopped at the bar for a glass of lemonade. They watched her silently for a minute.

Finally Mrs. Saltonstall broke the silence. "You may be ready—even Alice may be ready—but I doubt very much that Mrs. Lee would be willing to lose her daughter before her debut."

Theodore opened his mouth, but she held up her hand, gently silencing him.

"All I am saying is to wait a year," she said with a firm but compassionate look in her eyes. Then she walked away.

From across the room Dickey saw the baffled look on Theodore's face and quickly joined him.

"She too thinks I should wait until next year!" Theodore whispered.

Before Dickey could respond, he added in a firmer voice, "It is simply out of the question. In a few short months school will break for summer, and after that I will be hundreds of miles away, in New York."

He looked hard at Dickey. "I must make another plan."

The next day Theodore sent a telegram to the Roosevelt estate in New York requesting them to ship his horse, Lightfoot, to Boston — immediately.

Within a few days the horse arrived, and Theodore rode it the six miles from Boston to Cambridge where he rented a stable near his Harvard rooms.

The next day he set off with hunting crop and a beaver hat for Chestnut Hill, six miles away.

That afternoon he took a long walk with Alice; the entire time he romanced her. Theodore was lively and positive, but part of him felt there was not enough time to win her heart before he had to return to New York for the summer.

She held his hand while they walked, but got no closer, and although they talked animatedly the entire time, she steered away from any conversation revolving around their future.

By the time he returned to his rooms it was dark. After writing a few lines in his diary he collapsed in bed.

He rose early the next day to study and thus fell into a rhythm that would occupy the coming months.

Six to eight hours of his day were devoted to study, next came an hour of weight training. Then he showered, dressed, and rode Lightfoot the six miles to Chestnut Hill where he could romance Alice in the afternoon and evenings.

Over the next few weeks they took countless walks, had picnics, played card games, and told ghost stories. Theodore taught Alice the five-step waltz. They spent hour upon hour with each other, but she remained evasive.

At night, when he finally returned home, he confided in his diary about her: vowing one night that he would marry her within a year's time.

The weeks flew by, and soon there was only a month remaining before it came time for him to return home to New York. And then, late one moonless night, Lightfoot stumbled while Theodore ran him home through the dark woods. Horse and rider took a nasty fall.

Theodore was thrown and bruised his shoulder, but Lightfoot's injuries were more severe. In the darkness he comforted the horse as he methodically felt out its wounds. Lightfoot could barely put pressure on one hoof and it took Theodore hours to carefully walk the limping animal home.

Lightfoot's right, front ankle was severely swollen the next day. The vet spoke of putting him down, but Theodore would have none of it. Instead, he put all of his energies into carefully and patiently nursing his loyal horse back to health.

But he continued to visit Chestnut Hill in the evenings, now by foot. After his studies and after tending to Lightfoot he ran the six miles, carrying a pack with a change of fancier clothes. He stopped by some high shrubs just before Alice's house, where he freshened his appearance and changed into his other wardrobe.

As June approached he felt fitter than ever. Running twelve miles a day, Alice's smile always on his mind, he was now in great shape. The frail boy of a year before was merely a memory.

He had also done well at Harvard, placing in the top of his class. And with only one week left before his return to New York, he was now painstakingly planning every detail of his final day and night with Alice.

The night before, he went out with Dickey, who met him at a local pub. Dickey noticed as soon as Theodore walked through the door that his friend was as tense as a wire.

Although Theodore reveled in his newfound physical strength, and even enjoyed the efforts he put into his studies, all the planning—and worrying—he put into romancing Alice Lee was putting him over the edge and leaving him truly exhausted.

His eyes darted around the room nervously as he talked.

"You should see the day I have planned tomorrow," said Theodore excitedly. "It will be grand…"

Before he could say more a local lad fell backwards, knocking into them and spilling his beer on the floor. He was a large fellow and fairly drunk.

"Hey, you with the glasses," slurred the drunk, "watch where you're goin'." His friends howled with laughter.

"Excuse me," said Dickey, "but you bumped into us."

The drunk grabbed Dickey's head, pushed him back and was on the verge of swinging, when Theodore stepped in with a combination of punches and leveled the lad.

The two Harvard students stood back and looked down at the unconscious man. His friends stepped forward slightly, but once they saw the fierce look in Theodore's eyes they backed off. While one of them dragged their friend away Theodore noticed a cut on his hand.

"Looks like you cut your knuckle on that mucker's teeth," said Dickey.

Suddenly Theodore looked panic-stricken.

"Please do not tell Alice that I have been fighting!" he whispered.

On his final day with Alice Theodore had planned a full itinerary, hoping the combination of the day's events would overwhelm her conviction to remain elusive.

Through the course of the day they attended two tea parties, had lunch at the Porcellian, and then they danced until midnight. Throughout it all Theodore had remained tranquil and relaxed, and outwardly he showed no sign of the nervousness he felt in the pit of his stomach.

"What a royally good time I have had this summer," said Theodore as they danced under a full moon. The other guests had thinned out, but Theodore and Alice remained on the dance floor as if the night was young.

"Oh, you and Dickey have been having fun together?" asked Alice coyly.

"You know I am referring to my time spent with you," replied Theodore softly, as he smiled at her. While escorting her off the dance floor he noticed a bruise on his hand and casually tucked it behind his back.

"Yes, I do Teddy; I was only teasing."

He leaned forward and kissed her tenderly, just letting their lips brush. "We could be together all the time, Alice. We could start our life together."

He looked into her eyes. "Please marry me, Alice."

She laughed lightly, although Theodore could tell now that she took him seriously; the way she was wringing her fingers gave him the hope that she felt the same weight he did.

She said, "Just a little more time, Theodore. I assure you there is no one else I fancy."

Again, Theodore's soul filled with panic at the thought of not seeing her for the summer.

She could see it in his eyes and quickly tried to put him at ease.

"Teddy, come now, my parents both want to see my debut, and after that I will be eighteen and an adult. Enjoy the summer, and when you come back in the fall we can talk about marriage."

His eyes hardened for a minute as he thought over her words. She had rejected him, but she had done it in a way that did not leave him entirely despondent. She had even invited him to resume his suit in the fall.

He smiled and nodded, comforted by her words — which he repeated to himself over and over — and by the thought of another plan that would help him when he returned in the fall.

Under the moon's glow he memorized the features of her face; her pert, slightly-upturned nose, the soft curls of hair piled on her head, her dainty mouth, and finally her eyes — eyes that looked deep into his with such confidence, and even expectation, despite how evasive she'd become.

Finally, the night drew to a close and he walked her to her door; the entire time he felt he watched — helplessly — from a distance, unable to change the outcome of the scene. He smiled as she kissed him goodbye and then watched the door in horror as it shut on him for the summer...possibly for life.

Once Theodore was home in New York he dug out his journal from Maine and opened it to a diagram he'd made of the pung that Scout had pulled on their sleigh journey to Cecil's logging camp.

Although to some it appeared he had forgotten Alice completely, his entire motivation was based on her.

Taking a fresh piece of paper, he sketched it again — this time with two wheels instead of runners. When one of his uncles visited a little while later he showed him the drawing.

"The closest thing I know of to that drawing is a *Tilbury*, or a dog-cart," said his uncle. "They ride on two wheels — like your drawing — but they are very tight; and you must have a horse that is trained to pull it."

"Yes, I know," replied Theodore. "I wanted something that was close to the experience I had in the pung last winter."

In the city, all wagons ran on four wheels, and to his uncle, Theodore's sketch appeared to be missing an axle. He said, "I would think it would be like riding a unicycle."

191

The uncle shook his head. "Why on Earth would you want that contraption when you can afford a bigger, more comfortable carriage?"

Theodore smiled. "With my twenty-first birthday approaching I thought it time I learned to drive, and this seems like elegant locomotion."

His uncle glanced at the drawing again and laughed.

"It looks pretty crazy to me, but good luck."

The next week Theodore purchased a Tilbury whose seat was just large enough for two slim people, and he spent the rest of the summer getting Lightfoot used to the harness and training him to trot in front of the vehicle.

Family members who observed his prowess with the whip and reins commented on how Theodore reminded them of his father; but those close to him also noticed a confidant smile and a determined air about his movements, like his mind was fixed on a goal that was clearly in sight.

And it was—Alice. That summer while he worked Lightfoot tirelessly Alice's face always hovered just ahead of his every action. He felt not the summer heat, the dust on the road, or the ache in his limbs, just the glow of her presence and a strong desire to return to Chestnut Hill in the fall.

Chapter Twenty-one
Katahdin

One year from his first visit to Maine Theodore was again riding the train through the dark woods of the north. He traveled alone, staring out the window of his first class cabin as the countryside passed by.

His mind was uncharacteristically out of focus; the polite conversations and engagements of the last few weeks echoed in his head. In the end, the drawing rooms had become claustrophobic and he couldn't wait to get away into the wilderness again.

He had been in high courting gear and found it difficult to leave Alice; her image stayed with him, filling his mind to distraction, but deep inside he felt it was again time to clear his head — and chest — in the Maine woods.

When the train entered the deep forest he inhaled deeply, smelling the rich aroma, and already he felt his lungs responding.

He also missed Bill Sewall's council.

At the station he expected to find Bill waiting, quietly leaning against the wall with his black hat tilted down, but as the train pulled up he was surprised to see Bill's brother, David, standing on the platform instead.

Theodore stepped off the train, and they shook hands formally.

"Mr. Roosevelt."

"Mr. Sewall."

Then David smiled broadly and slapped the young man on the shoulder.

"Good to see you again, young fella."

Theodore nodded and David added, "I told Bill I had *bizness* down this way and he asked if I would mind meetin' you."

The young Harvard student simply nodded. David noted that he appeared withdrawn and sensed there was something on his mind, so he simply grabbed his small trunk and carried it to the buckboard.

Theodore didn't fight him for it this time.

At the buckboard Theodore stopped and stared at the team of horses.

"I was rather looking forward to seeing Scout."

David laughed. "I would'a too! I've been usin' the buckboard lately to move some loads, and it was too much work for one horse. These two belong to Wilmot."

He gestured at the horses.

"These knuckleheads are Cain and Abel. Cain's got the white mark on his forehead, but it don't really matter. They're brothers and work well as a team; and they don't fight with each other either which works for me."

Theodore again nodded quietly. As he climbed aboard, David looked him over and decided the long train ride must be responsible for his quiet mood. He'd done the journey himself and the motion of the train and sound of the tracks had stayed with him for days.

He kept up the one-way conversation while they stowed Theodore's trunk, adding, "Wilmot was probably glad to have them away for a while. They may mind well, but they sure can eat."

Slowly, the two horses pulled the buckboard through town. They were in no rush and — to Theodore — the ride contrasted sharply with the sleigh ride he'd done with Scout in February.

He remembered her eagerness when she tore off out of the town, dashing over the ice-covered street.

David tried to coax Theodore out of his silence, knowing they had a long ride ahead.

"Are you sure you're ready to rough it again?" he asked. "I know that brother of mine has quite a bit planned for you two."

At this Theodore's face lit up.

"Yes, I cannot wait."

David grinned a little as he added, "Bill said in your last letter you talked quite a bit about a woman named Alice, and he was afraid you might cancel."

Theodore flushed.

"Well, I may have considered it if he had been reachable. You do know it is perfectly impossible to communicate with you, the telegraph not going all the way to Island Falls."

At this David slapped Theodore's back.

"That's one of the nice things about livin' in Island Falls."

Then he added, "If you really didn't want to come you could always write…although the post does move slowly up here."

Theodore shook his head as he looked over the countryside which was alive with the colors of fall.

"I would not have cancelled and Bill knows it."

On the outskirts of town they passed a field dotted with a dozen cows.

David pointed at them and said, "Now there's an animal that gets a free ride. Just stands 'round eatin' all the time and all it has to do is put up with havin' its tits pulled twice a day."

Theodore looked over the cows.

"Well, there is not a real happy ending for most of them."

The Mainer shook his head.

"You'd be surprised how soft some of these farmers are; I'm tellin' you, them cows have it easy." He added with a loud laugh, "You bet yer bottom if they could talk they'd be using those weasel words I told you about."

Theodore stared at him with a quizzical expression.

"Sure," David continued, "they'd be tellin' you how good the milk was, and how important it was, and all these other things to convince you that they should be allowed to just stand around."

Finally, Theodore cracked a smile.

David pointed at his team and added, "These two lunkers may not be that smart, but they work hard for their meals."

He shouted, "Don'tchya, boys?"

The one on the left—Cain—actually neighed, as if he understood every word.

David watched the cows as they passed by.

"Those ain't nothin' but converters."

Grinning, he explained, "They convert food to..." he glanced at Theodore, still in his fancy traveling clothes, "...well, I'm sure you know what I mean."

Once out of town the road got rough, and they each did their best to just hold on for the next seven hours.

Bill had been waiting on the porch of his town house when they arrived. He looked Theodore in the eyes as they shook hands, quickly examined his dress and frame, and then wasted no time getting the young man into his canoe.

They remained only briefly at the house in Island Falls for Theodore to change into his outdoor clothes and pack a small backpack. Then Bill paddled them down the river to Mattawamkeag Lake and on to his camp.

The camp on the lake was made of notched logs which stood with a fine view of Mt. Katahdin: the mountain's massive silhouette dominating the western windows of the Sewall cabin.

Theodore sat on a handmade chair and took in every detail of the mountain, while Bill got the wood stove going and started frying up some venison on the burner up top.

From time to time he looked at his young charge, but he held his tongue. He knew it had been a lengthy day with the seven hours in the buckboard right after the long train journey.

Eventually Theodore asked, "How far away is that mountain?"

Bill turned to Katahdin for a minute.

"As the crow flies I'd have to guess 'bout thirty-five or forty miles...but gettin' there is a bit more indirect."

"Well, how would you get there?"

Bill stroked his whiskers, "That mountain sits between the east and west branches of the Penobscot River, but if you tried to get there by water you'd just go around it. I found the easiest way was with a buckboard for the first twenty miles, and then on foot when you got into the deep forest."

"You've climbed it before?"

"*Ayuh*, twice in fact; first time was with Wilmot and a small group — that was back when he was only twelve in ... I'd say '67. I would think I must'a been about your age then."

Theodore was still staring at the mountain.

"How long did it take you?"

Bill faced the mountain without speaking for some time.

"I'd speculate it was eight or nine days..." he finally said. "Quite a while ago, and my memory isn't to clear on how long we took."

The onions were sizzling and the venison was done so he emptied the pan onto two plates. As he handed one to Theodore, Bill said, "I do remember it was a good haul to the top. If the geographical survey is correct that mountain is 5,268 feet high, makin' it the highest mountain in Maine."

Theodore was silent.

He looked at his plate but didn't touch the food.

Finally he stated, "I want to climb it."

Bill stared looked at the mountain, then back at Theodore.

"*Ayuh*, we could do that."

With that decision, Theodore finally began to relax. He'd come to Maine this time with a mission, but he wasn't ready to talk about it yet.

For now, Katahdin would do.

Bill nodded at Theodore's plate of venison and onions and said, "That meal isn't gonna eat itself."

Theodore nodded as he took a bite, but then looked at the porch with its unobstructed view of distant Katahdin and asked.

"Bill, could we take our meal to the porch?"

Bill laughed, "Of course, Theodore."

Late in the afternoon Bill spotted a canoe making its way toward the camp. It only took a minute for him to deduce who was in it.

"Here come a few of your fellow New Yorkers."

From the distance Theodore could only barely make out a craft at all. "How can you tell who it is from this far away?" he asked.

Bill stared and said, "Well that's a nice canoe—birch bark, hand-made—but it's not an Indian steering it so I'd guess it's someone from out of town—and the only man I know 'round here that owns one would be your friend, Arthur Cutler. He recently bought a place on an island not far from here."

He looked at Theodore.

"If I remember correctly, Mr. Cutler was your tutor, wasn't he?"

At this Theodore looked a bit uncomfortable.

"Yes. When I was young I was too sick to attend public school and had tutors. Mr. Cutler was my final tutor, terminating his services when I began taking classes at Harvard."

Again Bill peered at the far-off canoe which was slowly approaching.

"And I would have to guess that it's one of your cousins sitting up front; most likely Emlen."

Theodore squinted again.

"What makes you say that?"

Bill smiled broadly. "Well, Emlen's a good boy, and he tries hard, but he still don't paddle like a Mainer."

When the canoe arrived Bill walked down to the shore and steadied it while Mr. Cutler and Emlen stepped out.

"Careful how you exit the canoe, Emlen. We cannot afford to have you puncture a hole in this craft," warned Mr. Cutler.

Theodore remembered how often his former tutor had talked about Maine and his time in Island Falls. In the end the area had been everything Mr. Cutler had said — breathtakingly beautiful, remote and wild — but he found it strange now to see the man here. Although only nine years older than Theodore, Mr. Cutler held himself like he was a much older man.

He was dressed in attire suitable to the area, but his clothing still had a flair to it that spoke of wealth and the city. He seemed comfortable in the canoe, although nothing like Bill and Wilmot.

It was only when Mr. Cutler addressed Emlen that Theodore saw flashes of his former tutor. Glancing back at the canoe, Mr. Cutler ordered his cousin around as if he were still a twelve year old in his charge.

"Emlen, get that package for me and bring it to the camp."

It wasn't rude as much as habit, but in this wilderness that Theodore had embraced it rubbed him the wrong way.

Emlen quickly did as he was told, instantly reverting to the obedient teenager he'd been when he had been tutored by the man. He gave Theodore a quick look in passing and grinned.

Once back inside the cabin Mr. Cutler opened the bundle and handed it to Bill.

"I appreciate you looking after my place while I was away and wanted to give this to you."

Bill opened the cloth bundle to reveal several high-quality butchering knives.

"Well now, this is a bit extravagant."

Mr. Cutler smiled; pleased he'd chosen a good gift.

"Nonsense, it's good to know someone is around when I'm not here."

Bill waved Mr. Cutler´s gratitude away.

Theodore watched the exchange with a little jealousy, the entire time observing how well Mr. Cutler seemed to get along with Bill.

As if noticing Theodore for the first time, Mr. Cutler said, "My, Theodore, it is good to see you here. I hope you are not pushing yourself too hard — I am well aware of your physical limitations."

Theodore went to reply, but Bill answered for him.

"Young Master Roosevelt is doing just fine."

Mr. Cutler nodded.

"And what adventures do you have planned for this visit?"

"Actually," began Bill, "We were just planning an excursion to Mt. Katahdin."

As soon as he said it Bill knew it had been a mistake. He also caught a look of panic in Theodore's eyes which backed up his hunch.

"Ah, that would be splendid," said Mr. Cutler. "Would you mind if Emlen and I came along?"

Theodore liked his cousin Emlen, and he actually enjoyed Mr. Cutler's company as well, but he'd been looking forward to some time alone in the woods with Bill.

His face flushed slightly as he said, "We were planning on leaving first thing in the morning and you really would not have any time to prepare."

Mr. Cutler paused for a minute, his eyes casually glancing at the new knives he'd just given Bill.

He hesitated before saying, "Tomorrow is rather soon."

Bill broke the uncomfortable silence by adding, "Perhaps if we left two days from now you would have time to get some supplies together."

At this Mr. Cutler smiled and nodded.

"Yes, I believe I would. So we will leave at first light, two days from now?"

Bill agreed, although Theodore sensed that he also would have preferred to go with just the two of them.

Emlen had been staring out the window, beyond the far shore of the lake where the entire view was dominated by Katahdin. He seemed not to be paying attention, but suddenly asked, "Are we going on an excursion?"

Mr. Cutler nodded, "Yes, we are going to climb Mt. Katahdin."

With that everyone turned and looked at the mountain.

Emlen suddenly grasped what they were saying. As his gaze moved to the faded ridges and peaks beyond the lake he said, "It looks to be more than a walk in the park."

On the morning of their departure there was a brisk chill in the air. Wilmot was waiting at the Sewall house in Island Falls when Bill and Theodore arrived by canoe.

"I asked Wilmot to get a buckboard and team ready, and set aside some supplies for us," said Bill. "Although once we are on foot we'll travel light and hunt and fish on the way."

Theodore nodded, still a bit unhappy with the situation, but thrilled with the idea of living off the land. While he waited for the others to arrive he walked to the front of the buckboard and rubbed the muzzles of Cain and Abel.

Soon Mr. Cutler and Emlen arrived, each carrying a backpack. Bill looked the packs over and said, "Those packs seem rather full."

Mr. Cutler hefted his and replied, "Not so bad, Mr. Sewall."

"When we leave the buckboard behind," said Bill. "I'll have to add some of our supplies and I don't see much extra room."

Mr. Cutler nonchalantly set his pack down on the buckboard. "We will just have to cross that bridge when we come to it."

Bill nodded, but didn't appear satisfied with the answer. Soon the buckboard was loaded with everything they needed and they set out with Bill and Mr. Cutler on the front bench, and Theodore and Emlen riding in the back.

A few miles from Island Falls they came to a river. It was low and they managed to ford it without unhitching the wagon.

Once on the other side Bill said, "To the left is the road to Patten, but we are going straight. This is Winding Hill Road and it will bring us in a more direct line to the mountain."

The road was hilly and they soon lost view of the distant mountain. Occasionally they passed farms that had been carved out of the wilderness around them. In the valleys between the hills the woods closed in and civilization seemed to disappear.

"These farmers are all lumbermen," said Bill. "They tend their farms in the summer, then work the forest through the cold months."

As they neared the top of a hill Bill looked around. "I always thought it'd be good to have a farm out here; nice and quiet with a view of the mountain."

Theodore looked around and was about to comment, when Mr. Cutler pre-empted him. "It certainly is nice land, Mr. Sewall." Over the next few hours he noticed that Mr. Cutler did this repeatedly, in effect preventing him from joining in the conversation.

As they rolled over another hill they stopped. Below them the road descended steeply into a dense wilderness, but in front of them Mt. Katahdin rose up.

"In the local Indian dialect, Katahdin means, *Greatest Mountain*," said Bill.

And it did look great. Katahdin's majestic peaks crowned a mountain which rose abruptly from flat country to a gently sloping plateau above the tree line. From their vantage point they could make out two peaks, with a long sharp line stretching toward a smaller peak to the left, and below sat two vast basins.

"I do have to say that from this distance it does not seem like a real destination, "said Emlen.

Bill laughed.

"Oh, it's real alright! The first documented climb of Katahdin was completed in 1804 by Charles Turner, Jr. who wrote an account of the ascent," said Bill. "But I'm sure the Indians were climbing it long before that."

Theodore took in a deep breath as he stared at it.

He then looked at his cousin and thought of how things had changed since they had come here together the previous year. After his winter visit, Theodore no longer looked to Emlen as the expert on Island Falls.

"I cannot believe it has taken me this long to finally climb it, I have wanted to since I first came here."

Bill laughed again.

"Well you haven't climbed it yet; and you weren't ready for it last year."

The young man replied defiantly, "I think we did quite well last winter."

Bill nodded. "*Ayuh*, we did, but that's a big mountain and you're still ridin' in a buck board. We'll see how cocky you are after a few days of carryin' a heavy pack."

Eventually the road rose up and led through a small town named Patten. A few farmers looked up and nodded a greeting as the buckboard passed by before returning to their labor of harvesting potatoes. The air smelled of fresh tilled earth and the poplars that lined the way shivered in the breeze.

The road continued on, Mt. Katahdin looming ever taller ahead of them.

When they reached a prosperous farm near the edge of the town Bill stopped the buckboard and walked to the door.

He knocked and was invited inside while the others waited by the buckboard.

About ten minutes later he emerged with a bent, old man. The man looked to be about seventy and wore a fur-lined hat that covered his ears. In one hand he carried an empty burlap sack.

"This is Rolland," said Bill, "he's goin' to watch our horses and the buckboard when we continue on foot."

Rolland looked over the group, nodded slightly, and mumbled, "*Ayuh.*"

Then he walked to the field that just about circled the house, bent down, and roughly yanked a potato plant from the ground. He shook it hard and then scooped up about twenty potatoes that lay on the ground and just under the soil, and put them in his sack.

Without another word he tossed the sack in the back, and then slowly climbed on to the front bench, unceremoniously forcing Mr. Cutler to the edge of the bench.

Bill hopped up front as well and they set off with Rolland in the middle, rocking from side to side.

They were still a ways off, but now the land slanted down, giving unobscured views of Katahdin. Theodore eyed the mountain the entire way, amazed how it could keep growing larger and more imposing. Harvard, New York, and even Alice were rapidly fading from his mind.

And then they left the farmland behind and entered a thick forest of spruce. It closed in all around them and insects now filled the air. The atmosphere was moist and rich with the smells of pines, growth, and decay.

The road had turned into a trail and frequently skirted small ponds and bogs. Every couple of miles moss-covered logs lay across the road and they had to stop to move them, but many were half-rotted and crumbled under their touch.

Here and there they had to cross muddy stretches of road using "corduroys" — multiple logs that had been laid out side by side in the mud, perpendicular to the direction of the road.

Although earlier the chill of fall had been ripe in the air, now they rode along steaming bogs and swampy areas that were a long way from freezing.

When the trail became ever rougher Bill's face turned grave with concentration. He was fully focused on working the horses, and he needed more room on the bench. Rolland showed no inclination of moving, so Mr. Cutler quietly volunteered to move into the back with the others.

Theodore watched the landscape pass by, fascinated; Emlen sat next to him with a look of dread in his eyes. Mosquitoes attacked him constantly, as if his blood was sweeter than everyone else's and he swatted at them excessively.

In the back, Mr. Cutler was trying to find a more comfortable position. The bugs seemed to like him as well. For some reason they stayed away from Theodore.

Up front, Rolland had somehow fallen asleep sitting up, occasionally leaning on Bill.

After a while Bill whistled and the team stopped before a fallen tree.

He turned to the three in the back and said, "We can either leave the wagon here, or you lads can help clear a trail ahead of us and maybe we can make a few more miles."

Not ready to leave the buckboard behind, Emlen was off and ready to help, making Theodore chuckle. Even Mr. Cutler lent a hand, and they continued on.

A few miles down the trail Bill gently nudged Rolland, who sleepily sat up. "Looks like the end of the trail, old timer, I can't get the buckboard any deeper into this mess."

They all got off and unloaded the buckboard while Bill staked out the horses. Afterwards, he got a fire going and started sorting through their supplies.

Emlen eyed Rolland and finally asked Bill in a hushed voice, "Do you really think that old man is going to make it up the mountain?"

Bill let out his boisterous laugh that echoed off the surrounding hills.

"No offense, sir, but I'd put more stock in him makin' it than you."

When he saw the insulted look on Emlen's face, he quickly added, "Rolland is just along to watch our camp and the horses after we head out on foot. He used to be one heck of a woodsman, but now he's old and bored and was happy to come along."

He eyed the woods around him.

"There's plenty out there that wouldn't mind takin' down a staked-out horse and it's a long walk back to Island Falls."

Emlen eyed the woods uneasily.

Chapter Twenty-two
Base Camp

Bill set down his sack on the shore of an expansive lake, and as the others caught up with him they did the same. They had covered twelve miles on foot, carrying almost all of their gear, and they all welcomed their destination for the day.

On the other side of the lake the land rose up until it was capped by the mountain itself. And behind it the sun was beginning to set, bathing the sharp granite ridge in an orange glow. In the descending shadows on its slopes, details began to fade, but the size of the mountain was intimidating.

Theodore arrived, limping along in one shoe. While crossing a rock-studded tributary of the East Branch of the Penobscot River he had dropped one of his shoes and lost it. Now he skipped along, trying to act like nothing was wrong.

Mr. Cutler came in soon after him, his face red and swollen from mosquito bites. Lastly came Emlen, looking worn-out and exhausted.

"Finally, we are at the mountain itself," said Emlen.

Bill laughed. "It's still a good four miles away, Emlen."

He added, "If we could cross this water we might shave off a few miles."

Emlen looked around hopefully.

"Is there, by chance, a boat or vessel of some sort?"

Bill smiled. "Do you remember carrying one?"

Sheepishly, Emlen looked away.

After surveying their surroundings again, Bill said, "This is as good a place as any to make camp. We can rest here for a few days and then take on the mountain."

Over the next few days Mr. Cutler fished while Theodore and Emlen hunted along the shore of the lake. They slept in the open, in a ring around the fire. Luckily the weather held and they stayed dry.

During one day Bill hiked all the way back to check on Rolland and bring back some more supplies. When he returned he found Theodore sitting by the fire with two ducks cooking on a spit; two more sat behind him, ready to eat.

"I suppose four ducks deserves some praise," said Bill, "but you better eat your fill because at first light tomorrow we're takin' that mountain."

Emlen sat down to eat, but as he looked at Katahdin looming over them he suddenly lost his appetite. Even the reflection of the mountain in the lake appeared overwhelmingly imposing.

The next morning they got up early and ate. Through the early hours they'd lain awake listening to a loon's cry echo across the lake. When the sun hit the water the insects swarmed and the trout started jumping.

Their bodies were stiff from sleeping on the ground, and the weather had turned overnight. It had gotten chilly. As they slowly sat up, they tried not to look at the mountain, which was lit up with the sun's first rays.

Bill was the first up, going through supplies and adding some wood to the fire. Theodore saw the squeamish expression on his cousin, and the hesitancy in Mr. Cutler's movements, and felt they were beginning to stall out.

While they finished their meal Bill tried to add a few things to each of their packs, but found them over-packed with no spare room. Although he was carrying the heaviest load, the others each had to carry at least forty-five pounds.

"Do you really need everything in that pack, Emlen?" asked Bill.

The young man looked around defensively.

"I would think so; it all depends on what you would consider essential."

Emlen looked down at Theodore's feet, one of which had a shoe and the other was bare.

"At least I have shoes," said Emlen.

Theodore turned red.

"I will bear responsibility for losing my shoe."

Bill looked at the bare foot, which was already cut and in rough shape, but didn't say anything.

Theodore turned his attention to Emlen's pack, looking in a side pocket and taking out three novels.

"You should empty that extra stuff out and only take what's necessary. I assure you, cousin," said Theodore, "that I am carrying only the essentials, and you should be similarly packed."

Bill listened and then decided to test Theodore, "Would you mind tellin' me what you have prepared for clothing?"

Theodore stared at his pack while he went over its contents in his mind. His eyebrows gathered in a bunch as he rattled of his list: "Two complete changes of clothes: woolen socks, flannel shirts, duck trousers, heavy under flannels, plus a heavy jacket and a blanket."

Bill weighed that in his mind, but before he could say anything Theodore was struck by a wheezing fit—something that had become less and less frequent.

When he'd regained control of his breathing he straightened up and said, "And plenty of handkerchiefs."

Bill turned his eye on Emlen, who stammered, "I guess I have about double that...plus some nonessentials."

With a smile he added, "Including double the footwear...and maybe not as many handkerchiefs."

"Good," said Bill, "Empty that pack and weed out some things."

Mr. Cutler watched Emlen discarding extra clothes and items out of his pack and then silently turned and lightened his own load.

The fire had died down. Bill kicked it apart doused the coals with some water from the lake that he had fetched in a pan.

He took his time, knowing the boys needed to prepare themselves mentally as well as physically for this challenge. While wiping down the frying pan he looked up at them.

"You gentlemen sure you're ready to take on that mountain?"

Theodore was excited and answered first.

"I am, Bill, I feel tough as a pine knot."

Bill's laugh echoed over the lake in the cool morning air.

"And you, Emlen?"

Emlen looked at the mountain while taking a deep breath. He then looked at Mr. Cutler who watched the entire scene with amusement, and then at Theodore as he stared at the mountain nervously.

When he turned back there was confidence in his eyes.

"Mr. Sewall, when I started this expedition I did not know what I was getting myself into, but standing here now with you—and my cousin—I will say that I will give it my best shot."

"Well said, Emlen, "said Bill sincerely.

Grabbing the frying pan and some flour, Bill opened Emlen's pack and stowed them, then he did the same with Mr. Cutler's with some other gear.

Both men watched him silently at his task.

After adding a few items to Theodore's pack Bill turned and asked Theodore about his guns.

"As we will be hunting on the way I brought both the shotgun and the rifle; and plenty of ammunition for each."

Bill nodded and said, "We're off then," and without another word he threw his sack over his shoulder and strode away.

Mr. Cutler winced slightly as he hefted his backpack. Emlen looked ready to protest, but held back when he saw everyone watching him.

Soon the four men were on a trail that skirted the lake. The mountain was not visible; the land had just started slanting upward and the thick trees obscured it.

As they circled the large lake Emlen said.

"Couldn't we just make some sort of craft to cross the lake? It would save time in the end."

Bill laughed and patted Emlen's shoulder.

"You're better off just hoofin' it from here."

Resigned now to completing the journey on foot, Emlen shifted his backpack and followed Bill along the trail. Mr. Cutler fell in behind him, and then Theodore.

Mr. Cutler glanced over his shoulder at Theodore and said, "Now Theodore, you watch your breathing and just step where I step. We have a long way to go so pace yourself."

Theodore flushed slightly and felt no better when he saw Bill, up ahead, turn and wink at him.

As the land slanted up the landscape changed. They walked along more alpine ponds and lakes, but the water was now flowing instead of stagnant, and the trail often ran along small streams.

Again and again, Bill took a baited line out of his pocket, attached it to a stick, and walked through the stream. The water was never more than a foot deep, and as he slowly walked upstream he tossed the baited line into the flow just ahead of him.

Theodore watched in amazement as Bill pulled a trout, and then another, and then a whole string of them. The fish were only six inches long, but looked healthy.

Before long Bill had collected a small sack full of them.

Later, Emlen slapped a mosquito so hard that he almost lost his balance. Then he vigorously scratched his neck.

"Mingies, mosquitoes, black flies," grumbled Emlen, "there certainly is no shortage of terrible insects in these forests."

From behind him Mr. Cutler commented, "Emlen, you would do better to just try to ignore them. Do not…"

The older man never finished his sentence because as he was speaking Emlen frantically slapped at another mosquito, and in the process let a branch swing past him into Mr. Cutler's face.

Mr. Cutler didn't see it coming, and the branch scratched him badly on the eye. He howled and went down on his knees.

Bill appeared and examined the eye.

"Take it out! Take it out!" screamed Mr. Cutler. Bill gingerly pulled apart the eyelids but could make out no debris.

"There's nothin' in there, Mr. Cutler. My guess is you scratched your eyeball."

"Heavens, it hurts," was all Mr. Cutler could say as he bent over and covered his eye with his hand. Bill had him tilt his head so he could flush out the eye with some water.

Eventually Bill bandaged the eye with a strip of cloth and continued on, but hampered by his impaired vision, Mr. Cutler began to lag behind and the party slowly split into two groups, with Bill and Mr. Cutler trailing the younger men.

The trail was easy to follow, having been used regularly by deer and moose; and although it always slanted upwards, from time to time they found themselves traveling through level ground with small alpine ponds and groves of spruce and pine.

Finally, a pond blocked their way and Emlen and Theodore were confronted with a decision. The pond wasn't more than fifty feet across, but it stretched off a ways to the left and right. To the left lay a flooded plain of mud, and to the right was a dense forest that would have to be circumnavigated as well; to go around was going to take some time.

"Cousin," said Emlen, "I cannot see why we should not simply wade across this. You can see the far side and it doesn't seem to be deep."

Theodore observed the section Emlen proposed to cross and noted that the water was still. In the center of the pond water rippled around a submerged boulder. It looked shallow enough.

But then Theodore looked over the far end and noticed how muddy it appeared.

He warned, "I saw Mr. Sewall drag himself through a similar bog and I would not recommend it."

Emlen looked at the far bank.

"You would rather spend an hour walking around this pond and that forest versus ten minutes of wading?"

Theodore laughed.

"You are going to come out of that looking like a bloody bog monster…is that what you want?"

Undaunted, Emlen began to take off his boots and roll up his pant legs.

"We will see who is man enough for this crossing," said Emlen, stoking his own courage.

Theodore watched from the shore as Emlen entered the water, his pack with all of his belongings held over his head. He did alright for the first twenty feet where the water was only a few feet deep. He was wading over layers of flat rock, and flashed Theodore a triumphant smile.

"You see, Theodore, how easy this is?" shouted Emlen, now in the water to his hips. "In a matter of minutes I will be on the other side, lying back in the sun while I wait for you to catch up."

But Emlen's next step under water did not land on rock. He suddenly sank into soft mud. It held his foot like a vice. He tried to pull himself out with another step, but now he was caught with both feet in the mud. The muck latched onto him like a pair of hands.

He turned his head in Theodore's direction, his body pinned with only his head and arms still above water, just barely keeping his pack up.

Theodore watched apprehensively.

Just ahead of Emlen he saw the large rock ripple the water's surface.

"See if you can swim to that rock," he shouted.

Emlen tried to yank free but could not.

"I'm rather stuck, Theodore. You have to help me."

Theodore cursed him under his breath as he stripped off his shirt and one shoe. As he stepped into the water he saw that Emlen had sunk a little deeper and had also allowed his backpack to sink until it was half submerged.

"Keep that pack up," said Theodore. "I will be right there."

And then, as Theodore was wading into the water, he saw the submerged rock in front of Emlen suddenly move. Emlen gawked in horror as the surface of the water moved and the rock lifted to reveal the head and back of a bull moose who had been feeding on the bottom of the pond.

It raised its head slowly, water and aquatic plants dripping off the massive rack. Emlen stared at it from water level, a mere fifteen feet away, but so far the moose hadn't seen him. He held his breath, trying not to make a sound.

The moose chewed for a moment and then submerged its head again.

Emlen shot a panicked look at Theodore who realized the danger of the situation and swiftly dove underwater to swim directly toward Emlen's feet. He grabbed Emlen's ankles and pulled to wrench them free.

Emlen sank underwater and twisted beside him. In a few seconds he was free and they both hurriedly paddled backwards, away from the moose, Emlen dragging his soaked pack.

They surfaced near the shore, scrambled out of the deep water and turned to see what the moose was doing. It had lifted its head again and stood chewing, and didn't seem to mind them.

Then it plunged its head underwater again.

Theodore dragged himself onto dry land, but Emlen sat in about two feet of water and just stared back at where the moose grazed.

"My god, that was horrifying."

His cousin nodded, "Yes, it was, but I would suggest getting out of that water."

Emlen sighed.

"I am already soaked, what more could come of it?"

When Emlen finally came ashore he was still coated with muck. Why he hadn't cleaned himself off while he was sitting in the water Theodore could not figure out.

After waiting for Emlen to put on his boots, which were now as soaked as the contents of his pack, they backtracked and circled the pond and met up with Mr. Cutler and Bill, who had just caught up with them.

Bill noticed Emlen's muddy clothing and shook his head. "I see you boys have been up to some mischief," was all he said as he took the lead.

A half hour later, their trail crossed a small mountain stream with a clear pool.

"Why don't you wash off here, Emlen," said Bill. "If you don't, you're gonna be all itchy and miserable."

Sheepishly, Emlen nodded and began taking off his wet boots, pants and shirt. As he took off the shirt and looked down on himself his face took on a horrified expression.

"Mr. Sewall..." was all he squeaked out.

Bill turned and saw a half dozen leaches on Emlen's white chest. He grabbed Emlen's arm, turned him around and found several more stuck to his back.

"Just hold still, Emlen, and I'll have you sorted out in a minute."

Emlen stood frozen, his eyes frantic.

Bill had opened his sack and dug through it until he pulled out a small container. He opened it to reveal a white powder which turned out to be salt.

In the meantime, Theodore had quickly taken off his shirt and searched for leaches on his own body.

He found none and said, "They must have gotten on you when you sat in the water."

"Enough lectures, Theodore," screeched Emlen.

His voice was quivering. Bill stepped forward and calmed him. "Okay, Emlen, this won't hurt, but you've got to let the cuts bleed freely after I apply it."

Emlen nodded and watched as Bill sprinkled salt on each of the leaches. One by one they dropped off.

The leech bites were still bleeding and the sight of it made Emlen queasy. Theodore examined them with interest and said, "I have heard that the leaches put an anticoagulant into the blood and that is why the wound keeps bleeding like that."

Bill grunted. "*Ayuh.*"

Within minutes Bill had freed Emlen of the leeches and the young man sat down on a rock, pale-faced.

"Just let it bleed for a while and it will stop," said Bill.

Emlen looked horrified at the blood flowing down his chest and asked, "Can I not, at least, wipe up the blood?"

Bill nodded.

"Sure you can, just don't touch the bites until I give you the word."

Mr. Cutler watched with a sick expression on his bandaged face and then looked in the direction they were heading.

A good ways ahead, an alpine basin slanted up before them, its left side was rimmed by a steep wall of granite. Several small ponds reflected the sunlight, and the far side was overrun by a long scree that lead up to a saddle between two peaks to the right of the basin.

"We will camp for the night in that basin, by the base of the scree, "said Bill.

Mr. Cutler and Emlen nodded miserably. Theodore´s expression was one of anticipation, but even he appeared to be having a hard time catching his breath.

Bill added, "We'll be going up in elevation, and I reckon by the time we get there we'll have left the mosquitoes behind us."

Emlen lay back against a rock. Mr. Cutler had also gone down on his knees, and Theodore followed suit. Bill looked over his weakened crew and decided a break might be in order.

He checked on Mr. Cutler's eye, which was swollen shut behind the bandages; he had made it worse by scratching and rubbing it. Then Bill turned to Emlen, whose bug bites were big welts between the leach bites that were still bleeding freely down his chest. He was wiping at the blood with a handkerchief, careful not to touch the bites themselves.

Only Theodore appeared in good spirits despite the fact that one foot was still bare, and his remaining shoe was soaked and covered with mud. His lungs had done well with the climb, but he still felt short of breath.

After examining the alpine basin, Mr. Cutler exhaled and said, "Mr. Sewall, I do appreciate all the effort you have put into getting us up this mountain, but I — for one — do not feel like I can go any further."

Emlen nodded in support.

"I think I am ready to turn around as well."

Bill looked to Theodore to see what his decision would be. The young man puffed up his chest as he said, "I am not ready to stop; the peak is within sight."

Bill agreed. "Yes, and as I said, once we get to the basin the bugs should be much less bothersome."

Mr. Cutler shook his head.

"I do believe you, but I just cannot go on. The trail back is easy to follow and I have no doubt I can make it back to our base camp without issue."

"I am retreating as well, Mr. Sewall, together we will be fine," added Emlen.

"As you will," said Bill, but before they set out he looked them over and quietly asked, "As you gentlemen have a fairly easy downhill walk, and we could be gone several days, would one of you consider giving up a shoe for Theodore?"

Theodore overheard the question and began to protest, but Bill held up a hand and silenced him, looking at Emlen and Mr. Cutler.

Mr. Cutler looked at the ground and fidgeted and finally answered. "I do see your point, Mr. Sewall, but with only one good eye I am afraid I will need my shoes more than ever."

Bill nodded reluctantly and focused his stare on Emlen.

He replied, "I think Theodore should have taken better care of his footwear. I don't see why I should pay for his mistake."

"It was an accident," replied Bill, "It could'a been you... and if I heard correctly, he just helped you out back there in the pond with the moose."

Emlen fidgeted with his backpack and stared at the ground, but before Bill could say anything else Theodore spoke up.

"He is correct, Mr. Sewall, and I am not interested in bagging this peak if it means I have to take his shoes." He glanced at his cousin, who looked very uncomfortable with the entire conversation, and thought, it will take more than the lack of footwear to keep this summit from me.

Bill nodded somberly.

"Alright," he said, "off you go then."

Bill watched the two New Yorkers set off down the trail, a little nervous seeing them depart unescorted.

From there on the ground rose and became drier and the pine began to look stunted. Often they passed patches of cranberries and blueberries which they would pause at long enough to grab a handful.

The ground was soft and Theodore limped along, placing his naked left foot carefully, and then confidently stomping forward on the shoed right foot. His left foot now looked horrible, but he didn't complain once and kept up with his guide despite his handicap.

In the late afternoon they reached the great basin, the circular formation of it created by a glacier that had long since melted. To the left impressive cliffs rose to the summit, and on the other a vast pond lay before them, bordered by a large ring of soft grass that led into a dense spruce forest. To their right lay another basin.

Beyond the spruce Bill pointed to a long rock slide that rose up from the basin, topping out between the two large peaks.

"It's too late to go for it today; in the morning we will climb that scree, right there between the peaks."

He looked around, sniffing the weather in that weird way of his. The sky was still bright with day, but the mountain blocked the sun's rays now and they set up camp in its shadow.

While they sat catching their breath Bill saw a flurry of movement, and with a smile he looked at Theodore and said, "I sure would love a bird to go with all those trout I caught."

Theodore grinned.

"Say no more," he said as he grabbed his shotgun and walked through the soft grass of the alpine meadow that surrounded the pond.

Within a few steps he stopped, took off his one shoe and went on barefoot.

In the meantime Bill got to work with his fire kit and in no time had a good blaze going. He propped two Y-shaped sticks on either side of the fire, and then stripped a straight, green shoot off a branch. This he ran into the mouth of the fish and out through the gills until about a dozen fish were dangling from it.

The flames were still too high for cooking, so Bill collected some blueberries to add to the feast while he waited.

As he was standing to return to the fire he heard several shots from Theodore's shotgun; they echoed through the basin after their first report.

By the time Theodore returned with two partridge the fish were dangling over the coals, sizzling away and ready to eat.

"I could smell that halfway across the pond," said Theodore.

"Grab a seat," said Bill as he gestured to a spot by the fire. "I've already had a few, why don't you eat while I prepare the birds."

The partridge were good size, but there wasn't much meat except for the breast. While Bill cut away the breasts he noticed Theodore's feet which were covered with dew and grass and looked cold. The young man stretched them out and let the fire help return circulation.

Once the meat was cooking Bill dug into his sack and retrieved a pair of moccasins. He held them up and then handed them to Theodore.

"I brought these along to wear at night when we camped, but I think at this point I'd rather you take 'em."

Theodore examined them.

"These are beautiful, but I cannot possibly take them."

Bill laughed.

"Of course you can, I'll just make another pair."

"You made these?"

Again, Bill laughed.

"You forget that my mother was a seamstress and we grew up making most of our own clothes."

He nodded at the moccasins. "You take 'em, they're yours. I would'a given them to you earlier, but the mud and water would've wrecked 'em. From here we'll be mostly on rocks and you should be fine in them...although I'm bettin' your feet are still gonna be sore when we get off this mountain."

Chapter Twenty-three
The Alpine Basin

Theodore put on the moccasins and began walking in circles, raving about how comfortable they were.

"I do say you have done a fine job, Mr. Sewall."

Bill cautioned, "You just watch your step and don't twist your ankle. It's a long way out of here yet and I reckon I wouldn't enjoy carryin' you."

The night had set in fully and the stars now blazed in the half of the sky not blotted out by the mountain.

"I am a bit worried about Emlen and Mr. Cutler," said Theodore as he sat by the fire.

Bill nodded gravely.

"I've been havin' second thoughts about 'em on their own as well."

"I gave Mr. Cutler my rifle just in case they had trouble," said Theodore.

Bill nodded. "I saw that. And I also told him if he got lost, or had any trouble, to fire three rounds."

He raised his head and listened and then whispered, "And I haven't heard anything yet so I guess they made it."

Later, the two men sat by the fire in silence; the warm glow of the flames hypnotizing them. Eventually Theodore broke the quiet by saying, "Bill, you know all about what I have been up to at Harvard, but you have not told me what you did during my absence."

Bill smiled.

"Well, son, I've been workin'. Someday you'll have to come back in spring and experience a river drive."

The young man from Harvard scratched his head. "I really enjoyed our visit to the logging camp last winter, but I am afraid I really do not understand how the log drive works."

Bill was silent for a minute, and then he began, "Remember at the camp you saw how the logs were all piled up on the shore of the lake by Cecil's camp?"

Theodore nodded.

"The winter's work is gettin' the logs ready for the spring drive. The piles of logs you saw by Cecil's camp would'a grown much larger by the time the ice thawed. By horse or wagon the logs are hauled to the streams or lakes all throughout the North Country. There they are stacked on the ice, or on steep banks of any height—some as high as forty or fifty feet. They were stacked in tiers, in huge piles ready to be rolled into the water when the spring freshets came and the streams opened up."

Bill leaned forward and adjusted one of the Y-shaped sticks that supported his day's catch. He had caught so many trout that during the course of the evening he had hung up several more sticks of the dangling fish. Now they slowly smoked above the fire, getting ready to become sustenance on their hike up the mountain.

After a few minutes, Theodore said, "But surely the logs do not just float to the mill on their own."

Bill let out a boisterous laugh that echoed off the cliffs around them. "They certainly don't! Often times there's so many logs that they reach clear across the streams, even when they're flooded. Breaking those landings is dangerous work, I tell you."

He chomped on a tasty piece of smoked trout.

"When the drives begin, men commence work on the opposite side of the stream that the logs are piled on—where the pile is lowest. Once a clear channel is made the logs are free to flow downstream."

Reaching into his bag he pulled out the small container that held the salt and sprinkled it over the fish he'd just taken off the stick.

"This job might sound easy, but it really requires men who are skillful and cautious. These landings hold tons of logs and their huge weight, combined with the flow of water can cause the log piles to collapse and trap men. It really is the most dangerous part of river drivin'—aside from log jams—and at times the men working them are forced to jump into the water and swim for their lives."

"It sounds dangerous," said Theodore.

Bill nodded. "Experienced men rarely get hurt. You'd have to be skillful for the boss to put you there in the first place, and generally those who do get in trouble find a way to escape."

He looked up sadly and added, "Well, most of 'em do."

Above them a full moon rose over the edge of the forest, looking down at them like a giant's head, and as they settled into their makeshift beds it slowly floated past.

Later the fire had died down to coals and Theodore sat listening to the night as he looked over the alpine basin. The moon had long passed and now the sky was littered with so many stars that there was good visibility.

Bill had been correct. At their current elevation it was too cold for mosquitoes, and the crickets were also absent, but the night was still alive with the sound of the frogs in the pond, and later an owl.

Theodore said, "Coty promised to cook me some frog legs when I see him again."

Bill went to say something, but then stopped and held his tongue.

For a minute he had a strange look on his face. Then he finally said, "You remember when I talked about the river run earlier?"

Theodore nodded, "Of course I do, Bill."

"Well, I had a bit more to say about log jams…"

Theodore stared at his Maine guide, suddenly uncertain about his unfamiliar hesitation.

"Well," started Bill, "the log jams are not dangerous to experienced men. Bad log jams are often made by a log swinging across the stream in a place where it narrows suddenly."

He reached for a piece of wood and added it to the fire.

"If the jam is in a falls with a considerable drop, and very swift water, the logs running down from above will soon load this log and keep piling up on it until the jam is ten or fifteen feet high. The logs pack so tight from the bottom upward that it dams the stream. If the banks are high above the stream a great head of water can collect. The key log will then have to be started out."

"The key log?" asked Theodore.

"*Ayuh*, the key log…" said Bill. "No matter how big the jam, there is always one log that holds everything up. Once that log is cut away everything flows again."

Theodore smiled as he said, "You sound like my father when he talked about politics."

Then he asked quizzically, "Is every jam like that?"

"Well, not all jams are made that way," said Bill. "They are sometimes formed on a rock or other obstruction near the middle of the stream. If they collect a great head of water behind them, it is always hard work to start them and sometimes dangerous; though I think the high landings are more dangerous."

Bill paused and glanced at the fire, and Theodore couldn't shake the feeling that there was something more to this story than Bill was letting on.

He continued. "Cutting away those key logs is only accomplished by picking and digging into the pile of logs until you find the one that everything hinged on."

Bill stirred the coals and added gravely, "This requires skilled and levelheaded men."

Theodore eyed his Maine guide. He felt that he'd gotten to know the man quite well over the last year. He watched Bill stirring the fire and avoiding eye contact with Theodore.

Finally, Theodore asked, "What's bothering you, Bill? Tell me now what you are holding back."

Bill looked up from the coals, into Theodore's eyes, and said, "Last spring, on one of the final log drives, your friend Coty lost his life."

This news hit Theodore like a punch in the gut; and after having spent the last year trying to cope with his father's death it was the last thing he wanted to hear.

Bill saw Theodore's jaw drop and his eyes lose focus. The older man averted his gaze and reached into his sack. He took out a bundle wrapped in a soft deer hide and handed it to Theodore, who inspected it suspiciously; silently he let his fingers trace the leather thongs that bound it.

"Coty made this for you last winter, after you left."

Theodore nodded absentmindedly, limply holding the bundle.

"Open it," urged Bill.

Theodore untied the package and discovered that the soft hide was actually the gift, not its packaging.

He stood to let it unroll and was soon holding a beautiful set of buckskins—the sides decorated with tassels.

A broad smile spread over his face. He stood, took off his damp clothes and climbed into the buckskins. Then he timidly looked at Bill, unsure if it was improper to be showing such joy after hearing of the death of a friend.

Bill noticed this and said, reassuringly, "Coty put a lot of effort into those buckskins—and I'm sure Cecil teased him the entire time. I'm guessin' he would'a been overjoyed to see how much you like 'em."

Theodore straightened up and paraded about the campsite. The buckskins appeared to be a perfect fit and he tried all sorts of moves to make sure of it: stretching, jumping, and taking wide steps.

Above them the sky had darkened and the stars were no longer visible. It started to rain and Theodore watched in fascination how the drops rolled off the buckskins.

Looking up into the heavens, the young Harvard man smiled at the drops of rain that hit his face. The rain swelled into a downpour, but Theodore made no move to get closer to the fire which was now hissing at the raindrops.

"I do believe I could live in this outfit," said Theodore.

He then sat and put on his moccasins which completed the outfit. He hopped to his feet and did a set of jumping jacks, then dropped to a plank position and began to do pushups.

"Don't get too brash there, young fella," said Bill.

While performing his exercises Theodore noted how they stretched but still offered support.

"Seriously, Bill, I do think this outfit was sorely missing in my repertoire of outdoor supplies."

He crouched down low and added, "With these I could follow you anywhere."

Staring at the older man from across the fire, Theodore added timidly, "With these I could even be on equal footing with you and Wilmot."

Bill watched him, not certain where Theodore was heading, and replied, "Well, you may be better prepared. But you just remember that preparation is in the mind — not in some article of clothing."

Theodore nodded and his features suddenly clouded with the same shadow of depression that had troubled him when he'd met David at the station. Although he was enjoying himself immensely, he had come north with a mission and he meant to fulfill it before returning.

Now was not the time though, so he again examined the buckskins and then said, "Tell me how Coty died."

Bill nodded somberly.

"Last spring I was working with a crew tryin' to break a dam up Dyer Brook. We were takin' a break when we saw Coty comin' along, headin' in our direction, on the other side of the river."

The Mainer paused and looked directly at Theodore.

"You should know that after Coty fell in the river last winter he never fully returned to his old self. He still joked around with us, but he looked frail and he rarely went outside. When he did go out he avoided any rivers—even though they were all frozen solid at that time of year.

Cecil teased him about it, but he only replied that his fate was sealed and it wasn't smart for him to go near water.

"That's one of the reasons that we found it strange when he came our way. It was one of the first nice days of spring, but the ground was still covered with snow. The snow was wet enough that it gripped everything, and Coty's boots were caked with it."

Bill paused long enough to add a log to the fire. It was obvious from his expression that this was not a story he relished telling.

Theodore found he was holding his breath.

Bill continued, "Anyway, Coty was starin' off—actually watchin' a chickadee on a nearby branch, and then he turned and started walkin' in our direction—evidently plannin' on crossin' the river on the logs that lay below the jam.

"These logs had been worked free and just floated there, and with the snow packed around the spikes of his boots I knew Coty would have little traction so I shouted for him to hold up."

Now Bill was looking pale and appeared to have a difficult time finding the words to finish his tale. He swallowed and continued, "When he heard my shout he looked up and smiled, and waved as well, but he didn't stop. I've often wondered if he heard what I said or just was acknowledging me.

"I stood and started in his direction but it was too late. He stepped across several logs and slipped. I saw him drop between two logs, into the water, and even though I was there in seconds he never resurfaced."

Bill watched the fire for so long that Theodore felt he was done with the story, but eventually he added, "The next day we found his body as the logs were eventually cleared. I must say it unnerved my crew."

He looked at Theodore.

"I don't know why, but he was smiling—even after floating under the logs for a day. Who goes to their death smiling?"

Theodore couldn't speak. In his mind he envisioned Coty grinning, a slightly bluish tint to his skin. He no longer felt as tough as he had a few minutes before.

The rain picked up again and Theodore moved closer to the fire.

Robert Louis DeMayo

Chapter Twenty-four
The Knife's Edge

The next morning was overcast and as they looked over the land below them they watched patches of fog lifting from the wet earth. The land steamed from the soaking of the night before, but Bill had kept the fire going through the night and most of their supplies had stayed dry.

Initially he'd strung up a small tarp to make sure their possessions would stay dry, but when the rain turned heavy they both sat under it.

Theodore eyed his buckskins proudly, brushing the dew off them while he marveled at how dry he still felt. He also examined his feet and tended to the cuts on the left one that had been shoeless, and then put on his moccasins.

Bill cooked breakfast slowly—fried trout and blueberries—in the hopes that the sun would break through, but it didn't. In fact, while they slowly prepared for their summit bid the fog thickened and started to rise up towards them.

"We better get up that mountain if we don't want to get fogged in right here," said Bill.

From their camp they could see a peak to their right, and a larger one on the left. Between them the land sloped up toward a natural saddle.

When Bill had finished extinguishing the fire he clapped his hands free of the dust—a sound that echoed across the basin despite the moisture-laden air.

For a little less than a mile they picked their way through a maze of large boulders, and then they started up the long scree that led up the side of the saddle. Bill had feared that the soles of the moccasins would prove too thin and Theodore would not be able to hike over the sharp granite, but the young man took to the change of terrain, hopping from rock to rock like a mountain goat.

Now the pines began to thin out, leaving only stunted birches, many half buried by landslides.

"It shouldn't take us long to get up this," said Bill, "but if I remember correctly, the last section is a bit of a scramble."

Theodore was breathing well and barely noticed the weight of his backpack. They'd been hiking for an hour and he felt he had a lot still in reserve. Looking over the saddle he couldn't image it taking more than an hour.

"Let us have at it," he said confidently.

Bill scowled, "You just watch for loose rocks and be careful."

Bill noticed a bank of fog had flowed into the alpine basin behind them and was currently obscuring their campsite, now a good ways below them.

The ground became looser as they neared the top, and at times they stepped up two feet only to slide back one. Theodore marched, undaunted, with Sewall surprised to find himself trailing the young man.

The top was rounded and Theodore kept going. He appeared ready to hike right down the other side. Between breaths Bill shouted, "Go to the left, Theodore, that's the main peak."

Theodore stopped, turned around, and surveyed the land they'd just covered. The basin where they had made camp was now filled with fog, and fog was seeping into the smaller one further north — on their left. This second basin's floor was covered with large boulders which now seemed to float above a carpet of fog.

The big peak lay about a quarter mile ahead of them, at the end of a line of weathered granite. It gradually slanted up and appeared to be no challenge, and Theodore grinned with the knowledge that he had the mountain conquered.

Below them the fog bank was quietly creeping up the saddle.

Bill doubled his pace until he caught up with Theodore. They covered the last couple hundred yards side by side, until they came upon the summit.

As they stood on the top a cold wind enveloped them: it seemed to blast them from every direction. The sunlight from above was harsh and gave no warmth, and the lichen covering the rocks appeared ancient and weatherworn.

"Well done, Theodore," Bill said as he sat down on a boulder and retied one of his boot laces.

The young man nodded proudly and looked over the land all around them. The fog was blanketing the mountain, but beyond that it had cleared. As his eyes swept the land he saw hundreds of lakes, including one whose expanses were so vast it seemed like an inland sea.

The sun was still visible above the rising fog bank, and all around the mountain it reflected off the many windings of the Penobscot Rivers.

And then the fog was upon them; when it was only fifty feet away the wind died completely and with it any sound.

Theodore was standing next to Bill when the change took place, and tried to step forward to see how far the blanket of white extended, but Bill held him back.

"Not a good time for lookin' around, Theodore," said Bill. "Just wait a few minutes and this will pass."

They waited, and sure enough soon breaks in the fog appeared. Through a hole below them Bill spotted a large Bull Moose standing in the middle of a pond. He pointed it out to Theodore who noted, "That pond is the one we camped beside."

Bill grunted in agreement.

"Do you reckon the moose could have been there and we just did not see it?" asked Theodore.

At this Bill laughed.

"You never know; if he was feedin' off plants on the bottom of the pond he might've spent half his time underwater."

For several minutes Theodore watched the animal, its huge rack impressive even from this distance. In the quiet of the mountain summit Theodore listened to hear the splash when it finally moved a few feet forward.

But then the fog overtook the men again and they were lost in a sea of white. Although Theodore had watched the clouds ascend he still found it surprising to be enveloped by them.

He looked around in the thick white soup, disoriented, and was suddenly filled with dread as he wondered how they would find their way off the mountain in this weather. He didn't even have a clue where the saddle was now.

And then it got so thick that even Bill, a few feet away, momentarily faded from view.

Bill watched Theodore and saw the flash of horror pass across the eyes of his young charge.

"Just sit tight, Theodore, this will pass."

Theodore nodded, crouched with his back to a boulder, and lay back against it; Bill lowered himself to the ground and did the same, using his sack as a pillow.

The fog now hid all except the rocks right around them, but Theodore still stared into it as if his gaze could clear it. For a second he thought he saw a figure standing a short distance away, but he blinked and shook his head and looked again and there was nothing there.

His breathing quickened as he strained to spot the apparition again. Was it just a trick of the fog? Nothing materialized, and he tried to shake it off.

Nervously he looked down at where the alpine basin had just been in plain sight and picked up the earlier conversation, "I have heard reports that when the Indians first saw the European ships some of them looked right through them and the image did not register in their minds."

Bill laughed.

"And why wouldn't an Indian be able to make out a ship?"

Theodore shrugged.

"I believe it was because it was too alien to them. It was simply too different."

The older man shook his head.

"Well a moose might be different for you, but I've seen my share of 'em—if there'd been one in the pond when we were there I most likely would'a seen it."

Theodore nodded and stared into the swirling fog again. The world seemed to have become so fragile in the fog on the mountaintop that he was beginning to question what was real.

Had there been a figure in the fog? And if he let his mind wander, would he soon recall that the figure had looked a bit like Coty?

Theodore was strangely unnerved, and he looked at Bill who appeared to take it all in stride. He seemed in no rush to move before the fog dissipated.

"Bill, have you seen many men die on the log drives?"

Bill sat quietly. He let the past seasons and the men he'd worked with pass through his mind.

"I saw a man killed once when he was working on a landing. It wasn't a dangerous landing and the accident seemed to me entirely unnecessary."

Theodore leaned a little closer and asked, "Do you mean to imply that the man could have reacted differently and avoided the accident?"

Bill scratched his beard.

"Well, I'd have to say he could'a."

A slight breeze started from below them and began clearing away some of the fog.

"During this incident I was workin' on a tier of logs, and to my side another man was workin' with his pick tryin' to loosen some of them. I noticed he was in a dangerous place, but he paid no attention to me when I warned him to step away. He did appear to hear me, but for some reason didn't care."

"Didn't care?" asked Theodore.

"Well," said Bill, "the pile of logs he was on extended down into the water, and he was using his pick to loosen logs that were jammed above him — do you see the problem?"

Theodore shook his head negatively.

"I really do believe I have to witness one of these log runs someday, because I am afraid I cannot envision it." Bill waved his arm through the air as if to wipe away the thought.

"All I'm sayin' is as he loosened the logs they would roll toward the water and he was standin' right in their way."

Bill held up his finger.

"Now it was a dangerous position, but it was still possible for him to run out onto the logs and jump into the water if need be and maybe that's what he intended to do."

Around them the fog seemed to clear briefly and Bill stood and swung his sack onto his shoulders. Theodore stood as well and shouldered his backpack.

"Let's try to make the second peak before this fog closes in again," said Bill. "This isn't dangerous if you stay in the middle. Watch out though, the side of this mountain is about to get steeper so don't stray."

As they started in the direction of the smaller peak Bill continued with his story.

"So this man persisted to work on the logs, jumpin' over them as they pulled free, and eventually he started one that didn't move out as the others had. As he moved to avoid it another log shot out from the top of the pile, completely rolling over him and crushing his head."

This story put fear into Theodore's mind as he thought about Coty's final minutes, and he tried to shake it off by concentrating on his foot placement. Ahead the second peak waited, and it looked no more than a half hour away — if they could get there before the fog closed in again.

Several questions passed through Theodore's mind, but in the end he simply asked, "How do you handle situations like that in wilderness areas?"

After a moment Bill answered, "Well, my crew was shaken up. This man had been warned by me not to do just what he'd been doing and they knew it. Death can linger around you during the dark nights of spring, and it's a bad thing to have on a job site.

"After the log rolled over him, one man shouted out, 'He's kilt. He's kilt' and that cry seemed to stay with us awhile. The crew seemed paralyzed while I went down and carried him up the bank. When we examined the body we all figured he'd been killed instantly. We were overcome and all but gave up workin'.

"I remember one older man showed no excitement and told us, 'Boys, it's what we all have to come to, and he has gone easy'."

They reached the second summit just as the fog closed in again. On either side the land seemed to drop away and they picked their way a bit more carefully now.

Just in time they came upon a small break in the ridge where a depression in the rock offered shelter on four sides. Quickly, they dropped into it.

Everything whitened out again as the fog rolled up and filled their shelter.

Theodore peered at Bill through the haze that had enveloped them and somberly asked, "What did you do with the body?"

"There was certainly no undertaker in our vicinity," answered Bill, "so we made a stretcher and carried him a half mile down the stream. He was a heavy man and it wasn't easy, but we got it done and eventually brought him to town."

Bill looked over Theodore with a stern expression as he added, "Out here we take care of others in the hope that someone will someday do the same for us...and there's never a charge for such cases."

Bill looked in the direction they'd been heading, beyond the peak they sat on, but could see nothing.

He was quiet for a little while, then he said, "My belief is that men die when their time comes, and his time had come."

Then he nodded into the fog.

"Up ahead is a part of this mountain that is shaped like a knife's edge. On either side the land drops off, at one point I'd guess for a thousand feet or more. It's a narrow path we'll have to walk so we're gonna wait for the fog to clear."

Theodore peered hard through the fog, occasionally seeing a thin ribbon of granite which promptly disappeared into the fog again.

Bill seemed to be quite comfortable despite the crazy weather. He looked relaxed as he observed the fog and said, "One of my Indian friends told me once there was an avenging spirit on this mountain called Pamola."

"Do you think climbing a mountain would offend a spirit?" asked Theodore.

Bill shook his head. "Can't say that I know anything about spirits...except what's mentioned in the Bible."

Then Bill leaned forward and slapped Theodore on the shoulder, "On the other hand, I've seen a man go under a jam of logs and go clear through it and come out unharmed, without any exertion on his own part."

He laughed as he added, "And this man couldn't even swim! I tell you it truly appeared that there was no possible chance for him to live; but he did. And another man, Ed Hillman, almost drowned in the rapids by our house, but he somehow survived and died in bed — an old man — surrounded by his children."

Theodore smiled, but then grew serious.

"And what of Coty; do you think his fate was sealed, as he believed?"

Around them the fog was suddenly blowing away, the winds from below now gaining momentum.

Bill stood and looked down at Theodore.

"I told you earlier that Coty was never the same after his swim in the river. He went through the motions of life, but seemed a mere shadow when compared to before. All I can say is that when a man loses his edge it's easy to die out here."

Bill took out a rag and wiped the moisture from his face.

He continued, "And when he crossed the logs below the jam that day he placed himself in exactly the right kind of position for something bad to happen — although I don't feel there was any intent of self-destruction."

Theodore said, "Just like the man you witnessed getting crushed."

"That's it exactly," said Bill.

Theodore pondered it all and then stood as well.

As he shouldered his pack he said, "I would have liked to have thanked him for the buckskins."

Bill smiled. "I'm sure he knows."

As they continued along the ridge Theodore remembered talking with Coty just after he'd pulled him from the river. Even then, he'd still smiled through his chattering teeth while he lectured him about leaving the lynx pelt behind.

Theodore turned to Bill and said, "After I pulled him from the river Coty stood there shivering. I remember he looked at me and said, 'Just because you fear for my life doesn't mean we should live life differently'."

Bill grunted in response.

Suddenly the fog was gone as if it had never existed.

On both sides the land dropped away in steep screes of granite boulders. Small ponds dotted the basins behind them, and before them lay a long, curved, serrated ridge of vertically fractured granite.

Theodore's heart pounded in his chest as he surveyed the line they were set to follow. The rock looked solid and clearly visible, but the exposure was incredible and even though he was sitting he still grabbed a nearby boulder for support.

In his head, he heard more of Coty's words from the scene on the frozen river.

"My people believe dat you should live your life in a way dat de fear of death can never enter your heart."

Theodore watched Bill as he set out to cross the knife's edge, his long step casually pulling him across.

Over his shoulder Bill called, "*Faces that have charmed us the most escape us the soonest.*"

Theodore called back in response. "So you are on to Walter Scott, eh? Well I can think of a few of his sayings that are appropriate for this trail..."

He stopped for just a minute and cleaned his glasses, the drop on either side of him momentarily forgotten.

As he started up again he said, "*One crowded hour of glorious life is worth an age without a name.*"

Bill approached a section where the ridgeline narrowed to just a few feet, but he continued on confidently. He passed over it as if it were a broad avenue, while reciting another Walter Scott quote.

"*One hour of life, crowded to the full with glorious action, and filled with noble risks, is worth whole years of those mean observances in which men steal through existence, like sluggish waters through a marsh, without either honor or observation.*"

As Theodore passed through the same section he stopped in the middle, stretched his arms in both directions as if walking on a tightrope, and said, "*For success, attitude is equally as important as ability.*"

Bill stared back proudly. "Well done, Theodore."

After they got off the knife's edge the mountain slowly diminished in size as it slanted back down to the lowlands. With one last glimpse at the ridgeline Bill added, "*Look back, and smile on perils past.*"

Theodore adjusted his pack, and then stood scratching his head.

He said, "I do believe I have exhausted my supply of Walter Scott quotes."

Bill laughed.

"I've still got a few. But it's a long way off this mountain and it's not worth rushin' or being distracted only to break a leg or worse."

"So you think we will make it to the base camp on the lake today?" asked Theodore.

Bill sniffed the air and said, "If not today, then tomorrow."

"Do you think Mr. Cutler's eye will be alright? I feel rather bad that he was not with us at the summit."

Bill laughed heartily.

"Oh, Mr. Cutler will be fine; you've just gone on to another level."

His eyes filled with pride, Theodore picked his way through the boulders, the dull yellow of his buckskins appearing to bounce from rock to rock as they descended.

Chapter Twenty-five
Island Falls and Bible Point

After Bill and Theodore had descended the mountain they slowly made their way to the base camp by the lake. Bill took a wrong turn somewhere and added an extra hour to their labor.

It had been a long day, but Theodore felt elated and didn't want to stop. In fact, even Bill's failure to find the trail made him feel better; the fact that his Maine guide could actually make a mistake seemed to level the playing field in his eyes.

As they lost altitude he became outright giddy. Theodore couldn't wait to march back into camp, triumphant.

By the lake Emlen and Mr. Cutler waited anxiously; they had had a day off, but the black flies had been relentless and they were desperate to get away.

As soon as Bill and Theodore were spotted Emlen went to meet them, and as soon as he was in calling distance he requested to be off at once. He did not even greet them.

Bill laughed and roused Emlen's hair, "Emlen, believe it or not, we've had quite a day already."

The young man indignantly straightened his hair and stepped aside to let him pass, then he looked at the ground and scratched his numerous bug bites. Bill could see his desperate condition.

He stopped and put a hand on Emlen's shoulder, looked into his eyes, and agreed to start back early the next morning.

After a good night's sleep and a quick breakfast they started back toward Rolland and the buckboard. To Theodore the twelve miles to the buckboard flew by, but they stretched endlessly for Emlen and Mr. Cutler.

The professor's eye was healing fine, and he could now open it partially, but the fire had gone out of him and he limped along listlessly and silently, just pining for the ordeal to be over.

Even Emlen was too tired to gripe.

When they approached the camp, Rolland had already spotted them. He nodded once to Bill as they approached, then turned and began breaking camp. Within the hour they were heading back to Island Falls on the buckboard. Theodore watched the countryside pass by, his heart saddened by the knowledge that this adventure was about to end.

For Mr. Cutler and Emlen it couldn't end soon enough. Once back at Island Falls they were quickly on their way, mumbling something about important events in New York City.

Bill suggested he and Theodore take a rest day in Island Falls, and he was glad when Theodore accepted the request. After the Katahdin climb Bill wasn't certain where he could take the ambitious young man next.

The next day was Sunday and Bill found Theodore at Bible Point, reading quietly in the early morning sun.

"I was hoping you might come by," said Theodore.

"Were you now," said Bill as he stepped out of the canoe.

Theodore grinned.

"Well, we have had our rest day, and I am anxious to discuss our options."

Bill shook his head as he tried not to laugh.

"Theodore, guiding you is certainly a different experience. Do you know that most of the New Yorkers I guide up here don't want to do any more than fish? And here you are all fired up only one day after you climbed Katahdin."

The younger man laughed, too.

"It is not my intension to be difficult; I simply want to acquit myself creditably."

Bill nodded.

"Well I think you did that admirably."

Off in the distance Mt. Katahdin was visible in the morning light and they both stared at it for a moment.

Bill said, "You should take some pride in the fact that you accomplished something your former tutor and a cousin your age could not."

Theodore's face sank a little as he thought of them.

"A few months ago that may have brought me some satisfaction," he said, "but at this point how *they* did on the expedition now seems irrelevant. And I am afraid that I did not find climbing the mountain a real challenge anyway."

"Not a challenge?" asked Bill.

Theodore sat up and looked directly at Bill.

"Mr. Sewall," he said, "it is not my cousin — or Mr. Cutler for that matter — that I want to measure up against…it is you."

The older man stared back at Theodore with a stern expression. He creased his brows and thought a minute before speaking.

"And how do you intend to measure up against me?"

Theodore stood nervously.

"I would like to join you in an adventure that pushes me, and pushes you, at the same time. I want to feel I can exist in the wilderness despite this body that has so often failed me."

Bill cocked his head and said, "Seems to me that your body is workin' just fine these days."

Theodore agreed. "It is."

Bill looked out over the lake. Then an eagle in the sky caught the men's eyes and they watched it soar over the lake and land on one of the big pines on the island.

Finally, Bill turned his gaze to Theodore and asked sternly: "I've been livin' like this all my life, Theodore. Do you really think in a few short weeks that you can be my equal in these woods?"

Theodore dropped his head and shook it.

"Of course I do not think I would acquire all of your knowledge just by following you around, but I would like to know if I can handle the same physical toil."

Bill stood and looked across the water. He skipped several rocks across its surface, and then looked at Theodore and quoted, "*My ambition is to win esteem, by rendering myself worthy of esteem.*"

Theodore smiled as he said, "That would be Lincoln again."

Bill nodded, "*Ayuh.*"

With the sun in the western sky they got in the canoe and made their way back to Island Falls. They both had retreated into silence; Bill trying to think up a worthy adventure, and Theodore's mind drifting back to Alice.

As tempting as it was to think of her, Theodore pulled himself away and said to Bill, "Tell me about the headwaters. What are they like?"

Bill's laugh echoed across the water.

"The headwaters...well, any headwater would have to be considered a magical place. You see, everything that happens here is based on water, and the headwaters are the source."

Theodore said, "I have listened to other woodsmen talk about them with the mystery of Genesis on their tongue...as if this was a place that was reachable only by select explorers or God-enlightened men."

The older man raised an eyebrow.

"Well, it is a special place," said Bill, "and it exists at the end of this world. Beyond the source there is nothin' else so your only option is to turn and go home."

"You have been to the headwaters?" asked Theodore.

"*Ayuh*," said Bill, and then he chuckled. "I've been to one, and you nearly have as well."

Theodore looked dumbfounded.

Bill continued.

"Last winter, when we took the pung up the Aroostook River to the Oxbow, we were most likely only thirty-five miles or so from the Munsungen Lakes—and they're one of the biggest headwaters around here."

Theodore shook his head in frustration.

"If we were only such short distance away...why did we not go there?"

Bill shrugged.

"Seems to me you had enough going on at the time; if I'd a known you wanted to go, we could have. That would have been the time to go, when it was all frozen."

Even as Bill spoke the next sentence his expression showed he knew he was in trouble.

"We could never get there this time of the year."

Theodore stopped paddling, turned, and looked Bill straight in the eye. "Why not, Bill? Why could we not go to the headwaters?"

The Mainer paused and set down his paddle while he tried to find a way to explain just how tough the journey would be.

Then he said, "In winter it would have been easy. All we would have had to do was let Scout pull us there. Granted, we had some rough weather on the way out, but we covered a lot of ground."

He looked at Theodore with knotted brows as he continued, "Now, there are no trails—haven't been any sleds on 'em since last spring. And you'd have to carry a boat along. Couldn't do it without a boat."

Theodore began to smile confidently and Bill sighed deeply, knowing he wasn't going to talk Theodore out of it.

He tried again, regardless.

"What I'm tryin' to tell you, son, is just to get to the Oxbow you'd have to wade up that river for fifteen miles — pushin' and draggin' a canoe with you the entire time.

"From the Oxbow you'd have to portage a ways, and then go upstream another thirty miles — and that's just to get you to the lakes! There are two lakes and to cross them is another five miles. And then you'd have to come back the same way."

Theodore picked up a paddle and helped his Maine guide paddle the canoe.

He grinned as he asked, "When do we set forth?"

"I'm tellin' you, Theodore, it would be a hard journey. We'd have to take a smaller boat, one that we could carry when the goin' was too rough, and there's some weather comin' in so we'd be doin' much of this journey in the rain."

Bill s face crumpled into a resigned frown as he saw the determined look in Theodore´s eyes.

Bill answered Theodore's question.

"I guess it would be first light tomorrow."

He slapped Theodore's back and added, "If that works with your schedule, Mr. Roosevelt."

Theodore grinned, looking relaxed at last.

"That would be just fine, Mr. Sewall."

Chapter Twenty-six
Up the Aroostook River

The next morning they hitched Scout to the buckboard and loaded up their supplies. They planned on hunting and fishing along the way, but they still needed a kitchen kit, pans, flour, one blanket each for sleeping and a tarp to create a make-shift tent — plus guns and ammunition.

Theodore wore the buckskins that Coty had made for him, and the moccasins that Bill had given him. When Bill tried to talk him into switching the moccasins for some heavier footwear he replied, "Bill, I fear my boots would never dry on this expedition, and I like the moccasins — even when they are soaked."

The Mainer had on his usual attire – heavy wool pants, a checkered flannel shirt with wool thermals underneath, and heavy boots. He kept all of his possessions in his sack which he was now rummaging through.

Buried deep was a bundle — his fire kit — that was as usual wrapped in layers to keep it dry. He took it out and carefully unwrapped layer after layer until he got to a container of matches.

He lit one, smiled before blowing it out, and then carefully put the rest away. After methodically rewrapping his fire kit he stowed it in the bag, then swung the whole load over one shoulder.

On this journey Bill also took a *pirogue*, or dugout canoe, which differed quite a bit from the canoe they'd been using. That one had wooden ribs and was a bit fragile; whereas the pirogue was made from one log, creating a narrow but solid boat.

"It'll be a bit tight once we load her up," said Bill as he watched Theodore inspect the craft, "but it's solid, so we won't end up hikin' out after it smashes on a rock."

Pleased by the look of the pirogue, Theodore stowed his backpack in the back of the buckboard and then greeted Scout with an apple.

They rode for most of the day, and much of the time Theodore fidgeted on the front bench, anxious to get on the river.

"Settle down, Theodore," said Bill. "That river's not goin' anywhere. If we rushed all we'd do is tire out Scout...and most likely smash the pirogue to pieces as well."

Theodore looked at the canoe, now tied down securely in the back of the buckboard. He said, "It looks to me like it could take quite a beating."

Bill nodded. "Oh, it's a stout little canoe, don't worry about that...the real reason I saw no point in rushin' is we are going to stay with some friends of mine tonight and tomorrow we can start fresh."

The older man winked at Theodore and then said with a softer tone, "I just didn't want Scout to think we were goin' easy on her."

Although Theodore had ridden this stretch of land on his winter visit it was now unrecognizable to him. Gone were the long stretches of frozen earth, and the trees without branches. The pine trees were heavy with pinecones and the foliage of the oaks was full of color. Theodore felt the joy the adventurous live for as they start out for a new destination.

Late in the afternoon, Bill said, "We´re going to be staying with the Pollards. I don't recollect if it was has him or his dad, but one of the family helped build a big fort around here about twenty five years ago."

Theodore looked around them and said, "It is beautiful, but there does not seem like there is much to defend."

Bill laughed, "Oh, it was during the Aroostook War when everyone was disputing the northeastern border between the United States and Canada. It's actually a strategic location because here the St. Croix and Aroostook Rivers meet up.

"This place is called Masardis, which is an Indian phrase that means *Where Two Rivers Meet*."

Theodore nodded. "A confluence? And who did they expect to invade them here?"

"Well, it would've been the British again—they controlled Canada. The U.S. built the fort for the artillery and the troops camped in tents. At the time they believed the British troops would come up the river and try to capture them."

Bill sat up a bit taller and began reciting a Ballard from the days of the Aroostook War, "*Come all ye noble Yankee boys, come listen to my story... I'll tell about those Volunteers and all their pomp and glory... They came to the Aroostook, their country to support... They came to the St. Croix, and there they built a fort.*"

Just before dark they came upon a simple cabin built on the shore of the St. Croix River.

Bill pointed at it and said, "Downstream a short way this joins the Aroostook River. When we start here enjoy it, for after we hit the Aroostook we'll be going upstream for fifty odd miles without a break."

The husband and wife that inhabited the cabin, the Pollards, welcomed Bill warmly and showed the two men where they could sleep.

That night, after dinner, Mr. Pollard told the story of the building of the fort—an action that took almost twenty years to complete. As he completed the story Mrs. Pollard served them all hot apple pie. Little did Theodore realize that he would be reminiscing over the delicious, hot meal for the next week.

Knowing they would have an early start Bill thanked them for their hospitality and retired with Theodore. But before allowing Theodore to drift off to sleep Bill made him unpack his things and sort through them.

"This will be your last chance to make sure you haven't forgotten anything."

Theodore nodded, and continued to nod as Bill recited a list of items he deemed necessary.

"And you brought a heavy wool sweater, good," said Bill. "One nice thing about wool is it doesn't lose its integrity when it gets wet. When you're in the water you should wear it under your buckskins. It'll drain fast and keep the water from your skin."

Then Bill did a last check on his own possessions before blowing out the candle and laying back.

The next morning they said goodbye to their hosts, and to Scout, who would be relaxing in the stable until they returned. Bill flipped the canoe over and examined every crack and imperfection to be sure it wasn't something that needed attention.

They dragged the pirogue to the edge of the river and loaded it, then stood back and looked downstream for several minutes without speaking.

Finally Bill broke the silence.

"It's gonna be about fifteen miles upstream when we reach Cecil's camp—he'll be gone of course—but that's gonna be the only real shelter we get on this trip."

"And what is after that?" asked Theodore.

"You just worry about getting that far for now," replied Bill. "I'm thinkin' it's gonna be a few days just to get there and we might want to turn around then."

Theodore smiled.

"Well, I will turn around if you are too tired to continue, but we will not be quitting on my account."

Bill reached over and squeezed Theodore's shoulder.

"So that's the way it's goin' to be, eh?"

Theodore looked back confidently, but then glanced up when a drop of rain hit his cheek. Above them the sky had darkened and looked ready to unload.

Once they reached the Aroostook River they turned upstream. The river here was wide and full, but the current slow. Bill sat in the back and paddled while Theodore looked for wildlife in the cool morning air.

The rain held off for a while, but eventually came down, sounding off as it hit the dead leaves that littered the forest floor.

"The further we go up this river the weaker the flow will get," said Bill. "We will pass several tributaries on the way, and each time we go beyond these streams that drain into the Aroostook River the flow will be reduced again, but our final destination is the Munsungen Lakes."

In the beginning the water was fairly deep and slow, but before long Bill started scraping the paddle along the bottom with his long, deep strokes.

After he'd scraped along the river floor half dozen times he silently paddled to the shore, stepped out of the canoe with axe in hand, and returned soon with a freshly cut long pole.

He stood in the back of the canoe, stuck one end of the pole into the water and put his weight on it. The pirogue moved easily ahead and they kept up a swift pace for several more miles.

Before the day was halfway over they came to the first log drift. Leftover timber from the spring run had jammed the river and made it impassable. Bill instructed Theodore to steady the canoe as he slipped over the edge and into the water.

"Thunderation! That cold goes right to the bones," he said with an intake of breath. The water was up to his waist.

Theodore watched Bill climb onto the log pile with apprehension. The logs were slippery and he thought it would be difficult to use an axe to clear a way because there was no hope of gaining sold footing. For the first time he sensed how difficult this journey was going to be.

Rather than wait for Bill to instruct him, Theodore slipped into the water and joined Bill on the log pile.

"How will we cut through this?" asked Theodore.

Bill looked it over and shook his head.

"You have to pick your battles out here. I think we're better off draggin' the pirogue over this one."

Together they carefully lowered themselves back to the canoe and each grabbed a side. Over the next thirty minutes they slowly hauled it up and over the log jam. It was exhausting work, and the shins and forearms of both men were soon covered with mud and small scrapes.

When they finally reached the other side of the blockage, they climbed back into the pirogue with a sigh of relief.

Maneuvering upstream now became a constant challenge. Through the remainder of the afternoon they labored hard, pushing and dragging the boat through rapids, hauling it over log drifts or other obstacles, while up to their hips in icy water.

They got lucky on a few jams: Bill hopped onto the pile and surveyed the chaos, and then after nimbly jumping onto a floating log he used his long pole to free one particular log.

To Theodore's amazement, when that log floated free all the timber around it followed it downstream. Theodore kept the canoe by the shore, out of the way, but when he saw the log Bill was on begin to float downstream he paddled to meet it.

The Mainer used his staff to help keep balanced, and when the canoe was close he expertly stepped in without upsetting the canoe.

"Not an easy task without caulked boots," said Bill.

"Excuse me?" said Theodore.

Bill pointed at his boots.

"If I was drivin' this river I'd have my caulked boots on: they've got nails stickin' out of the bottom and they give you better traction on the logs."

Bill feared that Theodore's moccasins would not hold up, but they seemed to do fine when the bottom was slimy, and even on the sharp rocks in rocky sections, Theodore was careful not to tear them. The young man was holding up well, but it was obvious to Bill that the effort they had to make was far greater than he had reckoned.

After ten hours of trudging upstream their hands and feet were numb from the cold; and when the sun dropped behind the trees Bill felt the first sign of a chill in the air. The rain had stopped and he knew it was time to call for a halt.

They were breathing hard as they dragged the pirogue to shore and made camp. Both men were exhausted, but they still needed to get a fire going, set up a shelter, and someone had to catch dinner.

While Bill lit the fire, Theodore circled the area with his shotgun, hoping to come across a partridge or duck. Once the fire had a solid base Bill dropped a line in the water and tried to land a few trout.

Over the next days, this became their pattern of making camp: Bill would get a fire going and fish while Theodore scouted for birds and rabbits.

Early the next morning they were on the river again, fighting their way upstream in the cold water. They'd awoken to rain coming down on their tarp and both scrambled to put the blankets away before they got soaked.

For hour after hour the challenge continued, and both men gave it everything they had. That night they were too tired to even eat and simply collapsed into their blankets, which had turned into a sodden mess from the rain and river water.

As Theodore lay down he feared the miserable conditions would deny him the rest he craved. But he was so exhausted that he passed out almost as soon as his head touched the ground.

On the third day they woke and had tea and cold, cooked trout. It had rained all night and small wisps of mist steamed off of them in the morning sun.

"Should we try to dry our things while the sun is out?" asked Theodore.

Bill scanned the blue sky and noticed more dark clouds moving their way from the west.

"Wouldn't make much difference," he said, "that rain is gonna start soon anyway and you and I are gonna be up to our waist in water."

Reluctantly Theodore climbed into clothes which he'd hung by the fire. They smelled of smoke, but hadn't dried, and in the cool morning air they felt miserably clammy on his skin. His limbs ached, and even though he knew the struggle to get upstream would warm him up, he didn't look forward to the days of hard labor that he knew lay ahead of them.

Late that afternoon they dragged the pirogue out of the water and sat down heavily on the shore.

"Well, we made it," said Bill.

Theodore looked around confused.

"Made what?"

Bill nodded inland, away from the river.

"We're just a short walk from Cecil's camp. We'll leave the pirogue here for now and bring our gear over first."

Suddenly Theodore brightened. Over the last few days he had worked himself numb, stumbling along as he toiled, and their destination had no longer seemed real. Now it dawned on him that they'd just knocked out one-third of the distance.

His legs were stiff from their cramped crouch in the pirogue, and numb from the cold water, but as they walked the distance to the camp over dry land he felt his energy return.

The camp was empty, as Bill had expected, but Theodore thought he could hear the voices of the woodsmen echoing when he swung the cabin door open. Then he remembered that the last time he had been here, Coty had still been alive. The memory of it weighed him down and he sat heavily on the half-hewn log that ran along the common bunk.

He caught a flash of movement upon entering the room, but it turned out to be a small animal scurrying for cover.

"That would'a been Tavish, the camp weasel," said Bill.

Theodore watched the weasel poking his head up from behind a log and staring at him

"Who named him?" Asked Theodore.

"There was once a woodsman named Tavish, and one morning he got up early to use the privy. When he was gone this critter showed up and sat in the warm spot he'd left behind. Another woodsman looked over and said, 'Look! Tavish done turned into a weasel.' And the name stuck."

Outside it had started to pour, which made the stout cabin seem like it was God-given. It felt incredibly spacious now that it was empty, and the yard was hardly recognizable without the snow.

Bill got a fire going with some kindling Cecil had left behind, and then sent Theodore outside for some hardwood.

As he carried in a load of wood, Theodore proudly said, "This is some of the wood Coty and I cut."

Bill nodded.

After the days in the cold and two nights wrapped in wet blankets the cabin felt very cozy. The rain drummed on the cedar shingles above and streaked across the only window.

When the fire was kicking out heat they lay their blankets down in front of it, and stripped off their outer layers and hung them to dry.

Before long the blankets were dry and they stretched luxuriously on them, the intense heat lulling them to sleep.

"We'd be set up pretty good if we had some food," said Bill. He glanced out at the rain and added, "We could try for a bird but I fear you'd have no luck."

During their last night on the river it had rained hard, and neither Theodore nor Bill had had any luck procuring a meal. Theodore nodded.

"We'll get something in the morning."

Bill shook his head.

"I do have to say, Theodore, that you have an incredible aptitude for survival. I know many a woodsman who would'a complained about no food after puttin' in a day like today — not to mention the last few days."

"I have gone four days without a thing to eat," said Theodore, "and I bet I could go another four or five days if I had to."

Bill somberly looked out the window.

"Let's hope it doesn't come to that."

They got the fire burning strong and repacked their clothing as it dried. From time to time Theodore could see Tavish's eyes glittering in a corner from where he watched the intruders.

Later, they were talking about the characters they'd encountered the previous winter — everyone but Coty — and Theodore asked what they were all doing now. Most were at one logging camp or another, and some would be heading back up to the winter camp on the Oxbow — the one they were currently in — once winter set in.

Then Theodore took some paper and began writing a letter to his mother. As he signed it, he looked at Bill and read aloud the final line.

"Tired out, and wet through, hungry and cold, but having a lovely time."

As they lay down to sleep Theodore looked at Bill and thought to himself, "I can endure fatigue and hardship pretty nearly as well as these lumbermen."

In the night he felt a brush of fur against his skin and realized Tavish was snuggling up next to him. The weasel eventually settled on the blanket by his feet and went to sleep.

By morning Tavish was gone.

Theodore woke to the sounds of Bill building up the fire.

"I've got a small piece of smoked venison in my sack. It's not much, but I can make a weak soup out of it."

Theodore nodded and Bill added, "We've got a long day ahead of us, we should get something warm in our stomachs first. Why don't you see if there's any game to help fill out my soup."

About an hour later Theodore returned with a partridge breast which Bill happily added to the stew.

From Cecil's camp they still had a three mile portage before they could meet the river again. They carried the canoe to its shore first, and then returned for their gear.

The wooded country they traversed had been ravaged by a fire the year before and now lay burnt and wasted. Theodore had started the day in a confident mood, but the scorched terrain depressed him and he found his limbs heavy as they completed the distance for the third time.

His stomach growled.

It was still early in the day but the lack of vegetation left them exposed to the sun. So far the rain had been their enemy, now they wished for it to return to keep the bugs down and the heat at bay. Soon they were covered in sweat. Theodore silently followed in Bill's footsteps, awkwardly trying to match his long stride.

Theodore felt as if he was in a dream. They walked and walked until eventually they stood in front of the canoe. He deposited his load and then stepped into the wonderfully cold water and sank under.

He surfaced with a smile and looked upstream, suddenly revived, even his hunger temporarily forgotten.

"So, how much farther, Bill? How far are we from the headwaters?"

The Mainer stared up the river as if he could see that far off place where all the rivers began.

"From here I'd reckon about thirty, maybe thirty five miles to Little Munsungen Lake, and then maybe another five to cross the two lakes."

Theodore grabbed the front of the craft, ready to lead it, but Bill's laughter stopped him.

"Slow down, Theodore," said Bill. "The water here is deep enough to pole, you just sit tight and I'll see how long this deep water lasts."

For the next ten miles they managed to alternate between paddling and poling. A few times they had to portage around obstacles, but all things considered, the going wasn't bad.

At night they camped on the shore and ate a few trout that Bill caught. At times the rain picked up again, but at this point they hardly noticed it. They just kept plodding ahead.

The next morning Bill continued to pole them upstream through a weak current. For a while Theodore sat back and watched the shore pass by, but before long he was restless.

"Bill, would you allow me to operate the pole?" he asked.

"At this point I'd let you do just about anything," said Bill, "but we've got some trouble ahead and I can't see either of us poling through it."

They both looked ahead as the land sloped upward. For almost a half mile the land rose and the river ahead of them came cascading down toward them.

The force of the water coming down was strong and both men knew that leading a dugout canoe up through it would be an epic undertaking.

Bill looked over the sides of the river and shook his head in dismay.

"Not much opportunity for portaging. Only when we reach the Mooseleuk River's confluence will the flow become less."

Theodore surveyed the river and saw it for the challenge that it was.

He stepped into the water, sinking up to his waist. His buckskins had darkened from the soaking but still fit snugly.

"Mr. Sewall," said Theodore with a mischievous grin.

"Are you ready to take this hill?"

Bill nodded somberly, but held up a hand of caution.

"I will not lose my gear on this adventure. Before we begin I want this craft unloaded."

Theodore nodded and after Bill had paddled them to the shore he obediently went to the task of unloading everything. Once they'd gotten the canoe beyond the rapids they would still have to return for it.

With determined looks on their faces they began to move the pirogue upstream. Theodore led with a rope while Bill pushed from behind. The water was thigh deep, but moving fast, and it was difficult to find secure footing, let alone control the boat.

Theodore's feet slipped out from under him and he floated right into Bill. Luckily Bill saw him coming and managed to absorb the blow without getting washed downstream himself.

As Theodore stood the two men laughed at each other and tried again. The weather had turned and the rain poured down cold and dark, but the worse it got the more their spirits rose.

Each had sustained splinters and scrapes but suddenly everything seemed trivial as they both felt the headwaters were within striking distance. Even the rain pelting down on them like pellets barely captured their attention.

But then, halfway up the long hill Theodore began to struggle as the combined exertions of the last few days caught up with him. The water pounding around him was deafening, and in his exhaustion he feared that one wrong step and he might be washed all the way down the long hill.

He struggled to find a clear path, but he was so tired that he felt like he was drugged — like there was a hallucinogen in the water that compelled him to quit — to lie down and rest.

He shook his head and tried to clear his thoughts, shouting, "Come on, Bill, give me some words of inspiration...what would Mr. Longfellow say about a situation like this?"

The top was within sight, yet he now questioned whether they would make it.

"Honestly, I think Mr. Longfellow might think we're crazy..." Bill went to say more but lost his balance and slipped under water.

Suddenly, only Bill's hands, still gripping the boat, were visible to Theodore. He watched the white knuckles while Bill fought to regain his footing. Soon he resurfaced, water flowing out of his beard.

Then Bill stood tall, rising out of the water as he glared at the rapids like he was looking at a man who had just struck him. He looked coldly at Theodore and then upstream again.

Suddenly, Bill was drawn into the same passion that had possessed Theodore all morning. Since they began their journey, he had tried to show the river respect and be aware of its dangers.

But now he was mad, and he just wanted to have at it.

Theodore tensed, unsure of this side of Bill.

Staring at the rapid they were about to storm past, Bill said, "*Half a league, half a league, half a league onward...*"

Theodore grinned as he recognized the first verse of Tennyson's Charge of the Light Brigade.

Grabbing the bow of the canoe Theodore steered it to the left of the next rapid.

He shouted, "*All in the valley of Death, Rode the six hundred!*"

Bill gave the canoe a mighty shove. The front of the craft rode up on a rock but the momentum sent it shooting upstream.

Theodore guided it forward, singing out the next line.

"Forward, the Light Brigade! Charge for the guns..."

With bold strides Bill forced his way upstream to help Theodore steady the canoe before the current sent it back. One on each side now, they pushed forward again, fighting the current for each foot gained.

Theodore looked at Bill and saw his exertion. Bill stole a quick glance sideways at Theodore and they both shouted together.

"Into the valley of Death, Rode the six hundred."

About a hundred yards ahead they saw the Mooseleuk Stream flowing in from the right. The water sprayed up and crashed down all around them. They reached an eddy, and while he steadied the boat, Theodore looked around at the angry white-water chaos that engulfed them. He continued with Tennyson's poem.

"Cannon to the right of them, Cannon to left of them, Cannon in front of them...Boldly they rode and well, into the jaws of Death, Into the mouth of Hell, Rode the six hundred."

With a concerted effort the men forced the pirogue forward, beyond the confluence and into the smaller stream that would lead them to the lake.

They stopped to catch their breath and looked downstream over the rapids they'd just overcome.

Bill shook the water from his beard and then continued with yet another verse from the poem.

"Was there a man dismay'd...theirs not to make reply, Theirs not to reason why, Theirs but to do and die, Into the Valley of Death rode the six hundred."

And together they added, *"When can their glory fade? O the wild charge they made!"*

As they lay panting on the river's bank, Theodore looked down at the cascades they had just come through.

"At least that is now part of our past," he said.

Bill laughed weakly, his exhaustion momentarily forgotten. "Are you forgettin' we have to return for our gear?"

The young man sighed and stood up stiffly for the return journey, but Bill stopped him.

"Wait, Theodore, there's no rush."

Gratefully, Theodore sank to the ground again.

"I think we need a fire before we continue," said Bill.

"And some food," added Theodore. "I will see if I can find a partridge..." His words trailed off as he realized his guns were at the bottom of the long hill.

"My guns are down below," he said with regret.

"Along with my fishin' gear," said Bill.

And then Bill sighed as he sank back in exhaustion, adding, "And my fire startin' kit."

The rain had started again, and for the first time both men were too tired to laugh off their fatigue. Theodore's stomach was growling so loud he thought Bill could actually hear it.

After ten minutes Bill sat up.

"Not much sense in waitin' any longer," he said. He got to his feet and started the return journey. Theodore followed.

Theodore tried to hop from rock to rock, but the banks of the river were steep and he soon found himself in the water again. Several times he lost his footing and was washed down by the current, frantically clawing at passing rocks. He eventually stopped himself and surfaced; his teeth chattered as he stumbled out of the water.

Bill's progress was slower, and more methodical, but even he lost his footing once and went under.

When they finally arrived at their pile of belongings Bill looked at Theodore and solemnly said, "This next section is critical if we plan on succeeding on this expedition."

He pointed at the gear and added, "We don't have much, but we need it all. Without the guns or fishin' lines we're gonna be hungry."

He smiled weakly, "And I mean a lot hungrier than you are now. And if we lose the fire startin' kit it'll be a cold ride out as well."

Theodore nodded. They shouldered their gear and over the next two hours they slowly—painstakingly—made their way up the long, cold hill. The rain had become a steady downpour, and in their weakened state they felt the additional water might actually wash them downstream where they wouldn't even have a canoe to retreat with. Stubbornly, they fought for each forward step and then held on bitterly lest the river take it back.

When they finally reached the canoe again both men collapsed to the ground in their wet clothes, too tired to light a fire or hunt for food.

Theodore woke some time later to the sound of Bill trying to get a fire going. In that cold world where he lay shivering in his soaked buckskins, the sound of a match striking and taking flame was food for the soul. It was late afternoon now and he knew that soon, darkness would descend on them. Silently, he grabbed the shotgun and set off to find some game.

He was so tired that he could barely lift the gun, and he wondered how successful he would be at hunting considering his muscles were bruised and spent, and his hands were shaking from fatigue.

In the end he returned with his pockets filled with blueberries, but no game. Still, he was so hungry that even one berry caused a wild sensation in his mouth, and a surge of energy in his veins.

They ate what Theodore had collected, lay on their sides by the fire, and were asleep in minutes. The dark sky let loose a cool mist just before dawn, luckily the heavy rain stayed at bay.

By the time they set off the next morning, Theodore could see that the flow of water had diminished; several hours had passed since the last downpour, but the going was still difficult. The stream was now less than twenty feet wide and for long distances they were forced to carry or drag the pirogue when it became too shallow to paddle or pole.

Within an hour of entering the water the rain began again. At times it stopped, but then the mosquitoes and midges came out and feasted on their necks, their faces, their ears and especially the tops of their hands.

Having spent several foodless nights, Bill called for an early stop so they could hunt and fish. Theodore set off with his shotgun while Bill dropped his line in a quiet pool of water and patiently waited for the first strike. Luckily it didn't take long, and soon Bill had a basket full of trout.

Just as they began to sizzle over the fire Theodore returned with a rabbit.

That night they feasted like kings, eating everything they'd caught. Theodore crunched on the rabbit legs—after he'd stripped them of all their meat—as he tried to get every ounce of nutrition available, and they ate all the trout Bill had caught, leaving nothing for breakfast.

The scenery around them was compelling and raw, with virgin pines towering above them and clouds floating low, obscuring the tops of many of the surrounding hills.

During the entire time they'd seen no traces of man and very little of game. The only animals present in abundance seemed to be beavers, but even then they saw only their dams, not the animals themselves.

"I feel like we are the only living things in this area," said Theodore.

"Maybe we are," replied Bill. "I told you, beyond the headwaters there's nothin'."

The next day they came to another confluence where the Millinocket Stream came in on the left. Here they veered right.

"Almost there, Theodore," said Bill. "I'd guess tomorrow we hit Little Munsungen Lake."

Theodore nodded, slightly dazed. He felt that his entire life had been condensed down to this one journey, and everything else had faded away. And even the days of the journey had blended into one long effort...always wet and cold, little sleep, sporadic food. His body felt as if it had never known another life.

They came across several dams, which appeared deserted but they still had to portage around them, and a few log jams too which made the going slow.

Each time they had to empty the boat, carry it to a manageable spot, and then return for their gear. At night they ate trout, which Bill continued to catch regularly, and bread that he cooked over the fire.

The quietness and the lack of people or even large game slowly worked on Theodore's subconscious and made him edgy. He wondered if this journey would cost him his sanity before it was over.

The next morning they reached the source of the Munsungen Stream — Little Munsungen Lake; here the water was too shallow to be passable so they dragged the boat through ankle deep water until they reached the lake itself.

The two men stumbled along, severely exhausted but neither willing to quit. The closer they got to the lakes the more it rained. They crossed Little Munsungen lake in a trance and it finally opened into the larger, Munsungen Lake. They continued to paddle numbly, automatically, as if they had forgotten how to stop this forward momentum.

Theodore had the feeling that the land around him was tilted, sending all of this water at them, and if he lost his footing he might just get washed downstream, beyond the cascades and the oxbow, all the way to Masardis where Scout waited for them.

For a brief minute the sun broke through and they caught a glimpse of the vast size of the lake. But then, as if to mock them, the clouds unleashed the fiercest downpour they'd experienced on the entire journey.

As the rain slowed down it got quiet on the lake; the raindrops whispered as they hit the water all around them. There was several inches of water in the canoe, but it wasn't enough to swamp it and they were each too tired to bail. After the punishing struggle it had taken them to get here their arrival seemed unreal.

Theodore felt depressed when he had expected to be elated. Low grey clouds hung over the lake, denying him the view of the far shore or the mountains beyond it.

He tried to shrug it off and just paddle along with Bill, noting his arms could just barely hold up the paddle. The urge to eat a good meal and sleep somewhere warm became overbearing — but at this point both appeared as far out of reach as the numerous stars that covered the night sky.

With slow but determined strokes Bill steered them to a quiet cove. They beached the pirogue and made camp.

Chapter Twenty-seven
The Munsungen Lakes

On the shore of the lake they sat under a tarp and surveyed the land. All was grey and subdued. Nothing moved but the rain.

Theodore could see low hills around them, covered in pine. The shore was rocky, and as he explored their surroundings he found pockets of mud with tracks in them, faded and filled with water.

He did feel like they were at some altitude and the way the land tilted toward the river made it look like it could be the start of a great water system, but in his exhaustion he just couldn't image the whole of it.

He sat back down in their camp and stared out over the water.

Glancing over at Bill he noticed the Maine woodsman looked pretty worn as well.

"Round here it don't get much wetter than this," said Bill. Their clothes were soaked and until the rain stopped there was little hope of anything drying.

"I would hope not," replied Theodore with a sad tone to his voice.

Bill looked him over and smiled. The young man was almost dazed in his fatigue. It was clear he'd forgotten why he'd come on this adventure in the first place.

"From the look of you I'd say you´re not findin' this place everything you thought it might be. Is that correct?"

Theodore watched the small waves that beached about ten feet away, their hiss drowned out by the downpour.

"I am sure it is a beautiful place, Bill," said Theodore, "but I thought I would feel different when I got here."

"Well, you did good gettin' here, and it wasn't easy."

Bill looked down at the waves and added, "And you stayed right with me the whole time — you know you did — and I wouldn't lie about something like that."

Theodore nodded.

"So what's botherin' you, son?"

It took awhile for the young man to speak, but they had all the time in the world. Bill noticed his moccasins had worn through in several big holes, and he could see cuts on his feet where they were exposed.

"We have completed an incredible journey and I should be rejoicing, yet part of me thinks I should continue...that I should keep pushing until I truly collapse."

Bill laughed loudly, the depth of his humor bringing Theodore around somewhat.

"Theodore, you really are something. You're gonna go far in this life no matter what you do, if for no other reason than the fact that you cannot stop yourself."

The young man's brows furrowed in anger.

"But how does one know when to stop? Why shouldn't we just push on until the next headwaters, or the next range? Why stop?"

The young man looked off, and somewhere deep inside he knew that this question would plague him for the rest of his life. But then he shrugged, and said, "How do I know that my body will not fail me down the line? Can I count on it from now on?"

Bill moved his head from side to side as if trying to work out a pulled muscle. He stretched.

"All I can say is you just keep livin' and hope for the best."

Theodore stared out over the water.

The rain continued to pour down.

Bill shook the tarp and adjusted a corner. There was just enough room for them both to sit under it.

"When this rain lightens up we can see about a shelter."

Theodore nodded.

Bill seated himself again and said, "You remember me mentioning my friend, Ben Brown, when we were back in Island Falls?"

"He was in the war, I believe," replied Theodore, "you mentioned him on my first visit and said he created the walnut ring that Emlen had found on your table."

Bill smiled, "*Ayuh*, but there was a lot more to Ben than that. I met Ben when I was young and we became instant friends. He had an honest face and dark hair. His mother was an Indian, and I guess you'd have to say he looked Indian too. Any spare time when we weren't at work we were fishin' or huntin'."

Bill paused for a minute before continuing.

"When the war started Ben left with the others, but I was too young, so I stayed behind. I didn't see him for a long time...eventually I heard that he'd been taken prisoner. At the time I'd come down with diphtheria and was fighting my own battle.

"I've often thought it interesting that while I was burnin' with fever he was goin' through his own terrible experience. Eventually I found out that he'd been in a close fight and been struck on the head with a musket that broke in the skull and rendered him senseless for some time.

"He said that when he came to he realized he was in water. He heard the rebel sergeant say, 'Damn him, if he doesn't keep up stick a bayonet through him.' And that's when he realized that a comrade was holdin' him up and wadin' to a boat. The man who helped him was named Hackett, and he was from Patten.

"Eventually they reached the prison in Columbia, South Carolina, but he got no medical attention there other than being allowed to wash his hair which was caked with blood.

"When we received the letter sayin' that he got paroled I was still confined to the house. I was very weak and when I tried to walk around my hands and feet would become numb as though they were asleep.

"The letter told us that he was wounded and would be home as soon as he could get there. I do believe on the way someone took pity on him and paid his passage on the train. The man who'd bought his ticket was himself poor, and Ben promised to repay him."

The rain had begun to slow down and soon it was only a drizzle. Bill looked the sky over and continued his story.

"Anyway, in due time he returned and paid me a visit; I could walk across the floor only with great difficulty, and when I fell, which I did frequently, I had to crawl to a chair before I could rise again. He wore a bandage around his head and moved a bit slower than I remembered. He said he couldn't remember much about the war previous to the experience — which he thought was probably for the best — and as I recall he never did get those memories back. "

Bill smiled at the thought of the two of them.

"We were quite a sight, him and I. I had also lost my voice and my eyesight was diminished – I could only read with the aid of my father's glasses. But since my two brothers had died and all the young people whom I had known were dead or gone to war I was very glad to have my old friend back."

The Mainer scratched his beard and added, "Even if he was a feeble specimen like myself we cheered ourselves by talkin' about what we would do when we got able. He had been to war and I had been to so many funerals, but we were hopeful and had good courage."

The mist around them had evaporated and the sky opened up a bit. Through the departing storm clouds they could see blue sky, but it was late afternoon and the light was already fading.

Bill reached behind him and grabbed his sack, and from deep inside it he withdrew his fire kit. As he unwrapped it Theodore watched anxiously, hoping the tinder and matches had stayed dry.

They had, and Bill laid everything out in preparation.

He got up and retrieved a dead pine, only about three feet high, which lay along the shore. He shook it vigorously to get the water off it and then started breaking it into small sticks.

When he had enough kindling he dug a small hole near the far end of the tarp. In it he placed an over-turned piece of birch bark and then his tinder on top of that.

Before striking the match he tested the wind and even though there was hardly a breeze he turned his back to it and squatted over the hole.

The match took, flickered for a moment, and then stayed lit—its brightness seemed completely out of place in this drenched world—and when he placed it under the tinder that took as well. As soon as he saw the flame growing strong, he began adding small twigs.

He smiled at Theodore and said, "Always keep your fire kit buried deep and well protected."

Theodore nodded and stared at the flickering flame, deeply cherishing its tender warmth after ten hours in the cold.

"It seemed like old times at first," Bill continued his story. "One of our neighbors had a sickly old horse and Ben and I offered to dispose of it—our primary interest to use it as bait.

"We led it into the deep woods and up the Mattawamkeag River and shot it, set our traps, and then began the long walk back. I believe we'd each overestimated our strength and it was a long time comin'. We were both so exhausted when we reached Island Falls that we each went straight to bed.

"Through the course of that winter we'd return again and again to the carcass—sometimes seein' tracks—but our traps were always empty. As we dragged our weak bodies back to Island Falls I often fell repeatedly. Ben teased me that I was becoming clumsy.

"Ben was not as inept, but I noticed through the long winter that his strength was returnin' slower than mine. Our remainin' family and friends all supported us and did everything they could. They had all lost loved ones to either diphtheria or the war and I think they needed us to survive for their own peace of mind.

"My brother Sam had a boy and girl die while I was sick, and two of his wife's sisters had come to help, one older and one younger, and they had both died of the disease. Hardly a family escaped without losin' some children, and I knew one family that lost five young ones."

Bill added some more fuel to the fire and then stared hard at Theodore.

"You asked if your body would ever fail you again?" said Bill.

Theodore simply nodded.

"Well, I don't reckon I know how to answer that," said Bill. "My personal experience leaves me questionin'. Through that long winter I got better but Ben didn't. He was sure glad to be home, and he made it a point to go check the traps with me whenever I went, but each time it was more difficult for him.

"When the spring came and the days got longer I began to feel my strength return, but Ben caught a cold and on rainy days he had bad coughing spells. We never spoke of it, but I could see in his eyes that he was fading."

Again Bill fed the fire and delayed his story.

"I used to think survival was about havin' the will to live, but I don't know anymore. Ben wanted to live and it seemed to me we should have had an equal chance...he had an iron will, a good constitution and a cheerful disposition.

"He was clever too! The guards had left him with a jackknife when they searched him at the prison, and with it he carved rings of wood and other trinkets. Like I said, he was likeable, and soon he made friends with the guards and traded for food. But he couldn't think his way out of his injury.

"Late one spring day we walked to check our traps and saw bear tracks everywhere around it. We reset the traps and returned in a few days, and sure enough there was a good-sized she-bear in it. Over the next few weeks we returned again and again and in all I believe we brought in five bear — with a two dollar bounty on each bear plus money for each pelt, we felt we'd done well."

He smiled proudly. "Ben took his money and sent it to that man who'd paid his train fare."

Bill looked up at the sky again and noticed it had darkened. The sun was gone and the temperature had begun to drop.

"I believe that was the last good time we had together. All summer he weakened and one evening late in the fall Ben and I went over to my brother Sam's. On the return journey he had a bad coughing fit that led into a hemorrhage.

"From then on he was confined to bed and he failed rapidly. Late in March of '63 he died. He's buried in our family lot as he had no livin' family ties."

Theodore looked over the water which appeared ominous after this sad tale. The rain began again, now colder and with a bite.

Bill leaned forward, making eye contact with Theodore, and said, "You just keep chasin' your dreams and don't worry about your body keepin' up. You lead, it'll follow."

Theodore nodded.

Bill looked over the small pile of kindling he had gathered and then at the rain falling around them.

"We're gonna need a good deal more wood if we hope to stay dry tonight," said Bill.

He pulled his sack a bit closer and reached inside to pull out his hatchet.

Handing it to Theodore, he nodded toward the nearby woods. "Theodore, would you mind choppin' us some more fuel for this fire?"

Not waiting for an answer, he added, "The drier the better."

Theodore took the hatchet and walked off into the rain. On the way he remembered another cold night with Bill when he'd refused to let him chop wood.

The next morning was clear and bright and as the sun rose across the lake the light reflecting off it was blinding. Theodore walked to the shore, his body stiff, and looked across the water.

By draping the tarp over the staff they'd used for polling Bill made a side-less shelter, but the constant rain had soaked the ground and their blankets had soon gotten wet as well.

Theodore cleaned his glasses but could still not see clear. In the middle of the lake he thought he saw something—something big—but he had great difficulty focusing.

And then he glimpsed a bull moose, standing up to his shoulders in the water. It had a massive wrack that dripped water and a long trail of fur hanging from his chin. As it exhaled a puff of mist shot out its nostrils.

The moose looked in Theodore's direction, but then the strain of looking into the glare was too much and he had to blink and wipe his eyes. He tried to look again, but the glare was almost blinding. He closed his eyes for a solid minute, and when he opened them again the moose was gone and he wondered if he'd imagined it all. Although he scanned the shore of the lake all around him, he never glimpsed the animal again.

As he looked around the alpine lake he saw how everything steamed and glittered. The shore was lined with immense pines, and just behind them stood a few oaks that blazed with the colors of fall.

Bill joined him and looked over the lake.

Theodore said, "This truly is a magical place."

Bill nodded, "I never doubted we'd make it here."

Theodore turned to look at Bill directly. "I would not have quit until we reached these lakes, but it appeared at times to be a destination that was unobtainable...like honor or virtue sometimes appear to be."

The older man smiled and quoted.

"To be ambitious of true honor, of the true glory and perfection of our natures, is the very principle of incentive and virtue."

Theodore thought for a moment and said, "President Lincoln?"

Bill shook his head.

"No sir, it was Walter Scott again."

They remained by the lake for a few days, hunting and fishing while their clothes dried. Theodore bagged a few ducks, trout were plentiful, and thankfully the sun came out and quickly dried everything.

When they had finally recuperated and once again loaded the pirogue to return they wore dry clothes and carried a good supply of smoked trout. The rain had left the rivers swollen and easier to navigate.

Going downstream, the river supplied most of the forward thrust. And some sections that they had had to portage around or drag the pirogue through they now found had enough water to support the dugout canoe.

Soon they had passed the confluence of the Munsungen and Millinocket Streams, and they sped downstream even faster. Theodore laughed at the ease with which they swiftly shot through sections that had taken them hours to fight their way upstream.

The two men were a ragged-looking lot. Neither had had a proper meal or bed for some time, but they were on their swift way home and the world seemed a vastly kinder place than just a few days ago.

Theodore sat in the front, exhilarated, and spouted poetry and quotations for much of the afternoon. Although Bill was busy steering the craft he sang along, his deep bass voice joining Theodore's.

Only one day after they'd left the lakes they came upon the long hill on which they had recited the Charge of the Light Brigade and as soon as they began the descent they shouted the words again.

By back-paddling, and maneuvering through the eddy's, Bill controlled their speed and the ride through the rapids felt not as dangerous as Theodore had feared.

Before they were ready for it they were again at the three mile portage to Cecil's winter camp. This time they carried their packs and the canoe at the same time to save themselves the six mile return hike.

They paused at the entrance to the camp. Theodore should have welcomed this first shelter in days. But he was overcome with nostalgia and the knowledge that he most likely wouldn't be back.

The long common bed appeared ridiculous without any other occupants so they put down their blankets closer to the fire, cleaning the area first with Coty's handmade broom.

Once they had their clothes drying on the stink pole they both quickly fell asleep. The heat from the fire was luxurious, and the crackling as the kindling took, hypnotic.

Now, in this safe and warm place, they finally allowed the exhaustion of the entire journey, the tiredness they had pushed aside so many times since they had loaded the pirogue into the buckboard in Island Falls and said goodbye to Wilmot, to overtake them.

Tavish was notably absent.

The next morning they were on the river early. They moved slower now and didn't cover as many miles as they could have had they not each been worn out.

In the previous days Theodore had learned how to work with Bill, paddling backwards when he needed help navigating through the tangle of boulders and rapids. He now watched what came their way and reacted instinctively, and while paddling they wasted few words and instead worked together like they'd been doing it for years.

"I feel like a native, like some noble savage on the river," Theodore rejoiced at his new canoeing skills.

"That's all fine," replied Bill, "but just remember that *the true nobles of this land were not the rich, but the farmers and backwoodsman who cleared the land and worked the soil.*"

Theodore laughed. "How could I forget that, in fact, Mr. Longfellow has not been far from me since I first entered these Maine woods."

As much as they both longed to complete the journey there was still work to be done: they had to navigate through or over beaver dams and log jams, portage beyond a few rocky sections, and every so often Theodore had to hop out and help lead the canoe through shallow water.

Both men had become silent; they'd each spoken what was closest to their hearts and the rain had washed away any remaining thoughts.

Early one morning they came upon the simple house where they'd started their river journey. The owners were away, so they hitched Scout to the buckboard, loaded up the pirogue and started for Island Falls.

As they left, Theodore said, "It's too bad the Pollards are away. I would have paid almost any price for another piece of her hot apple pie."

When they finally limped onto Bill's porch in Island Falls Theodore collapsed into a chair, sighed, and then paused to reflect on what they'd done. At the goal of their journey he had been depressed and saw no value to it, but now the adventure had expanded in his mind, and for the first time he took pride in it.

He looked down at his moccasins and saw that his feet had worn through them, and although his buckskins had held up, they now looked worn and in need of some repairs.

Bill sat down heavily on a rocker and started untying his muddy boots. When he had removed them he peeled off his damp socks and wiggled his toes.

Theodore wiggled his toes as well, although he had yet to take off the moccasins. Having worn clean through on both feet, they now rode up near his ankles like a pair of gaiters.

"Looks like I'm gonna have to make you some new moccasins."

Theodore grinned and did his best imitation of the Maine accent as he said, "*Ayuh.*"

Chapter Twenty-eight
Canoe Trip to the Station

Theodore sensed that this last visit had been different than the previous two and didn't want it to end. He'd broken through to something new and even once they returned to Island Falls he constantly pestered Bill to find new adventures.

Bill did his best to entertain the young man, but his ambition now knew no bounds. Be it hiking twenty miles, sleeping in the open, or dragging a pirogue up a raging stream, Theodore was ready for it.

One day as they paddled along the shore of Mattawamkeag Lake, they passed the outlet where the Mattawamkeag River began.

"Where does that lead?" asked Theodore.

"Well," said Bill, "It flows for about a hundred miles before emptying into the Penobscot River, just past Kingman."

"Kingman?" asked Theodore. "Why, I do believe the train stops at Kingman."

Bill nodded and said, "It does, just south of Mattawamkeag Station."

Theodore scratched his stubble, which was rapidly growing into a beard.

"Why not just canoe down to the station then?" asked Theodore.

Bill knew he was once again in trouble.

He said, "By buckboard it is only a distance of thirty-two miles to the Mattawamkeag Station, by river—like I said—it would be close to one hundred to Kingman."

Seeing the light in Theodore's eyes he shook his head and laughed.

"Theodore, you are truly tireless. Why not rest here for a day and just go by buckboard? Besides, the rivers have dropped after that rain and you wouldn't be able to canoe the whole way…you'd have to portage and drag the canoe a good part."

But Theodore's smile failed to waver and Bill resigned to the fact that he would be taking the young Harvard student on one last journey before he put him on the train.

Wilmot accompanied them on the trip to Kingman, and although it meant tighter quarters when on the water, having the extra man made portaging much less of an ordeal.

Rain fell constantly, and there were many stretches where they had to carry everything, but they were going downstream, not up, and they made the journey easily in three days.

At night they set up a tarp and kept a low fire burning near one end while they told stories and quoted poetry. Theodore tried to get Wilmot to recite some Whitman, but he remained silent, his eyes glittering with the reflection of the fire. This underlined to Theodore just how much Wilmot had opened up on the cold night of the caribou chase, standing by the fire in subzero temperatures.

Late that night Theodore woke and listened to the sounds of the forest around him. Downstream from them he heard an owl calling out, and a large pine behind their camp creaked in the wind. It was still several hours before dawn, and the Mainers were sleeping soundly.

He lay there, remembering the different animal encounters he'd had since coming to Maine, little over a year ago; and it wasn't just their physical forms that played out in his mind, but their essence as well: the vitality of the buck in the snow-covered pines, the cunningness of the trapped bear by the orchard, or the determination to live that he saw in the eyes of the caribou. He also remembered the moose he'd glimpsed one glittering morning, and how it slowly faded away like some creature of the mystic.

His thoughts lingered longest on the wolves – the one he'd seen at Bible Point, and the one that had run along the pung on their winter journey to the Oxbow. He remembered the gaze in their eyes and knew it would stay with him long after the journey was over.

When sleep still didn't come he thought of all the people he'd encountered: he saw Bill leaning over a fire while preparing his bean hole beans, and Wilmot watching him while he strutted around in snowshoes for the first time, and then Barry whispering to him behind the logging camp as he tried to trick him. With a smile he remembered the expressions on the faces of the woodsmen as he told them how he'd scurried up a tree after being scared by the frozen wolf.

With sadness he reviewed the time he'd spent with Coty trapping the lynx—and later on that fateful day when he'd fallen through the ice.

His mind settled on an image of himself when he'd first come north, and he realized just how much Maine and its inhabitants had changed him.

When he saw the first traces of dawn he added a few logs to the glowing embers of their fire, and lay there listening to it crackle as he waited for Bill and Wilmot to wake up. Before long he knew they would be on the river again, and soon the journey would be over.

The thought saddened him and he lay back quietly, hoping to revel a bit longer in this wilderness where he now felt at home, and delay the departure.

When they finally did pull into Kingman Theodore felt like a true explorer: his clothing was worn, his beard full, and although he may not have called himself a local, he didn't feel green anymore.

They dragged the canoe ashore by a lumber mill and left it with the paddles and some of their gear stowed inside. A few workers watched them, noting their confident manner.

After breakfast in Kingman the three men waited at the station for Theodore's train to arrive. Bill and Wilmot sat on a bench, while Theodore paced with relentless energy. In this last year he had developed a momentum that Bill thought would project him right through life.

Bill watched the young man, remembering the frail, skinny youngster that had arrived on his porch only a year before.

"So you feel good, Theodore, eh?" asked Bill. "Ready to take on the world?"

"Yes, Bill, I feel as strong as a bull."

Both of the Mainers laughed at his response—not in mockery, but in joyful respect. They had both seen just what he could do when he set his mind to a task.

For a moment Bill eyed his young charge and then said, "If someone had asked me what you were capable of last year at this time I never would'a dreamed that you had it in you to complete the expeditions we undertook."

Theodore absorbed the comment with a look of confidence and satisfaction. He weighed his next words carefully before speaking.

"I want to thank you, Bill—and Wilmot—for what you have done for me. I wanted to prove that I could overcome this weak body that has always let me down, and you have helped me with that."

He stared at Bill before adding, "I also needed to know that I could measure up to strong, tested men like you both."

The two men nodded and shook hands with Theodore, but said nothing; the look in their eyes was enough to affirm Theodore.

After an awkward moment Bill asked, "So what do you plan on doing now, Mr. Roosevelt?"

Theodore took a deep breath, his eyes alive with an energetic sparkle.

"I feel now there are great things in my future, and through your help I have realized that my body will not prevent me from obtaining them if it is my will."

Bill stood tall and looked down at Theodore.

"Well, you've managed to keep up with us, in our own environment, and proved yourself our equal. I don't believe I could say that about many men—especially city folk like yourself."

Theodore thanked him for his words and they sat, the three men remaining silent for a bit.

Eventually Bill added, "Theodore, when you leave here I want you to remember us—not just Wilmot and I—but the woodsmen you encountered, and the old timers, and even the gnarled old spruce towering above us.

"A new century is approaching, and it'll be forged by young men like you, but now is the time to look around and see what is passing. The old time people are nearly all gone, and as I look about me at the few like myself who are left I realize that the old forests are disappearing too."

Theodore smiled easily and said, "I will do my best, Bill, to remember everything, but on this day I cannot see how I will ever forget our Charge of the Light Brigade, or how Longfellow's Challenge of Thor accompanied me on the long trail that caribou laid out for me."

Bill added, "Or how the wisdom of Walter Scott allowed you to cross Katahdin's knife's edge without worry."

To Theodore's surprise, Wilmot quietly added, "Or how Mr. Whitman helped you through a cold night."

Theodore dropped his formality and embraced Bill just as the train blew its whistle and came into view. He then shook Wilmot's hand—and then embraced him as well. When the train pulled up the three men stood next to Theodore's gear, waiting for the metal beast to come to a halt.

Bill looked down on Theodore, proudly, "I see now that you are ready for bigger things. I can see it clearly. And I'm certain you're on the verge of gettin' pulled off into a larger world that might not include Maine."

Theodore held up his hand to silence Bill.

"I will always have time for a quick getaway to the Maine woods."

Bill nodded with a smile.

"*Ayuh*, I sure hope so, but I just want you to know that if you ever decide to set off on another adventure—wherever it may be—all you have to do is send for Wilmot and I and we will be at your side."

Speechless for once, Theodore nodded and boarded the train.

As he turned to wave Bill recited a verse from The Saga of King Olaf.

"*Olaf the king, one summer morn, Blew a blast on his bugle-horn, Sending his signal through the land.*"

.

Chapter Twenty-nine
Alice

Upon returning to Boston Theodore wasted no time saddling Lightfoot and making his way to the Harvard Campus. He felt in the very marrow of his bones that his entire future lay ahead of him. All that was needed was a little push and it would come into focus.

Lightfoot took to his mood easily — his eagerness was contagious — although the travelers whom they overtook on the road there didn't appreciate it.

Various horses and carriages made their way across the campus, but all moved casually, some with an air of importance. Not so with Theodore and Lightfoot who tore across the landscaped lawns, short-cutting the pathways.

Dickey watched them approach as he sat waiting on the steps of the Porcellian Club. From the distance he saw the horse rise up on its hind legs, rearing in response to an obstacle, but the rider held on tightly and shouted out to continue.

It wasn't until the rider dismounted his horse and tied off to a tree that Dickey realized it was Roosevelt.

Appalled, he said, "My God, Roosevelt, what has gotten into you?"

Theodore laughed.

"It is just good to be back."

He embraced his friend, who remained rather stiff, still staring at Lightfoot tied to the tree.

He said, "Why, might I ask, have you tied off to a tree — like an Indian savage — when there's a perfectly good livery nearby?"

Again Theodore laughed.

"I have someone delivering my Tilbury to this location and I wanted her ready."

"A *Tilbury*? My goodness, you've gone and bought a *dog-cart*?"

Theodore frowned at the word, thinking Tilbury had a much more romantic sound to it.

"Yes, and it should be here soon, so let us get some breakfast. I am starving."

As they entered the Porcellian Club, Theodore put an arm around his friend. "While we eat I must tell you of my adventures on the Aroostook River and the Munsungen Lakes."

An hour later they returned to Lightfoot, and from the look on Dickey's face it appeared that Theodore had talked the entire time.

"...so once we left the Oxbow region we still had a good journey to the lakes!"

Dickey asked, "How far away was...," but never finished his question. They both stopped in their tracks as they looked at Lightfoot, who now stood harnessed to a two-wheeled cart.

The cart's black lacquer shone in the morning light, gaudily reflecting two gleaming lamps that were suspended near the front of the carriage. It was a small vehicle, but very elegant.

Lightfoot waited — a bit impatiently — in a harness connecting the horse to the cart by two long, curving poles. After the thunderous charge from earlier it seemed the horse found its current situation a bit indignant.

"You do realize that you'll be the first on the Harvard Campus with one of these?"

Theodore nodded

"I have been training Lightfoot on our grounds in New York, and I feel quite ready."

He looked at the horse and added, "Lightfoot does not seem particularly taken by the idea of haulage but he does fine."

"Good," replied Dickey, "it wouldn't do to see you made a spectacle of." Then he hastily added, "And you do realize that these carts are known to have an erratic center of gravity?"

Young Roosevelt looked at his friend for a moment before replying. Every vehicle he'd ever driven had had four wheels and this was a change, but the thought of it — seemingly balancing on air as you are pulled along — was intoxicating, and he wanted it.

"I told you, Dickey, I have already been riding it in New York."

Theodore shook the carriage with his hand, testing its stability, and then climbed in.

"It is really not that different from staying afloat in a canoe, or a pirogue."

"And what, might I ask, is a *pirogue?*" asked Dickey. But Theodore didn't hear him. He grabbed the whip from its sprocket.

"See? You must hold the reins with your hands extended...like you are offering someone flowers," said Theodore. "And the reins should be flicked, like casting a fly."

"Off you go then," said Dickey, as he gently grabbed Lightfoot's bridle and led him onto the path. The two wheels pivoted behind him and spun around but Theodore remained upright, poised in place.

He flicked his wrist and Lightfoot responded to the light nick by rising up and lifting his front feet about a foot off the ground. Then he leaned into the harness and fell into a trot, quickly disappearing down the road.

Theodore and Lightfoot drew quite a spectacle as it appeared that they'd lost the back half of a wagon in their impatient ride.

And it wasn't just the design that fascinated observers. Without a back axle or a load to carry the Tilbury looked like it was propelling itself, moving faster than the other vehicles.

When Theodore and Lightfoot finally pulled up to the Saltonstall estate Theodore spotted Alice and her mother on the front lawn. As he approached, he could see her mother turning her head at the arriving vehicle, lifting her brows and frowning.

She said something to Alice and then returned indoors.

Theodore had visited several times since his return, and this was the first sign he'd seen that he may not be welcome.

Theodore waved and Alice met him by the driveway. As she inspected his cart, her hands followed the smooth black curves of the seat. Then she wrinkled her forehead and looked behind the seat for a cover.

"Is there no top? What if it rains?"

Quickly Theodore came to the defense of his vehicle.

"The top is still being designed, but I should have it next week."

She nodded and looked where, if she was to ride with him, her feet would go. Then she noticed a small blanket, neatly folded on the floor. It was barely big enough to cover both of them.

"And I would think I would be cold without more blankets."

Theodore nodded, a bit dumbfounded by her lack of enthusiasm. She looked back at the house and took a breath.

"Do you realize, Theodore, that everyone will notice you now when you come to visit me? This is very conspicuous."

"And what is wrong with that?" he asked defiantly.

"What is wrong is that my debut is approaching and you make it appear that we are engaged," she said impatiently.

"W...well, we are engaged," stammered Theodore.

Alice looked him in the eye.

She waited a moment before speaking, aware that her words would hurt him.

"My dear Theodore, you have asked me to marry you, but I have not yet agreed."

The words tore his heart into pieces. He tried to speak, but was unable. As he stepped off of the Tilbury he felt like the ground was about to disappear beneath him.

He looked into her soft eyes, imploring her to save him.

Alice leaned next to him, and whispered.

"Theodore, you must be patient. I cannot have a debut if I am engaged; and my parents want this."

He nodded, his gaze on the ground, then turned and climbed back into the Tilbury and drove away.

Through the months of fall Alice cooled even more. Dickey visited Theodore at his Harvard apartment and tried to console him, but it was pointless.

"Oh, the changeableness of the female mind!" lamented Theodore as he paced his rooms.

He stalled and stared at a photo he kept on his desk. In it he posed with Alice, and Dickey's sister, Rose.

Theodore blushed slightly as he said, "In the beginning I did not really think I could win her."

He picked up a pair of slippers by the foot of his desk and stalled again as he remembered the night Alice gave them to him.

When he continued his voice shook slightly.

"Now I feel I may lose my mind at the mere thought of losing her."

Dickey sat on a couch and rested an arm on the ebony armrest. He motioned for Theodore to sit.

"Rest, my good friend. Sit."

Reluctantly, Theodore complied and settled into a chair.

"Now you do understand that her parents are set on having her debut, correct?"

Theodore nodded.

Dickey continued, "Well the entire idea of a debut is to show off ones daughter to the eligible bachelors."

Horrified, Theodore's jaw dropped.

"Dickey, I was under the assumption that you were trying to make me feel better...or that you might have a suggestion."

The young man laughed.

"Don't worry, I do have a solution," said Dickey. "There is no reason why — when she has the debut — that she can't be in love with someone, is there?"

With a hopeful look in his eyes Theodore again nodded.

Dickey continued, "Theodore, as long as I've known you, you have always found a way to get around the obstacles that barred your way."

Theodore looked up, hoping for some advice which would help him see through the fog that now obscured Alice.

"Now, you say both families get along well? And they both approve of your union?"

Theodore agreed on both accounts.

"Good, because you will need their support to make this work. If I were you, I would try to get them all together for family events as much as possible. That way she will see the approval of those around her."

"Yes," said Theodore, "With the holidays approaching I can find numerous excuses."

"Good," said Dickey. "You're a likeable fellow, be around her as much as you can and it'll rub off on her."

And with that Theodore was out of his leather chair again and off, writing letters and paying visits while he arranged events. Alice's debut was just after Thanksgiving, but in the three weeks preceding it she found herself at four family get-togethers, and at each she was conveniently seated next to Theodore.

Sadly, for Theodore, she remained evasive on each occasion. At night he reviewed each word she had said to him, hoping to find a clue to her heart. But for the most part she left him with a sense of desperation. He had the feeling he was merely clinging to a few words here and there.

When Thanksgiving came — only a few days before the debut — Alice was no different. She was polite and always sought him out; at times they even took walks or went on picnics, which merrily felt like the old times, but when it came time to depart she was once again formal. A year before he'd made a vow to win her hand in marriage, but now he felt that vow slipping away.

For her debut Theodore dressed in his finest apparel, but in the crowd he saw every eligible bachelor he knew, all from the best families and dressed no less smart than himself.

From across the room he watched Alice being led through the introductions. She appeared radiant as she teased and flirted with the young men who came before her. When she'd first appeared Theodore believed he was going to pass out. She looked so beautiful that he found he couldn't catch his breath.

But then when they began introducing her to all the eligible men he experienced a little death each time one approached her.

Just watching made Theodore feel sick.

Dickey found him slouched in a stuffed chair, half hidden in the shadows, observing the spectacle from under his brow.

"Come, Roosevelt, you're being too obvious."

Theodore clenched his teeth as he said, "See that girl? I am going to marry her. She will not have me, but I am going to have her."

Dickey stood, offered his hand to Theodore, and said, "Alright then, Theodore, time for us to step outside for some air."

As he looked down at his friend, Dickey noticed he was pale and had lost some of the vitality he'd had when freshly returned from the Maine woods.

On their way to the door they came upon Alice's mother. Mrs. Lee was reserved, obviously determined not to treat Theodore any differently than the other men who sought her daughter's attention. But when she saw the downtrodden look in his eyes she took pity on him.

"My, Theodore, you must not take this personally."

He stared at the ground as he replied, "I do seem to be personally involved."

They both looked up and saw at least six men fawning for Alice's attention.

Theodore added, "At least I used to be."

Mrs. Lee looked adoringly at her daughter and then at Theodore.

She said, "Give her a few more weeks of attention and she will return to be the girl you love. It will be worth it in the end for her to have felt this way."

Theodore went to respond, but he didn't know what to say. Dickey nodded to his aunt and continued with Theodore to the door.

Over the next few weeks Theodore developed insomnia. At first he only slept a few hours a night, and then not at all. By early December he didn't even go to bed, considering it a waste of time if he couldn't sleep anyway.

His friends worried about him — Dickey among them — and wrote to his family in New York, where it was decided that the best hope lay in his cousin, West, who was going to school nearby to become a Doctor.

West talked with Dickey, hoping the reports had been exaggerated, but what he heard was far worse.

"He refuses to go to his rooms," said Dickey, "at night he roams the woods, trying to come to terms with this obsession — and I fear he will not!"

When they went to sit him down he was nowhere to be found. Together they searched for him as the day wore on, and not until after nightfall did West come upon Theodore. He sat under a full moon's glow on a nearby hill which overlooked a quiet forest.

"Cousin West," said Theodore, as if there was nothing strange in this late-night meeting, "how good to see you."

West sat down next to him; examining Theodore with the tools he was just now learning. He noted that he was not cut or bruised, but he looked worn-out and there was a slight wheeze to his breathing. The way his eyes darted around West wondered if he was delusional.

"Your friend Dickey was worried about you. Are you in some trouble?

Theodore huffed at the suggestion.

"Me? Of course not, I am fine."

West waited to see if Theodore would say more, but he didn't. "He said you do not even sleep in your rooms, that you are away all night…is that true?"

It seemed as if Theodore was confronting this thought for the first time. "Well, the room just feels too small," he said. "I cannot catch my breath in there during the night."

Then he added, "But I do return by day. In fact, I have begun to write a history of the Naval War of 1812…it really is quite fascinating."

West nodded, not certain what to say to his cousin, but determined to get him to shelter.

"Why not go back to your place, and you can lay it out for me there. I would really like to hear more."

Reluctantly, Theodore nodded, but before he stood he looked at West and said, "She shall always be mistress over all that I have."

West hoisted him to his feet.

"Come on cousin, I am freezing."

By Christmas Theodore had returned to his family home in New York City. He had finally resigned to the fact that he would never win Alice's hand and had decided to try to pull his life together again.

He quietly left his Harvard rooms and took the train to New York. There, he kept to himself for a few days, and spent Christmas Eve with his mother and sister; but on Christmas Day he tried to purge Alice from his mind by visiting ten of the prettiest girls he knew.

He appeared festive, and arrived wherever he went with an armload of gifts, but as he rode home from the final visit his heart was heavy again.

Not one of those women compares to my Alice, thought Theodore. The barren trees above him howled as the cold December breeze blew through their lifeless branches.

He went to bed that night, horribly bereft of all inspiration and enthusiasm. All the roads that lay before him, that had earlier filled him with such passion, now seemed boring and bland. He paced once again; knowing there was little chance of him actually sleeping.

His mother and sister were both sleeping in rooms nearby, but without his father's presence the large estate felt empty. The thought of returning to the wilds of Maine crossed his mind. But he waved even that way because he didn't want Bill Sewall—or Wilmot Dow—to see him like this.

Eventually, dawn came. As he walked through the quiet house—the house that had once echoed with his father's loving voice—he heard a knock on the door and went to get it. He didn't care that he looked disheveled and wasn't dressed properly.

He grabbed the solid brass handle, so cold and heavy, and pulled the door open.

In the doorway stood Alice, her hair lit up by the early morning sun, her eyes gleaming and full of promise. It was as if lightning had struck him. He just stood there, utterly lost and confused.

He stared at her as if she was a mirage.

"W...what are you doing here?" he finally stammered.

She shrugged with a sweet smile.

"When you failed to pay me a visit on Christmas Day I realized how empty the day was without you."

"You missed me," Theodore said with a coarse voice; he couldn't believe the words he was hearing.

She leaned in to kiss his cheek, and her perfume made him dizzy.

"Yes, I missed you."

With a coy smile she added, "And I was hoping you would show me around New York City."

The color was now slowly returning to his face. He took a deep breath and like the morning fog blowing off Mt. Katahdin, his mind cleared. In seconds he was back to his former self.

He said, "I would be elated to do so! How long do you have?"

Alice gazed into his eyes for an eternity before answering.

"I have as long as you need."

He didn't respond. Her words spoke so clearly of her intent, they said it all. They were together again, and the realization flowed through Theodore like a magic elixir, restoring his dreams, his vigor, and his optimism in mere seconds.

Suddenly he felt himself stand taller; and it was if his heart beat stronger, for he could feel his blood surging through his veins. The world again seemed full of potential.

He slipped his arm behind her as he escorted her into his home.

"Then what are we waiting for?"

As they closed the door Theodore excitedly called through the house for everyone to get up.

"We have some entertaining to do!"

Robert Louis DeMayo

Postscript

Five years later, Theodore summoned Bill Sewall and Wilmot Dow to New York to ask them to go west with him. They agreed, and eventually Sewall became his ranch foreman in the Dakotas.

But thaht's another story...

Robert Louis DeMayo

Sources

Island Falls Maine – 1872-1972
By Nina G. Sawyer   1972

Recollections of William Wingate Sewall (1945-1930)
        of Island Falls Maine
By Harriett S. Harmon and Harriett H. Miller   1972

The Rise of Theodore Roosevelt
By Edmund Morris
1979 Random House, Inc.

Bill Sewall's Story of T.R., Teddy Roosevelt
By William Wingate Sewall and Hermann Hagedorn
1916 Harper & Brothers Publishing

"We hitched well...from the first" – *Harper article*
By Michael T. Kinnicutt

Lion in the White House
By Aida D. Donald
2007 by Basic Books

The Last Romantic
By H. W. Brands
2007 by Basic Books

Becoming Teddy Roosevelt
By Andrew Vietze
2010 by Down East

Robert Louis DeMayo took up writing at the age of twenty when he left his job as a bio-medical Engineer to explore the world. Over the next 15 years he traveled to every corner of the globe, spending almost 8 years abroad, and experiencing around 100 countries. He is a member of The Explorers Club and The Archaeological Institute of America.

During his travels he has worked extensively for the travel section of The Telegraph, out of Hudson, NH. His first assignment for the paper was to drive from New Hampshire to Panama in 1988, writing feature articles on the way. He has written numerous novels and screenplays, four collections of poetry, as well as hundreds of newspaper articles. He also accumulated a photo archive with over 40,000 images.

Before 9/11 he worked as Marketing Director for a company called Eos that served as the travel office for six non-profit organizations. Tours marketed included: dives to the *Titanic* and the *Bismark;* Antarctic voyages; and African safaris; as well as archaeological tours throughout the world. After 9/11 he worked for three years as a driver/guide in Alaska during the summers (horseback and hiking in the Yukon, and historical tours of Skagway and The White Pass), and as a jeep guide in Sedona, AZ during the winter.

For the last few years he has worked as the General Manager for a Jeep tour company in Sedona (A Day in the West). Currently he resides full time in Sedona, AZ with his wife (Diana), and two girls, Tavish (11), Saydrin Scout (9), and Martika Louise (born 1/11/11).

Made in the USA
Charleston, SC
13 July 2011